AVENGER

The Sanctuary Series

Robert J. Crane

AVENGER
THE SANCTUARY SERIES: VOLUME TWO

2nd Edition

AUTHOR'S NOTE
This is a work of fiction. Names, characters, places, and incidents either are the product of the author's imagination or are used fictitiously, and any resemblance to actual persons, living or dead, business establishments, events, or locales is entirely coincidental.

For information regarding permissions, please contact cyrusdavidon@gmail.com.

Find Robert J. Crane online at
http://www.robertjcrane.com

Layout provided by **Everything Indie**
http://www.everything-indie.com

Acknowledgments

Writing a novel takes a lot of work, and a lot of help. For this one I had to round up the usual suspects. In no particular order:

Kari Layman was my trusted first reader, going through my unedited nonsense and repetitive prose (you think it's bad now? HA!).

Shannon Garza, Heather Rodefer and Debra Wesley spent countless hours fixing my numerous and prolific spelling, grammatical and punctuation errors. Any that are left remain mine... just as they were when I put them there.

Andrew Seager gave me a great, helpful critique on how my writing could improve from Volume One to Volume Two. For that, I am grateful.

Thanks also to Jon Burrell for being the first to buy my book.

Big thanks to Mary, Rocky, Monica and Derek Lyle for being so very, very vocal and early in their support. As far as I know, Rocky remains the first person to actually buy and finish my book after release, to which I say, "It may have been hot in Texas on that day, but you could have surely found SOMETHING better to do..."

To my grandmother and grandfather, for being helpful, kind and supportive.

The map of Arkaria was done by Robert Altbauer, a stellar cartographer (as in very good, not as in a mapper of the stars). His work is both fast and top notch. His website is http://www.fantasy-map.net/ and he can be reached via email at contact@fantasy-map.net Once I found him, getting the map made was the easiest thing about this book.

The cover for this, the second edition, was created by Karri Klawiter, whose name I only seem to spell correctly once out of every couple of times I try. Her work is exceptional, and can be found at artbykarri.com.

Thanks also go to Nicholas J. Ambrose, who has been an exceptional editor, formatter, and pretty damned cool guy to talk to about gaming and writing, two of my absolute favorite subjects. Since the very first book I wrote he's been instrumental in carrying my vision onto the page, and I appreciate his efforts.

To the GC Alums: Again. You guys rock. Thanks for being the inspiration for my some of my characters as well as being some of my biggest fans.

My thanks to everyone who bought a physical copy of book 1. My first order went faster than I could have predicted.

Thanks to my mom and dad, and my wife and kids. I couldn't have done it without you all.

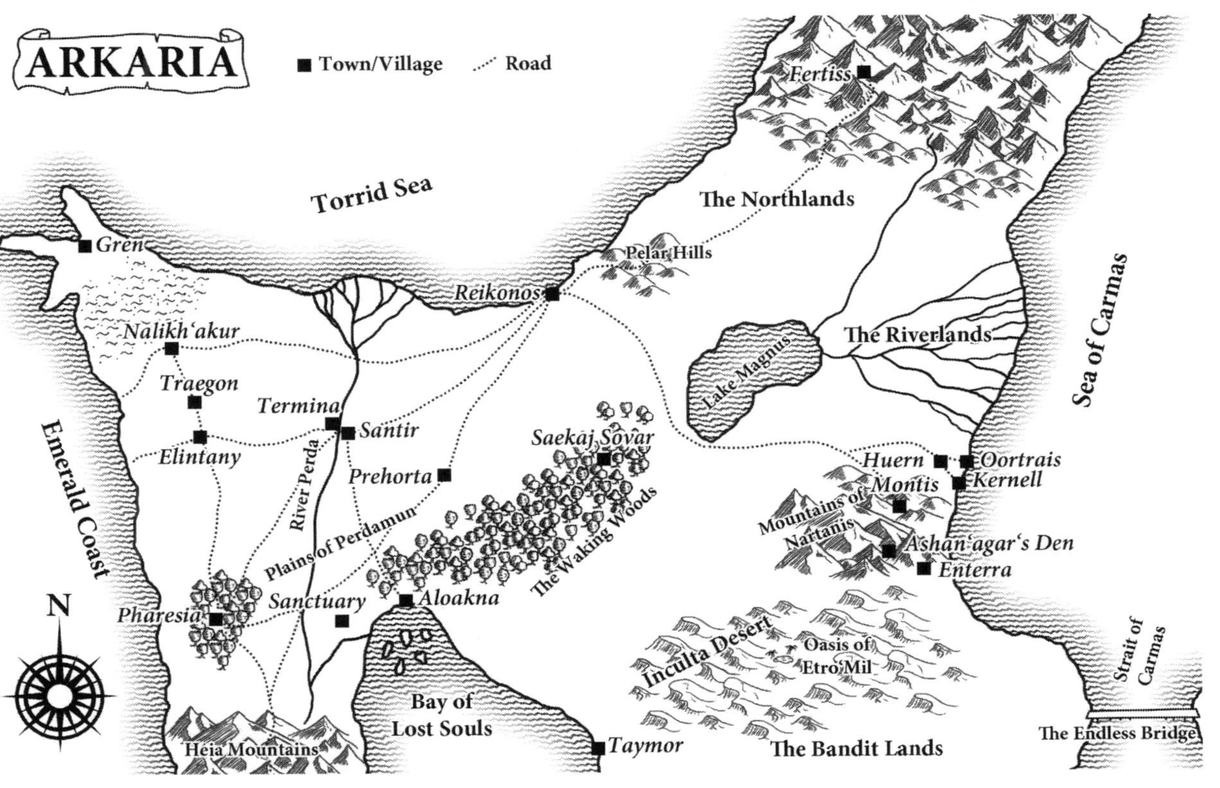
ARKARIA
Town/Village
Road
Torrid Sea
Gren
Reikonos
Pelar Hills
The Northlands
Fertiss
The Riverlands
Lake Magnus
Sea of Carmas
Nalikh'akur
Traegon
Termina
Santir
Elintany
Prehorta
River Perda
Plains of Perdamun
Saekaj Sovar
The Waking Woods
Emerald Coast
N
Pharesia
Sanctuary
Aloakna
Heia Mountains
Bay of
Lost Souls
Taymor
Huern
Oortrais
Kernell
Montis
Mountains of
Nartanis
Ashan'agar's Den
Enterra
Inculta Desert
Oasis of
Etro'Mil
The Bandit Lands
Strait of
Carmas
The Endless Bridge

NOW

Prologue

The warrior looked around at the wreckage of the place he had once called home. He sat in the archives of the ruined guildhall, a place where the ruling Council of Sanctuary had stored the records of their history. The hanging torches lit a room in chaos; books lay scattered across the floor, scorched walls showed where stone had been tested by fire and the furniture lay splintered and broken, pieces strewn over the chiseled gray block that made up the floors.

Cyrus Davidon was a man out of place. Even in the days when he called it home, Sanctuary had never looked like this. The archives were organized, the halls were clean and spotless at day's end and by day's beginning. He had seen the destruction stretch through the corridors as he climbed the tower to the archives, next to the room where the Council met. He stood and pushed through the door to the chambers for another look.

The table at the center of the room was smashed. The chairs that surrounded it were upended, their plush stuffing bleeding out in clumps. He knew that if he followed the call of his heart and wandered down the stairs to the foyer, the lounge and the Great Hall, he would find each of them in similar condition, wrecked, with all trace of life long gone. The fires that once burned in the hearths were long ago extinguished, the warmth of fellowship as gone as the souls that had once made this place great.

When did it all go wrong? Cyrus pondered. *How did we go from where we were to here?*

He didn't bother to answer himself. He crossed back to the archives and resumed his seat. He picked up the volume that he had laid down to stretch his legs and flipped to the page where he had left off. The inside page told its purpose: *The Journal of Vara – An Account of My Days With Sanctuary*. Her image sprang to his mind; her long, blond hair tucked in a neat ponytail; her armor shining in the summer sun; the way her red lips contrasted her pale cheeks, and curled in disdain when she scoffed at something foolhardy. Which was often something said by him.

The skies outside had darkened but the torches had relit

themselves, giving him enough light to read by. The words looped in a flowing script that spoke of long hours of practice in an attempt to make the handwriting more elegant.

It has now been a little over a year since I met the most frustrating person yet to come across my path in Arkaria, it began. *In addition to the ego and arrogance so common in humans who wield swords, this man seems particularly well disposed to raise my ire in ways that I have not experienced since... well... long ago.*

His grim mood broke for a moment as he chuckled at her assessment of him. His eyes skimmed further down the page. *Whatever my problems with him, though, he is a man, and he possesses certain frailties inherent in men. Never has this been more evident to me than tonight...*

As he read, his hand reached down and he stroked the hilt of his sword and the ghost of a smile sprang to his lips. A memory came rushing back to him, unbidden.

"We grow in times of trial," Alaric, the Sanctuary Guildmaster, had once told him, years earlier. He remembered the feelings, remembered the trials that had taxed him... and remembered the days that had followed the battle in the mountains with the Dragonlord and thought his troubles, finally, might be over...

7 YEARS EARLIER

Chapter 1

The sword swung past Cyrus's head, clashing against the metal of his helmet. He returned the favor to his attacker, impaling them with a vicious sword thrust that sent the monster spiraling away from him at an angle. A smile crept across the warrior's face at the sight of the next foe. Green scaled skin stood out against the sharp, pointed teeth and yellow eyes of his enemy. The smell of damp air filled his nostrils. His blade found the throat of the next goblin in line.

His eyes swept the room. A full force from Sanctuary was around him, engaged in battle. The Emperor and Empress of Enterra stared down at him from their throne platform, watching with red eyes as he cut his way through their Imperial Guard. Cyrus threw his gaze to the side, falling on Nyad and Niamh, two elves that could not have been more different.

Niamh was a druid, who controlled the powers of nature through her spells. Her long red hair was tossed back as she raised her hand, throwing blasts of fire into a cluster of goblins coming through the door to the army barracks. Her eyes were lit with the excitement of the battle, and she cried out as she loosed another burst of flame at the enemy.

Nyad, on the other hand, had blond hair that fell below her waist. She was a wizard who carried a white staff with gnarled boughs at the top of it, and it was taller than her. Her crimson robes fell to her feet, but deft movements kept her from tripping over them. Energies channeled through her staff, sending a blast of ice from the tip that froze three goblins in place.

Cyrus swept his sword through two more goblins in front of him. He caught a glimpse of Orion, the ranger, clad in green and with his bow in hand, arrows flying. A goblin ran at him but Elisabeth swept forward, her short swords moving with such speed he couldn't see anything but a blur from her hands. Cass, the warrior clad in gray armor, moved to Cyrus's left, carving his way through the goblin army, Andren, J'anda and Vaste behind him.

Things became hazy. Blood swirled on the floor. Niamh and Nyad were dead, then Elisabeth, then J'anda and Vaste. Cyrus watched as Cass was impaled by a goblin with a spear and

Andren's body hit the floor immediately after. Cyrus howled and attacked even harder.

The red eyes of the Emperor and Empress hovered just beyond his reach, watching him. Behind them, a black-cloaked figure watched with red eyes of its own. His sword moved of its own accord; goblin blood covered him - pungent and smelling of iron, he could not stop swinging his blade. For every goblin he felled another sprang up, claws reaching out for him, their clicking driving him mad.

"Hold it together!" a voice called across the madness. His eyes found Narstron, smile wide and wreathed in battle. *I have to get to him,* Cyrus thought. His sword danced, slicing through five more goblins and then five more after that, but there were more... always more...

Narstron battled, but every step Cyrus took toward the dwarf brought him no closer. Narstron was so deft with a sword that Cyrus could scarcely see it move. The red eyes of the Imperials drew closer, just beyond the dwarf's field of battle. Cyrus tried to move toward Narstron, but his sword was too slow and his feet were like leaden weights. The red eyes were coming for the dwarf; he could feel it.

A thousand stings pinched him in the ribs. Claws slipped between the joints of his breastplate and backplate, stabbing into his flesh. He did not care; he tried to move forward. More pain, more stabbing, and red eyes looking into his. The Empress grasped him by the neck, claws cutting into his throat. She was flanked on either side by the Emperor and the black-cloaked figure. He could not move.

The red eyes resolved, and her face began to clarify. It was Narstron - not G'Koal, the Empress of Enterra. The dwarf looked down at him, all trace of felicity gone. His face was creased with gashes, blood oozing from a dozen cuts. The dwarf's lips were cracked, and when he opened his mouth, blood dripped out. His voice was a rasp, the sound of death.

"You promised to... avenge me..."

The red eyes swallowed him and he screamed.

Chapter 2

"Wake the bloody hell up!"

Cyrus bolted awake, slapping away the hand that was on his jaw. His eyes focused on the face a few feet in front of him, lit by the moonlight shining through the window of his quarters. She was pale and wore a look of annoyed concern. The moonlight leeched the color from her normally blond hair, giving it a ghostly tinge. He sucked for air, his gasping so loud it blocked out all other ambient noise.

"Vara!" he shouted before lowering his voice. "What are you doing in my quarters?"

Her eyes narrowed and her lips pursed. "I was in *my* quarters, sleeping, and you had a nightmare that woke me from three rooms away." He smelled a faint scent of lilacs from her.

His eyes fell from her face to her attire. She wore a nightgown cut low; much lower than anything he had seen her in before. His stare caused her to fold her arms, as though she could cover herself. "I'm up here," she snapped, drawing his eyes back to her face. "You were thrashing about and shouting. I merely wished to be certain you weren't struggling with a lethal foe - which, in your case, could be your pillow."

His hands rubbed his eyes, massaging the sleep out of them. "I thought you were going to stop insulting me.

A slight smile upturned the corners of her mouth before disappearing back into annoyance. "I would never foreswear insulting you when great opportunities present. What was your nightmare about?" She stiffened. "Not that I care."

He cocked his head to the side. "So you charged down the hallway in your barely-there nightgown because you wanted the noise to cease?"

"Damned right," she said without a hint of humor.

"Do you remember our last excursion into Enterra?"

She frowned. "I remember being sick to my stomach upon hearing of Goliath's abandonment of it. I remember rushing to save you after you all died in the depths." Her voice faltered. "I remember your dwarven friend, Narstron. His funeral."

Cyrus's voice hardened out of necessity. "I remember that too."

Vara did not say anything for a moment. When she spoke

again, her voice was much softer. "Your nightmare was about Enterra?"

Cyrus stared straight ahead, not daring to look in her eyes. "Yeah. It was." When his words came again, they were halting and came in staccato bursts. "We went there the second day I was in Sanctuary. I don't think I believed someone could die - really die." His jaw set. "I wasn't prepared for that."

She was sitting on the edge of his bed. "You've been an adventurer for years. You never faced death before?"

He turned his head to look at her. "That night was the first time I've ever died. That was jarring, even though the resurrection spell brought me back. I can deal with dying." His hand clenched involuntarily. "But I swore vengeance over Narstron's coffin on the day of his funeral, and I have failed to deliver on my promise."

Her face became a sudden mask.

He looked at her. "You disapprove of revenge?"

Vara's face maintained its frozen state. "As a paladin - a holy warrior - we are taught that revenge is a self-serving emotion. The dead are gone. Desire for revenge is a trait of survivors." She looked out the window. "It's a mortal emotion, though, desire for revenge. I cannot say I have not felt it myself." Her gaze drew back to settle on his eyes. Hers were clouded, her expression tight.

"I was raised in the Society of Arms in Reikonos, the capital of the Human Confederation," Cyrus began. "There are few followers of Bellarum, the God of War, in mankind. I think it makes people uneasy, the desire for combat." He smiled. "In the Society, we were taught that battle is good, that revenge is good, and to pursue both with more ardor than you would give to wooing a lover - the instructor's words, not mine," Cyrus added as a flush crept across his cheeks.

Vara chewed her lip before she replied. "If you intend revenge, I would caution you in the words of one who once cautioned me. Hasty action is the domain of the fool; especially in the area of vengeance."

"I've waited over a year," Cyrus said. "I wouldn't consider that 'hasty action'."

Her eyes flitted across his features. In the pale of the moon he couldn't see the glittering blue that rimmed her pupils. "I would encourage you to..." She drew a deep breath. "- be careful."

"Worried about me?" he asked with a sly grin.

She rose, her expression stern. "I'm worried that you'll lead

Sanctuary into danger to satisfy your desire for revenge." Her arms crossed once more. "Regardless, I doubt you'll invade the Goblin Imperium tonight." A hint of mirth turned her lips up. "Especially not attired as you are." She looked down, saw her nightgown and her face fell. "Nor I. If you'll excuse me..."

He watched as she turned to leave. Her nightgown was silken and fell to mid-thigh. Her hair hung around her shoulders, hiding the points of her elven ears. She shut the door behind her - but not before she caught him looking again, which seemed to embarrass her more than it did him.

The window was open, letting the autumn air breeze through. A chill rushed through the warrior. *No more sleep tonight.*

It took him a few minutes to strap on his armor. He felt the curious absence of weight on his belt; his sword had been lost in a battle with a dragon only days before and he had yet to go to the armory for a replacement. Opening the door, he strode to the end of the hall and up the stairs.

Emerging from the spiral of the stairway, he found himself in front of double doors. Unthinking, he opened them and stepped into the Council Chamber. Voices halted and a burst of warmth encompassed him as he entered the chamber; fires were burning in the hearths on either side of the room, the logs cracking and spitting and filling the air with a lovely smell of burning wood.

"I had not thought that any of our brethren would be awake at this hour," came the voice of Alaric Garaunt, the Guildmaster of Sanctuary. The paladin stood to greet him.

Alaric Garaunt was just over six feet in height, with brown hair that fell at the base of his skull, streaked with gray. His face was weathered, and his left eye was covered by an eyepatch. In addition to leading Sanctuary, Alaric was also a paladin, a holy warrior that Cyrus knew from experience could wield a sword better than any other - as well as cast some spells.

"I don't know what time it is," Cyrus admitted. Terian Lepos and Curatio were arranged around the circular table. Curatio, an elf and a spell caster possessing the ability to magically heal wounds sustained in battle, was seated to Alaric's right.

Terian, on the other hand, was a dark elf, with skin of the deepest blue. The smirk on his face as he turned in his chair to face Cyrus was reflected by his posture; he had one foot resting on the table and was leaning back as far as his chair would allow. He raised a hand in a salute to Cy as the warrior walked in. Terian's nose was long and pointed, and the armored pauldrons that defended his shoulders from attack bore spikes that jutted six inches in the air to either side of his head.

Terian was a dark knight - the opposite of Alaric's paladin. Dark knights could also wield a blade but used black magics. He was able to steal life from an enemy, cause searing pain or even a plague of disease to fall upon his opponents. He had left his post as one of Sanctuary's officers a few months earlier during a dispute over his failure to intervene in a quarrel between guildmates, two of whom later turned out to be traitors that were conspiring with Sanctuary's enemies.

"It's three in the morning," Curatio answered. The elf wore the white robes of a healer, fastened around the waist by a brown leather belt. Very slight crow's feet were present on the healer's face, not the result of age but from his perpetual smile. "Having trouble sleeping, brother?" Cyrus was uncertain as to when Curatio and Alaric had begun to refer to the members of Sanctuary as their brothers and sisters, but it made him feel more at home.

"Yes," he replied. "I hope I'm not interrupting."

Alaric smiled. "We were discussing Terian returning to us following his assistance with Ashan'agar."

Cyrus restrained a smile as he took his seat. "You'd give up 'walking the world' to rejoin us?"

Terian's smile vanished. "You're such a smartass, Davidon. I'd say that I hope it lands you in trouble someday but I'd likely land in it with you."

Alaric's eyebrow cocked in amusement. "I will wait for the Council's opinion, but since he helped save the world from the threat of the Dragonlord's rise, I recommend we reinstate Terian as a member of Sanctuary - and an officer."

"Not Elder?" Cyrus said, referring to the title accorded the most senior officer of the Council.

"I don't want it." The dark elf studied his hand as he spoke. "Officer is almost too much for me - I don't like people enough to take on more responsibility."

The door swung open behind Cyrus and he swiveled to find Niamh striding into the room, red hair pulled back in a ponytail. "Nice to see everyone's working late tonight," she giggled, sounding like a teenager. Cyrus knew she was over six hundred years old - yet she looked less than thirty in human years. She shot a smile at him as she slid into the seat to his left.

"Ah, yes," Alaric began, but was interrupted as the doors to the Council chamber opened once more and disgorged Vara, now clad in her shining silver armor, and another.

"Vaste," Cyrus nodded with a smile at the being standing beside Vara. Vaste was a troll who stood close to seven feet in height with skin of a light green hue. A few scars stood out on the troll's head and face, all recent - enough so that Cyrus hadn't yet to had a chance to ask about them. Vaste nodded as he took his place between Cyrus and Vara, smacking his lips and yawning.

"I cannot recall when so many officers were rendered sleepless at the same time," Alaric remarked.

"Blame him," Niamh yawned as she pointed at Cyrus. "He woke up everybody in the officer's quarters with his howling."

Cyrus turned a deep crimson. "I'm sorry."

Alaric turned to Cyrus, brow furrowed. "Is everything all right, brother?"

Cyrus waved him off. "I'm fine."

Before Alaric could respond, the last of the officers breezed in, looking a bit fresher than the others. J'anda Aimant was a dark elf and an enchanter, a spell caster who could bend the minds of his foes with illusions.

Cyrus still remembered the night that J'anda had shown him a mesmerization spell - he paralyzed foes by showing them a vision of the deepest desires of their heart come to life - in Cyrus's case, it had been a vision of Vara, seductive and sweet. He had felt her touch against his skin and the warmth of her kisses. He shook the memory off before it had a chance to linger.

"You too, J'anda?" Cyrus grimaced. He studied the enchanter. "You look much more awake than the others."

The dark elf's distinctive, stitched blue robes swayed about his thin frame as he took his seat and waved a hand in front of his face. The skin rippled as the illusion spell fell away and his expression changed; the enchanter looked haggard, eyes half-lidded. "I took a moment to freshen myself up," he admitted, waving his hand again. The sleepless look was replaced by a smiling and bright-eyed visage. "What are we discussing?"

Alaric looked around the table. "We were discussing returning Terian to Officer status."

J'anda nodded, a subtle movement of his head. "All in favor, say aye." A chorus of ayes, most tinged with fatigue, filled the air around them.

"The motion passes," J'anda yawned. Cyrus looked at the dark elf in amusement. J'anda looked back. "I can't cast an illusion to cover a yawn, sorry." A pensive expression crossed his face. "Why am I apologizing to you, you're responsible for this..."

Alaric turned to Terian with a broad smile. "Welcome back to the fold."

Terian removed his foot from the table. "That's good, because I already moved all my stuff back into my old quarters." He looked at his fingernails, every one of which came to a vicious point. "It's a real bitch to move some of it, too."

Alaric turned his attention to the parchment in front of him. "Since we're all here, does anyone object to covering the items we were going to attend to in the morning meeting?"

"If it means we can cancel it and sleep, I vote yes," Niamh said without enthusiasm, face resting against her hand. "I need rest to keep up with you younglings." A wide grin split her face. "Except you, Curatio – old man."

J'anda leaned forward. "You have such a timeless quality, Curatio. How old are you?"

A sparkle lit the eye of the healer. "I am however old you think I am; it matters not to me."

A laugh rounded the table. Alaric smiled once it was finished. "The first item on our agenda is to discuss our recent glut of applications."

Curatio spoke. "We had around 850 people when we faced off with Ashan'agar. Nobody died, but we lost about 75 after the battle. We had recruited people that had never seen battle before, so they left after realizing it wasn't for them."

"That's not good." Niamh's frown was interrupted as she stifled an involuntary yawn.

Curatio smiled. "It's not bad. Our newfound prestige from slaying the Dragonlord netted us another 350 applicants in the last week. It's tapered off quite a bit the last couple days, but we're still getting a steady stream."

Alaric frowned in concentration. "I would have thought the surge would continue for a few more days."

"No complaints," Curatio said with a shrug. "We have over a thousand people at our command now." A gleam filled the healer's eye. "The new people that have joined us are almost all veterans, unlike those we were recruiting before the battle."

Cyrus cracked his knuckles. "That'll make my job as General easier."

Alaric smiled at the warrior. "In that department, I am curious as to what you believe to be our next step?" A long moment passed in which Cyrus did not answer. "Cyrus?" Alaric asked.

The warrior's attention was focused out the windows behind Alaric. Cyrus stood without warning, chair tipping over behind him. "Gods dammit! They got another one!"

He rushed past Alaric, throwing open the doors to the balcony. The chill of the night air rushed over his skin and the grassy smell of the Plains of Perdamun filled his nose, but he ignored it as his eyes stayed focused on the horizon. The night noises of the plains were drowned out by the sounds of the Council joining him.

Alaric's eyes narrowed at the spots of light in the distance. He turned to Niamh. "We must go to their assistance. We require the Falcon's Essence."

The red-haired elf nodded, and muttered a spell under her breath, giving them all the ability to walk on air.

"Is everyone armed?" Alaric asked.

"No," Cyrus replied.

"Take this." Terian pulled a short sword from under his back plate and tossed it to Cyrus. "But I want it back."

"Curatio –" Alaric cast a look at the healer. "Awaken the guild. I do not anticipate difficulty, but just in case..." Curatio nodded and hurried back through the Council Chambers.

"Whaddya think?" Terian asked. "Twenty miles?"

Cyrus looked at the fires on the horizon. "About that."

"With the Essence of Falcon," Alaric remarked, stepping over the edge of the balcony and off the tower, "we will be there within the hour." His voice receded into the darkness.

Without another word, they all followed him over the edge, running into the night.

Chapter 3

Alaric was barely visible in front of Cyrus, leading the charge across the plains toward the distant fires. Cyrus raised his gaze and felt his altitude increase; he brought it back down and joined the rest of them running low, skimming the tops of the tall grass.

"How many this week?" Vara said from his right.

"Four?" Vaste chipped in. "Five now, I think."

Terian whistled from behind Cyrus. "I've been with Sanctuary since almost the beginning. We've had bandits in the Plains of Perdamun for years. But they only attacked people traveling in small groups or by themselves."

"Whoever they are, five convoys in a week is a lot." Cyrus's face hardened as he added his opinion. "All from different places, with different destinations, and all destroyed, nothing left but dead bodies and burnt wagons. Whoever's behind it, they're putting a squeeze on the trade routes of the southern plains."

"Disappearing without a trace is a neat trick for bandits." Vaste spoke between gulps for air. "I wouldn't feel so bad if they'd left behind even one of their dead, or a clue of some kind to tell us they were there. Whoever they are, it's like they don't exist after the attack."

"Maybe it's a ghost," Terian said with a laugh.

"Don't being ridiculous," Vara said sharply. "You'll make Alaric think we're talking about him behind his back."

"I can hear you," came the voice of the Ghost from far in front of them. "And it is no ghost."

They ran in silence the rest of the way. Flames were roaring from several wagons. "Lighting them all on fire – was that really necessary?" Vaste asked as they crossed the last hundred feet to the site of the attack.

Cyrus stopped behind Alaric, who was hovering a few feet above the road, surveying the wreckage. "Whoever did this wanted it to be found. You don't light thirty wagons on fire for the hell of it."

"No sign of the attackers," Alaric sighed. "Let us see if we can trace their movements."

Bodies lay strewn around the burning wagons. A few corpses lay in the flames. The bodies were cut and bloodied; a few eviscerated. "No chance of resurrection spell - maybe give us a witness?" Cyrus asked, looking to Vaste.

The healer shook his head. "The time limit for a resurrection spell is an hour. These souls are lost to permanent death."

Cyrus stooped over one of the corpses, a dark elf. "Looks like this convoy comes from a dark elven city?"

Terian joined him beside the body. "I'd say this was a shipment from Aloakna, the port on the Bay of Souls. It's a neutral town - big dark elf population, lots of elves and humans too. Probably a shipment of cloth, silk, maybe even some gold - bound for Elven territory - most likely Termina."

Niamh was flummoxed. "You guessed that all from looking at one body?"

Terian frowned. "No, I guessed it because of the direction they're heading, the road they're on, and the types of trade that would go from Aloakna to Termina that would be done by dark elves."

Terian's head swiveled to look at Alaric. "It's a sovereignty convoy." He grasped the wrist of the corpse and held up its bracer, which bore a distinctive circular crest. "Sovereign's insignia. Not found on free citizens. This guy was a member of the Saekaj Sovar Militia. I see a few others as well."

"Who would want to attack these convoys?" Cyrus mused. "This is wholesale slaughter."

Terian answered. "Any group of bandits would want to. They're filled with riches, which is why they're protected the way they are. The question is, who possesses the strength to down a convoy? There have to be fifty soldiers mixed in with eighty or more traders."

Alaric spoke first. "I do not know, but it is an ill sign that these attacks are occurring so near to us."

"The Plains of Perdamun are vast," Vara agreed, speaking for the first time since they had arrived at the site. "I wonder if perhaps there are other convoys being attacked elsewhere in the Plains? If not, this is no coincidence."

Heavy footfalls padded behind them and Cyrus turned to see Curatio arrive with reinforcements. The elf's face fell upon arriving.

They scoured the remains of the convoy for the next four hours. By then it was well past daybreak and the fires were dying.

"I don't see anything," Terian said with a curse.

Curatio nodded. "Not a visible footprint, no sign of hostile dead - nothing to prove anyone attacked this convoy." The elf gestured at the wreckage. "Other than the ruin they left behind."

Alaric's hand came to his chin. "We have done all we can here. Have one of the wizards return us to Sanctuary." The Ghost turned to face them and his eye moved to each of the Council members in turn as he spoke. "We will meet in Council when we return, to discuss this and the other matters we left behind."

"So much for that nap," Niamh said.

Cyrus took a last look at the wreckage of the dark elven caravan before he grasped the orb of teleportation that the wizard conjured for him, and saw the last flickering flames of the convoy replaced by the bright blue energy of the spell that carried him back to Sanctuary.

Chapter 4

They reconvened in the Council Chamber almost an hour later. Alaric had yet to arrive, but the rest of the Council was seated. A thin mist filled the room, flowing toward the head of the table. It slid from the floor up the chair, and Alaric faded into view, demonstrating once more the genesis of his title, 'The Ghost of Sanctuary'.

Niamh pulled her head from the table at his appearance. "Maybe you can explain to us how a knight can disappear and reappear at will, 'cause I've never seen anyone but a full-on spell caster do anything close to that." She looked pensive for a moment. "And how do you do that thing with the mist? I have the forces of nature at my disposal and I can't do that."

Alaric smiled. "Someday, I may explain. For now we have more pressing matters to attend to. These convoy attacks have become concerning to me."

Cyrus looked around the table. "No one likes to see convoys get slaughtered, but is it our responsibility to get involved?"

"Are we not defenders of the weak and protectors of those who cannot protect themselves?" Vara bristled.

"Absolutely." Cyrus met her gaze, unflinching. "But we are also only one thousand strong - with about five hundred veterans - and the Plains of Perdamun are sizable. If you restricted us to within fifty miles of Sanctuary in all directions, would you feel confident that we could guard that territory?"

The heat of Vara's gaze fell upon him, and did not abate, although the intensity of her words was lost. "We would struggle to protect even that."

"Indeed," Curatio added. "That would be almost 8,000 square miles and we wouldn't even be watching halfway to Aloakna."

Cyrus looked around the table. "Whose territory is this?"

A shadow grew over Alaric's face. "The Plains of Perdamun are disputed territory for over a thousand years. The dark elves enforce a boundary at the eastern edge of the Waking Woods, the Elven Kingdom patrols west of the river Perda, and the human government in Reikonos has yet to stretch the Confederation's military presence south of Prehorta, which is a few hundred miles north of here."

"But," Cyrus realized with a start, "someone's been keeping the bandit population in check. How do they handle criminal matters in this part of the Plains?"

Alaric answered. "Each village has magistrates and lawmen to handle their own. We've swept the spaces between settlements as needed for the last twenty years, whenever a bandit group became problematic. While the elves, the humans and the dark elves don't fight over this territory, they all claim it and each race has settlements within it.

"This was originally Elven land, long before the rise of the current kingdom. Then it was claimed by the dark elves in a war about a millennium ago. They traded the territory back and forth in several wars since. It's been a hundred years since the last war when the possession of the Plains of Perdamun was contested."

"They fought over it for two thousand years?" Cyrus boggled.

"What precisely did you learn in the Society of Arms?" Vara interrupted. "Because they certainly didn't teach you how to wield a sword - unless they taught you to use a cudgel and you've substituted it for a sword."

He shot her an irritated look. "History was not my strong suit."

Vara threw her hands in the air in exasperation. "Fine. Yes, they fought over these lands, the imperialist dark elves and the fair kingdom of light elves, in another timeless battle between the forces of good and evil -"

"Who are you calling evil?" J'anda straightened, glaring at Vara.

"Me, I hope," Terian added with a nasty smile.

"Fear me, black knight," Vara shot back. "My point is whoever won the last war got the territory."

"So what changed?"

"This lesson in elementary history would go much faster if you would constrain yourself to shut up," she fumed. "But," her voice lightened a touch, "you asked the question, and you are the answer."

"Me?" Cyrus looked at her, tentative.

"Your people, the humans." Her frown deepened. "The coalition of human city-states that was precursor to your Human Confederation inserted themselves in the last war, tipping the balance of power in favor of the elves. There was a lasting peace after that war between the two major powers - now three, since you humans mastered the art of walking upright - and people from all three nations have settled the southern plains."

Alaric took over. "Now, the hundred years of peace in this region might be undone by three different factions sending armies into our quiet little area, starting a war that will likely spill into the rest of the world."

"You think," Cyrus asked in astonishment, "that bandit attacks here, hundreds of miles from any of the major powers, could start a war?"

The Ghost straightened in his seat. "The Plains of Perdamun have become the breadbasket of Arkaria, supplying enormous quantities of foodstuffs to every major power. I have seen wars begin for lesser reasons. For example, the dark elves once began an assault on the borders of the Elven Kingdom when the King failed to send an appropriate gift for the Sovereign of Saekaj Sovar's wedding."

"When was that?" J'anda said with a curious look. "I'm two hundred years old and I don't remember that. The current sovereign doesn't even..." His voice trailed off and he looked around the table. "...take wives."

Alaric brushed it off. "While this seems on the surface like mere banditry, there are deeper concerns. Which brings me to other items of great import on our agenda - the first being our entanglement with the Alliance and the second being the training of our army."

The eyes of everyone at the table subtly shifted to Cyrus. "I don't really have a list of targets in mind." He cleared his throat. "All my efforts right now involve training the new folks in basics. Elisabeth from The Daring informed me that they have a line on a time when Yartraak, the God of Darkness will be absent from his Realm, so she's scheduling an Alliance incursion there."

Alaric stared at Cyrus. "We need to host more audacious excursions if we intend to whip this army into shape and position ourselves to shed the Alliance."

"I don't disagree," Cyrus said, "but what could we attempt with half our complement being inexperienced?"

"Perhaps the Trials of Purgatory?" Vaste suggested with light humor. "After all, the last guild that succeeded –"

"Was killed almost to the last person," Vara interrupted, dour look on her face.

"A joke, only," Vaste said with a nod toward the elf.

"Regardless," the Ghost said, angling his head toward Cyrus,

"I'm confident when next we meet you'll have possibilities in mind."

"Yes," Cyrus stammered. "I will."

"Excellent. Then we are adjourned," Alaric gestured with a flourish. Cyrus stood, intending to be one of the first out of the Chamber. "Hold, Cyrus," Alaric gestured to him. "I have things to discuss with you."

The rest of the Council filed out one by one, Niamh yawning and Vara shooting him an indecipherable look on her way out. When the door shut, Cyrus found himself looking into the eye of the Ghost, steely gaze giving no hint of the paladin's intentions. "I have two things to discuss with you," Alaric began. "First, there is a matter that needs settling. I would have you meet me in the dungeons in two hours."

Cyrus blinked. "Okay..."

"Second, I typically do not meddle in the personal affairs of my officers, but when one of them has a nightmare of such intensity that it awakens everyone, I become concerned."

"I thought this was going to be about my lack of planning."

A wave of the paladin's hand dismissed that thought. "You have established that you will take care of that by the next meeting and I trust you to deliver on your word." The gray eye of Lord Garaunt pierced him. "This nightmare - may I ask what it pertained to?"

Cyrus felt a sudden rush to his head and a numbness in the rest of his body. "It was about Enterra."

"I assumed as much." Alaric stood and began circling the table. "I received a report from a source that indicated Orion's proclamation of the rising force of the Goblin Imperium is coming to fruition. They are stirring."

Cyrus's fingers found his temples and begin to massage them. "I thought Orion lied about that so he could stage an Alliance invasion as a diversion while he stole *Terrenus*, the Hammer of Earth, from the goblins?"

"All the best lies cloak themselves in truth. Orion knew that well. He failed to acquire the Hammer that night because one of Ashan'agar's other servants betrayed the Alliance to the goblins in exchange for it."

Cyrus's jaw tightened. "I have not forgotten. But what does this have to do with my dreams?"

The Ghost's gaze cooled. "Perhaps nothing. Perhaps

everything. At the moment it is impossible to say."

"Really," Cyrus stated rather than asked, "because you just inferred that events taking place in Enterra are influencing my dreams, which is a bizarre proposition for a warrior - one who has no magical ability whatsoever - to accept."

The Ghost smiled. "Did I infer that? How peculiar a thing for me to suggest of you who have 'no magical ability whatsoever'." The smile vanished. "It might be more peculiar if you fully understood magic."

"Enlighten me," Cyrus said with the slightest tinge of annoyance.

"Perhaps some other day," the paladin said with just a hint of regret. "I do not wish to antagonize you by making you think I am holding back some vital information; I merely have suspicions about the shape of events." He held up his hand to stop Cyrus from interrupting him. "Suspicions which I will, of course, share with you -"

"- in the fullness of time," Cyrus interrupted anyway.

The Ghost's smile returned. "I hope you will accept that."

"Do I have a choice?"

Alaric did not smile this time. "No."

Cyrus shrugged, faking a grin. "Then I guess it doesn't really matter." Without another word, he crossed the distance between his chair and the door handle.

The Ghost's voice came to him once more as he opened the door. "Should you have another dream, please seek me out... and we will discuss it further."

"I'm sure that will be enlightening for me," Cyrus said with unmitigated sarcasm. He turned to favor the paladin with a glare but the Ghost was already gone.

"Enlightenment comes to the patient," a final whisper filled Cyrus's ears.

He sighed and turned to leave. "Sadly, not one of my virtues."

Chapter 5

Cyrus descended the stairway and entered the foyer of Sanctuary. An enormous open space with a balcony, the foyer could easily fit the entire population of the guild in it, and was used for times when the officers' Council wanted to address everyone outside of a mealtime in the Great Hall. A hearth the length of three men laid end to end stretched across the wall nearest the stairwell. To his left sat the doors leading outside, and opposite him was the open entrance to the lounge where members spent much of their free time.

He had often admired the stonework around the walls, which were carved so perfectly that there was no sign of grout between them. The fireplace crackled even now, giving the entire foyer an aroma of sweet smokiness and a warmth that was comfortable but not so overbearing as to cause Cyrus to sweat. The entrance doors were mammoth, carved of a dark wood that was mysteriously light and easy to open.

They were open now, however, and Cyrus wandered over to a table resting close to the entrance with a familiar elf sitting behind it, inkwell and parchment before him and a quill in his hand.

"Andren," Cyrus intoned as he approached the elf from behind. A line of five people unfamiliar to Cyrus stood in front of the table.

Andren wore a scowl and was writing on the parchment in front of him, hand moving with angry flourishes. "They've got me handling applications for these new people," he said with a furious gesture that splattered ink on the red armor of the young human warrior that stood first in the line before him. The warrior did not flinch, standing at attention, arms straight at his sides and spine upright.

"Why would they go and do something like that during regular drinking hours?" Cyrus quipped.

"I don't know," Andren said, shaking his head hard enough that his long, dark hair fell off his shoulder. "Probably because I'm literate."

Cyrus frowned. "I thought all elves were literate."

"They are!" Andren scowled. "But you humans aren't! Why don't they teach you how to read and write?"

Cyrus shrugged. "I don't know; I learned at the Society of Arms."

The elf stared blankly back at him. "So they did teach you something there? I'm surprised."

"Hey!" shouted the warrior standing in front of Andren. "I was trained at the Society of Arms as well!" His face contorted with fury.

Andren turned his empty gaze upon the new applicant. "Would you like me to ask the application questions more slowly?"

"Perhaps I should take over for you," Cyrus suggested as the red-armored warrior's face began to match the color of his breastplate.

"Meh. I'll write, you talk." Andren turned his head down and began to scribble furiously. "First applicant... warrior... human... below average intelligence... sub-par personal hygiene..."

"Shut up!" Cyrus's voice came out as a low hiss, laced with urgency. Turning back to the warrior, whose expression had only gotten darker, he said, "What's your name?"

The warrior tore his eyes from Andren, who was still writing. "Thad Proelius, sir."

"At ease. You're from Reikonos?" Cyrus asked. The warrior met his gaze and nodded. "When did you graduate from the Society?"

"About three months ago," Thad answered. "You're Cyrus Davidon. You were graduating when I moved into warrior training." He outstretched his hand to Cyrus. "It would be an honor to stand by you in battle."

"...projects the aura of a perfect lackey..." Andren droned as he wrote.

"Ignore him," Cyrus said. "He's harmless to everything but an alcoholic beverage." He grasped the young warrior's hand in a handshake. "Glad to have you with us, Thad."

The next in line was an elven woman with brown hair pouring out of her chainmail headweave. She was pretty, Cyrus thought, and carried the look of someone who wore a perpetual smile. "My name is Martaina Proelius," she said.

Cyrus returned her smile. "You're married to Thad?" She answered him with a nod, her smile broadening. "I see more elven women married to human men than I do elven ones."

Martaina's smile turned into a smirk. "It's because human men are so young, vibrant, passionate and excited – they know how to satisfy an elven woman who's been around for hundreds or thousands of years. Elven men," she said with a glare directed at Andren, "are old, boring, stodgy and self-absorbed."

Andren's lips had narrowed and pursed. "You wound me, madam, with your words."

"If you'd prefer," she said, "I could do it with a blade?"

Andren grimaced and Cyrus laughed to the obvious delight of Martaina, who nodded and moved off to the side to join her husband. The next applicant in line was another human, clad in more maneuverable leather armor. "I remember you," Cyrus said, "you're from the Confederation's northlands – close to the border with the dwarves."

"Aye," the human said with a smile. A ragged beard of black hair covered the warrior's face and the pommel of a sword jutted from his belt. A smell wafted off him of sweat and dirt. "You met me when you came through my village while recruiting a few months ago."

"Your name," Cyrus said, pulling from memory, "is Menlos Irontooth."

The bearded human smiled. "Kind of you to remember; I know you must have talked to quite a few people since then."

"I did, but you were memorable. Where are your wolves?"

Menlos pointed down. Cyrus and Andren leaned forward to see three wolves lying in the shadow of the table, each gnawing on a bone.

"My gods," Andren said in surprise. "I thought that the gnawing noise was him –" pointing at Thad – "eating for the eighty-fifth time today." Cyrus tossed an apologetic look to Thad. Martaina's hand reached out to the red-armored warrior, soothing him.

"Are they always this quiet?" Cyrus asked.

Menlos shook his head. "They get loud during battle."

"You use them in combat?" Andren said with a raised eyebrow.

"Wolves are vicious fighters," Menlos confirmed, dirty fingernails running across the hilt of his sword. "They bring down my foes so I can finish them."

"Interesting," Cyrus said genuinely. He shook the northman's dirty hand and watched Menlos join Thad and Martaina at the side of the table.

Next in line was a man clad in dark blue armor, steel plate covered with a white surcoat, and a coat of arms on it: a black lion with an extended paw, as though it were swiping at a foe. The human had a lantern jaw, and his deep brown eyes watched Cyrus shrewdly, gauging him. "I am Sir Samwen Longwell," he said in a lilting accent that Cyrus couldn't place.

"Pleased to meet you, Longwell. Where do you hail from?"

Longwell hesitated. "Far away. I doubt you would have heard of my homeland."

A hint of curiosity went through Cyrus's mind as he studied Sir Samwen Longwell. "Very well, then. Are you a paladin?"

"No, sir," Longwell replied with a shake of the head. "I use no magics; where I come from, they do not exist. I am called a dragoon."

"What does a dragoon do?" Cyrus asked, curiosity increasing.

"I am a very skilled fighter on horseback," Longwell replied. "I prefer to use a lance, but I can also use a spear or my sword."

He nodded to dismiss Longwell, who joined the others. He brought his attention to the last person in line to find a beautiful young dark elf with a shy smile. "Pleased to meet you..." His words drifted off.

"Aisling," she said. "Aisling Nightwind." She wore twin daggers and light leather armor. A few thistles were entangled in her white hair; whether by accident or intention Cyrus did not speculate.

"I don't see a bow on you," he said, looking her up and down. "I have to admit, that's a bit unusual for a ranger."

She stepped around the table, cutting the distance between them. She was short compared to him; her head barely reached the base of his chin. "I'm an unusual ranger," she said in a throaty whisper. "I'm sure I have a bow around here somewhere... why don't you –" she winked as she smiled at up at him – "see if you can find it?"

Cyrus stared at the dark blue face for a moment without saying anything, his own frozen without expression. When he regained the capacity for speech, he cleared his throat. "I... I will... take your word for it... that you have a bow... somewhere."

"Are you sure?" She leaned in, brushing against him.

"Quite sure."

She shrugged, smile receding. "If you ever change your mind..." She took a few steps toward the rest of the new applicants then turned back, tossing something. He caught it nimbly, realized with a start that it was his belt.

"What the...?"

"This too," she added, pitching another object at him underhand. He caught it. "You're very nimble for a warrior," she purred. "That's an enjoyable quality in a man." Looking down, he examined the object – it was his coinpurse. He looked up to meet her gaze, which was bordering on salacious. "I told you I'm a very unique ranger."

"Looks like the roguish sort to me," a familiar voice crackled from behind him. Vara appeared at his shoulder, face contorted in a mask of annoyance. "Don't think that removing objects from this addle-brained oaf's person will endear you to anyone but him – and that's only because it requires you to touch him in a nearly intimate way."

"I wouldn't mind touching him in a very intimate way," the dark elf said with a grin. "And my touch has been known to endear me to more than just men." She looked at Vara with the same lasciviousness that had been directed at Cyrus.

"Oh, my." A clatter echoed in the foyer as Andren knocked over his inkwell.

Cyrus could feel Vara tense at his shoulder. Fearful of her reaction, he stepped forward and began to address the new arrivals. "Welcome to Sanctuary. We are glad to have you. You'll find our purpose very simple – we are a band of adventurers that prize honor above all. We travel to the corners of Arkaria in search of new places to explore, new items and experiences to enrich us, but strive above all to be protectors, saving Arkaria from the dangers that lurk outside these walls."

"And now, within it," Vara muttered, eyes fixed on Aisling.

"It is our solemn duty," Cyrus continued, "to defend those who cannot defend themselves. To assist the helpless, and to bring justice to those who would otherwise have no opportunity for redress. Does anyone have a problem with that?"

"I knew this was the right place," Thad said. "Is it true that you helped Goliath kill Ashan'agar, the former Dragonlord?"

Cyrus's jaw dropped. "What?"

The warrior stared at Cyrus, blank expression on his face. "I'd heard that you assisted Goliath in killing the Dragonlord in the Mountains of Nartanis last week."

A strange pounding in Cyrus's ears was suddenly all that was audible. He threw a look at Andren, who appeared stricken, then at Vara, whose fair complexion was flushed red, especially mottled on her cheeks and neck.

"I killed Ashan'agar," Cyrus whispered, menace crackling through every syllable.

"No, you didn't," Vara said behind him, voice choked. "Alaric finished him after you blinded and crippled him."

"The point is, Goliath had nothing to do with it! They barely arrived in time to reinforce our army in fighting the Dragonlord's minions!"

"That's not what the rumors around Pharesia are saying," Martaina breathed. "I heard that Goliath, led by Malpravus, killed the Dragonlord and that Sanctuary and the Daring helped in the battle."

"I heard the same thing in Saekaj Sovar," Aisling agreed.

"Wow," Andren said after a moment of silence. "We've been betrayed by Goliath. I can't believe it. If only there had been some warning - like if they had betrayed us before," he deadpanned.

"I'll bring this to the Council. Feel free," Cyrus said to the new applicants, "to ask around and see what your new guildmates have to say. Having actually been at the battle, they might be able to offer a different perspective than you've heard through rumor," he said, jaw clenched. "Do any of you have any questions?"

"Yes," Menlos interjected. "Can I keep my wolves with me?"

Cyrus raised an eyebrow and shot a look at Vara. "We'll have to discuss that in Council and get back to you. Anyone else?"

Martaina raised her hand and turned to Vara. "Are you... shelas'akur?"

Vara's face became flintlike, and the normal glitter of her eyes dimmed. "Yes," she said finally. "We will speak of it no more."

Martaina nodded. Menlos, Thad, Longwell and Aisling all wore the same perplexed expression as Cyrus. Andren was unreadable to Cyrus; a first in all the time they had known each other.

Another moment of uncomfortable silence passed. "I look forward to getting to know all of you in the coming days," Cyrus said, then turned his back and stalked toward the stairway, Vara only a few paces behind him. They did not speak until they had reached the top of the first landing.

"What the hell is shelas'akur?" Cyrus stumbled over the pronunciation.

"It's elvish for 'mind your own business'," she snapped.

"I'm not shocked at your reticence to have a peaceful discussion," Cy replied, trying to control his voice. "But you could let me know what questions I'm going to have to answer about you from applicants. It reflects poorly on us - on me."

"That's rich, coming from you!" Vara snarled. "Flirting with a new applicant as though she were some simpering courtesan from Pharesia!"

"Excuse me?" He looked back at her. "The flirting was one-sided, and it wasn't my side." His expression changed to a scowl. "Why do you care?"

"There is a certain standard of behavior expected from an officer of this guild," she said irritably. "You do not involve yourself with people below your station."

"How charmingly old-world elvish of you," Cyrus spat back. "And here I thought you were from Termina, where everyone is equal."

"It is not a matter of personal equality! It is a matter of positional equality - of you, as an officer, having power over whether they become members of this guild."

His arms snapped crisply back and forth, fists balled, as he climbed the staircase. "How would you have me handle it? Remonstrate the poor girl in front of her fellow applicants?"

"Yes, remonstrate her for bad conduct, chide her for making an unfavorable impression, and admonish her for having exceptionally poor taste in men."

"And women, it would seem."

"We have other problems to deal with," Vara changed the subject. "It would appear that Goliath is impugning our reputation."

"Finally, a point on which we both can agree."

They flew through the door to the Council Chambers to find it empty save for Niamh. "They did what?" she asked after hearing their explanation. "We need a meeting." Her face darkened. "*Another* meeting."

Vara nodded. "I'll go see who I can find."

"I'll check the officers' quarters," Cyrus added. Vara slipped out the doors without even a backward glance at him.

Cyrus started to leave, then turned back. "Niamh," he asked. "What does 'shelas'akur' mean?"

"Nice try." The red-haired druid regarded him coolly, eyes

indifferent. "No elf will answer that."

"I don't understand why no one can answer a simple question about her."

"It's a sensitive matter..." Niamh began.

"– one you don't discuss with outsiders. Yeah," he nodded. "I heard that line over and over from you when we were on our trek through the wilderness. But you know," he said with a smile, "someone, sooner or later, is going to give me the answers I'm looking for, even if they don't intend to."

Her eyes became haunted, but her mouth upturned, giving her just a hint of a wistful smile. He turned to leave but heard her whisper something else, just loud enough for him to hear: "I hope so."

Chapter 6

It took a few minutes to assemble the Council. By the time Cyrus re-entered the chamber he found Alaric waiting at the head of the table. He took his seat as Vara finished delivering the news.

Alaric folded his arms. "I am no more pleased than any of you. But we have no proof that this rumor originated with Goliath."

"I'm sure that some peasant in Reikonos started the rumor because Vara insulted him," Terian said, flecks of spittle flying out of his mouth in rage.

"That's plausible," Cyrus deadpanned. "She's offensive."

Vara cast a glare at him, but whatever reply she might have made was halted by one look from Alaric. "While odious and damaging to the ego, stealing credit for our efforts is not a criminal offense." The paladin placed his hands on the table in front of him. "We have many things to focus on; this cannot be one of them." He looked around the table. "Until we have evidence, we will not discuss this any further."

With grudging looks, the Council members stood to leave. "Cyrus," Alaric called. The warrior turned. "You and I have an appointment."

With a feeling of combined dread and curiosity, Cyrus followed him.

"Have you gotten yourself another sword?" the Ghost asked as they descended the stairs.

"No," Cyrus admitted. "I've been postponing it."

"Let us stop by the armory and see what Belkan can provide."

Alaric pushed through the doors when they reached the armory. A smell of fresh leather filled the air, and hooks stuck out of every surface. When last Cyrus had been here, they were covered with weapons of all kinds. Now they all stood empty save for a few axes that clinked against the stone walls, disturbed by the shifting air current of the opening door.

Belkan, the armorer, was an aged warrior, with gray hair and a face that looked as though it had been poorly carved out of granite. His nose had been broken on several occasions by the look of it, and a host of scars crisscrossed the wrinkles that lined his chest all the way down his open vest, which looked to be made of some animal skin.

"Davidon," the old warrior snapped in greeting. "I was expecting you days ago." The old armorer turned to look at Alaric, favoring the Ghost with a nod of deference.

"Belkan, our young warrior seems to have misplaced his sword whilst battling a dragon," Alaric said, voice dripping with irony. "Do you have a worthy replacement for him?"

A pained look crossed the armorer's face. "Unfortunately, I don't think I do." His gaze flitted around the bare walls. "With all the recruiting he's done, I've given out just about every sword that I had to get this army ready for battle." Belkan leaned over, reaching under the counter. "The best I've got left is this," he said as he placed a short sword on the counter in front of him.

The blade was as long as Cyrus's forearm and hand, flat steel separated from a rounded handle by a thin rectangular guard. The pommel was a half a sphere of unadorned metal. *This may be the plainest sword I've ever seen,* Cyrus thought. *And damned short.* Cyrus felt his heart fall in his chest. "I had a feeling there wasn't going to be much left."

Belkan's white, bushy eyebrows furrowed. "Now see here, son, this might not be as fancy as your mystically enchanted swords –"

"Or long enough to keep a gnome at arm's length," Cyrus said with a pronounced glumness.

" – but it's well made, it's well taken care of, and it's a fair sight better than using your gauntlets."

"Yes, it is," Cyrus said without enthusiasm.

"Take heart." Alaric clapped him on the shoulder reassuringly. "It is the warrior that makes the sword great, not vice versa."

"Alaric," Cyrus said in a muted whisper, "it's half the length of the blades I normally use. I'll take it because I've got no other options, but I'm going to be suffering until I get a better sword."

"Perhaps," the Ghost suggested, "you could go to Reikonos and acquire a sword that would be more fitting."

Belkan snorted. "I doubt it. The 'Big Three' guilds – Amarath's Raiders, Burnt Offerings and Endeavor – have bought every weapon in every major city they can get their hands on since they've begun expeditions into the Realms of the gods. The blacksmiths in Reikonos have a two year waiting list for weapons, and that's just for me – I send quite a bit of business their way." The armorer shook his head. "Sorry, son, but this is the only option unless you want a rusty blade."

Cyrus dropped his eyes to the short sword. It gleamed in the torchlight, showing a blade that, although short, had been impeccably taken care of. "No, this will have to do."

"Bring it back when you find better," Belkan said, tipping the short sword into its scabbard. "I know you will. What about that sword of legend you've been working on assembling?"

"Not even close."

"Pity," Belkan said as he handed over the blade. Cyrus placed the scabbard on his belt as they walked out the door. "Davidon!" Belkan called out, causing Cy to turn back. "Next time, come see me right after you lose your sword, not a week later."

"Would it have made any difference?" Cy asked.

"Yes," the old armorer said. "Yesterday afternoon I gave up the long blade I was holding for you; figured you'd made other arrangements."

Cyrus closed his eyes for a moment and let the words sink in. "Hopefully there's not a next time." He turned and left, following Alaric.

"Why are we going to the dungeons?" Cyrus asked as they crossed the foyer and entered a hallway that lead along the side of the Great Hall.

"We have a matter to settle," the Ghost answered without inflection.

"Do you ever get tired of being cryptic?"

"No." A slight smile upturned the corner of Alaric's mouth. "Does it annoy you?"

"Yes."

"You are in good company," the Ghost replied as they reached the staircase and began the descent to the dungeons.

"Is there any reason you can't just say, 'Cy, here's what I need taken care of and here's why,' and just be done with it?" Irritation rattled in every word.

"I could. I might say we are going to the dungeons to converse with a rock giant who until last week was a dedicated servant of the Dragonlord. But there is no anticipation in that. Life is full of surprises, and to have all them revealed at the outset would make a boring life, bereft of adventure."

"After the last year," Cy mumbled, "I could do with a little less surprise and a little more certainty."

"An odd comment from an 'adventurer'. Think how dull things would be if I simply spilled out all I knew instead of doling it a bit at a time." The paladin halted at the bottom of the stairs, his face a mask of seriousness. "There are secrets I know that could get you and everyone you know killed, that could rock the foundations of Arkaria. Should I spill them out on the table, let you sift through and choose which ones you'd like to know?"

Cyrus's eyes widened. "You're joking to make a point."

"Perhaps." The seriousness did not fade. "When I am being mysterious, it is either for your own good or because I would not argue with you to get you to do something that is in your own best interests."

Cyrus shifted back to annoyance. "So why won't you tell me your suspicions regarding my nightmare?"

The paladin sighed. "Once again we go back to my earlier statement about it being 'for your own good'."

Cyrus threw his hands in the air in a gesture of surrender. "Fine. Keep your secrets."

Alaric nodded. "I know you are not pleased with me and I do not blame you."

Cyrus brushed past him. "I'm sure hidden in my nightmare is a secret that could destroy Arkaria. Let's just get done with whatever it is you brought me down here for."

Alaric studied him for a long moment without speaking. "This way." He led Cyrus through a labyrinth of corridors until they reached a locked door guarded by two warriors that Cyrus knew to be long time members of Sanctuary, swords at their sides. Cy looked with envy at their weapons as they saluted Alaric. One reached for a key and unlocked the door, stepping to the side to admit them.

Cyrus walked through the door following Alaric's gesture that he should enter first. The cool air prickled his skin as he entered, and the lack of light sent his eyes into a scramble to adjust to the semi-darkness. There was a smell in the room that gave Cyrus a flash back to a time during a fight when he had been hit hard, dropped to the ground and his face landed in the dirt. A clacking of chains was subtle but audible against the far wall.

He focused his eyes, trying to find the origin of the noise. The stones on the wall opposite him seemed to be moving. His gaze moved up - and up, until it reached the apex of the moving rock in front of him. It was a rock giant: ten feet tall, brushing against the ceiling, with a skin that looked to be composed of living stone. Chains with steel links an inch thick were draped across both of its hands, binding them to each other and to its feet.

Cyrus hid his surprise, but only because he had faced this kind of beast before. "A rock giant," he muttered. "I thought you were kidding."

"Kidding makes it difficult to be mysterious." Cy's head whipsawed around to catch the smile on Alaric's face. "Don't be shy; introduce yourself."

Cyrus turned to face the giant in front of him. "My name is Cyrus Davidon. I killed your master and I've killed your kind before." The words came out in a snarl, all his frustration unbottled at once. His hand slid to the hilt of his sword.

The rock giant glared down, red eyes shining in the dark. They surveyed him for almost a full minute before it spoke in a voice that sounded like falling gravel. "You killed my master? You killed Ashan'agar?"

"Damned right I did, I took both his eyes and I rode him into the ground." Cyrus did not break off, staring down the wall of a creature in front of him.

"He only had one eye." The voice came out in a low rumble, the eyes still fixated on his.

"I took his other a year ago, when I invaded his den," Cyrus crowed.

The red eyes of the rock giant fell for a moment. "So you killed Ashan'agar?"

A small cough from behind him stopped Cyrus's reply. He turned to face Alaric. "I didn't think about it at the time, but you deprived me of the kill."

The paladin's helmet was under the crook of his elbow and he looked at Cyrus in amusement. "You had just been resurrected and were still weak. I assumed you wanted him dead – the sooner, the better."

"Good point." Cyrus turned back to the rock giant. "I blinded and crippled Ashan'agar." He gestured to Alaric with a thumb. "He delivered the killing stroke."

The chains rattled in front of them as the rock giant readjusted himself. The red eyes turned to Alaric. "Is this true? Did you kill my master?"

Alaric coughed. "I did."

The room shook as the rock giant fell to a knee and bowed his head. "You have killed my master. I, Fortin the Rapacious, am now your servant."

"We do not condone the keeping of slaves," Alaric said.

"I am not a slave." The rumbling voice filled the air. "I am a rock giant, a creation of the god of Earth, Rotan. My people choose to follow those who are strongest. I pledged myself to Ashan'agar because he was mightiest." The red eyes narrowed. "I pledge myself to you now, not as your slave but as a warrior in your service, because you have bested my former master."

Alaric shifted to rest his hand on his chin. "What are the terms of your service?"

Fortin returned to his feet. "If you order me to do something, I will do it, even if it is to my death. In exchange, you feed and house me."

Cyrus raised an eyebrow. "What does a rock giant eat?"

The red eyes found his. "I prefer gnomes."

Alaric shook his head. "That is unacceptable."

"Dwarves, then?"

"No."

The rock giant's head sagged. "I can feast upon other beasts you would consume - cows, deer, leopards... but I prefer gnomes."

Cyrus shook his head. "If only Brevis were still here."

"May I eat your enemies?" Fortin asked, his voice laden with innocence.

Alaric sighed once more. "We will discuss it on a case-by-case basis." The paladin straightened. "I accept your terms of service, provided you will restrain yourself in your choice of meals to options I deem acceptable."

The rock giant bowed his head. "I will serve you until you are killed by someone stronger. Until then I will follow your orders - even if it means I cannot eat gnomes."

Cyrus turned to Alaric. "Are you sure this is such a good idea? What if he turns on us?"

Alaric looked at Cyrus. "Then you will kill him."

A clinking behind him drew Cy's attention back to the rock giant, who was studying him. "How did you kill the rock giant you defeated?"

A flush crept up Cyrus's cheeks. "I knocked him off a bridge into a pool of lava."

The red eyes moved up and down with Fortin's head in a slow nod. "I knew the giant whom you killed. Well done. Were I him, I would have minded my footing."

"Were you there the day I killed him?"

The giant nodded once more. "I fought your compatriots on the bridge before you escaped. You were the warrior in black who challenged Ashan'agar on the platform."

"You recognize me now?"

"Not really," Fortin said, moving his shoulders in a shrug. "You tiny fleshbag races all look alike to me."

"I will have a guard release you from those chains," Alaric said.

"No need," Fortin grunted. The sounds of the clanking chains stopped, replaced by the straining of metal.

Something stung Cyrus in the arm, impact blunted by his vambraces. "Ouch," he muttered and stooped to pick up a piece of metal - a lock, broken open.

With a clanking, the chains fell from the rock giant. "Would you like me to sleep down here?"

Alaric's eyebrow raised. "I think the upper floors would be unsuited for your weight. We will prepare accommodations here in the basement, but not in a prison cell."

The red eyes surveyed the space around him. "Good. I find this underground space... homey."

"Very well," Alaric nodded. "We have a guard quarters down the hall from here. I'll have it cleared out for you."

"Where will your guards sleep?"

"We rarely have prisoners, but if we do they can remain in their quarters upstairs."

"I can assist you the next time you do," Fortin said. "Intimidation and torture are two of my specialties."

"I doubt you'll be needing those skills here." With a bow, Alaric moved toward the door. "I will send for you when the dinner hour approaches, Fortin. Welcome to Sanctuary."

Cyrus lingered for a moment. "You're bigger than me, stronger than me, and every inch of you is a weapon." His voice hardened. "But if you harm anyone in Sanctuary, I will smash through that rocky skin and disembowel you." The warrior straightened. "Just so we understand each other."

The rock giant's red eyes followed Cyrus as he began to back out of the room. "Consider me duly intimidated, fleshbag."

The look of intensity left Cy's face as he followed Alaric back to the stairs. "I don't know whether I should be excited or terrified that we have *that* fighting on our side."

"You should be thrilled - so long as he continues to fight on our side."

"Yeah, so long as someone doesn't come along and kill you," Cyrus said with a nod. A dawning realization crawled up his spine. "So if you ever die in battle, does that mean he would betray us then and there?"

The paladin shrugged with an air of unconcern. "It may."

"Should I be worried?" Cy fixed his eyes on the Ghost, who removed the helmet from the crook of his arm and slid it over his face.

"I wouldn't lose any sleep over it - you need all you can get at this point." An amused smile crossed Alaric's face as he turned and walked away.

Chapter 7

The days that followed were filled with training exercises; efforts to enforce martial discipline and teach the applicants how to be part of a large army. Fortin had shown up and responded to orders with more enthusiasm than almost any of the other new recruits.

"Fortin, refrain from swinging your arms when you're in the middle of a formation," Cyrus suggested after the giant had hit three rangers, almost decapitating one.

"I will try, because Alaric asked me to follow your orders, but perhaps it would be wise if you changed the formation to give me more elbow room."

"I've heard worse ideas," Vaste muttered from behind Cyrus.

"The only way I can change this formation," Cy explained, drawing on reserves of patience he didn't feel, "is to place you at the back."

"That won't work." The rock giant's boulder head swiveled from side to side. "I'm of no use to you in the back. Better I be out front and the others follow me."

Cyrus did not respond but turned away, expression suffused with frustration.

"He's not wrong, you know," Niamh said.

"Of course he's not wrong," Cy snapped. "If he was wrong, I'd tell him so and be done with it. It's because he's right that it's a problem. I've got an army trained with tactics that don't take into account that we've got the most effective fighter in Arkaria in our midst. So my choices are to hamstring the fighter and lose his advantages or retrain my whole army."

"But this is not a bad problem to have," J'anda whispered. "Three quarters of our force have seen battle once and been training for only a few weeks. If we must retrain, this would be the time."

"You're right," Cy muttered. "But I've never seen an army deal with this sort of... problem."

"It's a simple fix," came Vara's voice. "A rock giant is not much bigger than a troll warrior." She nodded at Vaste. "The bigger guilds, like Amarath's Raiders, would place him at the rear and use him as a strategic reserve in tighter spaces, like caves, knowing that he is a bottleneck that could slow down and kill them. In wide open spaces he becomes the front line, either replacing the primary warrior or becoming the secondary to mop up additional enemies. Either way, you give the biggest fighter the space to do what he does best."

A moment passed before Cyrus spoke. "Makes sense. Do we have enough time to retrain the army before the Alliance invasion of the Realm of Darkness?"

Vara paused. When she broke her silence, every word seemed to come only with great effort. "You are a... capable... General. I am certain you will have them trained sufficiently to handle the dangers of Yartraak's realm by the time you go."

Cy turned to her, unable to hide his surprise. "Did it cause you physical pain to say that?"

"Hush." Her eyes fell to his waist. "What is that?" she said, pointing to the scabbard in his belt.

"It's my sword."

"It's appalling. My arms are longer," she said with a distinct frown. "How are you to hold enemies at bay?"

"I'll find a way," he replied, nostrils flaring.

Things had been quiet in the Plains of Perdamun after the last bandit attack, with no destroyed convoys found in spite of several sweeps of the roads. "Perhaps they have given up," J'anda said with a shrug.

"Seems odd that they'd devastate convoy after convoy and suddenly disappear," Cyrus replied. "Why not keep doing what's working?"

No answer was forthcoming. The day of the Alliance invasion of the Realm of Darkness was soon upon them, the chill of autumn deepening as the winds howled across the otherwise peaceful Plains. Cyrus entered the Great Hall an hour before the time that Sanctuary's army would leave to meet the Alliance force.

The Great Hall was longer than the foyer but not nearly as wide. Along one side ran a hearth and fireplace bigger than the one in the foyer; along the other ran a window that opened into the kitchens with a long bar at the base, food resting upon it. Cyrus's nose always found the Great Hall a pleasing place; the smell of the cooking reminded him of very faint memories of his childhood. The ceiling reached up several hundred feet, wood beams as big around as him supporting the stone ceiling. Many stories above, he knew, was the Council Chamber.

He joined Curatio in line at the window, filling his plate with bacon, ham, fresh rare beef cooked in spiced juices, eggs and fresh baked bread. Carafes of fruit juices lay at the far end, along with boiling hot coffee and fresh milk.

Larana Stillhet, Sanctuary's resident cook, seamstress and blacksmith, was in the kitchen watching Cyrus quietly - which was how she did everything. Her eyes were green, and she habitually sported dingy robes of dark greens and browns. She was a bit older than Cyrus, but with stringy brown hair that looked as though it had never received half the attention she put into her cooking. Freckles dotted her sun darkened cheeks and when he caught her gaze, she blushed and looked away. He cast a smile her way, then followed Curatio to the Council's table where Niamh, J'anda and Vaste were already eating.

They ate in relative silence until Vara arrived with a bowl of oatmeal and, after a moment's hesitation, took the open seat next to Cyrus's. "What's that?" he asked between mouthfuls of ham. "Horse food?"

She rolled her eyes, a favorite expression. "Not all of us cart around as much padding in our armor as you."

He stopped. "You calling me fat?"

"Only that unused space betwixt your ears," she said before taking in a spoonful of her breakfast.

His brows furrowed together. He was wider than her, had more upper body strength and muscle mass. His eyes looked over her frame, which was thin and lean. She was not malnourished but neither did she have the heavily muscled look that warriors tended to sport. Her legs, even with their armor were less than half the size of his. And yet... he reached over, resting one of his hands on her shoulder.

The response was immediate and painful. Her hand was on his, his thumb was screaming in pain, and she knocked him off his chair with ease. "We keep our hands to ourselves during breakfast," she said without looking up from her food. "And at all other times, as well."

"Wasn't trying to get amorous with you," he grunted. "That was an experiment."

"To test your tolerance for pain?" She kept eating, not even deigning to look at him.

He smiled as he picked himself up. "I already knew that was high. I've seen you leap unreasonable distances, do considerably more damage than a little waif with your musculature should be able to do." His smile grew wider. "It's your armor. It's mystical."

"You're quite clever. It's taken you a year to realize this? I weigh one hundred and forty six pounds and carry a sword that weighs half as much as I do." She stopped eating to look at him for just a moment. "Your powers of deductive reasoning do truly fill me with a sense of awe." With a certain stiffness, she returned to eating her oatmeal.

"Wow," Niamh said. "Don't you two ever take a rest from having a go at each other?"

An awkward silence filled the air and Cyrus looked at Vara, who returned his glance for just a beat. "No," they chorused.

Curatio chuckled. "Vara, I take it you won't be joining us in the Realm of Darkness today?"

"You assume correctly. I shall be spending my time outside of the company of treacherous trolls."

Eyes widened around the table. Niamh shot a nervous look at Vaste. "She means me," Cyrus explained.

She frowned. "I mean the Alliance. I have never died, and I avoid Alliance expeditions because I wish to continue that winning trend." Her words hung heavy around the table.

"And what will you be doing while we're gone?" Cyrus asked.

She smiled, a mischievous look turning up the corners of her mouth and putting a sparkle in her eyes. "Plotting your demise."

The Sanctuary army assembled in the foyer in preparation for the trek to the Realm of Darkness portal. They took the path toward the Waking Woods. It was a merry bunch, the nearly thousand of them, most swooping along with the Falcon's Essence, hovering a few feet off the path.

The walk took several hours through very pretty terrain. The trees of the Waking Woods grew taller and taller as they ventured deeper into the forest, until after an hour the boughs twisted together above them, creating a canopy of darkness that blotted out much of the sunlight. The biggest trees grew hundreds of feet into the air and had trunks fifteen and twenty feet in diameter. Moss hung from the low branches and the whole place smelled of fresh leaves, even as the first tinges of red had begun to leech the green from them.

The noise of the forest diminished as the army moved through, drowning out the animals and insects that made the Waking Woods their home. The autumn breeze stirred the first fallen leaves around Cyrus's feet, bringing them around in small whirlwinds, dancing in the air.

"Don't see vegetation like this in the Plains of Perdamun," Niamh sighed. "Some of these trees are thousands of years old."

"Do you talk to trees?" Cyrus asked her, voice tinged with curiosity.

The red-haired elf smiled. "As a druid, I do share a deeper bond with nature. I can pick up on certain signs, things that a forest might be telling me by intuition and experience, but no, I don't talk to trees, unless they're talking to me."

Cyrus's eyebrow raised. "Do trees often talk to you?"

Her smile turned sad. "Not anymore." She did not elaborate.

Andren tromped up behind him. "So why are we going to Darkness again?"

"I don't know why *you're* going," Cyrus replied. "But I'm going because I like places where I can't see the things that are trying to kill me."

"You're a right funny bastard, you know that?"

"Adventure, Andren. It's what we do."

The elf sneered. "I haven't forgotten that. But we're talking about the Realm of a god here. I know they say he won't be home, but I have concerns about facing a god: that I'll be dismembered, or worse."

"Let not your heart be troubled. And don't forget that we've also got a personal stake in this invasion."

"You mean your sword quest?"

"Yeah." Cyrus looked away, staring into the woods. "That."

A flash of irritation cut through Andren's voice. "What's left?"

Cyrus shook his head and reached beneath his armor, removing a scrap of parchment and unfolded it, reading it once before handing it to Andren, even though he knew every word by heart.

> ***Serpent's Bane*** *– The guard and grip are in possession of Ashan'agar, the Dragonlord.*
> ***Death's Head*** *– The pommel is held by Mortus, God of Death.*
> ***Edge of Repose*** *– The Gatekeeper of Purgatory holds the blade as a prize for one who knows to ask for it.*
> ***Avenger's Rest*** *– G'koal, Empress of Enterra has the Scabbard.*
> ***Quartal*** *– The ore needed to smith the sword together is found only in the Realm of Yartraak, God of Darkness.*

Brought together by one who is worthy, they shall form ***Praelior, the Champion's Sword.***

"I need the quartal to smith it. I need the blade from Purgatory. And I need the scabbard from Enterra to enchant the sword."

Andren looked down at the parchment. "Because you got the pommel last year and someone left the Serpent's Bane on your bed a few weeks ago - still don't know who?" Cyrus shook his head at Andren's question and the healer gave a head shake of his own before returning the parchment. "Still sounds like a lot of work to me."

"It'll be worth it."

They reached a clearing, with a gap in the canopy above that let in the sunlight. At the center stood an ovoid ring of rock with runes carved around the edges. It had a gaping hole through the middle wide enough for several men to walk through side by side. It was filled with a crackling black energy that seemed to pull the light out of the air around them, darkening the sky as one drew closer, until finally, standing just before the portal, it was black as night even in the light of midday.

Forming around it was a small group that Cyrus knew was one of their Allied guilds - the Daring. Cyrus was greeted by three of their officers. The first was a human warrior with dark hair and light eyes. Unlike himself, this human had painted his armor a deep gray. "Cass," Cyrus acknowledged him with a smile. "It's been a few weeks. I hope you're well." Their hands met in a firm handshake that became a contest of grip.

"Boys, please - if you're gonna wrestle it out, at least strip down and coat yourselves in oil first," came the caustic voice of Erith Frostmoor, another of the Daring's officers. A dark elf, her white hair stood in marked contrast to her dark blue skin. She wore a robe of red silk that glistened in the low light of the clearing. Her slightly fanged teeth pushed her lips back in a grin. "Then at least Elisabeth and I could enjoy watching."

The third officer of the Daring frowned at being mentioned in Erith's comment. "I don't know that I'd enjoy watching that, Erith," Elisabeth said, her fine elven features contorted with discomfort.

When Cyrus had first seen Elisabeth a year earlier, he had thought her one of the fairest elves he had ever laid eyes upon. Her long brown hair lay across her shoulders, which were covered with a light chainmail with tiny rings half the diameter of Cyrus's little finger. Her features were perfectly carved and proportioned and her face was radiant, even with the slight cringe it now wore.

"Oh come on!" the dark elf harangued her lighter-skinned counterpart. "Two big, strapping men like that! How could you not?"

"Nice to see you, Cyrus," Elisabeth said, ignoring Erith.

He nodded at her, but before they could exchange any further pleasantries, they were interrupted. A blowing horn filled the air as hoof beats echoed in the woods. An army marched from the opposite direction that Sanctuary's had arrived from, a line of troops that stretched out of sight. Above came a winged griffon that landed in the clearing, the first of a dozen riders on flying mounts. Some rode on creatures Cyrus could scarcely imagine, including something that looked like a small dragon.

At the front of Goliath's army came a host of riders, most on horses but a few on war wolves the size of cows, as well as what looked like an elephant and some other fantastic beasts that were unrecognizable to Cyrus.

Malpravus, Goliath's leader, was a dark elf that habitually sported a dark blue robe with a hood that often covered his face. When it was exposed, his features were gaunt, almost skeletal. The black horse that he was riding looked impressive next to the smaller pony that Tolada, a dwarf and one of Goliath's officers, rode in on.

A tall elf Cyrus recognized as a Goliath officer named Carrack, a wizard, dismounted on the other side of Malpravus from a war wolf, wearing black robes with crimson highlights and a red sash looped at the waist. His robes had no cowl and an open neck, showing his muscled chest, surprising for a spell caster. A black tattoo was visible leading up to his neck, stopping just short of his Adam's apple.

"Remember," Niamh said in a voice of warning, "Alaric wants no mention of the rumors. He's saving it for the next Alliance officers' meeting."

"I'll keep my mouth shut if you do." Cyrus shot her a wry smile that went unreturned.

Malpravus dismounted and slid over to where Cyrus had gathered with the other officers of the Daring. "So wonderful to see all of you here today." Malpravus had a voice that was unnaturally smooth. "I see that Sanctuary has come in force, a pleasing sight indeed," the dark elf smiled, mouth visible beneath the hood. "Of course, our own numbers have swollen in the last weeks as well..."

"Wonder how that happened," Vaste said under his breath. If Malpravus noticed, he did not interrupt himself.

"With our additional forces, this should only be mildly difficult," Malpravus mused. "We will divide our armies into smaller forces, with a general at the head of each." His eyes flicked toward the small group of the Daring. "I would recommend we disperse your force into the Sanctuary group – I envision armies of about 500 combatants, making for easier movement and coordination. We'll be marching in a column along a straight line for the bulk of the invasion."

The dark elf swiveled to face Cyrus. "My boy, will you kindly divide your army in two? You lead half of it and pick another of your officers to lead the other half."

"Sure," Cyrus said after a moment of surprise. "Curatio will spearhead our second army."

"Ah, yes, Curatio," Malpravus said with an ever-widening smile. "Perfect." Something in the way he said it caused Cyrus to shudder. "I will place Tolada, Carrack and Yei in charge of the other Goliath armies... perfect, perfect." Now the Goliath Guildmaster seemed to be thinking out loud; though with his eyes covered, it was impossible to tell. Behind him, Carrack wore a self-satisfied smile while Tolada wore a blank expression.

Malpravus waved his hand vaguely and cocked his head at an angle. "You may disperse now; go and form your armies, and we enter the portal in a few moments. I will address everyone before we go." Turning, he swept away, seeming to glide across the ground.

"So comforting to be given a clear idea of what we're going into," Vaste muttered again.

"Relax, big guy," Elisabeth said in a soothing voice. "He'll tell us before we go charging in."

"I suspect he still won't have told us what we're facing by the end of the excursion," Vaste replied.

"Bah!" She dismissed him. "You're so negative."

The troll's eyebrows retreated up his massive and balding forehead. "And you're so trusting. Like a fluffy bunny just before the leopard eats it."

She gawked at Vaste. "You think he'd throw us into death?"

The troll healer's jaw hardened. "If it benefited him in any way, great or small."

"That's not a good position for an officer of this Alliance to take." Elisabeth's eyes were narrow, her lips pursed in clear disapproval.

Vaste did not answer her. Fortunately, Erith broke the silence. "It's not a good position, but it's a safe one." Elisabeth's gaze moved to her own guildmate in silent accusation. "Malpravus would sacrifice his own mother's soul in a flash if he thought he'd get a bronze piece out of it, Elisabeth."

Curatio spoke. "We have orders from our General to divide into armies." Nods around the officer's circle greeted that assertion, and they broke.

It took Cyrus ten minutes to divide Sanctuary's army. During training they had practiced breaking the army into smaller pieces. Moving them into the formations they had practiced allowed him to complete his reassignment before Goliath had begun theirs.

He placed Cass in Curatio's army as the primary warrior, with Fortin as the secondary.

"You have a rock giant?" Cass muttered. "What do you need me for?"

"Human sacrifice." Looking back he found Erith watching him from nearby and just behind her, Aisling. "What?"

Erith looked at him with amusement. "Sorry. Still thinking of you boys wrestling it out."

He shook his head and turned to Aisling. "And you? Are you concerned about the invasion?"

"Nah." She looked at him, black eyes shining. "I'm concerned with afterward. Any plans?"

Cyrus coughed. "After a successful expedition, there's a celebratory feast in the Great Hall that filters into the lounge afterward, with much drinking and merriment."

Erith watched Aisling with undisguised amusement as the blue skinned ranger slinked closer to Cyrus, her feet making no sound as she walked. Her hands rested on her hips, but almost seemed to caress upward along her sides, pushing her chest out. "What happens at those parties?"

Cyrus's eyes widened and he looked at Erith in a moment of panic. She snorted, turned and walked away. "Like I said – a feast, then drinking and merriment."

She took another step closer. He took a step back. "I won't

bite." She giggled. "Until you ask me to." Her eyes seemed to swallow his and he couldn't break away from her gaze. In a flash he was reminded of Ashan'agar, trying to bend his will. "Until you beg me to." A seductive smile creased her lips and now she was close enough that he felt her breath.

"Frankly, I'm more concerned with my gold at this point."

"I was just showing off before." She reached out to him and he counter-stepped away again. "I would never steal from a guildmate, especially not one so..."

"Stop," he interrupted her, closing his eyes in a bid to break the rising tension between them. "I am an officer, you are an applicant. This is not right; it's..."

"Wrong? Naughty?" she said before he could get another word out. He felt her brush against him, having taken full advantage of the second that he'd stopped to close the small distance between them. "Doesn't that give you a rush, knowing you could have your way with me?" There was nothing but mischief and desire in her eyes.

"That's appalling," he answered, but the words came out feeble. "What is it that so entices you about me?"

She shrugged, still looking at him with her lips pursed just so, and he closed his eyes again for a second and let out a sigh. "Until you can answer, I'm not interested." He turned on his heel to walk away.

"Maybe I just like a man who doesn't cave to me in the first five minutes," came her voice from behind him. He looked back. "Maybe I'm just looking for a man who can last longer than most." She smiled again, and it was back to the suggestive look she had given him earlier.

"Perhaps in the future, a serious answer," he said as he turned, leaving her alone on the edge of Sanctuary's army.

"May I have your attention?" Malpravus called out from the far end of the assemblage, magic boosting the volume of his speech to overcome the thousand voices talking in the clearing. "We will begin in moments, and I need to outline things so that we can move forward, comfortable in our roles and in this army."

He ticked off points on his bony fingers. "First, when you get separated from the army, do try not to panic. Screaming and thrashing about in the darkness will only hasten your death."

"I'm not comfortable with that role." Vaste had eased next to Cyrus.

"Second," Malpravus continued, "some of you will die. I would estimate something on the order of fifty to seventy-five percent of you. These are acceptable losses," he said, bringing a hush over the crowd. "We will of course endeavor to bring you back to life through the use of a healer's resurrection spell."

"My comfort is not growing," Cyrus whispered to Vaste. "Why is my comfort not growing?"

"I think it has something to do with the evil and treacherous General admitting that getting three out of four of us killed would be acceptable to him."

"Third," the dark elf went on, "even if you are gifted with the eyes of an elf, or the magical equivalent, it is unlikely you will see more than a few feet in front of you. Be assured," boomed Malpravus's voice from beneath the cowl of his cloak, "I know where we are going at all times."

"What if you die?" came a voice from the Sanctuary part of the crowd. A small rush of levity ran through the Goliath forces.

Malpravus smiled, visible beneath the cowl as a wide, knowing grin that was bereft of any warmth. "You need not fear, for I am a master of death."

"If possible," Vaste whispered, "that makes me feel less comfortable than the thought of leadership falling to Tolada." Cyrus nodded in agreement.

"My army will move first into the portal," Malpravus concluded. "All others, follow behind in order."

"Wait," Cyrus said under his breath, with a certain amount of alarm. "Did I miss the part about what we're facing or what to do after we're into the portal?"

"You did not," Vaste assured him. "I believe that other than the comments, 'Many of you will die,' 'Try not to thrash about in the dark,' and 'I'm a necromancer, watch me play with your corpse,' there was no helpful instruction in his speech."

"Well, the 'try not to thrash about in the dark' bit could come in handy."

"I'm more worried about the 'many of you will die' part."

The armies of Goliath began a steady march forward, disappearing into the portal in neatly ordered rows. When the time came, Cyrus marshaled his army into formation and led them through into the twisted, distorted black veil of the passage to the Realm of Darkness - and watched all light fade away.

Chapter 8

When Cyrus emerged on the other side, he waited for his eyes to adjust to the darkness. The only point of light visible to him was a lantern hanging from what looked like a lamppost, shedding a small amount of light on cobblestones below it. He took a deep breath that tasted of stale air and felt a sense of nervousness from the near-blindness of the dark cause a crawling sensation up his back. The background noise of the army around him was a low hum of conversation; from behind him were voices of alarm from those just entering the Realm and finding themselves unable to see.

"What the hell?" Cyrus muttered as he continued to move forward toward the lamp, following the elements of Goliath's last army. He could hear the pads at the bottom of his plate boots landing on cobblestones.

A sudden lightening filled his eyes, and he looked back to see Vaste, fingers twirling in the conclusion of a spell. "That help at all?" the troll asked.

"A little. I think Yartraak is pretty serious about his Realm being in darkness. We might need a lantern."

"I've heard that the Realm of Darkness swallows all non-mystical light sources." He pointed to Thad nearby, who was tinkering with a lamp. "Hey, warrior," he called out.

Thad looked up. "What?"

"How's that working?"

"It went out the minute we crossed over."

Cyrus looked at Vaste. "Any other ideas?"

His brow furrowed in thought; an unnatural look for a troll. "Nyad!"

The wizard broke through the crowd to come over to them, pale skin even more washed out in the lamplight. "Yes?" she asked, her tone meshing with the formal red robes that she wore. Nyad was royalty; the youngest daughter of the King of the Elves, yet Cyrus had seen her start blazing fires with a few words and a shake of her staff.

"Start a fire; we need light," Vaste suggested.

She waved her hands in a series of gestures and pointed her staff into the distance. A jet of fire burst forth from it and shot fifteen feet before its arc carried it to the ground below. The light it put out flickered, illuminating the area around them. "I can cast a bigger flame," she told them. "Just didn't want to waste the magical energy if it didn't work."

The flames continued to burn from her last spell for several minutes, illuminating the edge of the cobblestone road and revealing dead grass and sand at the roadside. The army of Sanctuary marched along in silence, still following the last of Goliath's forces. Cyrus walked at the fore of his group, struggling to see into the darkness.

A tingle once more ran down his spine. He turned to say something to Vaste only to find the troll gone from his place in the formation. "Vaste?" Cyrus called out. There was no answer. He looked at Nyad. "Where's Vaste?"

Nyad looked around. "I... I don't know, he was here a minute ago."

"Formation halt! Everyone check to your left and right," he shouted. "See if anyone's missing." Shouts filled the air around him.

"We've got one missing here!"

"A whole row missing in front of us!"

"One here!"

"Two here!"

"Andren... is missing here," Erith said.

Cyrus craned his neck. There was a gap in the line where his old friend had been. His stomach dropped and a memory sprang to mind of a dark tunnel, with row after row of bodies, with one missing. "What is going on here?" he muttered.

"We're in the middle of the Realm of Darkness, and we seem to be disappearing in ones and twos," a voice answered him from behind. His head whipped around to find Aisling staring at him. "You asked," she said with a shrug.

"Sounds sinister when you put it like that," Cyrus agreed. "I wonder if they wandered away from the formation in the darkness?"

"You think they might wander back?" Nyad's face was lined with concern.

"Sounds like going in circles," Aisling said. "I don't like going around; I prefer going down –"

Cyrus grunted. "Must you use everything for innuendo?"

A grin split her blue face, all he could see in the darkness.

"Yes."

"Where's Vara when I need her?" Cyrus shook his head.

"What do you need Vara for?" Nyad replied from behind him. "Other than the obvious."

"Quiet, you," he shot back with exaggerated menace. Nyad had been a constant thorn in his side in the matter of Vara, telling him to confess his feelings for her. He had thus far refused, not wishing to expose himself to that particular hell.

There was a stir in front of them and his thoughts of Andren and the other missing souls receded. Screams echoed in the darkness, coming from the Goliath army in front of them. "Nyad," Cyrus said in a low voice. "Illumination."

The wizard nodded and grabbed one of her fellows out of the line behind them. Setting themselves at the front corners of the Sanctuary line, they sent twin bursts of flame at an angle on either side of the army's formation. The fire was long and sustained, lighting the scene before them.

Scattered movement filled their view as the Goliath army scattered in all directions, most surging backward in retreat, running right into Cyrus's lines. Faces frozen in terror passed him, breaking to either side of his army as they ran. In front of the remains of the Goliath army something else was moving, a shadow that seemed to absorb the light.

Twisting, turning, a shade lit by the wizard's flame, it stood thrice the height of any of the mortals - and it struck down again as Cyrus watched, knocking bodies aside and causing screams of agony and pain as the firelight dimmed.

"Hold the line!" a voice shouted above the retreating Goliath army. "Stand your ground and fight!" Carrack stood at the very back of the Goliath army that was breaking, hectoring them onward. The elf brought a hand down, slapping one of Goliath's retreating warriors and dragging another by the collar forward. He pushed the two of them forward and then took several steps back himself.

"Carrack!" Cyrus called. "March with us and we'll help marshal your forces as we move forward!"

The elven wizard watched the two men he had sent forward disappear into the carnage of the battle with the shadow. Sickening screams cut through the dark. "I don't think so," he said with a shake of the head. "Best you go on without me." A cockeyed smile twisted the wizard's lips. "I'd only slow you down."

Cyrus turned away from the Goliath officer, rage filling him at the blatant display of cowardice. "Nyad, keep the flames going! Sanctuary, move up and get ready to engage!"

He charged, army at his back. The Goliath forces were broken, scattering to either side of the road, screams filling the air, all martial discipline forgotten. Carrack tipped a salute to Cyrus as the wizard shoved past a Goliath ranger who got in the way of his retreat, knocking the human into the dirt as he passed.

Cyrus reached the last vestiges of the Goliath army's front line. The wizards cast fire as they advanced, providing a horrific view of the carnage that was befalling the Goliath army.

Shadowed appendages swept down, shaped into blades and clubs, killing the Goliath guild members. Cyrus watched a dwarf impaled as he tried to run and a shadow slipped from the darkness and cut through him, black protrusion jutting from his chest. Inky blackness from the shadow spread from the wound, consuming the dwarf, covering him in a skin of darkness as he fell.

It struck again as Cyrus closed to sword range. With a ferocious strike, it seemed to sweep down on Goliath's forces, knocking them out of the way of its advance as though it were a child kicking little dolls out of its path. The cries of Goliath's wounded filled his ears - the specter made no noise at all and would have been invisible if not for the firelight cast by the wizards behind him. He saw more of the fallen, all covered in the darkness, it sliding over them like an inky skin.

He leaped forward to attack, sword raised, and brought it down on the specter. His sword swept through the darkness, making no contact with anything solid. Something moved in the specter and hit him in the breastplate, knocking him off his feet. He heard a cracking noise as he hit the cobblestone road and felt the wind knocked out of him.

"I need a healer," he rasped, trying to pick himself up off the road.

"I've got you," came Erith's voice from behind him.

Cyrus vaulted to his feet after the mending spell knitted broken bones together within him. A shadowed appendage struck out at him from the body of the creature, grazing him and leaving a shallow open wound along his side.

"My daggers are having no effect!" Aisling shouted from

behind the creature, her blades singing as she struck at it over and over again. She shrieked and narrowly avoided a strike by the specter that sent five members of Goliath sailing through the air, one of them in several pieces.

Fire filled the air above Cyrus as one of the wizards cast a powerful flame spell. It burned a translucent blue and streaked through the air above him, wrapping itself around the specter. An otherworldly sound - a high pitched wailing - left the warrior in no doubt that the creature was vulnerable.

"It's immune to physical attacks! Spell casters, blast this thing!" he ordered, dodging three of the dark appendages as they struck at him in rapid succession. "I'll keep it distracted!" Three prongs shot from the specter's amorphous body at him and each found their mark.

The first one broke his jaw and knocked his helmet askew. The second landed against his ribcage, bruising him. The last was the worst by far, hitting him mid-thigh, breaking his femur and dropping him onto his already-broken jaw. He yelped in pain and rolled to his back. The specter extended above him, taller than even Fortin. It was engulfed in a series of flame spells from Sanctuary's druids and wizards. A few of Goliath's survivors were contributing their own spells to the fight, keeping the shadowy beast hemmed in by a circle of spell casters.

It howled once more, buffeted between attacks from all directions. The flames pitched it left and then right as it tried to avoid that which was causing it such agony. It swelled like a balloon then shrank to a thin state, wriggling in the light of the flames. At last, it focused on the only other thing within the fires that encircled it: Cyrus.

"Oh bugger," he whispered through his broken jaw as the specter formed six appendages and drove them down one at a time. The first possessed a dull edge, an overlarge hammer, and he did not entirely avoid it, rolling as a searing pain engulfed his left arm from the elbow down, a crunching noise coming as it hit his wrist.

The second and third ghostly appendages carried a bladed appearance and snaked down at him, each skimming off his breastplate and missing his side as they hit the ground. The fourth and fifth were both smaller blunt instruments. The fourth missed him on the swing as he rolled across the ground and scrambled to get away, but the fifth hit him square in the backplate, smashing his face into the cobblestones.

The sixth appendage was sharp like a dagger and Cyrus looked behind him in time to see it slam down into the gap between his greaves and backplate, cutting its way through the chainmail beneath and stabbing him in the kidney. He felt the point of the blade dissolve, snaking its way up into him.

The first appendage returned with a brutal smash to his shoulder, driving him back to the ground as the sixth continued to cut inside him. A sharp pain was slowly driving its way through him. A howling filled the air. He couldn't be sure whether it was the specter or himself, so great was his agony. Two more bladed limbs came down on him and he felt his arm go numb.

Urgent shouts filled his ears and the fires got hotter around him. The smell of something burning was strong in the air as the lightheadedness threatened to overcome him. He tasted the dirt between the cobblestones as he forced his head down to cope with the agony. The pain inside was getting duller and duller, and he thought it was somewhere around the bottom of his lungs, because it hurt to breathe.

"Where are you, Andren?" His words came in a wheeze. It was getting darker now; the flames were licking at him; he was sure of it even though he couldn't lift his head to see them. It was so hot.

"Hold on," came a voice to his left. Even with his cheek pressed to the road, he could see Aisling. *Is she dying too?* he wondered. Thoughts were becoming difficult to form.

Her face was next to his now. "It's okay," she whispered, and her hands were running through his hair. In spite of the heat and the fire above him, it seemed to be getting darker. Rough hands seized him and he was facing upright. The specter was gone and there was no fire. *Still so damned hot.*

"My spells are having no effect on him," Erith's voice faded in from above, her face looking down at him.

"That thing cut his arm off..."

"Help me put it back on," Erith ordered, voice frantic. "Hold it in place, I'm going to try another mending spell." She breathed a few inaudible words, then cursed. "Nothing! What the hell did it do to him?"

Aisling's voice was clear, but he couldn't see her anymore. "Did it get him with the darkness, like it did those others? Would that keep your spells from working?"

"I don't know. Did someone go to get Malpravus?"

"Nyad left as soon as the specter died," Aisling answered. "He won't make it if you can't mend these wounds; he's bleeding to death."

Cyrus coughed and a horrible, metallic taste filled his mouth as he began to choke.

"Roll him over!" Erith ordered. "He's coughing up blood!"

"The darkness is enshrouding him," came a calm voice. "It's blocking your spells."

"What?" Erith said, looking up in surprise. "Vaste?! Where the hell have you been?"

"Facing the darkness," came the troll's calm reply. "Stand back." The troll began to speak low, almost a hum in a steady stream. Light blinded Cyrus, then was blotted out by darkness, then light cut through it, burning his eyes, filling him. He tried to breathe, but it choked him, as though something heavy was on his chest, forcing the life out of him.

I can't breathe, he wanted to say. *I can't...*

With a flash, the light was gone, and darkness crept back in. Faces stared down at him once more - two of the darkest blue, one green and leering. Vaste murmured a few words and Cyrus felt the wounds begin to close.

"How did you know that was there?" Erith regarded him with suspicion. "And what the hell is it?"

"The specter is composed of living darkness, a creation of Yartraak," Vaste replied. "It seeped into him, gave him a fever and blocked healing by draining the energy of any mending spells. Not a pretty way to die."

"Indeed." Erith regarded him with suspicion. "Good thing you saw it. How did you do that, through his armor?"

"I saw it draining his spirit."

"What?"

Whatever further reply Vaste might have made was stifled by Cyrus staggering to his feet. "You should rest for a few minutes," Erith insisted.

Cyrus dismissed her. "Yeah, I'll take a nap right here in the Realm of Darkness."

Nyad arrived in a huff. "I spoke with Malpravus. He says it's unfortunate that Cyrus is dying, but he's preoccupied with other things at the moment."

"What's he preoccupied with?" Cyrus looked at her with undisguised curiosity.

"Three of those specters are attacking his army."

"He'll need help." Cyrus put aside once more the thought of Andren, even as another flash of Enterra crept into his mind - the two of them, side by side in the tunnel, waiting for Narstron to return. *He'll be fine. He has to be. It can't happen again.*

"Why can't his armies help him?" Erith looked at him with undisguised irritation.

"His armies will break and run at the first sign of trouble," Cyrus replied. "Sanctuary, we're moving! Spell casters to the front." Splitting into two columns, the Sanctuary forces moved on either side of the formations of Goliath's army in front of them. The Goliath soldiers milled about in scattered lines and allowed them to pass. A clamor of battle could be heard in front of them as they passed both Tolada's and Yei's unmoving armies.

Nyad cast a burst of fire, revealing the forward Goliath army. Malpravus stood back as his forces battled the specters. They attacked in force, spells flying at the specters and combatants trying to strike with swords and other melee weaponry. Cyrus paused for a moment - there was something very unnatural about the movements of the Goliath forces.

"Malpravus!" Cyrus shouted as the Sanctuary army streamed into place behind Goliath's Guildmaster. "What's the situation?"

The cloaked dark elf turned back to him, face marked with strain but a malevolent grin creasing it. "Ah, dear boy, I must say I am pleased to see you. We've run into a bit of a snag." The necromancer turned back to the battle and waved his arms without saying a word.

The specters were attacking Goliath's forces much as they had Cyrus's army only moments before. Bodies, limbs and other pieces flew through the air as they turned loose their weapon-shaped appendages. Cyrus watched a ranger hit the ground in front of him, dead, neck at an unnatural angle.

"Ye gods," he muttered. "Healers -"

"Ah ah ah!" Malpravus cut him off. "Healers would be most inconvenient for me right now. Save the resurrection spells until we are done."

"What?" Cyrus gasped. His eyes dropped to the corpse of the ranger, which had begun to rise, head hanging to the side. Understanding dawned on Cyrus and his eyes swept the scene. "Malpravus," he said with a sick feeling, "how many of them are dead?"

"Of my army? All. You really are quite bright, boy; most would not have picked up on that before charging into battle. You show such promise."

"You're... controlling them?" Erith's face was lit with shock as Cyrus felt the nausea rise in his stomach. "Casting spells for them? Ordering their corpses to attack?"

"Indeed." Malpravus's grin grew wider still. "But I could use some help. If you'd care to add your efforts to mine."

"I feel I should add my breakfast to the ground," Vaste said with a scowl. "What's to stop you from taking over our corpses if we fall?"

A surprised look crossed the Goliath Guildmaster's face, eyebrows raised. "Your comrades are in the fight of their lives. Wouldn't you assist them, even in death?" Malpravus turned back and waved his hands once more, bringing another twenty bodies lurching back into the fight.

"I honestly don't know which monster is more deserving of our attacks, the specters or him," Vaste said, face grim.

"Alaric will be most aggrieved if we attack Malpravus." Cyrus's hand masked his expression.

"I know you're trying to cover how disturbed you are with a joke, but this isn't funny!" Vaste thundered. "He's subverted the bodies of his comrades and now he's preventing them from being resurrected!"

"No, it's not funny," Cyrus agreed. "But we can't attack him."

"The sooner you help me kill these specters," the voice of Malpravus chimed in, "the sooner we can start the resurrection spells on these poor, unfortunate souls."

"Who follow you for some reason," Vaste spit at Malpravus, "gods know why – perhaps ignorance."

Malpravus's gaunt fingers reached out as though he were taking hold of something delicate, and another body rose on the field of battle. "Strength. They follow my strength. If they fall, they know I will avenge them." He turned back to the Sanctuary officers and smiled, locking his gaze on Cyrus.

Cyrus ignored the sudden drop his stomach took and held up a hand to stop Vaste as the troll took a step toward the necromancer. "We fight the darkness first."

"If I die and he takes control of my corpse, I'll kill him." Vaste pulled himself to his full height, eyes narrowed and green skin glaring in the reflected light of the spells flying in front of them. It was strangely silent; none of the dead bodies vocalized as they swung their weapons, creating an atmosphere of metal clanging, flesh being hit and the screeching of the specters as spells impacted.

"Such misunderstandings do not help our cause," Malpravus chided without turning around.

"Shut up," Cyrus breathed. "Weapons are ineffective, so the spell casters attack from here. I'll have the warriors and rangers form a line to protect them."

After a moment to organize, the spell casters lined up in ranks behind Cyrus and the others and let fly a barrage of spells that struck down the first of the specters. Corpses of the Goliath army swarmed over the fallen enemy until it discorporated, fading like dust in the wind.

It took several more volleys to bring down the second specter, but when it finally fell, a ragged cheer rang through the Sanctuary army. Goliath's first army, already throwing themselves after the final specter, was still silent – but at least this time, Cyrus knew why.

Another specter's scream tore across the dark landscape. The last of them flung a wave of Goliath's fighting corpses out of its way and slithered across the ground toward the Sanctuary army. The bodies it threw landed in front of Cyrus, and each of them was covered in the black tar-like substance that the specters gave off. *Is that what I had in me?* he wondered.

Cyrus moved forward to meet the specter, dodging the first attacks. A tentacle of shadow swung at him, followed by another and another. He dodged the first two and the third hit him on the breastplate, staggering him. He swung his sword, cutting through the specter's appendage to no effect; it reformed as soon as the sword passed through it.

"Without a mystical blade, you can't hit it," Aisling's calm voice whispered in his ear. He jumped in surprise and felt her push him to the side as another volley of the specter's limbs flew at him and missed thanks to her efforts. Her breath was warm against his neck as she pressed against him.

"I know that!" he snapped. "I'm not trying to or I'd have ordered the whole army against it." He lunged back to his feet and dodged another swipe from the specter. The next attack connected, drawing blood from a superficial cut to the side of his neck. "I'm trying to distract it," he shot back at her. Another strike connected, this time a blunt instrument, and knocked him off balance.

"Marvelous job," Aisling's dry voice found him as his head was spinning. "It is focusing on splattering you on the cobblestones."

"So nice to be paid attention to," Cyrus muttered, ducking another attack.

"You talking about from me or it?" Aisling said from a few feet away.

"Get back! I'm trying to draw its attacks; I don't need you getting killed." A stabbing blow glanced off his shoulder. Fire lit the scene as Nyad and the other spell casters hammered at the shadowed fiend, flames of blue, red, yellow and orange lighting up the battle. Screeches filled the air and small shadows flaked off the specter's mass.

"Don't worry about me," Aisling said with a grin that spread from ear to ear. Before his eyes, she began to fade from his view, slipping into the shadows.

"Wait!" he cried, a vision of Andren filling his head. She paused for a moment, shrouded in the shadows, flickering in the light of spells. Her smile froze and her eyes widened.

Cyrus felt the specter land three hits in rapid succession, pummeling him. Something snaked around his waist and yanked him upside down into the air. He swung the short sword in the direction he was pulled, but made no contact with anything. A sense of disorientation took over as he was pulled into the air. He could see flashes of his guildmates, a hundred feet below. He had a sudden memory of the feeling when Ashan'agar spiraled to the ground. A lurching twisted his stomach and for a beat he wondered if the specter would drop him.

A blur raced past, a feeling of lightness crept through him and an explosion of flame a few feet away drew a final scream from the specter. He braced himself for the inevitable fall, but it did not come. His feet floated below him as he began to drift to the ground. A flash of red blurred through the darkness in front of him, and he felt the caress of a small mending spell.

"Saved my ass again, Niamh," he breathed.

"Pretty sure I saved the whole entirety of you."

"Yeah, but I'm all ass, all over, so..."

She giggled and they floated to the ground to find Malpravus, expression passive as the invasion force's healers labored to resurrect Goliath's first army. "My boy," the necromancer began as Cyrus descended, "you do have quite the flair for theatrics, don't you?"

"I don't know what you mean."

"Getting captured by the specter like that?" Malpravus had a grin filled with smooth, even teeth, all of which gleamed a pearly white. "Pulled hundreds of feet into the air? I was certain I'd be adding you to my army, but you survived, once more, and quite admirably." The smile dimmed a bit. "Of course, I am pleased to see you make it back to us in one piece."

Cyrus suppressed a shudder at the thought of being in the control of the dark elf. "Not half as pleased as I am." He turned to face the Sanctuary army, forming up in the gap between the ragged first army of Goliath and the second, which had distanced itself during the fighting.

Wizards kept the flames in the air, lighting the scene as the Alliance force recovered. Cyrus looked around, scouring face after face, until his hopes sank and the familiar feeling rose once more in his stomach – a feeling he would forever associate with a night of agony spent in the caves of the goblin city of Enterra, waiting for a friend who would never return.

Chapter 9

When the invasion force was reassembled, Cyrus found Malpravus standing next to him, fingers steepled. "Dear boy, why don't you take the lead for a bit? Give my fighters a chance to recover from the beating they took and a chance for us to reorganize and help Carrack's army... regain their courage?"

The way he said it sent a chilled knife to Cyrus's guts. He could feel the looks of the officers of Sanctuary behind him in the loose circle where they had been talking. "We'll be happy to lead the way."

"Excellent, excellent." Cyrus's eyes were drawn to the ornate rings decorating each of Malpravus's long fingers. One seemed to cover half his hand, a circle of metal with a red ruby the size of a walnut mounted in the center. It made his already slender fingers seem almost bony by comparison.

Niamh restrained herself until the Goliath Guildmaster was out of earshot. "What are you thinking?!" Her face flared an angry red to match her hair. "If Vara were here she'd tell you what a fool you are for playing into whatever devious plan Malpravus has in mind."

"Let's not be hasty," Curatio stepped in. "I'm sure Cyrus has good reason."

"Yes, I'm sure it's something reasonable." J'anda's hands folded in front of him. "Like, 'I don't feel I've been possessed by a wicked sorcerer enough today.'"

"I agreed because by being up front, we're leading this expedition," Cyrus said. "Malpravus can't issue orders to us from the back of the action, not when I'm in the thick of it. And we're about to come up against something nasty. I'd rather have us facing it than them."

A moment of silence passed over the circle of officers, broken by J'anda. "Say again?" The enchanter's eyes were wide with disbelief, mouth forming a perfect o. "You would rather us face the deadly peril waiting ahead than throw three or four Goliath armies at it?"

"Yes."

"Explain the bizarre troll logic behind that!" Niamh exclaimed, shock written across her face. She ignored Vaste's scowl. "You'd rather throw our lives away than theirs? What if this creature causes permanent deaths? You'd rather have that visited on us than them?"

"No." Cy shook his head. "But I think we're walking into a tricky battle, something that is going to require more finesse than Goliath is capable of." Cy's eyes narrowed. "I think Malpravus knows that, and he's drained – he doesn't have another battle like the last in him."

Niamh's look of shock turned to confusion. "So we're not facing peril ahead?"

"Oh, no," Cyrus said, voice nonchalant. "We are. But we're the best hope the Alliance has of overcoming it; Goliath has no military discipline in place. If they run into something nasty, they will break. They're the barely-trained rabble that Vara was afraid we'd end up with – they've got a lot of people, most of them are even more experienced than ours, but they don't fight as a unit – no one can trust the person next to them."

"That feeling tends to flow from the top," Curatio said. "I'm guessing it's not encouraged by Malpravus."

"What was the first giveaway?" Vaste said, voice dripping with sarcasm. "That their Guildmaster decided to delay their resurrections by commanding their corpses to save his own ass?"

"That would be a strong indicator." Curatio turned to Cyrus. "How will you prepare for what's ahead?"

Cyrus stroked his chin once more. "Sanctuary's armies need to combine; I want Fortin up front with me and the spellcasters in the middle of a ring of warriors and rangers to protect them. I need a count of how many are still missing. Be ready to move in five minutes."

As they broke, Niamh remained behind for a moment. Her expression was skeptical. "How do you know you're reading this right? Everything you're doing is based on assumptions – the biggest being you've figured out Malpravus's motives." She shook her head. "I'm not sure he's that easy to read."

A moment of doubt hung in the air between them. Cyrus looked down as he answered. "You may be right. But our alternative is to let a Goliath army lead us."

She said no more, and within five minutes they had consolidated the army. Cyrus marched alongside Fortin, leading the way down the road, the rocky skin of the giant bathed in the light of the fires cast by the wizards.

The thought of Andren nagged in his mind as the minutes wore on. Vaste interrupted his thoughts with a report. "All of our people have returned except one. All the missing reported feeling trapped by darkness, unable to escape it," the troll said, face impassive. "Care to guess who hasn't come back?"

"Andren." Cyrus studied Vaste's face. The troll had a plethora of scars; his life's tale had been tragic. Only a few weeks earlier he had returned home to the troll homeland to try and recruit members of his tribe for Sanctuary's expansion. Leery of associating with the races that had broken their empire in a war only twenty years prior, they had reacted unfavorably to his attempts, beating him nearly to death.

"You got it."

"Think it's coincidence?"

"That your oldest friend disappears in the Realm of Darkness and is the only person that doesn't return?" Vaste's eyebrow raised. "No, I don't think that's coincidence."

"Why does it matter that he's my oldest friend?" Cyrus looked around, trying to see past the army at his back and through the veil of darkness beyond.

"This place crawls." Catching the quizzical look on Cyrus's face, Vaste went on: "There are creatures lurking in the darkness and they can see and hear us but we can't see them. Yartraak also makes fear his domain and a weapon in his arsenal. These servants are looking for leverage against a leader on this expedition. Malpravus has no weak points; at least not in the form of a person."

A pang of fear for Andren hit Cyrus in the gut. "But I do."

"Yes. And if you're going to attack someone and make them fear something, why not tap into a loss that's fresh in their mind?" Vaste's eyes honed in on him.

"You're delving into the territory of a mind reader, my friend."

A smile cracked the troll's face. "I'm just someone with good hearing that sleeps in the room next to yours." The smile evaporated. "I don't know what we face, but I know that it is staging a campaign of fear against us, trying to take us off guard, trying to make us doubt ourselves. Whatever it is, it's close, and it wants us fragile."

"You're painting a grim picture."

Vaste snorted. "Be ready for the worst."

As their conversation concluded, Cyrus realized that he and

Vaste had been the only ones talking. An ominous silence fell around them as Cy's thoughts turned once more to Andren. A flash came to him, an image in his mind of the elf, injured in the darkness, dying, trying to find his way with no light. He suppressed a shudder.

The dark surrounded them, flames licking into it as they marched forward in uncertainty. Every few minutes, even over the tramping sounds of the army on the march, Cyrus could hear movement beyond the black. *Maybe I shouldn't have listened to Vaste. I'm hearing things.*

There are things all around you. Dark things. Things that are coming to get you. Like they got Andren.

Another vision of Narstron's body fell into his mind, the sight of the dwarf's corpse, lying on the floor of the tunnel at Enterra. Now it seemed more real than in his nightmares. He blinked, trying to expel the thought from his mind, and for a flash he thought that red eyes were staring back at him.

He'll die too. Just like Narstron. So will the others.

Dark thoughts clung to him like the stench of rot fills a bog. Cyrus blinked again, suddenly aware that like a snake, these dark ideas had slithered into his mind. "Vaste," he said, sotto voce, "whoever is running this 'fear' campaign you talked about? They're worming their way into my thoughts right now."

"Mine too," the healer muttered back. "We're not alone."

Cyrus glanced around. Nyad was closest to him, sending gouts of flame in front of them, her expression laced with fright. Niamh stood behind her, all color sapped from her face, contrasting with the shock of bright red hair atop her head. Fortin's rocky face was expressionless, but his gait had slowed. "Be ready to execute a formation change!" Cyrus called out to those around him. "Something is out here, and it's playing with our minds."

Found me out, did you? Or are you just talking to yourself?

My inner monologue isn't this ominous, Cyrus thought. *I can feel you, creeping through my thoughts.*

But you can't see me yet. Doesn't that worry you?

Once you've faced a dragon, Cyrus thought with a steely calm, *unexplained voices in your head don't terrify nearly as much. Especially when they're in the Realm of Darkness.*

You should be afraid. For what I'm going to do to you. For what I'm going to do to your friends.

Cyrus's eyes narrowed. *Now you're just pissing me off.*

They struck without sound: a hundred slimy arms from out of the dark, weaving their way through the feet of the Sanctuary force, grasping and wrapping them like snakes. A shock ran through Cy as one slithered up his leg and he brought his sword down. He heard a wet, sucking noise as his blade sliced through. *Not quite so slippery as those specters, are you?*

They are my harbingers. A laugh sounded in his head. *They are nothing compared to me; I am the greatest servant of the Lord Yartraak, God of Darkness.*

"They're vulnerable to blades!" Cyrus called as he brought his sword down on another, this one wrapped around Nyad. A blaze of fire from her hand lit the area around them. Cyrus looked down to see what he was fighting - it was half his size, a purple octopus moving on eight tentacles across the ground. It had two of its tentacles wrapped around Nyad, pulling her toward an open mouth, fangs glistening. Cyrus sunk his sword into its forehead and the tentacles relaxed.

He looked past it to find thousands, swarming around them, filling every inch of available ground. Longwell had a spear in his right hand, three of the octopuses impaled on it and with his left he fended off attacks from two more. Fortin waded forward, splattering their foes with well placed stomps. Sanctuary's neatly ordered formation had degenerated into a melee, octopuses scattered through their lines, dragging people toward those insatiable mouths.

Cyrus attacked, a blur of motion, striking at the creature nearest to him. It screeched as he sliced his way through three tentacles and plunged his sword into its head. It went limp, releasing Martaina, who pulled the bow from her back and shot three arrows into the next nearest of the creatures. Thad lay dead at her feet, a dead octopus on top of his body.

Erith stood in a whirl of activity, sending healing spells in all directions toward the wounded. Cyrus watched as she turned, mending Cass's injured arm after a tentacle wrenched it, knocking his sword free. It was killed by a man of the desert that Cyrus had recruited into Sanctuary months earlier, Scuddar In'shara, his scimitar catching the light when he brought it down, cleaving the head of an octopus in two.

"We're getting overwhelmed!" Vaste's normally calm voice was infused with urgency. He held his staff with both hands, beating one of the fiend's tentacles as it snaked toward him, one of

Menlos Irontooth's wolves already in its mouth.

Cyrus felt something slip around his leg and yank him to the ground. His head hit the cobblestones, knocking his helmet aside, and he felt a pressure on his chest as one of the octopuses climbed onto him. Tentacles slipped around his neck and arms, trapping and choking him as it eased his face toward the gaping mouth, a sucking noise of anticipation coming from within.

Light flashed from the back of the formation, causing Cyrus to flinch from the sudden brightness. The tentacles relaxed and he freed his sword hand, stabbing forward into the open mouth, and out the top of its head. The octopus slumped and fell off him.

Light filled the air around them. It glowed like the sun, illuminating everything, as the octopuses squealed and released their captives, blinded, eyes unable to cope with the darkness stripped away from them. The light source hovered into the sky, ascending from the back of the formation to hover a hundred feet in the air, bathing everything in light strong enough to make it look like midday.

"That looks... big," Vaste said aloud. "At least half the height of Sanctuary." Cyrus looked in confusion at the light until Vaste hit him in the back with a staff. "Over there." He pointed in the direction they had been heading. Lit by the brightness, in their path stood... something.

It had a dozen legs on each side of its body, which appeared like the body of an insect. Vaste had been right: it was mammoth, a face that was blanching against the light streaming at it, but black eyes, a mouth big enough to devour a building whole, and a carapace of blackened skin that looked thick as stone blocks. Its torso stretched back to an engorged abdomen. It stood in the distance blocking the road and behind it lay a white city, fallen into ruins.

"What the hell is that and how do we fight it?" Erith asked, jaw dropped.

"Where is this light coming from?" Vaste said.

"Gift horse, my friend," Cyrus replied. "We need to strike now – whatever that thing in the distance is, it's the last of Yartraak's servants." He turned to shout, "Sanctuary, kill these things fast! We have more trouble ahead!"

The light... it hurts... so painful... suffer...

Good, Cyrus thought. *Keep suffering.* He plunged his sword into octopus after octopus, watching them quiver helplessly as he killed them. Their dark eyes rolled back in their heads, trying to retreat from the brightness, but their eyelids were flimsy and transparent.

The sounds of battle filled his senses, along with a smell of rot as he slashed his way through the octopuses.

You come to me... you bring the light... I hate the light...

"Let us hope that this light continues; it's crippling that thing," Cyrus said as he brought his sword down on another octopus.

Not crippled... but hurt... I hurt...

I'll hurt you more, Cyrus thought.

A scream of mental shock ran through Cyrus; images invaded his mind of the night in Enterra, Narstron missing, the feeling of sorrow and loss thick in his chest. It shouted in his mind, and a wrenching insecurity ran through him.

You cannot protect them. You cannot protect them any more than you protected Narstron.

Yes I can! Cyrus clenched his eyes shut as the voice in his head exploded through his being.

You will fail.

I won't stop, the thought came to his mind.

It does not matter. When the time comes, there will be no one left but you. You will be alone.

Cyrus opened his eyes. He was on his knees, octopuses struggling around him. His army was down, hands clenched on their heads, the voice overpowering their thoughts. In the sky, the light twinkled, dwindling, then a burst of pure blue flame streaked from it and hit the creature in the distance, rocking it back.

"We have to move now," Cyrus muttered as he forced himself back up. "We have to move NOW!" he shouted to the Sanctuary army. "On your feet! Leave the octopuses behind! We have to fight the giant insect now!"

"It's called an incubus," came J'anda's voice, louder than Cyrus had ever heard it. "Its skin will be nearly invulnerable to your swords."

"Doesn't matter," Cyrus said. "We have to face it now or it will destroy us; only the light is keeping it in check." As if on cue, a bolt of lightning streaked from the light in the sky, arcing at the head of the incubus. "Where is Niamh?"

"Here," she replied. Cyrus turned to see her, pale and waxy, barely on her feet.

"I need Falcon's Essence." Cyrus watched the incubus rock back and forth, unsteady on its legs from the stunning light above. "Fortin too. Vaste, move the army forward to engage, Fortin and I will distract it."

Vaste cast his eyes to the glowing orb in the sky. "Isn't it already distracted?"

"Fine – we're going to kill it. But we might need help."

"Like a healer?" Erith chimed in. "Niamh, me too. I'm going with them."

"Stay behind me," Cyrus cautioned.

"I'm not going to stand between you and serious injury," Erith said with a grin.

"Let's go," Cyrus commanded. He and Fortin sprinted into the air, Erith a few steps behind them. Cyrus fixated on the incubus head as he ran, feeling his feet climb invisible steps, watching the black eyes that were as tall as he, the head swaying as the light threw another bolt of lightning followed by three balls of fire the size of a human. "Whatever that light is, I hope it keeps the pressure up – it's keeping the incubus from invading our thoughts."

"I'd be interested to know what that light is," Erith said.

"Questions for later," Cyrus replied. "The biggest threat first."

"Reminds me of an old story," Fortin rumbled. "The gist of which is that not everyone that helps you is your friend."

"Let's not make any new enemies until the multistory mind-attacking incubus is dead, shall we?" Cyrus turned his attention to the incubus, now only a few hundred feet away. Its legs wobbled beneath it and a weak voice came to Cyrus's mind.

You brought this upon us... I will make you suffer.

"Is everyone else hearing a voice in their heads?" Erith asked.

"Yes," Fortin replied. "I find its incessant prattling annoying and wish to smash the speaker's mouth to pieces."

Erith cast a look at him. "If it's talking directly to your head, don't you think you should smash the brain?"

"I'll smash everything."

The face grew closer and Erith hung back, keeping her distance while Cyrus and Fortin closed on it. "Orders?" came the rumble of Fortin's voice.

"Look for weak points," Cyrus replied.

"I see one." The rock giant sprinted ahead, legs moving with nothing under them, and surged toward the mouth of the incubus, which opened as if to devour him. Fortin slammed his fist into the open mouth, smashing past the teeth into the soft tissue. With a battle cry he leapt upon the tongue, which bounced him into the back of the incubus's throat and he disappeared as a swallowing noise filled the air around them.

"Uh... that thing ate your rock giant!" Erith called from her position behind him.

"He'll regret that," Cyrus said aloud as he ran atop the head of the incubus. His sword was in his hand, and he aimed himself toward the opening in the side of the head that he assumed were ears.

"Regret what?" Erith said. "Dispensing with one of his attackers in about two seconds? I think he'll be rather excited about it; one less of you to deal with! We should have brought more people."

"Or one less," Cyrus said, so low that she could not hear him. He plunged his sword into the open ear hole, then used it to swing down into the ear canal.

"What are you DOING?!" Erith shouted to him.

He did not reply. He made his way into the canal as the incubus began to jerk and move once more. It tilted to the side as the Falcon's Essence spell dissipated, causing him to lurch backward and nearly fall out. He held onto the edge of the ear hole, looking below at the ground - a dingy brown mess of dead grasses. The incubus righted itself again as it completed its turn, now pointing toward the wrecked city.

Towers extended above them, some of which were taller than the Citadel, the tallest building in Arkaria. The incubus was moving fast now. A glance back revealed the Sanctuary army moving toward it at a run, and a mass of Goliath's forces behind looked disorganized and scattered. The writhing octopuses had settled down - most had to be dead, Cyrus concluded, as there was little movement where they covered the ground.

Another rumble from the incubus shook him and his grip loosened. He looked over to see Erith running alongside where he hung, one hand on his sword, the other gripping the edge above. "If you fall from this height," Erith shouted, "you're going to splatter!"

"I'm not going to fall," Cyrus muttered, plunging his sword up and into the ear. He felt rather than heard the cracking of the exoskeleton, and his sword sank into the incubus's flesh. He pulled, bringing himself back into the ear. Another turn nearly tossed him out again and he held to the hole he had created with the sword and looked out, cracked facades of buildings moving past at an alarming rate. "Where are you going?" he murmured.

Away. Away from the light. Away from the pain.

Cyrus dived deeper into the ear canal, plunging his sword forward when he could go no further. *No escaping the pain,* he thought.

The incubus shook once more, an inarticulate howl filling his mind. *It hurts, it hurts, it hurts....*

What did you do with Andren?

It hurts, oh, it hurts...

He brought his sword back once more, prepared to plunge it into what he knew was the creature's brain when his feet left him; the incubus tilted forward, as though its legs had been cut from beneath it, and Cyrus felt it drop. He threw his hands up and braced himself with his legs as the head plunged down, falling hundreds of feet to the ground. The impact brought his hands forward, breaking through the wall of the ear canal and into the tender flesh beyond. The light visible at the entrance to the ear disappeared and once more Cyrus was lost in darkness.

Chapter 10

It smelled awful, Cyrus reflected as he awoke. A pain radiated from his left collarbone. He could hear pounding in the distance, and the walls vibrated around him. He lay in a pool of something wet and sticky that felt like the insides of a pumpkin. He felt around with his left hand and found his sword. Pushing off it, he pulled himself to a crouch, cradling his right arm against his body.

A faint flickering light was visible, and after a moment he realized he was looking at the aperture he had used to enter the ear. Stooped over, he worked his way toward the light. He crawled the last feet out of the ear and onto the cobblestone street below. Bringing himself to standing, he navigated away from the incubus, which lay stretched out, three wrecked buildings buried under its abdomen.

"There you are," Erith called out. He looked to see her waiting past the jaw. "He's over here!" she shouted to the army, waiting beyond the carcass. The flickering was the fires of the wizards, lit once more against the darkness. The light in the sky had disappeared.

"Where's Fortin? And Andren?" he asked, looking around. "And where did the light go?"

"Fortin never came out of the mouth. Still haven't seen Andren," she said with a shake of her head. "Not sure where the light went; it disappeared when the incubus hit the ground. How did you kill that thing?"

"I didn't."

A tearing noise was audible as a craggy hand ripped through one of the beast's eyes and tore an opening large enough for Fortin to extract himself.

"That was fun," the rock giant said, voice deadpan. "Got any more?"

"Not right now," Cyrus replied. "I doubt there are any more of these."

"There aren't," came a high, hissing voice. Cyrus turned to find Malpravus gliding up to him. "I certainly do have an eye for talent, don't I?" the necromancer cooed. "Perhaps one in a thousand Generals could lead their army to victory against an incubus and the octopuses." His fingers steepled together in front of his face, dark skin contrasting against his grin. "Well done, my boy. Who cast that light?"

"I don't know," Cyrus replied. "I don't even know what it was."

"No matter." Malpravus spread his hands wide in acceptance. "I have no doubt that you, dear boy, would have prevailed and overcome it even without that assistance."

"That's okay," came Vaste's voice, laced with sarcasm. "The rest of us had nothing to do with this victory."

Malpravus raised an eyebrow in surprise, but before he could respond to the troll's comment, the deep, rumbling voice of Fortin filled the air. "The General should receive all glory from a battle won; his troops should be grateful to be associated with such a skilled Warlord."

"I'm not a Warlord," Cyrus said, glancing back at the rock giant, voice quiet. "And I could not have done this without the assistance of our army. Or that light, whatever or whomever cast it."

"All evidence to the contrary," Malpravus mused, glee evident. "You *are* a Warlord. You are a follower of Bellarum, yes? Why deny your true nature? Why turn away from the greatest honorific that could be bestowed on a devotee of the God of War?"

Cyrus cast another look back at the assembling ranks of the Sanctuary officers. J'anda and Curatio met his gaze with measured neutrality while Niamh blanched.

Vaste made no attempt to hide the disdain with which he held Malpravus, his face a darker green than normal. "He doesn't accept the title because he's not a bloodthirsty beast."

Malpravus raised an eyebrow. "A narrow definition for such a beautiful title." His fingers flexed, steepling further. "Very well, we shall discuss semantics some other time. For now…" The gleeful look spread to the necromancer's eyes with a light that became almost frightening. "The way to Yartraak's treasure hoard is open, the last of his servants slain." He turned to his army, formed behind him, gesturing for them to move forward. Looking back to Cyrus, he added, "Dear boy, I'll lead the way from here."

"Malpravus," Curatio said with a smile. "Erith and Niamh will accompany you so we don't have any 'misunderstandings' in regards to the treasures in Yartraak's chambers."

The necromancer stopped and turned at the waist. "But of course, Curatio, whatever the Alliance requests, I am more than happy to render."

"On behalf of the Alliance, I'd like you to render yourself over an open fire," Vaste muttered.

"I doubt I'd be open to that, my green friend," Malpravus said after a moment's pause, without turning back. "Let us keep our discourse civilized, shan't we?"

"How did he hear that?" Niamh asked, mouth open in shock.

"Dead men tell tales," Vaste replied, expression unreadable.

The army of Sanctuary was arrayed around the corpse of the incubus. Fortin stood next to it, face inscrutable, admiring his handiwork. Lost in thought, Cyrus almost didn't notice Aisling approach.

"So," she said as she sidled up to him, "that was impressive, leading us to victory against an enemy like that. What's your secret to success?"

Cyrus was distracted by the activity around the corpse. "I look for weak points to attack; feet, knees, eyes, groin."

"Ouch," Aisling winced. "The groin?"

Cyrus shrugged. "Given a chance, my foes would do the same to me."

"Do enemies often attack your groin?"

Cyrus stared ahead, preoccupied while he answered. "Not often, but it does happen."

"I'd like to attack your groin –"

"For the love of the gods, woman!" he exploded.

"– I'd do it with enthusiasm –"

"Shut up! Just stop!" he shouted as he hurried away from her.

Cyrus joined the reformed army, falling in behind Goliath's forces. They marched through the streets of the decrepit city. Absent the light, it did not appear to be in as bad a state of decay. Wide avenues were flanked on either side by tall buildings, steps leading up into them. Columns were a prevalent theme; white marbled ones that reminded Cyrus of the library in Reikonos. Rubble from collapsed buildings and ruined columns littered the streets.

No wind moved through the buildings. The air was stale, reminding Cyrus of a crypt. The sounds he had heard in the darkness were gone, replaced by the good-natured joking of the armies surrounding them, already overcome by a feeling of victory.

After marching through the streets for a half-hour they

approached a building at the center of the city that stretched several stories into the air. It was built like an overlarge cylinder that tapered to a rounded top. Stretching up the side were doors big enough to fit three Fortins, stacked on each other's shoulders. The armies stopped outside the doors, but Cyrus moved forward with the other Alliance officers, catching up with Niamh and Erith, who stood next to Malpravus and the Goliath officers.

"Does no one else feel the anticipation of glorying in our spoils?" the necromancer asked with an expression of unguarded surprise. His gaze locked on Cyrus. "Surely, my boy, you must feel a desire for some object herein?"

"Not everyone has a price, Malpravus," Erith said hotly.

"Everybody wants something, dear lady," he replied.

Curatio answered before Cyrus could. "We're all here. Perhaps we should get some wizards ready to cast flames inside so we can see –"

"That won't be necessary." With a wave of Malpravus's hand, two of Goliath's warriors cracked the door to Yartraak's chambers, and a beam of light spilled out, bright as the sun, illuminating the darkness all around them.

"That hypocrite," J'anda breathed. "God of Darkness, Father of Night, living in a lighted space?" A bitter dark elven curse filled the air, bringing an even bigger smile to Malpravus's face.

"We all have our idiosyncrasies, don't we? But it rather casts certain things in a different... light, doesn't it?" Malpravus and J'anda shared a knowing look.

Cyrus strode forward while they talked, into the blinding brightness and seized hold of the door opposite the Goliath warriors. Applying all his strength, he pushed the door, moving it a few feet.

"I'm not sure that Yartraak has ever opened this door all the way," the necromancer cautioned. "I believe he keeps this door closed but for a sliver to let himself in and out."

Grunting, Cyrus pushed the door, widening the crack. Light spilled out, casting brightness upon the ruins of the city once more. The two Goliath warriors had moved to the opposite door and were opening it as well, after receiving a nod of approval from Malpravus. Vaste added his strength to Cyrus's, standing with his back against the door, shoving it.

The brightness within Yartraak's chambers lit the Realm of Darkness. The cobblestone road was bathed in a warm glow and the plains on the path out of the city were exposed in the light, showing dead grass and the occasional withered tree. The ruins of the city stretched in all directions.

"Why is there grass in the Realm of Darkness? Trees? Who would have lived in a city of perpetual night?" Niamh looked around the circle of Alliance officers. Blank looks greeted her, save for on two faces. Malpravus wore the same malicious grin as always. Curatio's eyes were closed, his lips pursed.

"A most interesting question," Malpravus opined. "Best discussed at a time when we are not trespassing on the domain of a god."

"Oy there!" a shout came from behind them. Cyrus turned at the sound of the familiar voice. Blinking into the light of the open door was Andren, staggering toward them from the wreckage of the city.

Cyrus ran to greet his old friend. Vaste, Erith and Niamh followed close behind. Cy caught Andren just as he fell. The warrior turned to Vaste. "A healing spell?"

The troll shook his head. "No, I suspect he's just wickedly tired."

"Not tired," Andren said. "I'm starving! And I could use a nip, if you know what I mean. My flask ran dry while that thing had me captive. Wish Larana had come with us; she could sort it all out."

Vaste shifted his focus to Andren. "Do you remember what happened?"

The elf's face grew haunted as they carried him into the light of Yartraak's chambers. "I remember getting lost in the dark, and something talking in my head, for what seemed like forever. Then all the sudden it screamed and was gone, and I'm wandering as blind as can be until you lot shed some light on the subject."

"Nimrod," Cy breathed. "Why didn't you just cast the return spell and go back to Sanctuary?"

Andren flushed. "I tried that; no use."

Vaste frowned. "I wonder if there's a barrier to keep us from teleporting out?"

"There is," Malpravus said without emotion. Cyrus turned to see the Goliath Guildmaster standing between Elisabeth and Curatio. "It emanates from that." The necromancer pointed into the chamber at an orb no larger than a crystal ball.

With two strides, Cyrus crossed the chamber and grasped the

orb, crushing it in his gauntlet. "Try your return spell now," he said to Andren. "Get back to Sanctuary and rest."

"That was *valuable,*" Malpravus breathed, exasperated, as a twinkle of light encompassed Andren and he faded away. "There are other solutions besides smashing things."

Cyrus's eyes were drawn to a pedestal in the far corner. An axe hovered above it, with a long hilt and a double bladed head that was bigger than any Cyrus had seen. "Ah, yes," Malpravus said with a grin. "That would be *Noctus,* the Battle Axe of Darkness. We'll not be able to defeat Yartraak's barrier around it. Excellent eye, though, seeing that first."

Cyrus's gaze darted past the pedestal to a smaller one a few feet away. On it sat a block of metal, bigger than a brick. He couldn't feel himself walk as he approached it; all the sound around him faded as he picked it up and stared. The metal glinted, a prismatic effect running across the surface with a bevy of different hues shining on it; only on the Serpent's Bane had he seen anything approaching the look of the metal he held in his hands. It felt warm to his touch, like a dinner roll fresh from the oven.

A rattling breath over his shoulder took him by surprise. "Quartal?" Malpravus wore a look of pleasant surprise. "Mined in small chunks from the Mountains of Blackest Night. Quite valuable. Were you interested in it, dear boy?"

Cyrus held back for a moment. "Yes. I am."

Malpravus's grin returned and he nodded. "Everyone wants something." Turning to the other Alliance officers, he called out, "I believe that Cyrus, who has been of invaluable assistance on so many expeditions, deserves a special reward. Would anyone object to him being given this Quartal?"

Heads nodded around the room as Cyrus stared in shock. Malpravus interlaced his fingers. "There you go, my boy, all yours now." He lowered his voice as he said to Cyrus, "Whatever you do, don't let them catch you selling it, it might earn you bad will."

The warrior blinked. The Quartal now seemed heavy in his hands and he looked at the necromancer, studying the dark elf. "I've never seen you give up a piece of treasure. What do you want?"

The smile deepened on the Goliath Guildmaster's face. "Want? I was merely... showing my gratitude for such excellent effort." Malpravus glided away, leaving Cyrus with an unsettled feeling that was far from gratitude.

Dividing the treasure among the guilds took less than an hour. Once it was over, Cyrus found himself standing next to Niamh.

"I've been wanting to talk to you about something, but I didn't want to do it until this invasion was over," she said, chewing her lip.

"What is it?"

"Not here." She lowered her head and murmured an incantation. With a blast of wind, Cyrus found himself at the portal in the Plains of Perdamun, only a few minutes walk from Sanctuary. Fields of wild grass swayed in all directions around them. With another incantation he felt his feet leave the ground as the Falcon's Essence gave him flight. "Now, let's move away from the portal so we won't be interrupted by anyone else who teleports in."

The crisp breeze blew past him, and an involuntary chill rippled across the flesh hidden under his armor. A putrid smell crinkled his nose involuntarily and he heard the braying of a horse nearby. Cyrus's eyes stopped on something just through the hole in the portal. Climbing through the gap, he paused at the apex, a sick feeling taking hold in his stomach that had nothing to do with the smell.

"What?" Niamh said from behind him. She clambered through and froze next to him, hands covering her mouth in horror.

Before them lay the scattered remains of a convoy; human bodies were arrayed around it. The wagons were emptied but not burned, a silent monument to the souls that had died defending their precious cargo. Horses stood, still lashed to the wagons, stomping. Cyrus stepped out of the portal and walked to the nearest body, pulling off his gauntlet and feeling the cheek of the corpse.

Shaking his head, he slid his hand back into the gauntlet. "They've been dead for a day, not much beyond that." He surveyed the carnage around them and shook his head once more.

"What is it?" Niamh looked at him with undisguised curiosity. "You're holding something back."

He nodded. "They've stopped setting fire to the convoys. We thought they'd stopped attacking, but they haven't, and we haven't been searching." He looked at the wreckage of the convoy. "By now there could be dozens more... just waiting to be found."

Chapter 11

The red eyes stared at him from the darkness. Once more, his sword found claws, and the clash jarred his teeth as though he had hit a wall. Cyrus brought his short sword back to attack again, but missed. A spear pierced him and he grunted. His eyes drifted to where Narstron had been fighting his battle, alone.

The dwarf was near dead. Blood dripped from him, and chanting filled the air. *Gezhvet... gezhvet... gezhvet...* repeated over and over again until it was maddening.

The red eyes of the Emperor and Empress of Enterra lingered just out of reach, the black cloaked figure's high and taunting laugh filling the air as Narstron's body surged toward Cyrus, born by a horde of goblins, their claws impaling the dwarf. "Vengeance..." Narstron rasped. "I died alone... no one to remember me..." The dwarf's eyes locked on Cyrus, and they had turned deepest crimson. "*AVENGE ME!*"

With a start Cyrus woke up, sheets wrapped tight against his skin. Light streamed into the window as he sat on the edge of the bed, face buried in his hands. He stood and padded to the bathroom, looking in the mirror that was suspended over the stone basin of the sink. He splashed water over his face and looked up; for a moment he could swear his eyes blazed red instead of the usual blue.

The days had passed slowly since the Realm of Darkness. The frequency of Cyrus's nightmares had increased and become more intense. He sought out J'anda, who had experience in matters of the mind. When pressed for an opinion, the dark elf had been very frank.

"The incubus awakened fears of all sorts in people that were part of the invasion force. Others have told me of nightmares they've had, things buried and long forgotten that have resurfaced since we returned from Darkness." With a shrug, the dark elf looked at him. "The nightmares will fade in time, as your mind's resistance returns."

Cyrus shook his head. "I don't understand. We faced the incubus days ago. Why is it still affecting us?"

"It's not affecting everyone. In Darkness, everyone else was more paralyzed by the attacks of the incubus than you were. The only reason they were able to function was that you were shouting orders at them; very basic ones they had trained with a thousand times, that gave their minds structure to fight through the fear."

"I didn't realize that."

"Even though they weren't in the fight, three of Goliath's armies fell apart, just sat there and quivered, or ran into the darkness when the octopuses attacked."

"So why are the aftereffects hitting me so hard if the attacks affected me less?" He stared the enchanter in the eyes.

"What the incubus does is the opposite of mesmerization. Where my spell controls you by showing you joy, the incubus paralyzes with fear. Either way a strong mental defense is required to resist, which," he nodded at Cy, "you have.

"However," J'anda continued, "the mind's defenses are a like muscle. When the mind grows tired, resistance wanes. Breaking a mesmerization spell, the aftereffects would be a pleasant feeling of basking in the joy you experienced.

"But if it were fear attacking your mind?" The enchanter clasped his hands together. "Much less pleasant, and perhaps more lingering. And if one were already having nightmares about the subject of the incubus's attack?" J'anda's eyes were agleam and he favored Cyrus with a sympathetic smile.

They had conversed two days after the return from Darkness. In the intervening time, the nightmares had gotten only slightly better.

Cyrus strapped on his armor and walked downstairs, mind on one task for the day. As he entered the armory, Belkan looked up from behind his counter, monocle clenched on one eye as he examined the tip of a spear. The armorer was talking to himself and did not stop as Cyrus approached. "Lousiest metalwork I've ever seen, smiths oughta be ashamed..." He blinked, his right eye comically enlarged in the monocle. "Davidon," he acknowledged.

Cyrus's hand fell to the hilt tucked away in his belt. "This thing damned near got me killed, Belkan. I'm used to having something with a few more inches of length on it -"

"Bet you hear that from all the girls," the grubby old armorer said with a chuckle.

Cyrus rolled his eyes. "I don't fight with a short sword. I need something better."

"I still got nothing, so unless you want to go shake down some poor new recruit, you'll be swinging that sword 'til you find a replacement." The armorer leaned over the counter. "But... I contacted a smith I know in Reikonos. He's busy, but he can make a sword that'd be more a fit for you... in a few weeks."

Belkan dropped the monocle into his palm and slipped it into the drawer to his side. "'Til then, be grateful for what you got." The armorer turned back to the spear and shook his head in disgust. "Your sword may be short, but it's solid - new crop of smiths sprung up in Reikonos since this arms shortage. Try and fight with this."

Belkan brought the spear tip down against a block of steel on the edge of the counter, hard, and it shattered. "Don't even know what they made that of! And selling them for twice what a good sword would have gone for a year ago. Count your blessings."

Cyrus started to respond but stopped as shouts echoed through the hall. Ducking out of the armory he hurried toward the noise and found a small crowd in the foyer when he arrived. Vara and Alaric stood at the center of the disturbance, along with Terian.

"Cyrus!" Alaric called. "There is a convoy under attack...!"

Cy did not wait for Alaric to finish speaking; he was already charging out the entrance and down the steps. He could hear Vara paces behind him and a herd of footfalls after that. "Which way?" he called back to her.

"Follow!" she shouted and ran under the portcullis at the northern gate in the wall that surrounded Sanctuary.

Cyrus thundered ahead to take the lead. Stealing a look back, he realized the small force following was comprised of new recruits; not a single spell caster was among them.

His legs pumped for ten minutes before he caught sight of the convoy over a rise. Another ten of hard running drew him close. A few flashes caught his eye as teleportation spells flared around the wreckage of the wagons. At the edge of the convoy, he drew his sword and began to creep forward.

There was no sound but the small army behind him and then a clatter from one of the wagons. He crept around the side to find a dark elf, in armor, breath heavy and bleeding from several wounds. He looked back at Vara, sheathed his sword and knelt by the wounded dark elf, whose eyes found him and locked on.

"My name is Cyrus Davidon," he said as he unfastened the elf's breastplate and pulled it loose. Below, the chainmail was soaked with crimson and when the dark elf exhaled, a fine mist of blood sprayed into the air. Cyrus cringed and shot a look at Vara. "Can you...?" he asked. She shook her head, but murmured anyway. Her mending spell did not stem the tide of blood flowing from his chest.

The dark elf turned his head to focus on Cyrus. "Yellow," he breathed and was gone.

"Dammit," Cyrus muttered. "We need a healer here!"

"I believe we emptied Sanctuary as we left," Vara said, voice lifeless. "Alaric stayed behind to summon the others back, but who knows how long that could take?"

Feeling his jaw clench, Cyrus turned back to the body. "Where is everybody?"

"It's after midday and most have gone on various adventures or errands, as always. We can't all sleep until afternoon." He met her glare, but looked away after a moment.

"We need a healer that can cast a resurrection spell. This dark elf could tell us who's been attacking the convoys."

She did not answer him, but her eyes looked around at the destroyed wagons. "They have doubled the detachment of soldiers that would escort a convoy of this size."

"Cyrus?" A light voice drew his attention to the edge of the wagon where Martaina Proelius stood, Thad in her shadow.

"Yes?"

When Martaina hesitated, the red-armored warrior straightened. "Martaina is one of the best trackers to ever come out of the Wanderers' Brotherhood." She blushed at her husband's words.

"That's... nice." Cyrus smiled, unsure of what to say. He felt a sudden sharp pressure on his shoulder as Vara punched him. "Ow! What was that for?"

"The Wanderers' Brotherhood is the ranger version of your Society of Arms," Vara said, voice high. "She can perhaps shed some light on – at least – where the attack came from, and possibly even some detail on who did it."

"Oh!" Cyrus blinked and focused on Martaina. "Did you find anything?"

She frowned. "Not much. No discernible footprints. It looks as though someone wiped them clean. The attack came –" she turned and pointed to a slight rise at the edge of the road – "from behind that berm, and it appears they were overwhelmed by superior numbers. Some of the scorchmarks on the wagons indicate that the attackers have magic users working with them; because of the fire damage I would assume a druid, although it could be a weak or inexperienced wizard."

"How do you know that the magic didn't come from the guards escorting the wagons?" Vara asked, voice curious.

Martaina strode to the nearest caravan and pointed at one of the scorchmarks. "That's a possibility, but unlikely. If you look at the damage, most of it is found on the wagons and the ground near them. If the defenders were using magic, there would be damage to the berm; there isn't any. Also, magic users are more likely to be found in a guild than in a guard detail."

"Fascinating," Vara said coolly. "Thank you, Martaina."

"One other thing," Martaina said. "There are a number of riders heading toward us from the north."

Vara's head snapped around and she muttered a curse. "Damn. Right you are."

Cyrus stared north. "I don't see anything."

"Nor I," Thad added.

"With your human eyes, you wouldn't," Vara said as she drew her sword. "They are still at some distance."

Cyrus pulled his short sword from its scabbard as Thad mirrored him, drawing a full sized longsword that caused Cy to stare enviously. "You think it's the raiders?"

"Unlikely," Martaina chimed in. "None of the attack sites I've seen have suggested horses were used."

"Best to assume defensive positions," Cyrus said, tension mounting. "We don't have any healers on hand, after all."

"Perhaps we should take cover behind the wagons?" Martaina suggested.

"Because it worked so well for the last chaps that tried it," Vara muttered.

"Do it," Cyrus ordered. "I'll stand out front, the rest of you take cover," he said with a look that silenced Vara's already forming protest. "And send someone back to Sanctuary for reinforcements!"

He stood in the open air of the Plains of Perdamun, buffeted by the chill wind as the others took shelter behind him. Dust stirred on the horizon and Cy watched, silent, in the minutes it took for the riders' approach. When they got close, he spotted the gold and black on the lead rider's tabard that identified him as a member of the Reikonos militia.

"Hail," the rider said as he approached Cyrus, bringing his horse to a halt. The rider's comrades kept their distance as he bored in on Cyrus.

"Hail, friend, I am Cyrus Davidon. I presume that you are here to investigate the attacks on convoys?" Cy kept his tone pleasant.

The other rider didn't bother. "I am not, but it shouldn't surprise me to find one of Sanctuary's army in the remains of an attacked convoy."

Cyrus glanced back. "This is hardly an army, friend. We came to assist these dark elves, but arrived too late."

The rider spat on the ground at Cyrus's feet. His helm masked most of his expression, but his mouth and eyes were visible - and unpleasant. "I am no friend of yours or Sanctuary's. While it does not trouble my heart to see a host of dark elves killed, it enrages me that you have brought the same fate on countless of my countrymen and our convoys."

Cyrus felt a flash of heat run through him. "Neither I nor my guildmates have had anything to do with the attacks, and you are bold to make such an accusation. What is your name?"

"Your denials and lies matter not to me; I am Rhane Ermoc, Captain of Reikonos's Lyrus Guards. I bring a message to Sanctuary from the Council of Twelve."

Cyrus heard a gasp behind him but did not turn away. The Lyrus Guards were elite warriors; the best of the Reikonos militia. That they were in the Plains of Perdamun was cause for concern. That they had come to deliver a message was more concerning. "I am an officer of Sanctuary. I await your message."

Rhane reached into a saddlebag and pulled out an envelope. Slinging it to the ground in front of Cyrus, he spoke: "Know this! The Lyrus Guards will be in the Plains of Perdamun until this matter is settled. If ever I catch you and yours so flagrantly involved in the destruction of a human convoy, I will crush you and your pitiful guild without a second thought."

A flash of annoyance broke Cyrus's restraint. "You're gonna need a bigger army for that, jackass." He glared at Rhane and gripped his sword, wishing that the Guard Captain would draw his own.

"I have one." The contempt radiated off the Guard Captain in waves. "The longer these attacks persist, you can expect to see more and more of us encamped in the Plains. Unlike the elves and dark elves, the Council of Twelve will not stand for this attack to our interests. Do not expect me to turn my back on you and yours; do you think us fools?"

"Yes," Cyrus agreed, "I think you're a fool. Even more so if you believe Sanctuary is involved in these attacks."

Rhane's eyes narrowed but he ignored the interruption. "Do you think it has escaped the Council of Twelve's attention that there is an army growing here in the south, outside the reach of the major powers and not acting like any guild we've ever seen? And further coincidence that they sit in the center of countless attacks?"

Ermoc tugged on the reins of his horse. "We will be watching, and waiting for you to expose yourself. The day that you do will be your last." The Guard Captain turned his horse and rode back to his comrades.

Cyrus felt Vara at his shoulder. "Arrogant human," she said in a voice that reminded him of steel. "I should like to be there on his last day."

He stooped to pick up the envelope from the dirt and turned to her as he ripped it open. "This presents a problem."

She scoffed. "You think that this egomaniacal, overconfident field full of horse dung presents a problem? It wasn't that long ago we faced a dragon; armored goons on horseback don't concern me."

"It's not the Lyrus Guards that concern me," Cyrus said, pausing to read the letter. He handed it to her. "It's what they represent. It's a summons to appear before the Council of Twelve and defend ourselves against the accusation of colluding to attack the Human Confederation's shipping in this area."

"Who cares?" She rolled her eyes. "Let them think whatever they wish; we have no part of this."

"If we fail to defend ourselves," Cyrus said, "our members will be arrested anywhere they're found in the Confederation then imprisoned and killed."

"So we stay away from Reikonos," she said acidly. "And the outlying human areas."

"Easy for you to say, since it's not your home," Thad said from behind her. "I like to visit my family every now and again."

"This will not be the last," Cyrus continued. "If the Council of Twelve is considering this, no doubt the other powers will send a similar message." He looked her in the eyes. "Our people will be persona non grata in the Elven Kingdom and the Dark Elven

Sovereignty as well. And I doubt the dwarves and gnomes will be enthusiastic about us shopping in their towns if we're pariahs everywhere else."

He watched the Lyrus Guards as they rode toward the horizon. The bitter memory of Ermoc's words stirred something in him, an anger as the realization set in. "Soon... we of Sanctuary will stand alone against every power in western Arkaria."

Chapter 12

Cy and Vara entered the foyer as Alaric was exiting the stairway. He met them halfway across the floor. He gestured to the stairs and the three of them climbed in silence. The Ghost opened the door to the Council chambers and closed them once Cy and Vara had entered. "What happened?"

"We didn't have a healer with us," Vara snapped.

"We didn't have a healer with a resurrection spell with us," Cyrus amended. "The raiders teleported as we arrived. There was a survivor but he died without saying anything."

"Wrong again," Vara corrected. "He said 'yellow'."

Cyrus threw up his hands in surrender. "Let me know if you figure out what that means. It could refer to their attackers' clothing, their hair or the doll that the guard played with as a child."

Vara stared at him, failing to mask her amusement. "Did *you* play with dolls as a child?"

"Your verbal sparring will get us nowhere," Alaric interrupted them.

"We have nothing more to go on," Cyrus said. "We're already going nowhere." He tossed the envelope across the table to Alaric. "I shouldn't say that - there is one place we're going."

Alaric did not reply as he read through the summons. Upon finishing, the paladin let out a deep sigh. "I feared something of the sort would be coming along. It is unfortunate, but I suspect it will be the first of three."

The door to the Council chambers opened to admit the rest of the Council. Vara proceeded to inform them of what had happened. Cyrus listened to her, half paying attention while his head swam.

"...Martaina concluded that they had a druid with them, although she conceded it could have been a wizard that was somewhat unskilled –"

"Excuse me?" Frost dripped from Niamh's voice.

"I am only repeating what Martaina said."

"I'll have a word with her later. Maybe give her a show of what these 'unskilled wizard' powers of mine can do –"

"That is unnecessary, Niamh," the Ghost said. "Anything

further, Vara?"

"If we'd had a healer with a resurrection spell, we would know who was responsible," Cyrus interjected.

"And if we had possessed magical unicorns that could fly faster than the wind, we could have saved the entire convoy and been home in time for a drink before dinner," Vara quipped.

"There are magical unicorns?" Cyrus's brow was furrowed and he stared at Vara with a vacant expression.

"Dolt," she said dismissively. "We can wish all day for what we do not have, but it is pointless –"

"No, I have a point," he interrupted. "We have five healers and only two that can cast a resurrection spell – and over a thousand members now. We had three healers that could cast a resurrection spell when we had two hundred members." He looked around the table. "We need healers – and the ones we have need to learn that spell."

A silence fell around the table, broken by Niamh. "That's an advanced spell. Magic can only be taught by the Leagues, and only at their halls, through their instructors. It would take years –"

"No," Vaste said, voice quiet. "It would take a day at most."

Niamh's head swiveled to the troll. "Stop joking." She shifted her gaze back to Cyrus. "If you want someone to learn the resurrection spell, then they're going back to the Healer's Union for a minimum of two years."

"I'm a healer that casts the resurrection spell, and I'm telling you we can teach any healer that wants to learn in a day." Vaste's face remained neutral and his eyes were fixed, staring straight ahead.

Niamh's lips parted, twisting into a grimace. "That is ridiculous. I know it takes two years to train the resurrection spell –" Vaste's head shook, back and forth, a slow denial of her words – "there are advanced meditative techniques –" she ignored Vaste's shaking head, even as it gained speed – "there are different aspects of the enchantment to learn – STOP SHAKING YOUR HEAD! Fine," she hissed, "how can they learn the resurrection spell in a day?"

Silence fell once more. Alaric's hand covered his mouth, but his eye was closed. J'anda and Terian surveyed the table without speaking. Vara's eyes were pointed down, not looking at anyone. Cyrus had a sudden feeling that he was in the midst of a card game where one of the players had just alluded to cheating. The tension was such that when Curatio finally broke the silence, his soft words seemed as loud as a warcry.

"You don't use League instructors and you don't do it in their halls." The elf hesitated. "I taught Vaste the resurrection spell - and yes, it took less than a day."

Niamh's complexion turned nearly the color of her hair, and she physically shook for a moment before she exploded. "WHAT THE HELLS, CURATIO!?"

"I don't get it," Cyrus admitted. "So Curatio taught Vaste some spells. What's the problem?"

Niamh's words came out in a low hiss that gained volume until it turned into a shriek of outrage. "By doing that they've risked making us all HERETICS!" The last word came out as a curse and her eyes blazed as she looked at each of them in turn. "A healer's training, through the Leagues, is supposed to take ten years! Ten years to master spellcasting whether it's druid, enchanter, healer... you cannot tell me you've instructed him in..."

"About six weeks?" Curatio said. "I did. He received the rudimentary training at the Healer's Union in Fertiss, but his instruction was very basic and they kicked him out after a year because he's a troll. I filled in the blanks. He was hardly a master, but after I finished I would have put him against anyone who spent the ten years in the 'complete' training."

Cyrus looked around the table. "I know I'm not well versed in magic since I don't use it, but I can't help but feel there are things that some of you know," he nodded to Vaste and Curatio, "that others of us don't."

"That's because," Niamh replied, her words suffused with righteous indignation, "everything *they're* discussing is the stuff of heresy, the kind of things that could bring the full weight of the Leagues upon you. You know what heretics have in common? They aren't just hunted in the kingdom they've committed the crime in, they're hunted in all Arkaria by every power; the Leagues see to that."

"Like the Wanderer's Brotherhood and the Healer's Union?" Cyrus asked, uncertain.

"Yes, but as a group they're referred to as *the* Leagues." Niamh's fury had died down only slightly. Her complexion still struggled to dominate the red of her hair, coming damnably close. "They train paladins, dark knights, enchanters, druids... all of us."

Alaric broke his silence. "This discussion is unprofitable for us, friends. We will consider the possibility of training additional healers in the resurrection spell later. At the moment, we have Reikonos to deal with –"

A knock interrupted them and Nyad, face gray, opened the door and carried forth two envelopes to Alaric. Without another word, she left and the Ghost stared at each in turn.

"You're not going to open them?" Terian asked.

"I know what they say." Alaric's hand moved from his mouth to his forehead and began to massage his temples. His other hand reached down and slid one of the letters to Curatio and the other down the table to Terian. "Be my guest."

The room was quiet as the letters were read. "It's a summons to appear before the Sovereign of Saekaj Sovar to answer for the crime of robbery and treason." Terian looked around the table. "It's addressed to me and J'anda."

"The other is a notice to appear before the Elf King," Curatio said as he refolded the letter and placed it back into the envelope. "It names all of Sanctuary."

"They will seek monetary recompense for the lost shipments," Alaric said. "I expect that in light of the fact that we do not have the financial resources to make restitution they will resort to sanctions."

"I would have expected them to employ the death penalty," Vaste muttered darkly.

"In the case of the Sovereign of Saekaj, I wouldn't rule it out," Terian said without enthusiasm.

J'anda looked at him with curiosity. "I thought he was gone?"

"He's back," Terian replied, looking like a child submitting himself for punishment. Looking around the table, he answered the unspoken question. "The Sovereign led the dark elves into the last war, a hundred years ago, which we lost. He... recused himself for a while. All governance was through a tribunal, but as of a few weeks ago... he's back." Terian took a deep breath. "And he's not a merciful Sovereign."

"Who is he?" Alaric asked.

Terian grunted but said nothing. J'anda answered for him after casting a sidelong look at the dark knight. "It's not anyone you'd have met."

"But perhaps someone we've heard of," Alaric said.

"Perhaps. It is not my place to say." J'anda's face was inscrutable.

Cyrus buried his face in his palms. "Are there... any... of you at this table that aren't keeping secrets?" Frustration edged into his voice.

Vaste raised his hand. "I don't think I have anything to hide, so no."

Cyrus's head swiveled to fix on the troll. "So how did you find me in the Mountains of Nartanis? And how did you know what the specter did to me in the Realm of Darkness?"

"I stand corrected."

"Now, now," Alaric said, "think how boring life would be if you knew everything?"

"Speak for yourself," Vara said. "I know everything and am rarely bored hanging around with you lot."

"Let us focus on what must be done," Alaric said. "Terian, J'anda, you will stand before the Sovereign of Saekaj Sovar and present our defense."

"Great," Terian muttered.

"Curatio, you will take Nyad and speak with the King of the Elves in Pharesia," Alaric said, turning to the wizened elf. Curatio nodded in acknowledgment. "Perhaps hearing from his youngest daughter that we have no involvement with these attacks will soften his resolve. Meanwhile, Cyrus and I will present our case before the Council of Twelve in Reikonos. I doubt it is coincidence that the hearings are set for the day after tomorrow. We have an Alliance meeting at the same time, so needless to say, that will not be attended unless Vara and Vaste would like to go in our stead..."

"No," Vaste said in a tone of voice that offered no room for argument.

Vara smirked. "I think I'll do something more enjoyable, such as light my entire body on fire."

"So long as you keep your personal pyrotechnic displays out of the common rooms," Alaric replied without expression. "We have an opportunity to stem some very unfavorable consequences if we act properly. By presenting our case, we may buy the time necessary to uncover the real culprit."

"What do we do when we find them?" Niamh asked, complexion returned to normal.

Alaric's eye narrowed. "They have slaughtered hundreds of guards and traders and are besmirching our honor. When we find them, they will be made to suffer consequences so great that they shall never ponder a course of action such as this ever again."

"Oh," Cyrus said. "I just assumed we would kill them."

"That too."

Chapter 13

On his way to dinner that evening, Cyrus ran across Andren in the foyer, drink in hand, skulking outside the doors to the Great Hall. After a nod of hello from the healer, Cyrus launched into the question that had been on his mind for hours. "Why didn't you ever learn the resurrection spell?" Cyrus looked at the elf in curiosity.

Andren shrugged. "Never bothered to go back to the Healer's Union to study it."

The inner turmoil of his emotions over recent events overrode whatever tact Cyrus had. "There's a spell that can teach you how to master death and *you never bothered to go back to learn it!?"* The last words came out in a bitter scream, one that echoed in his ears long after their conversation had ended.

"It takes years!" Andren said in protest. "And the Healer's Union has a certain standard of conduct. For some reason," he said with a shrug, "drinking is not allowed. So I'd have to give up ale for AT LEAST two years. I decided it wasn't worth it."

Cyrus bit back the first response that came to his mind. Then the second. And third. "Your drinking," Cyrus said in a hollow voice, "has gotten worse since Narstron died." Cy looked around to make sure no one could overhear them. "I thought it was better when we were chasing the godly weapons and going after Ashan'agar, but it's gotten worse. And I don't know how it was the six months before that –"

"Because you were gone, yeah." Andren flushed. "You were gone a fair sight before that, though, weren't you? Adventuring every day, morning 'til night – never asking me if I wanted to go along."

"When you sleep until noon, you miss out on things," Cyrus said, an accusatory note creeping into his voice. "I'm not going to argue with you. It's your business; keep it under control."

"It is under control!" Andren shouted, voice filling the foyer. Cyrus looked around to find that everyone was already either watching them or pretending not to. Andren noticed as well, and lowered his voice. "It is under control. I'm fine. I just don't want to go to the Healer's Union in Reikonos almost two millennia after I finished my training, all right?"

Cyrus frowned. "Why would you go to the one in Reikonos? Didn't you get your training in Pharesia?"

"Yeah, but that one's closed." Andren dismissed it with a wave. "Point is, I don't want to do it."

"Fine," Cy nodded. "I might have an alternative. Could take less time too."

"Sounds dodgy."

"When have you ever cared how dodgy something was?"

"Good point."

They filed into the Great Hall and Cyrus took his seat at the officers' table after going through the line last with the other officers. "Bigger quarters, private bathrooms, but we have constant meetings and get the last pickings at supper." He frowned at his plate. "Not sure if this officer thing is worth the tradeoffs."

Niamh sat down beside him. "I need to talk to you about something."

"I hope it's not a mutiny." All the color drained from his face as her expression remained serious. "Please tell me it's not a mutiny. I know you were upset by the heretic talk in Council today –"

"It's not that," she interrupted, "although I'm not pleased at the thought of being an outcast. It's something else. I meant to talk to you about it after the Darkness invasion, but we –"

"Found that convoy. So what is it?" She winced at him. "Uh oh. Out with it."

"Well..." she began, struggling for words. "We have a new applicant. I'm afraid you're going to be upset."

"Why?" Cyrus laughed. "He's not a troll, is he?"

"What's wrong with trolls?" Vaste rumbled from a few seats away.

"They're violent, ill-tempered, stupid and they smell like the chamberpot at the Reikonos Inn after meat pies are served."

"I can't argue with any of that," Vaste admitted and returned to eating.

Cy turned back to Niamh. "You know Vaste and I made our peace after our... excursion to the bandit lands. If you're looking at additional troll candidates that are as good as Vaste, I think we'll be fine."

"No one is as good as me," Vaste corrected.

"It's not a troll," Niamh said with hesitation. "But you're on the right track. He is an outcast among his people."

"We already have a troll, a rock giant... is it a titan?"

"No."

"I don't know what I would have a problem with." Cyrus's eyes narrowed. "Unless it's Orion."

"It's not Orion. His name is Mendicant and he's a wizard. Which is unusual because magic is feared among his people."

"Mendicant?" Cyrus shrugged and smiled. "I'll give anyone a fair chance, regardless of where they come from, Niamh. My experience with Vaste has taught me that much, and there's no other race that has wronged me as badly as the trolls have." His smiled evaporated. "Unless... he's..."

"Yes." She grimaced. "He's a goblin. I've known him for years and he's not like other goblins; he's been out of Enterra for a very long time."

A long pause hung in the air. Cyrus looked away, caught up in the background noise of dinner in the Great Hall; plates clinking against silverware, voices raised in merriment. The smell of succulent cooked meat wafted through the air and Cyrus realized he hadn't touched his plate. "They don't know yet, do they?"

Niamh blinked, confused. "Know what?"

"About the trouble that's headed our way. The hearings."

She looked out across the sea of their guildmates. "No, they don't. Alaric won't announce anything until after the hearings."

Cyrus stared over them. "I remember my first day, when we had a fifth of the people we do now. I felt an army of that size could shake the foundations of Arkaria." His smile faded. "Then Enterra came, and I wondered if any victory would ever matter again."

He leaned forward, resting his arms on the table, eyes still scanning the crowd. "I predict a poor outcome for us in the hearings. And I don't know when we'll catch those responsible for the attacks, but I know that every day that passes between now and then, the likelihood grows that an army marches on the front gate of Sanctuary with violence in their hearts." He looked back at her. "I don't care if your applicant is a goblin or an ant-man. If he's honorable enough for you to call him friend, I'll judge him on his actions."

Niamh swallowed. Tension bled from her shoulders as she relaxed. "Thank you. I just wanted be sure in light of your recent..." She floundered, searching for the right word.

"Nightmares. I appreciate your concern but I have bigger

worries than my nightmares right now. Dark days are coming, and when they arrive, people will leave." Cyrus swept his gaze back over the crowd. "Soon I may wish for hundreds of goblins to fill the gaps left by those who chose to depart rather than face the trials with us."

Chapter 14

"Do they have the power to disband us?" Cyrus asked Alaric. They were in a wooden box, pulled by a thick twine through a system of pulleys, making its way to the top of the Reikonos Citadel, the tallest building in Arkaria. The squeaking of the wood as the elevator climbed did nothing to soothe his nerves. The box was open on the sides save for a small rail, and as they passed each floor he caught a glimpse of the Confederation's bureaucrats going about their daily routines.

"No, but they believe they have the power to invade Sanctuary and kill us all, which might be worse," Alaric replied, helm masking his expression.

"Only 'might be'?"

The Ghost shrugged as the pulley above them screeched. "Sanctuary is my purpose. For me, death would be preferable to losing the guild I have spent the days and years of my life building. For a new recruit being disbanded would be preferable. As always, it is a matter of perspective."

"Indeed." They reached the top floor and stepped out as the elevator box banged to a halt. A stone wall stood in front of them, obscuring their view of the rest of the floor. A sign mounted on it indicated the double doors on either side of the wall before them held their destination.

Alaric led the way through the double doors to their left, which were opened by two guards wearing a different coat of arms on their tabards than the Lyrus Guards. They were announced and Cyrus found his way into a circular chamber that was big enough to house combat in its center. Against the far wall sat the Council of Twelve, seated behind a long wooden stand that concealed them below the chest and elevated them above the rest of the chamber. A mixture of men and women peered down from the council bench, which was a rich, dark-stained wood.

A podium stood in the center of the floor before the council and had been the focus of their attention until Cyrus and Alaric entered. A gesture from the member of the Council seated in the center of the bench moved several of the guards into action. The speaker that held the floor took no notice that the focus had shifted from him and continued to drone on about the city water supply.

Two of the guards approached Cyrus and Alaric as they made their way through the rows of benches toward the rail separating the spectator seating from the open area with the podium where the speaker stood. "Good sirs," the guard said in a polite tone, "I'll need your swords for the duration of the hearing. You may collect them on the first floor when you leave."

Alaric chuckled. "Very well, but if I meant to assassinate the Council of Twelve I would hardly telegraph my intent by carrying a sword."

The guard gave him a smile. "It's a concern when people receive unfavorable judgments."

Alaric returned the guard's smile. "I'm already expecting one of those, so it should not come as a great surprise or cause me undue rage. But as you wish." The paladin reached down and handed his sword to the guard.

Cyrus grunted, almost in pain. A warrior of Bellarum never relinquished his weapon willingly.

"Let it go," Alaric whispered. "If they intend mischief, we can fight them hand to hand."

Cyrus reached into his belt and withdrew the scabbard, handing it to the guard without meeting his eyes. The guard stepped aside.

"Yes, yes," came a raspy voice at the front of the chamber. "We get the gist of what you're suggesting." The man in the center of the council table interrupted the speaker on the floor at the podium.

"But I have five more minutes!" came the protest.

"I am a man to whom time matters a great deal," came the resigned voice of the chairman. "Five minutes or five hundred won't make a difference in your case," the chairman concluded. "All in favor?" No hands were raised. "The nays have it, and thank you for bringing this to our attention."

"But you haven't done anything about it!"

"Yes, but at least now we are aware of the problem, and perhaps we will explore it again at a later date. Thank you," the Councilman said, dismissing the speaker.

Cyrus opened the gate of the railing for the retreating speaker, a small man with considerable years. "Better luck to you," the little man said as he hobbled down the aisle.

"Will the representatives from Sanctuary come forward?" The

chairman stared at them over rimmed lenses, something Cyrus had rarely seen. The chairman was at least sixty years of age, he estimated, and had jowls at either side of his mouth that shook when he spoke. Deep crimson robes flowed from a cowl that rested around his neck, a scrawl of symbols written around them.

Alaric halted Cyrus, whispering under his breath, "Do not underestimate this one based on his looks. He is one of the most fearsome wizards you could face and I suspect his influence extends far beyond the borders of the Human Confederation."

Cyrus looked at Alaric, perplexed. "What, you think I'm going to insult him or challenge him to a fistfight?"

Alaric's eye bored through the slit in his helmet. "Even if you were armed, I suspect it would end with an unfavorable outcome for you, my friend."

"Noted. I'll keep my rage to myself."

The chairman cleared his throat. "Would the representatives from Sanctuary please come forward?" he reiterated, a note of impatience in his voice.

Alaric strode to the podium, Cyrus a few steps behind.

"If you could identify yourselves, please..."

Alaric did not remove his helmet. "I have spoken before this august body on numerous occasions. Must I identify myself?"

"For the record," the chairman added with an imperious hand motion.

"I am Alaric Garaunt, Guildmaster of Sanctuary and this is one of my officers, Cyrus Davidon."

"Davidon?" The Chairman's eyes narrowed and he hesitated. "Very well. For the record the Council of Twelve stands in judgment of this matter, Chairman Pretnam Urides presiding." The chairman raised his nose when he spoke his own name, as though catching an enjoyable scent on the air. "We are here to discuss the complicity of Sanctuary in the attacks on Confederation shipping in the Plains of Perdamun."

"Let me also state, for the record," Alaric interrupted, "that Sanctuary has no complicity in said attacks."

"No admitted complicity," Urides corrected.

"No complicity," Alaric said with quiet finality.

"I see." The chairman looked down at the desk in front of him. "In the last few months we have lost fifty-eight shipments, creating a total loss of 5.8 million gold pieces, counting the loss of slaves killed or missing in the attacks and not counting the loss of manpower from the deaths of the guards and traders." His eyes raised and found Alaric and Cyrus standing below him. "That is a sizable number."

"To which number are you referring, the gold or the number of lives?" Alaric's voice contained just a hint of irony.

Urides eyes narrowed as he regarded the Sanctuary Guildmaster. "Both."

"To say nothing of the losses to the Dark Elf Sovereignty and the Elven Kingdom," Alaric added.

"Their losses do not concern me," Pretnam Urides said. "I am concerned with human affairs."

"I am afraid that the raiders of your convoys do not seem to share your narrow interest," Alaric said with a trace of sarcasm.

Urides ignored Alaric's comment. "We have seen your numbers grow in recent days, Alaric Garaunt. You have taken it upon yourself to go out into the world and drag people into your army that have never had a day of League training. You equip them with swords and bows, daggers and spears and call them warriors and rangers, even though their names have never been written on the rolls of the Wanderers' Brotherhood or the Society of Arms."

"I apologize," Alaric said, stiffening. "I was not aware that swordplay had joined spell casting in becoming the sole province of the Leagues."

The small man's eyes peered down at the Ghost of Sanctuary. "Spell casting is a sacred power, and none but the Leagues have the ability and means to instruct in its subtle and magnificent craft."

"And now you make the same claim for those who use a blade?"

"You border on heresy, Lord Garaunt."

"That would be a matter for the Leagues to decide, would it not?"

A smile cracked Pretnam Urides lips for the first time since they entered the chamber. "Perhaps." The smile faded. "Your army's growth is a matter of concern to all who have an interest in the Plains of Perdamun. What is your purpose in assembling this force?"

Alaric's hands gripped the podium. "I did not realize as I assembled my guild that I needed to explain my intentions to this body. We do sit far outside your borders."

Urides's smile returned, and it gave Cyrus a moment of disquiet. "Those lands have been long in dispute between the elves and the dark elves, and it is likely that they will never come to resolution. For that reason, the Council of Twelve believes that establishing our stewardship of those territories will be necessary to bring about peace."

Alaric paused for a moment before leaning forward to speak. "I apologize, perhaps I misunderstood you. Did you just announce your intention to annex the Plains of Perdamun?"

"By no means," Urides said with a derisive laugh, as though the idea were absurd. "We intend to steward those lands to avoid armed conflict over incidents such as this. We have already mobilized an army for that purpose." He removed the glasses and his eyes were beady without them. "The force in place will keep the peace by ensuring Sanctuary attacks no further human convoys and will protect our interests by removing any other threats to peace in the area."

"Meaning any other army that should cross into the southern plains," Alaric said with a sigh.

"We would also consider any large-scale movement by your army to be a hostile action and a threat to peace." Urides' smile had returned, almost taunting. "In addition, because of Sanctuary's role in the attacks and given the damages, we hereby levy a fine of 10 million gold pieces upon your guild, payable immediately, before any further commerce can be transacted between Sanctuary and any party in the Human Confederation."

"Is the Council of Twelve's treasury so empty that you would shake down parties innocent of any wrongdoing for gold?" Alaric asked with disgust.

"So you'll not be making payment today?" Pretnam Urides said.

"I will not." Alaric's voice overflowed with revulsion.

Urides head bobbed up and down in a nod. "Very well. It is ordered that every member of the guild Sanctuary shall be exiled from the Confederation until they make restitution in the amount of 10 million gold pieces. The accounts of said guild members at all banks in the Confederation shall be appropriated but not counted toward restitution."

Cyrus's eyes widened as Urides went on. "Any member of Sanctuary found in Confederation territory shall be arrested and executed for crimes against the state until the fine is paid. Any citizen who trades or does business with a member of Sanctuary shall be arrested and imprisoned for a term not less than fifty years." He looked around at the rest of the Council of Twelve. "I think that covers it."

Dark clouds gathered around Alaric. "I presume the 'arrest and execution' clause of your judgment does not go into immediate effect."

Pretnam Urides took a breath and exhaled, pleasant expression filling his jowly face. "I think we can be a little generous here. We can give you ten minutes." He leaned forward. "Our intention is not to kill any of your number, although we will if pressed. But you will make restitution for the losses of our convoys and for the loss of face we suffer from the rest of Arkaria. And let this stain upon your honor remain until then."

Alaric removed his hand from the edge of the podium and Cyrus could see an indentation pressed into the wood where the Ghost's gauntlet had rested. "Make no mistake, Councilor; you will never see a single piece of gold in restitution from Sanctuary because we have not committed this crime. You will, however, eat your words and your insults to our honor when we find the guilty parties."

"Very well, then." Pretnam Urides dismissed them with a wave of his hand. "But don't set foot in my Confederation again without either 10 million gold or your 'guilty parties' and an overwhelming amount of evidence to back up your assertions." The pleasant expression returned. "Until then, you are unwelcome here. Gentlemen... your ten minutes is ticking away."

Cyrus turned to leave, but Alaric was already moving. They entered the elevator and Alaric did not speak as they watched floor after floor go past. When they reached the first floor, Alaric ducked and jumped out of the elevator before it had stopped. He grasped his sword from the weapon's rack at the entryway and tossed Cyrus his short sword.

Cyrus followed the Ghost outside, and as he looked back, five of the Citadel guards followed them as they walked toward the square. "How much time do we have left?" Cyrus asked as he caught up with the paladin.

"Not much." Tension was evident in the Ghost's voice.

"Gentlemen, your time is up," came a voice from behind them. Cyrus turned to see the guard that had taken their weapons in the Citadel tower, standing behind them with his sword drawn.

Cyrus reached down to match the guard's motion but felt the pressure of Alaric's hand restrain his arm. "That won't be necessary." Cyrus turned back and a blur of red behind Alaric caught his eye.

"Hang on, boys," Niamh said as she squeezed between them, wrapping her arms around them in a tight embrace. Cyrus felt a tingle through his body, something far different from the winds of druidic teleport, and then a burst of light as the streets of Reikonos disappeared from view.

Chapter 15

The foyer of Sanctuary appeared around them as the light of the spell faded. Niamh gave them both a squeeze and released her hold on them. "Nothing like ending your afternoon sandwiched between two big, strong men."

"Your timing was impeccable," Cyrus said with a smile. "You just keep saving my ass."

"Should you keep eating at your current rate," came Vara's icy voice from over his shoulder, "that will involve more and more heavy lifting."

Alaric's head whipsawed around to Vara. "Has there been any word yet from the others?"

She shook her head. "I take it by your sudden appearance that things did not go well in Reikonos?"

"They threatened to have us arrested and executed if we didn't pay a fine of 10 million gold," Cyrus said. They were alone in the foyer; the rest of the guild were in the Great Hall for dinner.

Silence filled the air, broken at last by Niamh. "Did you say 10 million?"

"Yes," Cyrus confirmed. "They threatened to do the same to any of our members found in human territory."

"I see," Vara replied, face inscrutable. "And what did you do to precipitate these sanctions?"

"Me?" Cyrus said with indignation, looking to Alaric for confirmation. The Ghost was absorbed in his own thoughts and not paying attention. "I surrendered my sword and didn't say anything!"

"I sometimes find myself offended by your face," Vara admitted. "Perhaps you should have surrendered that as well."

"This is not a joking matter, Vara." Niamh's voice was stern, almost scolding.

"If we can't laugh about this, we may end up crying about it," Vara said.

A flash to Cyrus's left surprised him, and he swiveled to find J'anda with Terian clinging to him.

"You can let go now," the enchanter mumbled. Terian unwrapped his arms and took a step back.

"I take it your hearing did not go well?" Niamh eyed them

with a glimmer of hope.

"The Sovereign ordered our executions after demanding a fine of 5 million gold pieces," Terian admitted.

"That's not bad," Cyrus told him. "Reikonos ordered Sanctuary to pay 10 million gold pieces."

"The 5 million is for personal betrayals committed by the two of us as well as any other dark elf members of the guild," J'anda clarified. "The Sovereign has levied a 25 million gold piece fine against Sanctuary, and declared a death mark for all members."

"Until it's paid?" Cyrus shook his head.

"No, he expects us to pay the 30 million and *then* submit to our deaths," Terian said, face serious. "We barely got out alive. If it hadn't been for some quick thinking on J'anda's part we'd be dead."

Another flash of light brought Nyad and Curatio into focus. "I hope your meeting with the King went better than the rest went," Niamh said.

Nyad's face was pale. "We were expelled from the Kingdom and are required to pay a fine of 10 million gold to return."

"He's your father," Cyrus commented. "Doesn't he believe you when you tell him that we weren't involved?"

"He removed me from the line of succession," she said in disbelief. "And disowned me."

"I'm sorry, what?" Cyrus looked to Curatio for explanation.

"Nyad was next in line for the throne." Curatio's mouth was turned down in a frown; one of the first times since Cyrus had met the usually chipper elf. "She's been removed and all members of Sanctuary are banished from the kingdom."

"Happy day for the next poor sod in line," Vara muttered.

Nyad turned to Vara, mouth hanging open, but could not muster a response.

"Fool!" Alaric exploded, seemingly oblivious to the officers gathered around him. "He's engaging in a land grab against two of the oldest powers in Arkaria, believing the human army to be their equal or better." Alaric shook his head. "They will disabuse him of that notion, but not before a considerable number die."

"I'm sorry, I must have missed the first part of that," Vara said.

"Pretnam Urides, the Chairman of the Council of Twelve, is planning something arrogant and foolish," Alaric began.

"As he is a human, I remain unsurprised," Vara interjected. The squeak of a hinge filled the air as the front doors of Sanctuary opened.

"He intends - what the blazes are you doing here?" Alaric's voice rose on the last few syllables and the assembled officers turned to find Malpravus, Carrack and Tolada standing in the entryway, flanked by Cass, Erith and Elisabeth. Erith in particular wore a more sour expression that was standard even for her.

"I had assumed that with the difficulties you are experiencing, you might forget the Alliance officer meeting scheduled for today," Malpravus said with his usual skeletal grin. "Then I had heard that your entire guild was to be forbidden to enter the city of Reikonos, so I contacted the Daring immediately to find a more... hospitable location for us to meet."

Malpravus continued, gliding across the foyer toward them, "Then I heard that you experienced a similar fate in the Elven Kingdom and the Sovereignty. So rather than meet in a gnomish city or some dwarven hole, I presumed we should meet here since it appears to be nearly the last place in Arkaria where you would be welcomed." His fingers steepled in front of him and the Goliath Guildmaster's grin grew deeper. "You have been causing quite a stir, haven't you?"

"You know we have had no involvement in the convoy attacks," Alaric said, aggravation edging through the restraint in his voice.

"Of course, old friend, I know you would protest to your last breath your lack of involvement in anything so foul as thieving attacks on wealthy convoys that pass by your door. It must be rather like starving, then seeing ripe plums hanging over your neighbor's fence. What is the harm in plucking just one... then another..." His voice trailed off, but the grin widened.

"I don't hear a suggestion of our innocence anywhere in that statement," Vaste muttered as he appeared behind Cyrus.

"Probably thinking that if it were him in our shoes, he'd have been attacking the convoys long ago," Cyrus replied, voice low.

"Such uncharitable thoughts do not become you, dear boy," Malpravus said, not turning from where he stood, fingers caressing a torchlight mounted to the wall. His fingers slipped along the stone almost as if he were touching a lover. "But it matters not; we have many things to discuss. Where shall we meet, Alaric? Your Council Chambers, perhaps?"

"I think not," the Ghost replied icily. "There is a room behind the Great Hall that will be adequate for our purposes." Alaric turned and walked to the hallway that ran along the side of the Great Hall. Malpravus followed, gliding along with Carrack and Tolada in his wake and the Daring's officers a few paces behind them.

Cyrus felt a hand on his shoulder and stopped to see Erith looking at him with concern. She pulled him down to an embrace, surprising him. "This is going to be bad," she whispered in his ear. "Whatever happens, please try to remember that we are not all your enemy." She pulled away from him and looked him in the eye, biting her lip, then turned and followed the rest of them down the hall.

A sense of dread and curiosity filled Cyrus as they walked down the long corridor. Through the wall he could hear the sounds of merriment that always accompanied dinner. *I wonder how happy they'll all be when they find out they can never go home again just because they're members of Sanctuary? I'm upset about it, and I don't even have any family left!*

He reached a turn in the hallway and watched Erith disappear into a door. Almost across from it stood Malpravus, standing before another door. His fingers reached out and touched it as he turned to look at Cyrus. "Such a lovely guildhall, dear boy." He extended a hand toward the door that Erith had disappeared through. "After you, lad."

Cyrus watched the Goliath Guildmaster as he entered the room, a large chamber, bigger than the Council chambers upstairs, and laid out with tables along three sides. Malpravus followed behind him.

Cyrus looked around the room, amazed. Niamh gestured for him to join them at the longest table. "I've never seen this room before," he said.

"We have realigning rooms," she said as she took her seat.

"What?"

"They have enchantments that allow them to change based on what we need them for."

He shook his head in amazement. "I'm not well-versed in magic, but I've never heard of that."

"It's not common nowadays."

"What kind of spellcaster would even cast that spell?" he marveled.

She shrugged. "I don't know, an enchanter?"

"If we could begin?" Malpravus stood behind his table, taking command of the meeting. Cy shot a quick look at Alaric, whose arms were folded and whose face was unreadable under his helmet. "We have much to discuss. Instead of normal Alliance business, we find ourselves forced to deal with the difficulties of our members."

Cyrus looked around to find Cass unable to meet his eyes. Elisabeth stared straight ahead and Erith looked like she was ill. He locked onto Vara's face, which was already twisted with rage.

"How did he already know about our exile?" Niamh hissed. "We only found out in the last thirty minutes!"

Cyrus's eyes narrowed. "He must have spies in all the governments."

"I'm sure he does," Vaste said, leaning over from Cyrus's other side, "but he also communes with the dead, and there are so many dead listening to everything said that he wouldn't need any spies." Cyrus gazed at the troll for a moment in bewilderment before Malpravus dragged his attention back.

"Sanctuary's attacks on these convoys," Malpravus continued, turning a pointed gaze to Alaric, whose helm was lowered like a bull ready to charge, "have called possession of the southern plains into question. The Human Confederation has already sent an army, an action that is being mirrored as we speak by both the Sovereignty and the Kingdom. The humans also have additional armies marching this way, which will, inevitably, lead to armed conflict."

"I'm sorry," Cyrus interrupted. "How do you know that?"

"He's right," Elisabeth said, taking her feet. "This will escalate into a war here in the south, and once it starts, it will spread north. Armies will begin sacking the towns and villages along the borders and all of western Arkaria will mobilize." She looked around in dismay. "The governments will activate the homestead clause in our guild charters, and then we'll all be at war."

"What's a 'homestead clause'?" Cyrus looked at her blankly.

"Those of us headquartered in a major city," Elisabeth began, "had to sign a homestead clause before locating our guildhall there. It states that if the country goes to war, the guild will fight under their banner." She looked at Erith and Cass. "Because the Daring and Goliath are headquartered in Reikonos, we would be required to fight for the Human Confederation."

"Not quite," Malpravus said with a smile. "Those clauses are flexible if you have the proper connections. I have a great deal of latitude when it comes to Goliath's homestead clause. But that is neither here nor there. In the eyes of the three great powers of the west, Sanctuary is responsible for beginning this conflict; they have levied fines to force restitution, and if restitution is made and the attacks cease, this war can be stopped before it begins."

"No restitution will be made," came Alaric Garaunt's quiet voice. "Sanctuary has had no part of these attacks and we will not be made to pay."

"Is it because you don't have the gold in your treasury?" Malpravus said. "Because while Goliath has in excess of two hundred million gold pieces, I recognize that not everyone is so proficient at amassing wealth –"

"Corrupt and thieving, you mean," came the barely audible rumble from Vaste. Malpravus shot the troll a dirty look but did not answer his accusation.

"It matters not whether we have the money," Alaric said. "We are not culpable, and to pay would be an admission of guilt. We will catch the raiders and prove our innocence; it is the only course we will entertain at this time."

"Very well," Malpravus said, voice cold. "Your intransigence will have repercussions beyond those you have already been dealt. In the wake of these sanctions, your fellow Alliance members have held a discussion to determine your status with us. To have such renegades allied with us is a mark upon our reputations that we do not wish to bear without comment. Therefore, jointly, the Daring and Goliath have taken the following actions."

The Goliath Guildmaster reached into the folds of his cloak and produced a parchment which he read. "First, Sanctuary shall be reprimanded for their conduct, and marked among the Alliance. No Alliance voting rights shall be acknowledged during this time of shame.

"Second, in participation on Alliance expeditions, no loot rights shall be acknowledged for Sanctuary or any of its members.

"Third, no calls for aid will be answered from Sanctuary and no Alliance members will take part in any expedition, adventure, excursion or invasion run by or involving any Sanctuary members except those run by the Alliance.

"Last, these sanctions shall be in effect so long as Sanctuary remains a renegade guild operating outside compliance with Arkarian governments. For you who have chosen to shun the bounds of civilized society, you shall be cast out of our fellowship." With that, Malpravus rolled up the parchment and placed it within his cloak.

Cyrus sat there, a low hum echoing in his ears as numbness crept through his limbs and he felt a slight sway in the room. Niamh, next to him, was open mouthed in her shock, and a small flame glowed around her hand. Terian's spiked pauldrons had matched his forward lean and the dark knight looked as though he was ready to charge through the table and impale Malpravus. Alaric remained with his arms crossed and head down, while Vara offered a look of utter contempt hot enough to melt Quartal.

"While the Daring regrets to take these actions," Elisabeth said softly, "our guild is a democracy, and every one of our members has a vote. An overwhelming majority of our members felt that the stain upon Sanctuary's honor is not one that we wish to bear with them."

"It's good to have friends," Vaste said. "But even better to have ones that will abandon you at the first sign of trouble."

Elisabeth blanched, while Cass stared down at the table in front of him. Neither he nor Erith looked pleased.

"If these things seem unpleasant, know that we undertake these actions with great personal pain," Malpravus said, voice dripping with sincerity. "And as your allies and friends, we come to you as well with a proposal, one which we believe will help remedy this situation before it spins out of control."

"Oh, this should be good," Vara said.

"Indeed, it is," Malpravus agreed. "Your reputation is soiled, irrevocably, in the eyes of all the major powers. As word of their judgment spreads, it will become sullied in the eyes of the people of Arkaria as well. The Daring and Goliath, by association, will be viewed in unflattering terms, but less so. If we were to disband our individual guilds and reform as one, it would give a fresh start to all of us. The fines could be paid out of Goliath's treasury and we would be the fourth largest and most influential guild in all of Arkaria."

Malpravus's eyes glowed as he expounded on the possibilities. "With numbers such as ours, who could challenge us? Within months we could be uncontested in the top three, and in the course of a few years become the top guild in Arkaria." He surveyed the officers of Sanctuary. "The Daring has already voted and approved this proposal, pending acceptance by Sanctuary.

The problems you're having could be dispensed with, all at once."

"We have the money to buy you out of your mistake, no questions asked," Carrack added, face twisted in a smirk.

"We did not commit these crimes, you repugnant toad." Vara's reply lowered the temperature in the room by several degrees.

"Very well then." Malpravus nodded. "Think of the force we could bring to the plains. Of course we would headquarter ourselves here, and we could assist in stopping these attacks and put an end to this war before it starts."

Alaric stood so abruptly his chair tipped over and broke. "I think I've heard quite enough. Sanctuary will not consider that request."

Malpravus flushed, his complexion turning a darker blue before he unveiled a nasty smile. "I am aware of the bylaws of your charter, Alaric. You need to bring this to a vote before your members. And what do you think they'll say when they are given a golden out, after being placed in such a bitter position? We can make this problem go away, all of it, right now. They can all be welcomed home rather than be shunned in their own lands. And all it takes is one tiny formality - solidify the bonds of Alliance between us."

The Ghost was silent. Vara was not. "It would seem you intend to use the bonds of Alliance like a rope to strangle us."

"Vara, that's unnecessary," Elisabeth interjected. "If this proposal is to be decided, it should be decided by your members, not by a group of officers that have grudges that are based more on rumor than truth."

"Speaking of rumors," Cyrus said with unrestrained irritation, looking directly at Malpravus, "you spread a rumor that Goliath single-handedly killed Ashan'agar."

Malpravus favored Cyrus with a pitying look. "Such an accusation seems petty when we are dealing with matters of war."

"So you don't deny it?"

The Goliath Guildmaster sighed. "Of course I deny it. Prove otherwise."

"In this Alliance, it appears you need no proof of wrongdoing," Vara said.

"I think we've made all the progress one could hope for," Malpravus said with an air of finality as he stood. "We'll look forward to hearing the results of your vote."

Without another word, he gestured for the other officers to

follow him. Carrack cast a cocky smile backward over his shoulder as he disappeared through the door. Elisabeth breezed out behind them, sending a reluctant look to Cyrus and the others. Cass hesitated, looking as though he wanted to say something, but left without expressing it.

Erith paused at the door. "This sucks," she said without hesitation. "Cass and I were outvoted by our guild members but we think this is just as ridiculous as you do." Without waiting for a response, she walked out the door.

Niamh was the first to turn inward. "What do we do?"

Alaric's voice was strangled but unmistakable. "Council Chambers. Now."

Chapter 16

They trooped up the stairs in silence, until the door was shut behind them and all the officers were assembled within. No one spoke for a beat as they looked around the table and Alaric finally removed his helm. The Ghost's face was suffused with rage, and Cyrus felt a momentary urge to back away; he had never seen Alaric as angry as he appeared now.

"Why didn't we leave the Alliance just now?" Vara demanded before Alaric could speak. "They have insulted us, stolen recruits from us, and now they have placed us in a subservient position. I see no reason to continue our association with these flagrant jackals."

Alaric's response was barely above a whisper, but heard by all. "When we leave the Alliance, it will not be with our tail between our legs and a stain upon our honor; it will be with our heads held high in triumph and with the knowledge that we need not ever associate with the remnants of those horrors ever again."

"Also, members have to vote on forming and leaving alliances, according to the charter," J'anda added.

"I give less than a damn about the charter right now," Terian said. "Malpravus is intending to use it to force us into a marriage with Goliath. I say we suspend the charter right now."

"We can't do that," Niamh said, face pale. "Isn't it possible our members will understand? These are difficult times, they should be reasonable about it."

Vaste laughed. "Our members are about to be told that with the exception of the gnomes, dwarves, the rock giant and myself, none of them can go home again under penalty of death. I'm sure our human, elven and dark elven guildmates will be very understanding about that."

"Especially when they find there's an alternative, and all it requires is to tighten the bonds to an Alliance that we have played up as being good and useful," J'anda agreed.

"We have been hiding the difficulties with the Alliance for far too long," Vara said. "We should have been frank with the members long ago, when our troubles with them first began."

"It's not a secret that we aren't fans of the Alliance," Cyrus noted. "People have noticed that you, Terian and Alaric don't attend Alliance expeditions and have asked why. Under normal circumstances, I think the members would go along with a call from the officers to remove ourselves. Unfortunately..."

"These are not normal circumstances," Alaric finished for him. "And many of them will see a 'golden out,' as Malpravus called it, and go along just to return to the status quo." He shifted his gaze to Curatio. "I foresaw that things would go unpleasantly for us in Reikonos and Saekaj Sovar, but I am puzzled that you did not fare better in Pharesia."

Curatio frowned. "It was not for lack of trying, I assure you. It would have gone much worse were Nyad and myself not the representatives - I have a personal history with the King, stretching a long ways back. Weighing against us, however, was our suspected involvement in the theft of *Amnis*, the Spear of Water." The elf looked around the Council table. "With its loss in Ashan'agar's den, we were never able to clear our name in the Kingdom."

A knock on the door halted conversation. Nyad entered the room with an envelope that she handed to Alaric and then departed. She was still quite pale, Cyrus observed, even an hour after the events in Pharesia.

Alaric grunted after reading the contents of the envelope. "This letter is from a friend of mine, a member of the Council of Twelve. As I suspected, Pretnam Urides prearranged the results of our hearing. He intends to force a war to annex the southern plains and is blackmailing us to fill his treasury in preparation."

He crumpled the note and cast it away. "His support is not strong, but enough to carry a majority. If we can find evidence to cast doubt on our role, we can remove the sanctions. If we find the true bandits, we may be able to break his support for war."

"What about in Pharesia and Saekaj?" Cyrus asked. "Surely they can't want a war?"

"The King of the Elves does not," Curatio agreed. "My sense is that he is in a politically tenuous position right now because of... certain events that have occurred back home regarding the shelas'akur..."

"What does it have to do with Vara?" Cyrus asked. Vara flushed red but remained silent.

"I've said too much. Sorry, friends," Curatio replied with a sad smile and a tone of apology. "Those of us who are not elves will have to understand that this is not a topic for discussion outside the Kingdom."

"Thanks for bringing that up that titillating piece of information just to tell us we're not allowed to know about it," Vaste said. "Would you like to tease us with any other secrets we're not allowed to know?"

"We all have secrets," Alaric said. "We will respect their wishes and table any discussion of this topic in public."

"But in private, we'll be discussing it later in the lounge," Vaste added.

"I'd appreciate you not talking about me behind my back," Vara said, cheeks burning red.

"You're more than welcome to attend," Vaste agreed. "Perhaps you can answer some of our burning questions."

"The burning you will feel if I find you discussing me will not leave you with many questions."

"DAMMIT!" Alaric's fist hit the table, splintering it down the middle. "We are embroiled in a fight for our lives here; we have no time to bicker and discuss irrelevancies! I don't care about anyone's secrets at this table - we are losing face, recruits and money every day this madness continues, and that will expand to include members, as well, when we announce this to the guild."

"Screw the Leagues," Niamh said in a whisper when Alaric finished. "They're involved with the governments that have condemned us without any evidence." She looked around at all of them, quiet determination on her face. "They've basically branded us all heretics. If you can do it, we should go ahead and teach our healers the resurrection spell."

"I'm glad we've settled that, but it's tied to a discussion that we had before all this broke loose," Vara said with a healthy dose of sarcasm. "Perhaps we can focus on the matter at hand - namely, catching the bandits, clearing our name and sticking our victory so far down Malpravus's craw that it gets lodged in his skinny throat."

"What I'm discussing does pertain to that." The red-haired druid surveyed her fellow officers with an air of hope. "We need to step up our efforts to catch the bandits but we also need to do something to fight against a slide of guild morale. We need a bold undertaking, something to involve the members." Her green eyes danced, alight with possibility.

"You mean a distraction," Vara said acidly.

"I mean a challenge," she clarified.

"Yes," Alaric agreed. "Something that will inflame the excitement of our guildmates, give them something to focus on, some positive news in the wake of the terrible blows we have suffered. Something to unite us in these dark times." He nodded. "We need an expedition, something that would be of great note."

"Why can we not just focus on catching the raiders?" Vara shook her head in disgust.

"We shall, but we also require a challenge," Alaric stated. "This army is not well served by garrison duty, especially in light of the dismal news that they cannot return home. To have them stew on it for long hours while watching the plains with nothing else to look to will reduce morale further." A fire entered the Ghost's eyes. "We need a victory," he pronounced. "A big one. Cyrus?"

Cyrus blinked, stunned. "I came up with a list of targets we could explore, but they're on the edges of Arkaria, and none of them is well known."

"It matters not. Find a target and let us attack." The paladin's jaw was set. "Make it something that will challenge us, that will tax our abilities, something that will fire our imaginations."

"I'll come up with something definite in the next twenty-four hours," Cy agreed, a pool of nervous thoughts swirling in his head.

"Very well," Alaric said. "I am pleased that we were able to reach a consensus on what needs to be done. While we may argue and discuss as much as necessary within the walls of this chamber, we must be united when we leave. In light of the trials that are coming, we must provide a bulwark of strength for our guildmates to look to in these troubled times. We will only see our way through this morass if we draw together."

Curatio nodded. "We have, in the bylaws, a way to postpone any vote that is to be presented to the members for as long as six months, but only with unanimous officer agreement. I suggest we do that now. The measure must be validated every month for it to be kept in effect."

"Agreed," Alaric said. "Any disagree?" A shaking of heads from every officer sealed the vote. "Tomorrow evening at dinner I will address the issues at hand to the members. I suspect by then the rumors will have made their way to almost everyone."

They adjourned and Cyrus moved toward the door. Alaric stopped him once more. When the door closed, the Ghost spoke. "Find a target, quickly."

"I will."

"I know we are in the midst of a considerable crisis, but I must ask you - have your nightmares returned?" Alaric's voice was soft, understanding.

"Yes," Cyrus admitted. "And there's another element to them now. The word 'gezhvet'. I heard the goblins say it the night of the Enterra invasion. Do you know what it means?"

"No." Alaric shook his head. "But I believe Niamh told you we have a goblin applicant making his way to us in the next few days? I would suggest you ask him."

Cyrus blanched. "All right."

"Do not let revenge consume you now, my friend. It is a dangerous path, to obsess about vengeance when we are in the midst of a storm such as this. I need you to focus on helping us get through this."

The warrior looked down at his hands. "I can't stop thinking about that night in Enterra." He brought his gaze up to meet Alaric's. "We're in bigger trouble than I've ever been in, and I can't get myself to stop having nightmares about something that happened over a year ago. You'd think I'd be having nightmares about things that are happening here and now."

Cyrus felt the pressure of Alaric's hand on his shoulder. "I know of the strong calling for vengeance that you feel. I have felt it myself, and it is natural to desire retribution for so strong a loss as the one you suffered. I would tell you to let it go, but I doubt I would heed those words were I in your position." Alaric gave him a knowing look. "Instead, I caution you that vengeance will not bring you peace. Disassembling the goblin capital stone by stone will not silence the memory of your lost friend."

"I did not believe it would," Cyrus said with a nod. "And although this vision haunts me at night, I worry less and less about it during the days. In a way," he said with a tinge of guilt, "it's good that these nightmares are plaguing me or else I would forget Narstron - and the promise I made."

"We move on with our lives," Alaric agreed. "It is not a betrayal to their memory if we do not think of them constantly - or if we were to pass on an ill-considered vow."

"I know you've lost a lot of guildmates," Cyrus said with quiet certainty, "but I have a hard time imagining you as close to any of them as I was to Narstron. Because if you were... I don't see how you could dismiss the idea of revenge so easily." Even through his gauntlets, Cyrus's fingers pressed the metal into his palm.

Alaric's expression did not change. "I daresay I was closer to one of them; Raifa Herde was my wife."

Cyrus blinked in surprise. "Raifa Herde? Wasn't she one of the founding members of Sanctuary?"

"She was," Alaric said. "She was also the first member of Sanctuary to die permanently."

"How can you not have wanted to hurt whoever killed her... as bad as they hurt you?" Cyrus asked.

Alaric did not answer at first. He walked toward the window and stared out across the Plains of Perdamun toward the horizon. "I believe I told you once that the titans were responsible for her death, as this was in the days before the elves controlled the pass through the Heia mountains to the southern lands. The titan that murdered her still lives."

The Ghost turned to him. "I likely could have killed him by now, had I a single-minded intention to do so. I could have led assault after assault into the heart of Kortran, hunted him down and murdered him in his sleep if necessary, but I could have done it. Even so, Raifa would still be dead." He turned back to the window.

"She was so delicate," he said with a faint smile. "I could lift her with the greatest ease, as though she were a flower being hefted on the wind. When he hit her, she spun away like one." His noble features darkened at the memory, the smile disappeared and was replaced with a look that sapped all the kindness from the Ghost's face.

"Life is too short to exhaust it in mourning the loss of loved ones and trying to bring about the ruin of those who are responsible for taking them from us. We are adventurers who live by the way of the sword, and to swear revenge on all who aim to kill us and ours is to foreswear living any sort of life at all.

"When the day comes that Talikartin the Guardian meets his end, if it is by my hand it will not be because I have plotted and directed all my efforts to striking him down; it will be because he is a threat to my guildmates and in defense of them, he will die." His point made, Alaric faced the window once more.

Cyrus, taking it as his cue to leave, walked toward the doors. As he opened one of them, he turned back to the paladin. "You said vengeance would not bring me peace. But you also said Talikartin still lives. Since you never took vengeance, how do you know that it wouldn't give me some measure of peace?" His voice came out choked, more like a desperate plea than he wanted.

Alaric did not stir from his place by the window as he answered. "Talikartin the Guardian was hardly the first person to ever wrong me, Cyrus." Alaric turned back to him, and Cy caught a glimpse of a flash of cold fury that passed as quickly as it appeared. The fact that it glimmered and was gone in less than a second disturbed the warrior more than even the righteous anger he had seen earlier in the Council meeting. Expecting some final, reassuring message from Alaric, his unease grew with the Ghost's final word on the matter: "He is simply the only surviving one."

Chapter 17

Cyrus descended the stairs to find Andren in the lounge, post-dinner ale already in hand. He sat across from the healer, who did not speak, and looked away at Cyrus's approach. "What do you want?" He took a ferocious slug of the ale in his hand, pitching it back with more intensity than usual.

"Sorry I yelled at you."

"It's all right," Andren replied with a shrug. "You have a few things on your mind lately. Vaste told me what happened in the Council meeting."

"You going to let him teach you the resurrection spell?"

"He already did. I used it this afternoon; works just fine."

Cyrus stopped, surprised. "How did you use it this afternoon? Who died?"

Andren flushed. "Well, no *person* died, so I used it on one of the cows that Larana was going to slaughter for dinner. He sprang back up and vomited grass gunk all over my boots." The elf shrugged. "I guess they feel the effects like we do."

"So you just tried it the once?"

"No, we killed it over and over again, just to be sure. Probably did it about ten times."

Cyrus winced at the thought. "I feel kind of bad for that cow."

"Yeah, he was wobbling quite a bit at the end. We decided to let him live; figured he'd been through enough for one day." Andren took a pull from his ale. "Larana was not happy; her workshop stunk when we were done."

"How could you tell she was angry? Did she yell?"

"Oh, yes. Very scary when she gets mad, that one."

Cyrus chuckled. "She's dead quiet around me."

"She asked me about you once - figure maybe she's got something for you?" Andren's eyes were suggestive, then after a moment of looking at Cyrus, his eyebrows arched and lips thinned. "You okay?"

"No." Cy shook his head, looked around and lowered his voice. "We're about to hand out some very bad news."

"You mean about how we're banished from everywhere and everybody hates us?"

Cyrus blinked. "Yeah. That."

"Everyone knows," the healer scoffed. "Lot of talk about it, too. Not very happy tidings."

"Yeah, well, we need to plan an expedition somewhere - something challenging that could profit the guild and give everyone something to focus on outside of our own problems." His eyes narrowed. "Something that could cut through the bad reputation and make people think twice about leaving us, because we're a guild on the move."

"I don't think a successful excursion to kill the God of Death would make people think becoming a pariah is an acceptable trade-off for joining us."

"If we could just stem the tide of those who will want to leave, give them enough doubt to keep them here while we find these bandits..."

"There are rats already talking about jumping ship," Andren warned. "I wouldn't, because I have no family I care about seeing and give less than a damn if I ever lay eyes on the elitist Kingdom again, but there are some who are already homesick and heartsick and nothing you could plan would cut through that."

"Those are the ones we're going to lose anyway." Cyrus straightened as a realization set in. "Since we're pariahs and the whole world is against us, we might as well add a few thousand more people to the list." He grinned. "Especially since it'd net us so much money."

Andren did not look amused. "I can tell you're having a right nice thought there, but would you care to share?"

"The Trials of Purgatory," Cyrus said. "That's our target. The big three guilds - Amarath's Raiders, Endeavor and Burnt Offerings - are busy trying to make inroads into the Realms of the gods; the Trials are empty, no one's even making any attempts." His grin widened. "We're going to do it. We'll launch ourselves into the top tier of guilds."

"Correct me if I'm wrong," Andren adopted a pensive look, "but the reason no one has attempted Purgatory in the last year is because the last guild that did successfully execute that particular expedition was slaughtered in the streets of Reikonos moments after they emerged from the exit portal - which, by the way, is the ONLY way out of the Realm. Not to mention it exits in REIKONOS - you know, where we're all in danger of being executed if we show up?"

Cyrus shook his head. "First of all, the minute we step out of the portal, we can teleport out - before any other guild tries to slaughter us, and before the Reikonos guards show up." He scoffed. "Actually, with the entire guild behind us, the Reikonos guards would be helpless against us."

"Yeah, but there's the fact that the big three *slaughtered* - right there in the streets, with every other guild in the city *and* the Reikonos guards watching - the last guild to do what you're proposing we do!"

"I told you, we can teleport out before they assemble. That guild, Retrion's Honor - some of them escaped, but their guildhall was in Reikonos; they didn't know they'd have to run. We do."

"Wasn't their guildhall sacked and burned? You think the big three won't take a little trip to the Plains of Perdamun if they want to make an example out of us?"

"I don't think they'll care enough to pursue us, no." Cyrus's eyes darted around as his mind raced. "None of them has been through Purgatory in over a year. Everyone else is too scared to try. Even if they make an attempt on us afterward, we'll run and they'll decide it's not worth their time to unite forces and chase a guild whose days are already numbered in their eyes. If they chase us, we'll seal the wall and make a stand here. They'd have a hell of a time trying to storm Sanctuary."

"Fine. Assuming you're right - and I'm not saying you are," Andren said with practiced skepticism, "we still have a major obstacle in that we know nothing about the Trials of Purgatory! How are you going to plan an expedition when you don't know what we're facing? I mean, do we even know anyone who's been on a successful run through the friggin' Trials of Purgatory?"

"I have," said a cool voice from behind them. "I can tell you everything you'd need to know about how to get our army through safely."

Cyrus turned. Light from the entrance glinting off the shiniest armor he'd ever seen, and shone in her blond hair, which was loose and hanging around her shoulders for only the third time since he'd known her. Vara returned his stare, face impassive.

"I will help you lead us through the Trials of Purgatory."

Chapter 18

"You know Purgatory?" Cy raised an eyebrow.

"I was an officer in Amarath's Raiders when they succeeded in conquering the Trials." She straightened. "I was involved in the planning."

"You said 'when they succeeded'," Andred said with a tinge of caution. "So there were times they failed?"

"Horribly," Vara confirmed. "Hundreds dead, rather like your experience in Enterra; those of us who survived returned to collect the dead and prepare them for resurrection - but we lost dozens to permanent deaths."

Andren shot a pleading look at Cyrus. "I don't want to die again."

"If it makes you feel any better," Vara said in what could only be described as (for her) a soothing tone, "I have never died. And I have been on expeditions much more challenging than the Trials of Purgatory."

"Never?" Cyrus said, taken aback. "How long were you with Amarath's Raiders?"

"Five years," she replied.

"Impressive."

"Thank you. I did come very close once, close enough that I know I would not care to repeat that experience." A smile upturned the corner of her mouth. "So let us attempt to keep that trend alive, shall we?"

The planning had taken almost a week, during which Cyrus had called the Sanctuary army together every day to practice maneuvers that would be employed during the expedition. Each night he spent in planning with Vara, examining every point, no matter how trivial, related to the Trials.

"This is crucial," she said. "When you reach the fourth island, it becomes the point of no return. There is a gateway here -" she pointed to the hand-drawn maps on the table before them - "that is your last exit before the Final Guardian. If we choose to go forward and face the guardian, we are forced to exit into the Reikonos guildhall quarter."

"So we need to be prepared to fight a rear-guard action for a few minutes in Reikonos before we leave the guardian's island."

"We should prepare for the possibility that they may place wizards in position to block our exit with a cessation spell that could cut off teleportation in the vicinity."

"How do we counter that?" Cyrus's eyes widened in alarm.

"Kill the wizards in question," she said with a thin smile. "They'll be exposed, close by, and they'll have to continue the chanting in order to keep the spell in effect. It requires concentration, so they won't be able to move or the enchantment will break."

She pulled a map of the guildhall quarter to the top of the stack. "They'll have to place the wizards here or here," she said, pointing to the map. "Either way, since we know what we're looking for, a ranger will be able to kill them or disrupt their spellcasting ability with some well-aimed arrows. And we'll be out of there before they can re-establish the cessation field."

Cyrus sat back and looked at the pile of maps in front of them. Exhaling, he felt a rush of panic. "Can we really do this?"

"Yes," she answered without hesitation. "You know where the sticky points will be, and how we'll need volunteers for... that," she said.

"If that's the worst," he said, "I can take that myself - at least two thirds of it."

"Yes, well -" She hesitated. "I'm certain you can find one other willing soul in all of Sanctuary to bear the other part of it. Everything else we face is a matter of preparation, strategy and effort. The first challenge is likely to be a problem, since the brute force that Sanctuary can bring to bear does not compare to the sheer power that Amarath's Raiders has at their disposal."

"I'm more concerned about the third trial," he said, pulling the map in question from the pile. "This is something we've never practiced."

"It's easier than you would think. I worry about the power of the fourth trial; you will be in great peril during the entirety of that fight and it could be fatal." Concern etched her face. "You will have to be quick on your feet to survive."

"Don't bet against me," he replied with a smirk. "Remember what happened last time you did?"

"I won, as I recall."

He frowned. "You recall incorrectly. I stood there with you on the bridge in the garden as you insulted me."

"That was basest chicanery; you had deceived me about the

timeframe on the bet."

"You're an adult, physically if not emotionally; take some responsibility - it's not my fault you thought the bet had ended a day earlier."

"I thought it had because you told me it had." Irritation creased her brow, despoiling her pretty features. "You lied to me for the express purpose of collecting your prize." The annoyance on her face turned into self-righteous satisfaction. "If you won, then why haven't you tried to collect the 'date' you 'won'?"

"I've been rather busy with other things of late. If you thought you won," he said with a smirk, "why haven't you collected on the favor you were owed?"

"I haven't had need of any of your rather limited services yet, but be assured, when the day comes that I need a poorly brewed cup of tea or a slab of ignoramus to rest my feet on, you shall hear from me."

"I'm also a reasonably good pincushion and a fair dancer."

"I've seen you dance; I think you're overstating it."

They laughed for a moment before her expression became guarded once more. "Why did you choose Purgatory?"

He stared back at her, trying to mask his feelings. "It's one of the biggest challenges out there. It's high profile; it'll give our name a boost right now - which we could use."

"Of course the fact that you lack only two components for this weapon you've been assembling and that one of them is in Purgatory has no influence on your decision." Her blue eyes pierced him.

"I can't deny the appeal," he admitted, "but that's not the main reason. Since the 'Big Three' have been focused on exploring the newly opened Realms of the gods, all the tradespeople and merchants that were used to selling the exotic goods that came from their regular harvests of Purgatory have gone wanting. The goods we bring back will fetch a hefty price - enough to come close to paying off Reikonos, at least."

She looked down. "So money's the motivation."

He exhaled. "It's not just one thing, it's a combination of factors. And why does it matter? This expedition is a good move for us; it can provide answers to a lot of different problems we're facing right now."

"Alaric will never consent to paying Reikonos - nor anyone else."

Cyrus paused before answering. "If it gets desperate enough, he may change his mind - not for him, but for his guildmates."

She shook her head. "He is a man who does what is right in all things, no matter the cost. He would sacrifice *everything* in order to do what is right." Her eyes flicked up to meet his. "Not to '*appear*' to do what is right. To *do* what he believes is right, always."

Cyrus stood, smiling. "I admire him for it. I'll follow his lead, but I want to give him the option to pay if necessary. And if that fits with giving us a boost and a challenge to aid our retention, all the better." His smile disappeared. "Can I ask you something?"

Her face turned wary. "What?"

He leaned forward, peering at her. She stared back, eyes wide, not sure what to expect. "Do you ever think about the night we had dinner in that little village..."

She sat back and breathed in. "Elintany, it was called. South of Traegon."

He almost chuckled. "You remember."

"I do." Her eyes held a certain reserve, and a glimmer of sadness.

"That night, I felt like I finally got to know you better, and the next day it was as though you had shut the door to the Vara I saw there." He moved his head, trying to meet her gaze, but she was looking away, focused on the maps in front of them. "I've seen glimpses of her since that night, but it's rare."

Her head snapped up, a fire burning in her eyes. "I do not wish to discuss this any further; it is a dangerous path to consider."

"It's dangerous to consider what?" he fired back. "That you could melt that icy shield around you and come out and talk to me like a human being?" She rolled her eyes as she flipped her hair to reveal her pointed ears and stared him down. "Poor choice of words - like an elf being - whatever you'd call it. Like a person," he said with urgency, "rather than as someone constantly worried about being harmed."

"If I worry about being harmed," she said with a tinge of outrage, "perhaps that says something about what I might expect from a man like you -"

"A man like me?" Cyrus reeled back in shock.

"A human," she snapped back. "Let me ask you this: do you still want to kill every goblin in Enterra?"

He tensed but did not answer.

"I see." Her eyes pulsed with a self-righteous fury. "Do you still dream about them at night, wish to claw at the Empress and Emperor and visualize their slaughter?"

"Of course I do!" Cyrus erupted. "He was my best friend and they killed him!"

"This sort of human bravado can get us killed!" she shouted back. "When we go into the Trials of Purgatory, the Gatekeeper will know your very soul! Part of the Trials is facing his attack on your very essence - he says things to undermine your confidence. He knows your weaknesses and he will nettle you with the things you fear and the things you're obsessing over, try to hurt you with words and thoughts."

"Words don't concern me. Words can't harm me."

She laughed, but it was a bitter and scornful sound. "I have seen him use words to turn guildmates against one another. So perhaps I'm not as worried about his words harming you as his words causing you to harm another."

"You really think I'd harm anyone?" He straightened, trying to meet her gaze, but she had once more turned her eyes away. "Do you think I'd harm you? I know you don't hate me anymore -"

"I never did; do not presume to tell me my own emotions -"

"Well you acted like you did, and you don't anymore -"

"We'll see about that -"

"Fine," he said with a burst of fury. "I can see this was a stupid topic of conversation for me to bring up. Let's get back to focusing on the plans," he said with a shake of the head. "But we'll do it tomorrow morning; I'm done for the night." Without waiting for her to say anything else, he walked from the room, slamming the door behind him.

Chapter 19

"Cy," the female voice interrupted his stride halfway across the foyer. He turned, ready to spit venom, only to have the desire fade as he took in the speaker.

"Niamh," he acknowledged. The red-haired druid stood next to a goblin - dark green, scaled skin, almost the size of a dwarf, and possessed of long ears and sharp teeth. His eyes were cast down but his pupils were ringed with a yellow iris, visible even a few paces away because of their striking color. His body was covered by a light blue robe and bore the lettering given to wizards. Cyrus looked closer at the goblin, who appeared nervous and was almost twitching.

"My name is Mendicant," the goblin said with a bow, still not lifting his eyes to meet Cyrus's. "I am pleased to meet you, Lord Davidon."

The internal tension that Cyrus had felt upon spying the goblin dissolved. "I... can't say I've ever been called Lord Davidon before," Cy said with a smile. "I am pleased to meet you, Mendicant. Niamh has told me good things about you."

The goblin bowed again. "I only hope to be able to live up to her expectations, m'lord."

"Stop calling him 'm'lord'," Niamh commanded. "You'll swell his ego."

"Don't stop on my account," Cyrus replied. "She's just jealous because you don't call her Lady Niamh."

"Oh, he does," she said with a smile. "But as a more mature, stable individual, I can take a compliment without letting it go to my head."

Mendicant looked back and forth between them. "Let's remember the new recruit in our midst, Niamh, and keep the focus on getting to know him better," Cyrus said with an ingratiating smile. "Mendicant, you seem different than the goblins I've met in the past."

Mendicant's eyebrow arched. "Because I'm wearing clothing and not clawing at you?"

Cyrus studied him for any sign of sarcasm. Finding none, he replied, "That's a start."

"There are more goblins like me than you'd think," Mendicant said. "Our city is ruled by the royalty, and they are the warrior caste; all else is secondary to them. They take the strongest fighters and indoctrinate them into the ruling class, and lord over the rest of us with an iron fist. Most of my people hate life in Enterra."

Cyrus rubbed the stubble on his chin. "The Emperor and Empress are not beloved of all the goblins?"

Mendicant shook his head. "Only the warrior caste, but that's all it takes. We have no magic users trained in Enterra for fear it would diminish the power of the warriors." He looked down. "I may not look it to your eyes, but I am average for a goblin, too small to be a warrior. So they would have me be a worker, always doomed to be a second-class citizen. If a warrior wants to have his way with your life-mate, they may."

His teeth showed at the thought, but Cy noticed they were smaller and less pointed than the goblins he had fought previously. "So I left. Better to live under my own conditions, with no goblins around me than the way they would have me live. But they do not let you leave voluntarily - I had to escape."

A curiosity welled to the surface of Cyrus's mind. "I need to ask you something, Mendicant."

A nod. "Anything, Lord Davidon."

"What does gezhvet mean?"

Mendicant recoiled and blinked several times. "You have heard of the gezhvet?"

"I've heard the word. I need to know what it means."

Mendicant looked around, as if he were afraid of someone overhearing them. "Gezhvet is a tale of hope among the non-warriors, and a nightmare to the ruling class. Warriors have not always ruled our city. Several hundred years ago, we had a society that was wise, ruled by thinkers, scholars, workers and soldiers equally. Then came the days of upheaval when a strong General protected us from a great scourge that came from across the Sea of Carmas, and afterward came to believe that only martial strength was fit to rule. And so the ruling class was born.

"But the Prophecy of the Gezhvet is from the last of our magic users - a seer of some renown, who made many prophecies, all of which have come true after a fashion."

"After a fashion?" Niamh asked.

"Prophecies are bullshit." Cyrus shook his head.

Mendicant hesitated. "Prophecies are vaguely worded - the story of the gezhvet states that a dwarf shall come forth and be the ruin of the warrior caste and free the goblin underclass. It produces a great fear of dwarves in the royalty."

Cyrus had a stricken look on his face. "You know that my friend who died in Enterra was a dwarf?"

"I did not. It could be they considered him the gezhvet, and killed him to trumpet their defeat of the prophecy. The royalty would pay any price to avoid the doom brought by the gezhvet."

Cyrus set his jaw. "Even trade away their Hammer of Earth for a warning that he was coming?"

"They traded away *Terrenus*?" Mendicant's jaw dropped in outrage. There was a beat of stunned silence before the goblin spoke again, his voice high. "That is the birthright of my people!"

"You sound surprised."

Mendicant shook his head. "I should not be surprised. The powerful hold onto that power with all their strength. And with a race of warriors, that strength is considerable."

Cyrus nodded back. "Although we are embroiled in our own problems at present, the day may come when we delve into the depths of Enterra once more. I trust that won't be a problem for you?"

"So long as you don't wade through the streets of the city, filling it with the blood of my people, there is no problem," Mendicant said with a shake of his head. "If your intention is to storm the keep of the Imperials, you have my assistance every step of the way. And," he said with a jagged-toothed smile, "I believe I can be of great assistance in that."

"It would seem we have a common foe. I am pleased to make your acquaintance, Mendicant," Cyrus said with a smile.

Mendicant bowed. "I am proud to enter the service of so noble and honored a guild as Sanctuary."

Cyrus closed his eyes for a moment. "I wish I could say that we were as honored as we used to be, but unfortunately events have turned against us recently."

"These are but temporary problems," Mendicant said with a wave of his clawed hand. "Niamh has informed me of the difficulties and I am certain that you will clear this matter up."

"I appreciate your confidence."

Mendicant bowed once more as Niamh led him away, up the stairs toward the applicant's quarters.

"Cyrus," came a quiet voice from behind him.

He turned and exhaled, the energy rushing from his body. "I

don't have the energy for another argument tonight."

Vara stood before him, hands in the air in surrender. "I did not seek you out to fight you. I overheard your conversation with the goblin. I am impressed," she admitted. "You handled that well; better than I would have given you credit for."

"Because I didn't sink my teeth into his throat like the vicious dog you think I am?"

"Perhaps I spoke in error." Her hands fumbled at her sides, flitting from the plates of her greaves, where they left marks of perspiration in the shape of her palms on the shining metal. "My last experience in Purgatory was not a positive one. Amarath's Raiders barely won the day and it was a vicious final battle that ended in a rather unfortunate spot as the Guildmaster was slain by one of his most trusted officers at the urging of the Gatekeeper."

Her eyes looked up and behind them was a sheen of fear, something Cyrus had never seen from Vara before. "The Gatekeeper is one of the most frightening fiends I have ever faced, but he does not fight in battle; he undermines using every insecurity you could imagine. I am... afraid of him, which is the most difficult thing that any paladin could admit."

"I would never harm you," Cyrus promised. "Nor would I allow any harm to come to you."

"I believe you," she said, voice unsteady. "I am ready to resume planning on the morrow when you are." She turned and began to walk away.

He watched her go and turned to find Aisling watching him from the shadow of a nearby doorway. "Doing a bit of eavesdropping?" he lashed at her in an accusing tone.

She shrugged, languid smile across her face. "I like to listen. It's nice to stay informed." A smirk lit her dark blue features. "She's not just afraid, she's terrified of this 'Gatekeeper'. Unattractive trait in a fearsome fighter, isn't it?"

A surge of inarticulate anger straightened his spine and tingled across his scalp. "We all have our vulnerabilities. There's nothing wrong with that; it's natural."

"Nah." She tossed her shoulders back in an even more casual shrug. "Not all of us do."

"I don't have time to search for it, but I'm sure you have a soft spot for somebody, somewhere." He covered his eyes and bowed his head as the realization of what he'd said hit him. "You know what I mean."

"I have a very soft spot for you –"

"Just stop," he said in irritation. "Stop trying to convince yourself that you want to sleep with me."

Puzzlement covered her face. "But I do."

He laughed mirthlessly. "You do? You cannot possibly think that these ridiculous double entendres are doing anything other than irritating the hell out of me. You don't strike me as a stupid person, yet time and again you persist in following the same pattern of attack, and I rebuff you every time. It's wearing thin." Dark clouds gathered above his eyes. "If you were really serious, you'd find a different method of approach, since the current one isn't working... at all."

She recoiled as though stung. "This is who I am. I'm not going to change for you."

"Then I've got news for you," he said with a cold smile. "I don't like who you are. I don't find you cute or amusing, and I've had my fill of your ridiculous attempts to 'seduce' me with stupid one-liners and over-the-top displays of sexual aggression. Stop wasting your time and mine with your childish attempts."

"I don't think you need to worry about any of my attempts in the future," she said, acidity filling her tone. She turned back to the shadow of the doorway, her white hair standing out in the darkness.

"By the way," he tossed at her disappearing back, "looks like you're as insecure and vulnerable as the rest of us."

Deep, rumbling sounds resonated from a nearby grating. Approaching with caution, Cyrus saw a red eye gazing up at him from below and realized that the noise was laughter. "You really have a way with the ladies, don't you?" came a voice from below.

"Fortin?" he asked, peering into the grating. The eye blinked, showing a hint of rocklike-skin around it. "Do you listen to all the conversations that happen in the foyer?"

"Only the ones that interest me."

"These are private conversations," Cyrus said in irritation.

"Then have them in private." As Cyrus shook his head and began to walk away, the rock giant's voice rumbled at him again. "Don't get snippy with me because the woman you don't like likes you and the one you like doesn't," the rock giant called from behind him.

"You don't know what you're talking about, Fortin," Cyrus

threw back over his shoulder.

"Then why are you walking away in such a hurry?" came the rock giant's voice one last time as Cyrus stormed up the stairwell.

Chapter 20

Although they planned together for several more days, Cyrus and Vara did not discuss her admission about the Gatekeeper in Purgatory. During their planning sessions, her eyes rarely met his and then only seemingly by accident. He had not seen Aisling since telling her off in the foyer; he suspected her considerable skill at evasion and stealth allowed her to avoid him without difficulty. Every time he passed the grate that looked down into Fortin's quarters, he heard a hearty chuckle.

The day of assembly for Purgatory came at last; although reaction to the banishment and shunning of the guild had been unpleasant, the announcement of the Purgatory expedition coupled with Alaric's promise that they would do all in their power to resolve it had cushioned the blow. Patrols left on horseback every morning and evening, scouring the plains for any sign of the raiders. With only a few exceptions, most of the guild had accepted it to be a temporary situation that would be remedied soon.

"After all," Andren said when Cyrus had asked for his feeling on how the the guild was taking the news, "they know we're not responsible for the attacks, so they assume the rest of the world will figure that out as well."

Cyrus nodded and cast a glance down the corridor they were standing in to make sure no one was nearby. "And what do you think?"

The elf looked at him warily. "Most of our guildmates are from you younger races. Few of the elves here are as old as I. They're all a bit taken in by your human optimism."

"But not you?"

"It's not that I don't want to believe that we'll find the raiders and all this will be resolved peaceably," Andren said with a grimace. "The problem is that whoever they are, they've been exceptional at avoiding us so far. So who's to say they're going to get sloppy now? And without them, we've no evidence, which leaves us..."

"Still accused," Cyrus agreed. "So the question becomes, after we finish buoying guild morale with this Purgatory expedition, what can we do to speed up the capture of the raiders?"

Andren pulled his flask from beneath his cloak and held it up in a salute to Cy. "That's the question now, isn't it? How do you catch them when they almost seem like ghosts?" He looked around. "Uh, no offense to Alaric."

Cyrus chuckled. "I don't think he's lingering in the air watching you."

Andren took another swig. "After what you've told me about his disappearing act, I don't rule anything out. But if you could disappear into the air," he said with a conspiratorial smile, "wouldn't you take a wander through the female applicant baths?"

"You think," Cyrus said with a disappointed shake of his head, "that Alaric Garaunt, the Guildmaster of Sanctuary, the most honorable man we've ever met, gifted with the power to disappear, is going to spend his time and effort misusing that power to peep on our new female applicants?"

"Just the pretty ones," Andren said, looking mildly offended. "I wouldn't accuse him of spying on that new dwarven gal or any of the gnomes."

"In my culture, you would be considered a 'dirty old man', Andren."

"Thank you," the elf said as he took another swig. "I think."

Cyrus shook his head as he began to walk toward the foyer, the point of assembly. Andren followed him. "What, you're all high and mighty, you're telling me you wouldn't at least want a peek? Can't say some of those new recruits aren't attractive."

"Didn't say they aren't." Cyrus tossed a glance back at Andren. "I just said I wouldn't use a power like that to spy on them."

"What do you think of that Aisling, eh?" Andren said with a wink. "I'd always heard dark elf girls were a little dirty. She might be a good chance to prove it."

"Not interested."

"Oh, right," Andren said with a nod, face impassive. "I forgot I was speaking to a man for whom the necessary elements of attraction include being roundly insulted at every turn."

Cyrus stopped just short of the foyer. "That's hardly a requirement –"

"But you can't deny that she castigates you constantly," Andren said with a cocky smile. "I mean, why would you be attracted to that? I mean, other than the obvious physical attributes. Are you a glutton for pain?"

"Well, I am a warrior..."

Andren rolled his eyes. "There are a great many good looking women in these halls, my friend. You could take a bit of an interest."

"I'm an officer now. I have to uphold a certain standard, and pursuing recruits and members is not in line with that."

"My, aren't you an oak of resolve?" Andren said with a tsk-tsk sound. "I wouldn't be so reluctant if I were you."

Cyrus snorted. "Why does it matter what I do? Why don't you worry about yourself? I haven't seen you rolling in the female company of late."

"I'm not the one lacking, friend. I've found as much companionship as I can handle here." The elf smiled. "Just thought I'd try and help you out."

"I appreciate it," Cy said, tone softening. "But I have more pressing matters on my mind."

"More like repressing matters. When all that bottled up energy finds an outlet, it's going to be one hell of an explosion."

"I have an outlet," Cyrus replied as he resumed walking, entering the foyer to find an assembled crowd. "It's called battle."

"Oh, well, that should fix everything."

Cyrus started toward the staircase leading to the balcony. Vaste fell into step next to him. "Need me to clear a path for you, oh exalted General?"

Cyrus surveyed the room, packed with people standing shoulder to shoulder, gnomes lingering around the edges for fear of being trampled in the middle. "I may; we'll need a bigger foyer if we expand any more."

"I wouldn't go wishing for us to atrophy," the troll replied.

"Might not need to wish for it if we can't find these raiders," Cy said while peering over the head of a human in front of him.

"If you want, you can clear a path for me, Vaste," Andren said. "I want to get to the lounge; Larana usually sets a fresh keg out in the morning and I want a mug before we leave."

The troll stared down at him. "You can make your way through on your own."

Andren looked back at the assemblage. "Not all of us are eight feet tall and built like a titan," he grumbled.

"Nor are you as pretty as I am, or as well hung," the troll added lightly, "but you've got to work with what the gods gave you."

With Vaste's assistance, Cyrus made his way to the staircase. He passed someone in gray plate mail and his eyes flew back to see Cass standing before him with a wide grin. "What are you doing here?" Cyrus asked.

Cass wore a sly smile. "You didn't think I was gonna throw you to the wolves and run, did you?"

Cyrus looked at him warily. "After the last Alliance meeting, yes. Yes, I did."

"Ouch," Cass said, feigning hurt. His expression turned serious. "Our guild is a democracy; as one of the three officers leading, I have to follow the members' wishes, and their ignorant wish was to follow Goliath's lead, in spite of mine and Erith's objections. If I could have done it differently, I would have." He smiled. "But I am here to help, if you'll have me."

"And pretend it was your idea the whole time, no doubt," came Erith's voice from beside Cass. "*We* are here to help," she amended.

"You know what? We can use all the help we can get."

"Knew you would," Cass said with a wink that sent an infuriated look across Erith's face. She turned to argue with him as Cyrus moved on, Vaste in front of him.

"Nice to know we still have a few friends left, isn't it?" Cyrus asked the troll.

"Speak for yourself. I have many, many friends - you antisocial cur."

They ascended the grand staircase to the balcony to find the other officers waiting for them. J'anda looked appropriately calm, Terian sported his usual cocky grin, Vara appeared lost in thought and Niamh surveyed the crowd with a look of nervous anticipation. Curatio and Alaric spoke to each other in hushed tones, but looked up at Cyrus upon his arrival.

"We're ready for this," Curatio pronounced with an air of youthful enthusiasm that belied his years.

"You seem excited," Cyrus said with a hint of amusement.

"We haven't been this on-the-move in years," the healer pronounced. "I've lived... uh..." He halted and coughed - "...a long while and this is one of the most exciting times I've witnessed."

"Yes, a death sentence that stretches across multiple nations tends to inject a bit of excitement into one's life," Vaste agreed.

"You know what I meant," Curatio said to the troll with a smile.

"I agree," Alaric said, "if not for the onerous clouds hanging over our heads at the moment, this could be perhaps our finest achievement as a guild."

"I don't know about that," Cyrus said, pensive. "I think it will be our finest achievement *because* of the other adversities that we're battling against right now."

Alaric looked at him with a glint in his eye that almost looked like pride. "Well said." The Ghost made a gesture toward the crowd. "Your army awaits, General."

Cyrus stepped forward and gripped the rail of the balcony as applause echoed through the foyer. "We go now to a place that few guilds have seen and fewer have conquered," he began as the applause began to die out. "When we walk out of the last gate of Purgatory later today, we will be only the fourth guild in Arkaria to have conquered it." Another smattering of applause greeted this statement. "All the troubles we are facing will pale in comparison to this triumph. The nations that have accused us will wonder if perhaps they have viewed us wrongly."

Alaric leaned in. "You're going a bit over the top; the fools who govern those nations will likely not re-evaluate anything but how many troops they send our way."

"Sorry," Cy whispered back. Returning his voice to normal volume, he continued.

"We will face countless perils, but through our training and discipline, we will be triumphant. Maintain order at all times, be prepared for the worst, and watch out for your guildmates." He straightened and looked over the crowd with undisguised pride. This was *his* army. "Follow my lead, and we'll be out of the portal in Reikonos before you know it."

He turned and raised his hand to Nyad, who nodded back at him in acknowledgment.

"I know that the exit leads out into the Reikonos guildhall quarter, but where is the portal to go into Purgatory?" Niamh asked.

"There isn't one," Cyrus said without looking up. His eyes roamed the crowd, falling from Longwell, who gripped his lance across his chest and stared ahead to the desert man, Scuddar, whose face was masked by the cloth he habitually wrapped around his head before battle, to Larana who looked at him with a nervous anticipation and then averted her eyes when he met her gaze. "A wizard has to know a special spell to teleport us there."

Nyad muttered under her breath, and after a moment's pause a flash of red light sent glowing orbs flying in all directions. One of them settled in front of Cyrus and he grabbed it, blinding him with a blast of crimson, searing his eyes and clearing the vision of the Sanctuary army from his view.

Chapter 21

A wave of energy blasted around him as Cyrus landed, stunned from the force of the impact. The sound of others around him getting the wind knocked out of them told him he wasn't alone.

"That didn't feel like a normal teleportation spell," J'anda said, looking around while shaking his head. "That hurt."

"We just tore out of the Realm of Arkaria and into a Realm of gods," Vara replied as she stood up from landing. Dust filled the air around them and others picked themselves up. "It's not as simple as crossing a street."

"I've crossed the world with teleports," Terian mumbled. "Never had one feel like that."

"Can we save the chatter for another time?" Cyrus brushed a thin layer of dust off his black armor. "I had intended to lead an invasion of this place and your discussion is interfering with my ability to give orders."

"Sorry, *sir,* won't happen again, *sir* - get bent." Terian shot Cyrus a grin.

"Now, Terian," Alaric chided, "you should have added a *sir* to your last comment."

"What a merry band are you," came a voice from behind.

Cyrus pivoted, sword drawn before he had time to assess the situation. The speaker had not made a sound as he approached.

"Now, now," came the voice again, from a wizened, middle-aged human, "I wouldn't get too overeager with that blade or I should have to force you to eat it." Gold robes draped a man who possessed a long nose that came to a point. His expression was severe, and his eyes were a shining black. His face was thin, which only added to the overall scornful look he carried.

"I'd like to see you –" Cyrus snapped before feeling Alaric's hand on his shoulder. He cleared his throat. "You need not threaten us, Gatekeeper; I'm sure your trials will do worse than try and make me eat steel."

"Quite right," came the Gatekeeper's reply. "My trials shall make you eat a sizable helping of crow, reducing your rampant ego to a manageable size."

"No force created could keep his ego in check," Erith commented from a few rows back.

"You're a guest," Cyrus hissed as he looked back at her.

"So I should lie to spare your feelings just because I've been invited to die with you?"

Cyrus turned to the Gatekeeper to find him shaking his head. "Ah, Sanctuary, a fractious lot." A smile creased his worn face. "This should be most amusing."

"You should know better than to underestimate anything," Alaric said without expression.

"And you, Lord Garaunt, should know better than anyone that the Trials of Purgatory do not come without sacrifice." The smile broadened on the Gatekeeper's face, but Alaric did not rise to the bait and remained impassive.

The Gatekeeper shifted his attention to Vara, who since his arrival had remained quiet. "You, I am surprised to see again. I assumed after our last meeting that I would not see you again." The smile turned wicked. "But you have returned, once more, to challenge the Trials. I trust we shan't test you quite as hard as last time? Or shall we?"

There was a mutter of curiosity among the army that Cyrus silenced with a look. "Gatekeeper, I, Cyrus Davidon, General of Sanctuary's army, inform you that we intend to challenge the Trials of Purgatory."

The elder human raised an eyebrow. "And I, as Gatekeeper of Purgatory, do hereby open the gates to the Trials to you and your brethren. I hope your deaths are unpleasant and that your flesh serves as sustenance for our fiends."

"A simple 'good luck' would have sufficed," Terian muttered.

The Gatekeeper threw his head back and laughed, a long, malicious cackle that reminded Cyrus of Malpravus. "I do not wish you good luck but rather ill," the Gatekeeper scoffed. "Only four guilds entering this Realm have left triumphant and for one of them, the triumph was short lived," he said with a smirk. "I have nothing but hope that you will fail."

"Yeah, who knows what could happen if we were to emerge victorious?" Vaste said with a trace of sarcasm. "You might have every guild in Arkaria knocking down your gates next week, and then you'd never have time to sit in your private sanctum and practice being an insufferable jackass for hours at a time."

"Rein in your troll, Lord Garaunt, lest I remove his tongue," said the Gatekeeper, ice in his voice infusing the air.

"I have no desire to rein him in, Gatekeeper. I find his wit amusing." Alaric did not break the Gatekeeper's stare. "Do you intend to open the Trials to us?"

A long pause hung in the air before the Gatekeeper spoke again. "They are already open," he said, frost still falling from every word. "Should you survive," he said with a bow, "I shall see you on the other side of the first trial."

"Back to your sanctum to practice!" Vaste said with a smile and a wave.

The Gatekeeper did not respond, but his face thinned and he seemed to fold in on himself, disappearing.

"I would caution against taunting the Gatekeeper," Alaric said. "He will latch onto any overconfidence on our part and turn it to our disadvantage later."

"Seems harmless," Terian said with a shrug.

"He's not," Vara croaked, paler than usual. "He has power and is not above using it to influence the outcome of the Trials."

"He's a foul old man," Vaste opined.

"He is not a man - at least not anymore," Alaric replied.

"He's a foul old sonofabitch, regardless of species," Vaste corrected.

"Can we move this expedition along?" Cyrus snapped. "Vara has been here before and if she says avoid taunting the old bastard, then I don't care if he's a ferret, a gnome or that creepy pederast that skulks around the Reikonos market, don't taunt him! Now let's go! Fall into formation!"

They moved forward, and for the first time, Cyrus got a good look at the Realm of Purgatory. It was not dark, but there was no visible light source; a pall hung in the air that gave the place a feeling of perpetual twilight. The ground was rock and a light dust filled the air as the army moved, causing Cyrus to gag from the dry, chalky taste of it filling his mouth and nose. There was no sign of greenery to break the horizon.

They stood upon an island, hanging in the middle of the air. From where he stood, Cyrus could see in the distance an end to the ground and nothing beyond it. "What's out there?" he asked Vara, who had fallen into step beside him. Silence filled the air around him, save for the noise of the Sanctuary army.

"Oblivion," she replied. "Anyone who is lost to the edge shall not be returned until you have conquered the Trials."

"Sounds ominous."

"We lost several in our first attempts at Purgatory when I was with Amarath's Raiders," Vara agreed. "When they were returned to us months later, after we defeated the Trials, they were scrawny and haggard, but alive. Every one of them described a torturous existence for those months, however." She shuddered at the memory.

"Avoid the edges." Cyrus nodded. "Got it."

They marched forward, not in lock step, for their discipline as an army was not so formal, but in rows. Following Vara's lead, Cyrus directed them to a short bridge that narrowed and led off the island to another. Standing before them at the entrance to the bridge was a magnificent gate, with an arch made of stone. The gate itself was large enough to admit several of Fortin.

They walked through the gate and Cyrus found the terrain had changed; instead of flat, dusty ground it became sloped and craggy. The dust subsided and the ground became solid rock, reminding Cyrus of the foothills of the Mountains of Nartanis, without the volcanic ash.

They began to ascend a short hill, and at the top Cyrus could see the far edge of the island and another bridge, leading to another gate. "That is our course," Vara said.

"When will we be attacked?" Cyrus kept his voice low enough so that only she could hear him.

She answered him in the same hushed tone. "It could come at any time; there were occasions when we scarcely made it through the gate that they set upon us, and others when we had to take up a defensive position at the far gate and wait for them to appear."

"Make ready!" Cyrus ordered to the army standing ready behind him. They began to move slower, in anticipation of attack. *It could come from any direction, at anytime,* he thought. *Marvelous. It's like Vara's insults.*

The thought caused a smile to spread across his face and a chuckle to escape him. Vara's head whipsawed around to him. "And what do you find so funny at a moment such as this?"

"Nothing," he said with great certainty. They lapsed into silence. The crunching of Fortin's feet hitting the ground lulled Cyrus for a moment; the heavy footfalls caused small tremors across the ground. Cyrus turned to look at the rock giant, and felt a tremor that did not match Fortin's stride.

A thrill of anticipation ran through him. "They're coming!" Cyrus shouted. "Defensive positions!"

The army broke their square formation and moved into a

circular perimeter, with warriors and rangers on the outside and spellcasters in the middle. The footfalls became louder until Cyrus heard a shout from behind him, at the point where Thad was stationed. "Incoming! It's a golem!"

Cyrus nodded and heard the shout taken up by Cass to his left. "Another one!" He turned his attention back to his segment of the perimeter in time to see a creature made of solid rock crest the hill in front of him.

His eyes scanned it as it ran down the hill toward them. It was twice the size of Fortin, and while the rock giant had rocky skin, the golem appeared to be made of solid rock, given motion by some magic beyond the skills of any wizard Cyrus had ever met. There were no eyes, nor a mouth, ears or other weak spots visible. *Damn.*

It charged down the hill, and Cyrus had a moment of discomfort as a realization hit. "I wish we had set up at the top of a hill instead of the bottom," he muttered.

"What?" came Terian's voice next to him.

"It's coming at us on a downhill charge," Cyrus said. "I can't stop that thing before it runs through our ranks like a bull. Which means –" He shifted to turn around and began to yell. "Move out of its path!" he shouted to the spellcasters behind him. "Warriors, get out there and engage them in front of our lines!"

Without waiting for acknowledgment of his orders, Cy charged out from behind their defensive perimeter. The golem was easily four times his height, invoking a memory of the time he had invaded the titan city of Kortran, where the combatants were also giant. *But they were flesh, not rock,* he thought. *How do I hurt this thing?*

It barreled toward him at high speed. *To hit it full on means instant death,* he realized. *Which means I have to...*

As the golem reached level ground, it did not slow down, and as they closed on one another, Cyrus at a dead run and the golem moving faster than should have been possible for something so giant, Cyrus leapt at the last moment, evading one of the giant's legs by inches and raking his sword along the golem's skin as he passed. Rolling as he hit the ground, Cyrus returned to his feet and watched the golem break through the scattering ranks of the Sanctuary army.

The other two golems had effected a similar charge, and they all ended up at the center of the Sanctuary army, which had parted for them. Cyrus could not see if there were any dead as he ran back toward the army, where the golems had begun to swat at the creatures crowding around their ankles with swords and daggers.

Spells flew through the air, fire marking with scorches where it hit upon the skin of the beasts, and small pockmarks of ice checkering the torso of the giant he had charged past. There was no sign on its leg that his slash had done any damage as he passed and when he stabbed forward with his short sword, there was no effect on the rock where he hit.

Three more rapid attacks did little more damage, chipping away only bits of rock, and Cyrus felt a pang of discomfort - in none of their plans had they discussed how to defeat the golems if their weaponry could not penetrate the skin. Cyrus's eyes searched for Vara and found her behind the same golem he was attacking, but her sword was gouging large chunks out of the skin without difficulty.

The golem brought a leg up and stomped down. When it stepped again, Cyrus realized that several people had been killed underfoot. The golem's hands swung through the crowds below it, killing wherever it struck.

Cyrus worked his way toward Vara, dodging three stomps. "Vara," he shouted when he had moved close enough. She looked up for only a second, sword still dancing her hand. She had cut a deep hole in the leg, extending almost a foot into the golem. "Our fighters don't have mystical swords as powerful as Amarath's Raiders; they're not doing much damage to the skin of these things."

"I had noticed that," she replied crossly, not looking at him. "Unfortunately, I'm rather busy trying to make up for it."

"These things are made of solid rock! I don't think even the spellcasters can get through that!" A quick look revealed the others around him attacking the golem were experiencing similar results, save for a few of their more experienced combatants that had better equipment. Longwell's lance was gouging pockmarks an inch deep and Scuddar's blade carved heavy lines wherever his blade found purchase.

I can't break through solid rock with this piece of junk, Cyrus thought when he looked down at his short sword. *I'd need a pickaxe to do any damage.* He snorted at the thought then cut it off as he remembered a similar battle where he labored to cut through the skin of a dragon. *That almost didn't turn out well, either,* he reflected. *Wouldn't have made it out of that cave if not for...* a jolt ran through him.

"Niamh!" he shouted into the spellcasters, huddled away from the golems. "We need ice spells! Focus them on the legs!"

A flash of red as the druid turned her head to address the spell casters told him that she had complied with his orders. A volley of spells flew over his head and struck the legs of the golems. Ice spread from the impact sites, crusting as it ran down the legs of the stone creatures. Cyrus moved toward the nearest section of frost and struck with all his strength, shattering the ice and cracking the rock beneath it.

Rolling away from the golem's next stomp, he returned to the same damaged spot and slashed at it again and again. Chunks of rock fell from the wound he had created, and he saw his efforts repeated in other places where ice spells hit; all the wizards and druids had unleashed their frozen magics, and ice was forming around the golem's lower body. Vara had seized on a vulnerable spot and was wreaking tremendous havoc. A rumble made its way over the army as her last strike produced a satisfying CRACK and the golem's leg broke off, sending it tumbling to the ground and killing several of their guildmates upon impact.

Far from being finished, the golem lashed out from a prone position, striking Nyad and sending her through the air. The spell casters unleashed a volley that completely encased its head in ice. Vara jumped into the air and landed on the head sword-first, shattering it. With its head destroyed, the magic binding the golem together released and the arms and remaining leg fell apart, turning into pebbles that spread from the spot where it died.

Vara's face did not register a smile of victory as she moved to the next golem, similarly indisposed and delivered another shattering blow to end it, and then to the last as well.

"Next time," Terian said to Cyrus as Vara was killing the last golem, "tell us about mystical skin before sending us up against something like these. My axe was only marginally effective," the dark knight groused. "You and the new recruits didn't do squat with your steel weapons. I hope there aren't more of them."

"I don't think so," Vara answered as she returned to them. "Each of the Trials is based off of one of the elements, save for the last island. This is the Earth island, so naturally the defenders would be..."

"Rock golems," Terian said, shaking his head. "Of course. Why didn't you mention the mystical skin, if you've been here before?"

"In truth, I did not know the skin was mystical," Vara replied. "When I was here with Amarath's Raiders, we all had mystical weapons and no one had any difficulty causing damage to them."

"Must be tough to have such nice things."

"Yes, truly your burden is great to be so ill-equipped for battle, but worse than that is the burden of your father's disappointment in his son," came the voice of the Gatekeeper. "Yes, I speak to you, Terian Lepos - great must be the shame of your father."

Terian's grip on his axe increased. "You don't know what you're talking about."

"Oh?" The Gatekeeper's eyebrows leapt up in amusement. "Your father, one of the greatest dark knights to walk the face of Arkaria? Did he not want his son to follow in his footsteps and become strong in the ways of the blackest of the black knights? Yet here you stand, a shade of what you could have become - closer to a paladin than a knight of the shadows."

Cyrus stepped forward to bar Terian's movement, matched on the dark elf's other side by Vara. "It's not worth it," Cyrus whispered.

"It would be so worth it," Terian said with undisguised loathing. "To hold his severed head in my hands as he died would be so enjoyable, it would be the benchmark by which I could judge all other joyous events in my life." He did not struggle in Cyrus's grip, but the dark elf's eyes whispered murder.

"You take umbrage at the thought of being a noble paladin?" The Gatekeeper's amused look was now taunting. "Take heart. Did you ever tell your friends what you were doing after you left Sanctuary last year? Does Lord Garaunt know what sins his pet knight was committing while out of his sight?"

"I have not asked and he need not tell me," came the voice of Alaric. "I expect him to live up to the standards of Sanctuary while he is with us." The paladin strode forward, interposing himself between the Gatekeeper and Terian.

"If only you knew..." the Gatekeeper said in a chiding tone.

Cyrus took his eyes off the Gatekeeper's bemused expression long enough to confirm that Terian was focused on Alaric, a stricken look written on his face.

"There will be no need for explanation now," Alaric spoke over his shoulder. He returned his cold glare to the Gatekeeper. "You will open the next gate."

An accommodating nod from the Gatekeeper and a wave of his hand in the direction of the next bridge followed. "Your path is open. Many guilds before you have come this far and no further. I am required to offer you an exit, should you wish to leave now." His hand moved to indicate a portal in the distance and it flared to life. The Gatekeeper's smile evaporated. "I advise you to do so, as the next island shall be much more difficult than what you have experienced here." Once more, he seemed to fold in upon himself and was gone.

"Charming bastard," J'anda commented. "Are you sure we can't kill him?"

Vara shook her head. "He is some sort of Emissary from the gods that serves as the steward of this place. Every one of the elemental gods is responsible for an island of this Realm, each according to their type. We just faced Rotan's creations, for example."

"But aren't there five islands?" Niamh asked.

"Yes," Vara replied.

"Fire, air, water, earth... who commands the fifth?" the red-haired druid asked, curious expression on her face.

Vara pursed her lips. "It has long been rumored that the last island and its monstrous creation are the product of the God of Evil, whose name we know not." She looked down. "I would say, having been there, that it is a fair guess, since what is housed there is possibly the greatest evil I have ever seen."

"Well that was nice and foreboding," Vaste commented. "Are you going to act like Malpravus or will you tell us what we'll face there?"

"I do not know how to describe it, but those who have faced it have called it the Last Guardian." She hesitated. "Everything that the Gatekeeper has done thus far, preying on our weaknesses, stirring up doubts – the Last Guardian does as well. I believe that the Gatekeeper works to bring those insecurities to the surface to allow the guardian to better exploit them."

"So it's more of a mental battle?" J'anda asked.

Vara shook her head. "No, the guardian is also a fearsome fighter."

"Vara and I have discussed the guardian," Cyrus interjected. "We have a strategy in place to deal with him when the time comes. We have three more islands to deal with first."

Vaste spoke up. "We've brought the dead back to life and should be ready to move in the next few minutes - but I would advocate a short break."

Cyrus nodded. "That seems wise, to give those who died a chance to recover before our next challenge." He turned to Vara. "Unless you think we shouldn't?"

She shook her head. "No, we need to be at full strength to deal with the Wind Totem."

Erith shouldered her way through the crowd surrounding the officers. "I need to talk to you about something," she said with a curt nod toward Cyrus. "Alone," she said with emphasis, grabbing him by the arm and dragging him away from the army.

He did not protest. "What is it?" he asked when they were out of earshot.

"Not yet," she said, releasing him. "Keep going." He followed her over a nearby hill.

She stopped and turned to face him, then bit her lip. "You're going to find out eventually, but I wanted to tell you here so none of your guildmates could see your reaction."

His eyebrows arched in concern. "What is it?"

"When Sanctuary was dishonored among the Alliance," she began, still looking tentative, "Malpravus rallied us all to turn against you. He came and spoke to our members, persuaded them."

"Yes," he nodded. "I know. It stung, but it's done now."

"He told us something else," she said. "He claimed that this act of dishonor cast in doubt every other act Sanctuary had done and every accusation you had ever made."

"Why?"

She laughed mirthlessly. "Why does Malpravus do or say anything? To justify what he's done or get what he wants."

"Dishonoring us?" Cyrus shrugged. "He's been trying for years to force a merger of the Alliance guilds. He wants us all under his control, knowing that with Goliath's numbers, any kind of democratic process would work to his advantage."

"That's certainly an intent, but that's not why he made that announcement," she said, shaking her head. "He was giving himself cover for what he did next. He told us that you and the Sanctuary Council had conspired to release Ashan'agar into north with the understanding that he would elevate Sanctuary to rule over all the lesser races - that you had stolen the godly weapons, that you were known in Pharesia to be involved - and that you only took action against Ashan'agar and called in the allies after the Dragonlord betrayed you."

"This does not surprise me," Cyrus said, shaking his head.

"Then this might," she said, biting her lip. "He didn't just make the accusation - he brought one of his officers along to tell the whole sordid tale - of how this officer confronted you in the mountains while we were fighting. That he fought you and through treachery you killed him, and of how he narrowly escaped."

"You're joking," Cyrus said darkly. "He didn't bring back –"

"He did," she confirmed. "Orion is back - and Malpravus has made him an officer of Goliath."

Chapter 22

Cyrus returned to the army several minutes later, cloud hanging over him. Alaric sent him a questioning look as he approached, and Cyrus waved him off. "Later," he said in a choked voice. "We need to speak in Council once this is over."

Alaric nodded, his helm moving slowly downward in what seemed like an exaggerated bow of the head. "Of course."

"We're moving," Cyrus announced after a moment to calm himself. They headed over the hill and toward the direction he had come from.

Vara once more fell into step beside him. "What's wrong with you?"

"We'll talk about it later," he said, dismissing her.

"Fine," she said tersely. "If you wish to pout about whatever it is, I will respect your wishes to act like a child. However, you know that we must plan and act accordingly for what we are about to face -"

"I'll take it," he said, cutting her off. "I will."

She started. "You are the leader of this expedition. For continuity of command you should not be the one who -"

"It's me, decision made. Stop arguing," he said in a voice that brooked no further discussion.

"Very well, then," she said, face inscrutable. "I won't try to stop you."

"Didn't think you would."

Shaking her head in annoyance, Vara drifted away from him and Cyrus turned to his own thoughts. *Unbelievable. Orion, back in the Alliance. What do you do with a treacherous ally? How do you get rid of an enemy when you've got no weapon to use against it?*

They crossed the next gate and the terrain turned once more to dirt. Another flat, dusty stretch of land filled Cyrus's eyes, all the way to the edge of the island. In the distance, he could see the lights that denoted his enemies. He held up his hand to stop the army. "Hold here. I'm going to lead the way and I need you all to follow a few hundred feet behind me."

Alaric surveyed him from the front rank, eye narrowed visibly through his helm. The Ghost took a few steps forward, drawing even with Cyrus. "Perhaps I should go with you, brother."

Even as Cyrus faked a smile, he felt the unease grow inside him. "It's all right, Alaric. Just follow behind me with the rest of the army. I want to lead the way during this battle."

"Your bravery is unquestioned," Alaric said under his breath. "You don't have to do this."

"Do what?" Cyrus's smile grew wider, and more strained. "I'm just leading the way, like a General should." The Ghost hesitated and Cyrus caught a flicker of emotion in his eye. "What do you think is going on here, Alaric?"

"Very well," Alaric said with a bow of his head. "Lead the way." Alaric rejoined the line as Cyrus opened the distance between himself and the army to almost three hundred feet before signaling them to follow once more.

The lights in the distance began to move closer, then they streaked towards him, lighting the skies.

Pegasus, Cyrus thought. They were winged horses that shone with an energy that made them glow white. Their red eyes shimmered against the soft light of their skin. The first of them flew at him and he caught it with a swing of his short sword. Blood spattered the ground as the pure white of the pegasus was marred by red. It slammed into him with a hoof, knocking him sideways. The others landed in a crashing attack, hooves raining down on him as he dodged. A strong kick hit his arm, numbing it and causing him to drop his sword.

Cries from the army behind him reached his ears only faintly, drowned out by whinnying above. *Where are you, you bastard,* he thought as he dodged one pegasus and felt another crash down on his shoulder. A snapping sound was followed by an exquisite burst of agony that ran the length of his collarbone. He was on his back now, rolling to dodge another beat of hooves. He looked up and saw the largest of the pegasi, a horselord, among them. It was twice the size of his own horse, Windrider, and each hoof was as big as the watermelons Larana had served at the end of summer feast.

Its red eyes locked onto his and he felt himself freeze. *The Wind Totem. Damn, he's big.* Energy filled the air, and Cyrus knew his army was still at a distance – that Vara would keep them back. *Just a moment longer.* The Wind Totem glowed brighter than the other pegasi, and was getting lighter by the moment. He looked at its red eyes until his could bear the growing brightness no more, and an explosion of light filled his vision, even with his eyes closed –

Chapter 23

I have to hold them back, Vara thought as she watched the pegasi stomping on Cyrus, *until that damned Wind Totem shows himself for the kill.* "Hold! We must hold our position until the Wind Totem reveals itself!"

The winged horses attacked with a ragged ferocity, and she could not see the black-armored warrior through the half-dozen pegasi milling around him. *Come on,* she thought. *Show yourself already.* An inexplicable urge came over her and she started forward, but felt an iron hand clamp down on her upper arm. She looked back to see the gray eye of the Ghost staring into hers.

"Act now, and you nullify his sacrifice," Alaric cautioned. "Wait a moment."

Her shoulders clenched, and her feet wanted to charge across the ground but she restrained herself, waiting. She held up her hand to her right, holding back Terian as another light appeared above the herd of pegasi, a horse more massive than any she could imagine. It stared down into the circle of its fellows and gave off a glow brighter than the rest before exploding into a flash of blinding light that made her look away while a shockwave knocked her back a few steps.

"Let's go!" Terian's words came in a shout as he shoved her arm aside.

"There is no need to hurry," she replied. Her voice was dull, bereft of feeling. "He is already dead."

"What!?"

"He is dead," she said, the lack of inflection in her voice belying every emotion tearing at her from inside. "He went ahead to draw it out and thus spare the rest of us from the shockwave that the Wind Totem uses when it reveals itself."

"You knew?" Terian's eyes darkened and his head seemed to shrink between the spikes on his shoulders. "You knew and you let him be slaughtered?"

"We all have our sins," she said, hand on her sword. "We must retrieve his body for resurrection after we've defeated these pegasi."

The Wind Totem hung in the air before them, ringed by a dozen pegasi that took flight one by one, leaving behind in the dirt the body of Cyrus. Niamh gasped behind her. *You stupid, stubborn man,* Vara thought. A fearsome, bellowing warcry filled the air and it took her a moment to realize that it came from her as she charged toward the pegasi. Arrows and spells filled the skies above her, and the pegasi scattered, three falling to the ground from the ferocity of the first Sanctuary volley.

She brought her sword down on the first pegasus she ran past as it was struggling to its feet and struck a killing blow. She watched as Terian's axe cleaved the next one's head off and then saw the dragoon, Longwell, arc his lance through the air into another pegasus, catching it in the wing and causing it to spiral to the ground, where it was finished by the desert man, Scuddar In'shara. Martaina delivered a coup de grace to the last one writhing on the ground with her short swords.

"Is this thing going to blast us all now that we're near it?" Terian said from beside her.

"No, it will take several hours to recoup the spent energy before it can perform the shockwave again." She pointed at the Wind Totem. "But we should make killing it our first priority!" It swept through the air above them, flying in a tight circle.

"Great, well, you kill the last two pegasi, and maybe the big guy will land."

Vara turned and vaulted, sword in hand, reversing her grip in midair and plunged it into the neck of a pegasus that swooped down to attack Martaina while her back was turned.

"Yeah... uh," Terian said in mild surprise, "like that."

A volley of arrows filled the skies above them once more, followed by a blast of spells. The last pegasus fell to the ground and was dispatched, this time by Aisling, daggers twirling from her fingers. In spite of being hit by a flurry of spells, the Wind Totem remained aloft.

A burst of fire flew through the air, then another. The Wind Totem's wing was engulfed in flames, burning away. Vara looked back to see Niamh's hand inflamed, and a long, scorching blast of fire flew from her and engulfed the Wind Totem, who disappeared in the blaze as it fell to the ground. Niamh's spell reached its end and she fell back, waxy pale, but the Wind Totem was grounded and struggling. The druid's eyes fell to Martaina, who was nearby. "How's that compare to a wizard?"

A host of Sanctuary warriors and rangers fell upon the Wind Totem, its white coat burned away and bloody, scorched muscle and sinew showing where once the fairest white hide had been. Vara did not hesitate: she leaped into the fray and brought her sword down. Even with all her strength behind the blow, she did not kill it in one strike - repeated blows finally brought the Wind Totem's struggle to an end and drew a ragged cheer from the throats of the Sanctuary army.

Vara's eyes fell to the black armored body nearby. A tremor ran through her hands, down her legs as she resisted the urge to run to it. "Curatio." Her voice came out as a low, croaking sound. "Please resurrect Cyrus." The healer nodded and trotted off to where a small crowd had gathered around the body of Sanctuary's General.

Vara surveyed the damage around them. The pegasi lay dead, struck down by a vengeful Sanctuary force. Her eyes fell on Niamh, still looking weak from exerting so much magical energy. Terian and Vaste stood next to her, each catching Vara's eye in turn. Terian turned to look at the group gathered around Cyrus, which included a near-hysterical Andren. Aisling and Larana both slunk around the edges of the crowd, sneaking furtive glances toward the downed warrior.

"You and Cyrus have kept a few secrets about your plans," Alaric said, appearing beside her.

"We didn't want to worry anyone," she breathed. "Someone was going to have to die on this island and he chose to run headlong into it." *Like the noble idiot that he is,* she thought.

Alaric nodded and shifted his gaze to the horizon and the gate in the distance. "It's a shame he is bereft of magical talent in the eyes of the Leagues." A mysterious smile hung on the Ghost's face. "He would have been a magnificent paladin."

"Stubborn nobility alone does not make a paladin, Alaric," she snapped back. "He has no crusade, no cause but the conquest of enemies and the acquisition of pretty baubles and better equipment to aid his own aggrandizement."

Alaric did not respond at first, prompting Vara to look to make certain he had heard her. "I think you misjudge his intentions. While treasure and conquest certainly motivate him, I suspect that Cyrus could find a cause that he could get behind had he been inculcated in the ways of the Holy Brethren, as you have."

She snorted. "His only other focus is retribution for the loss of Narstron." A worried sigh escaped her, and she looked at Alaric to see if he had noticed. A slight smile peeked from beneath his helm, telling her he indeed had. "I wonder whether he will move beyond the petty desire for revenge or if it will consume him completely."

"You speak as though that desire has never filled your heart."

"I made the right choice," she snapped. "I set aside my desire for vengeance –"

Alaric interrupted. "I know. I was there during the time you spent trying to decide whether to pursue the reckless course. But you forget that you had counsel during that period, forewarning you about the perils you would face if you sought revenge."

"I have not forgotten," she said archly. "I remember standing in the doorway of Sanctuary, sword in hand, ready to set out in slaughter for the wrongs heaped upon me." Her voice softened. "And I remember you stopping me." Her tone rose again. "But he is different, Alaric –"

"We are all the same, you, he and I," Alaric chided. "We all have reasons for wanting to punish those that have wronged us, we have all made ill choices that lead us to the places where we were wronged, and we all have the ability to walk away rather than give in to hatred and obsess over it day after day, letting it consume our lives."

"We are not the same, he and I," she said with a snarl.

"So you believe him doomed to the path of vengeance?"

"I did not say that. I do not know." She sighed. "It is perhaps too soon to be sure."

"If it is any comfort, I still say that about you." Vara's head turned to find the Ghost chuckling under his breath. "I also say it about myself, if it helps." He turned to look at her. "Do you think that if Talikartin the Guardian crossed my path today, that I would not have to consider my actions? I believe that should... he... cross your path, you would do the same."

"He..." she said with a pronounced air of superiority, "has crossed my path. Twice. And he yet breathes."

"When not surrounded by his lackeys. When you have a chance at cold-blooded revenge. There is, after all, a difference between killing and murder."

"Does that distinction matter to the victim of either?" Vara asked with a shake of her head.

"Perhaps not. But for us, it is an important distinction, because a noble guardian fights with a code of honor at all times. Shallow pursuits such as killing for base reasons – robbery, revenge – are to be avoided, as you well know. Justice, honor, defense of those who cannot defend themselves; these are noble reasons to engage in battle. You know that. I believe he will come to see that as well, before it is too late." Alaric nodded at her and moved off through the Sanctuary army.

A moment of silence filled the air around her, interrupted by Terian. "I haven't seen the challenge yet. Where's the challenge?"

"The challenge, you nimrod, is steadily increasing, in case you failed to notice. We also have a much larger army than even Amarath's Raiders possessed when last I was here with them. But we have had quite a few deaths thus far. It will get worse as we proceed."

Her eyes flew unintentionally to the place where the warrior in the blackened armor was sitting upright. He tried to stand and was rebuffed by Curatio. Her pulse was racing, and she let out a mental sigh of relief when she saw him moving once more.

"You should go check on him," Terian said with a nasty grin.

"You have known me too long, dark knight, and because of that, you think you know something that you do not."

"Oh, I'm sorry." Terian shook his head while rolling his eyes. "You two are the most ridiculous, stubborn fools I've ever seen. You're so damned combative by nature that you'd rather fight when it's clear to everyone you'd prefer doing something much more pleasant."

A flush of crimson hit her cheeks along with a burning sensation in her stomach. "You're a moronic one, aren't you? Perhaps he has spoken to me of such possibilities and I have rebuffed him. Did you ever consider that?"

"I would consider that likely. You have always been your own worst enemy, after all."

"I have much more dangerous enemies than myself," she said, eyes narrowed. "But you won't find one more dangerous than me, Terian, and you would do well to consider that before speaking."

"Oh, my," he said with an unconcerned air. "I give you deep and inspiring insight into your own soul and you become defensive and tell me we're not friends anymore?" He favored her with a wounded look that gave his already pinched face even more of a squeezed appearance that relaxed after he'd made his point. "If you're sensitive about it, all you need to say is, 'this topic of conversation is closed, why don't you move along and chop some wood with your hatchet' and I'll be on my merry way, keeping my opinions to myself."

She let the words hang in the air for a moment before replying, still staring him down through narrowed eyes. "This topic of conversation is closed. Why don't you go take that hatchet and apply it to sensitive parts of your anatomy with aggressive force from now until morning?"

"Ouch. You're not even nice anymore."

She turned and began to walk away. "I never was," she said without looking back. Upon walking away, she hesitated. *Tend to the army or check on the General?* A moment's pause gave her no aid in making her decision. *The army is in my charge; they are my responsibility; I need to be sure we are recovering and ready to move.* Finally, despite the best intentions of her head, her feet carried her directly to Cyrus.

Chapter 24

Cyrus watched as Vara approached him, stopping for a moment to speak with Erith. *I feel sick,* he thought. *I'll never get used to this.*

She stuttered for a moment before speaking. "I... uh... we did well against the pegasi and the Wind Totem; only a few deaths. Erith informs me that we will be ready to move in a few minutes."

His head lolled back and forth before turning up to look at her. "Thank you. I take it everything went smoothly while I was out?"

"Of course." She stood ramrod straight in front of him, searching for words. "I... am pleased to see you're all right." She hesitated. "I was concerned."

He rubbed his eyes. "I would have been too, if it had been someone else in my place." He pulled himself gingerly to his feet.

"You should not be up yet." Her voice was cross.

"You've never died, right? So you've never known the loving touch of a resurrection spell."

"I hear it is quite unpleasant." She paused. "Thus, you should rest before you throw yourself back into the fray."

"Small price to pay for coming back from the dead. I've got a lot to do," he said with a shake of the head. "There will be plenty of time to rest when I'm really dead."

"An event which cannot happen soon enough," came the acid voice of the Gatekeeper.

"Spare me your insults and open the next gate," Cyrus said, dismissing the human. "And when this is over – I want the Edge of Repose."

The Gatekeeper studied Cyrus. "You are the first to ask me for it. Very well: it shall be your prize if you complete the tasks set before you."

"Thank you," he said without any sincerity. "You may go now."

A look of outrage crossed the face of the Gatekeeper upon being dismissed, but he folded upon himself and was gone.

"I didn't think he would be that easy to get rid of," Vara said in amazement.

"He's not," Cyrus replied. "I think he's humoring me."

"Shall we proceed?" she asked. "Water is next."

"I haven't forgotten," he said, and marshaled the army into

motion. A few minutes later they crossed through the next gate to find themselves at the edge of a lake that stretched into the distance. The water was dark, almost black, and nothing was visible beneath the surface. Cyrus felt the dust and rock beneath his feet turn to the dark sands of a beach. The water smelled, an odd, sulfuric stink, like rotting seaweed.

"Spell casters," Cyrus called out. "I want you to hit this lake with every lightning spell you have."

Thunder filled the air around them and lightning bolts flew from all directions, striking the lake; bolts of energy coursed across the surface, and a hum could be heard from the water. The stink of ozone filled the air.

"You don't believe that will work, do you?" The voice of the Gatekeeper did not even turn Cyrus's head as he studied the surface of the water.

"No. But it was worth a try." Cyrus turned back to the army. "I need Terian, Thad, Cass, Vara and Alaric with me. The rest of you, stay back." His eyes caught another face in the crowd. "Menlos Irontooth, come with me as well. Leave your wolves."

Menlos, the northman, came forward, a smile on his face. "Rather feel like the first whore picked in the house for the evening."

"You'll likely feel like one afterward, too," Terian cracked.

"Charming," Vara commented.

"Do you intend on having us swim, brother?" Alaric asked Cyrus.

"I doubt that gearing you up for a dance performance will get you across the lake," the Gatekeeper mocked. "Although it will surely have more effect than whatever you have planned."

"I do," Cyrus said, ignoring the taunts. "There's a monster in the depths and I don't think it will be efficient to bring the whole army. You can all swim, correct?"

"I can," Terian said with a note of protest. "But I don't wish to."

"Fine," Cyrus nodded. "You can stay behind and guard the spell casters until we get back."

Thad looked at the dark knight in amazement. "Are you a coward?"

Terian cast a loathing look at the red-armored warrior. "All right, you sold me; I'm coming."

"Vara, care to explain what we can we expect from this

creature?" Cyrus nodded toward her.

"It is a very large eel. He has thick skin," she began. "His eyes are a weak point but will be difficult to hit."

"Eel?" Menlos asked. "Isn't that like a snake?"

Vara tried to disguise her irritation but failed. "It would only appear to be a snake to the ignorant. It is an eel; it has a vertically flat tail that allows it to swim."

"Snakes swim, don't they?" Menlos's earnest face showed that he had not caught Vara's annoyance.

"It is highly mobile," she continued, ignoring him. "It is difficult to catch and difficult to hit."

"How did you defeat it in the past?" Terian asked.

"Very much like this," she answered. "You don't chance sending your force across the water until it's dead because it... jumps."

"I'm sorry... it does what?" Thad's eyes were wide, fixated on Vara.

"It jumps. It can leap from the water over a hundred feet into the air. Use Falcon's Essence and it still devours your army. If you send them all into the water..." Her words trailed off. "All but the most advanced spell casters are useless underwater; only those that know sublingual casting have any effect, and only then if they stay away from casting lightning, ice or fire spells."

She shook her head. "The only effective strategy we found was to send an elite corps of our strongest fighters and let them deal with it."

She paused, pondering. "If the lot of you possessed better armor, that gave you more strength, speed and dexterity, I would suggest you wear it into the water for this battle." She shook her head. "As it is, I must suggest that you don't. You will be more mobile without it."

"So now I have to swim, do battle with a giant eel, and I get to do it without the protection of my armor?" Terian shook his head. "This keeps getting better and better." He reached up and began to unstrap his breastplate.

They took off their armor in relative silence. "You should take off your armor as well, Alaric," Vara said, more gently than usual.

"Although it looks battered, this armor has more power than you realize, old friend," the Ghost said with a smile, then returned to a conversation with Curatio.

"Giving the ladies of Sanctuary a real thrill here," Terian

grumbled as he dropped his breastplate.

Vara rolled her eyes. "Speaking for the ladies of Sanctuary... no, no you are not."

Cyrus was first to finish removing his armor and slipped the short sword into his belt. "Are we ready?"

"Never," Terian replied.

"Everyone else ready, then?" Cyrus asked. "Perhaps our two paladins would consent to lead the way, since they are armored and we are not."

Vara nodded, as did Alaric, who took the lead, walking into the water until it reached his waist.

"Hold!" came a shout from the shore. Niamh moved forward, casting a spell as she walked. A faint glow of light ran across all of them. "That should give you protection from the deep; you'll be able to see and won't have to worry about drowning while you're down there."

"Yeah, the last thing I want to worry about when facing a giant eel is the thought that I might not be able to see him coming to kill me, followed by the thought that I might also drown," Terian deadpanned.

They proceeded into the water, walking across the shoals until the water reached over their heads, submerging themselves and swimming into the depths. Cyrus could feel the chill creep through him as the water crawled up his skin, and the inevitable shock of cold when he plunged in over his head was almost painful.

Niamh's spell aided their sight, giving light in the murky water beyond where the twilight from above failed to reach. Cyrus looked over to see Vara, swimming confidently, not seeming to be weighed down at all by the metal armor that encased her body.

Her body...

He shook the thought out of his head as he drifted to the bottom of the lake. There was no movement but for the group around him as his bare feet settled for a moment on the lakebed. He felt the mud between his toes and kicked off, swimming a few feet over the bottom.

Menlos and Thad swam to one side of him while Terian and Cass stuck to another. Vara and Alaric stood upon the lakebed, allowing their armor's weight to keep them down while looking in all directions. As Cyrus looked up, he could not see the light of the surface; Niamh's spell was all that was allowing them to see in the depths. *Thank Bellarum for her*, he thought.

A sudden movement caught his attention as Terian began to flail in the water. Cyrus looked past the dark elf, who was pointing into the distance, and a shadow began to slide out of the murk, slipping through the water.

The eel was long; perhaps a hundred feet or more in length, and even at this distance Cyrus could see the yellow eyes. A ridge ran the length of its back, scaled spikes sticking out every few feet, reminding him of Ashan'agar. He tried to speak, to warn the others, but only bubbles came out.

Fortunately, Terian's flailing caught the attention of the party. Alaric and Vara kicked off the lakebed as the eel closed, jaws open in anticipation of a meal as it darted toward Terian. A blast of concussive force exploded through the water, knocking the eel off course. Alaric's hand was outstretched and another wave of power burst through the water toward the eel, radiating a trail behind it. The eel staggered again, giving Thad time to clutch onto the side of its neck.

Thad's sword moved up and down slowly, and Terian joined him, grabbing onto a gill for leverage and moving his axe in a sawing motion along the side of the eel, which whipped its tail, trying to avoid Alaric, who sent another burst through the water but this time missed.

Blood began to cloud the waters around them as the eel struggled. It turned and swept toward Vara, who brought her sword around and held it straight for the eel to run onto as it charged at her, clamping down with its jaws.

Bubbles streamed from Vara's mouth as the eel bit down on her. Her sword found its mark inside the eel's mouth and the head whipped around in pain, crimson clouding the water around him. It became so dense that Cyrus could not tell if it was coming from Vara or the eel.

He swam toward the battle and reached it just as Vara thrashed away from the fiend, blood trailing behind her. Alaric's hand raised and the trail of blood that followed her stopped as she turned to join him and Cyrus. The eel circled, and Menlos sprung from behind some weeds and clamped on behind one of the eel's gills, joining Terian and Thad in holding on while it jerked to shake them off.

Cy gestured to Alaric and Vara and the three of them spread out as the eel came around at them again. This time it streamed through the water toward Cyrus, who rolled out of the way, catching a glancing blow from the eel's teeth as it slid by and giving it only a small cut in return.

The head jackknifed more quickly than he could have anticipated, and swirled around in a spiral, coiling in the water and clenching onto his midsection. Cyrus felt the skin rip and tear as the eel caught hold of him. He drove his sword into its upper lip, but a vicious jerk from the eel forced him to surrender his grip. Vara grabbed onto the eel and buried her sword in its side.

It began to struggle and its teeth released him. Cyrus felt himself fall out of the jaws of the monster, and looked up to see Menlos had opened up the gill. It thrashed about, sending Thad and Terian clear of it. Menlos and Vara held on as she continued to cut down the belly, but she was finally forced by a whip of the tail to let go.

The eel thrashed once more and Menlos fell back along the body as it darted off at high speed, slicing through the water with him attached to it. It came around at them again, yellow eyes enraged and pulsating with the power that a god had bestowed. A feeling like a thousand gentle touches ran along Cyrus's belly as Alaric cast a spell that healed his wound.

Cass intercepted the eel halfway to them, swimming out from where he had been lurking to plunge his sword into its tail. Another shadowy figure joined him, a thin body grabbing onto the tail with speed that Cyrus could scarcely believe. Small blades sprung from the figure's hands, cutting off almost ten feet of the tail.

The figure released the eel, which turned and struck; the figure dodged, and through the murkiness Cyrus realized it was Aisling. The eel missed again with another strike aimed at her, but her blades found its right eye, and she rolled into its blind side, plunging both daggers into its neck and riding along with it as it moved through the water toward Cy and the others.

Without the last part of its tail, it moved slower, allowing Cass, Thad and Terian to grab hold and continue their attacks. Blood flowed from dozens of open wounds on the beast. Cyrus swam at the jaws, open wide and coming at him again. He could see his sword jutting from the eel's face and grasped for it as it moved to bite him.

His fingers brushed the edge of it and he felt the barest touch of the teeth against his skin before the eel went slack. He pulled his sword from its lip and looked in the remaining eye to find it lifeless; the yellow was already fading and the body drifted past him to the lakebed. It came to rest and the members of his group departed from it one by one, save for Menlos who could be seen through a cloud of blood, still stabbing away without mercy.

Cyrus swam up, breaking the surface and taking a deep breath for the first time in over an hour. Another head sprang up beside him, and he looked to see a matted blond ponytail hanging over Vara's shoulder. She turned toward him and spoke. "That went rather smoothly, don't you think?" The trace of a smile on her face was the only sign that she might have been joking.

He smiled. "Could have gone worse. I should get some of that armor that increases your strength because I don't ever want to fight a battle like that again."

"It does hurt, doesn't it?" she asked as other heads broke the surface around them.

"Can you imagine how many spell casters we would have lost to that thing?" Terian said in amazement. "It would have taken out half our army, easy."

"And now you can see the peril we face," Vara said, grim. "We use time tested and proven strategies against these creatures. Those who faced them for the first time with no knowledge had much uglier results. It took almost two years of expeditions, twice a week, before Amarath's Raiders became the first to conquer the Trials of Purgatory." Her gaze fell, down toward the water. "We lost over a hundred members to permanent deaths during that time, because of this Realm."

"And replaced them with a hundred more willing bodies, I'm sure," Terian added. "It's not like any of the big three have a shortage of volunteers."

"Indeed not," Vara agreed. "Especially since in the year after Amarath's Raiders conquered the Trials for the first time, every member received a portion of the spoils - to the tune of over a million gold pieces each." Seriousness filled her eyes. "But it does not diminish the sacrifice of those we lost in the process of conquering it for the first time."

"Is everyone accounted for?" Cyrus's eyes searched and saw Aisling's head bobbing in the water a few feet from Menlos. He was rewarded with a tight smile from the dark elf. "Thank you for your help, Aisling. You were invaluable."

The dark elf nodded. "I... decided to try something different...

than what everyone else was doing, sitting on the shore." Her eyes found Cyrus's and she looked away again.

"Why were you here?" Vara snapped. "I did not hear your name mentioned as one who would be facing the eel."

"I apologize," Aisling said without a hint of remorse or sincerity. "Won't happen again."

"Now, Vara, there's no need to get upset with one of our guildmates simply because she wanted to be of service in battle," Alaric chided. "Quite the opposite, in fact."

"Martial discipline be damned, then," Vara muttered under her breath. "Very well, she can help us drag the corpse of the eel to the shore."

"I'm sorry, what?" Aisling's white eyebrow was cocked in confusion.

"It's valuable, and we'll be selling off parts of it for gold."

"I didn't realize we were doing that," Aisling said with a frown.

"Larana has been harvesting the useful parts of the creatures we felled, and this eel is no exception. But first," Vara said with a vicious smile, "we drag it to the edge of the lake."

"This thing is heavy," Terian complained for the first time as they broke the surface of the water near the shore. It had taken over an hour to get the corpse even this far, where their feet rested on the shoals below.

"Our guildmates will help when we get closer," Cyrus said. "Oh, look, here comes one now." He pointed to a figure heading toward them.

"That's not one of ours," Vara said.

"Damn you and your elven eyesight," Cyrus said as he squinted, barely able to make out the Gatekeeper's robes as the Realm's guardian strode across the water to them.

"Another challenge bested," he called out upon reaching earshot. "I suppose I should be impressed? I am not." He halted and looked down at them from his vantage point, sneering.

"You can open the gate and leave now," Cyrus said.

"Unfortunately for you, I do not respond to your commands except when I choose to," the Gatekeeper replied with a thin smile. "I have things to say to each of you before I depart.

"I know the hearts of each of you, the fears that consume you, the things that wake you in the night." He cast a glance at Cyrus, who remained impassive as he hefted the remains of the eel with his shoulder and pushed. "I know the sins in your past that you wish you could forget. Some, of course, I am... intimately familiar with." At this, the sneer turned into a vicious smile.

"You." He turned to Aisling. "You, who claim to be fearless and invulnerable - but we two know the truth, the reason you cling to everything and everyone you can get your hands on, until they become too close - and see your vulnerability, and you leave before they can exploit it." His head turned to Vara. "It's funny that you detest her, since you and she are different sides of the same coin."

"You're a mighty one, aren't you?" Thad said. "Trying to poke at the sensitive spots in people. Fine, then. Have at me, coward."

The Gatekeeper laughed. "Coward? *You* would call *me* coward? That is amusing. You, a man who has run from danger –"

Thad began to redden. "Shut up!"

"– at every turn –"

"SHUT UP!"

"Did she cry when you left her behind?" the Gatekeeper asked in a mock whine. "Did you hear her sobs as you left her to die? To save your own skin?"

"I didn't..." Thad's voice was barely above a whisper; he had dropped his burden and was beginning to shake, face pale.

Terian looked as though he wanted to say something, but remained silent. Cass, too, did not speak, while Vara and Aisling kept their heads down. Menlos's head remained under the water. Cyrus looked around and found himself staring at the Gatekeeper, who returned his gaze with cold amusement. "All right, then," Cyrus said. "What have you got to say to me, you heaping pile of troll dung?"

"I would have had kind words for you, about your destiny, about your strength, about how you could become the greatest Warlord ever seen in Arkaria. But instead, let's revisit the death of your best friend, shall we?"

Cyrus felt a fire fill him. "Yes, let's. Narstron died in the dark catacombs of Enterra, at the hands of the goblins. We were betrayed by someone from within our own Alliance, and I swore vengeance."

"A vengeance you have yet to deliver."

Cyrus's eyes burned as he looked at the Gatekeeper. "'Yet' being the key word in that statement."

"When it comes to vengeance, 'deliver' is the key word. Your poor, dwarven friend, left to die alone... he was alive, you recall, when they took him... how do you think he died? Do you think it was painful? Do you think he kept his courage to the end? Or do you think he screamed and begged for mercy that would never be shown?" A twinkle lit the eye of the Gatekeeper, coupled with a smile that could only be described as sadistic. "Because I know."

"So do I," Cyrus said with a calm realization. He could see Narstron's face in his mind's eye, the last image of him being dragged off by the hands of a hundred goblins. "He lived like a warrior. He died like a warrior. And everything else you have to say is lies. I will deliver vengeance in the time of my choosing."

The Gatekeeper turned back to Vara. "It would appear your fears are justified. Listen to him sit there and plot his vengeance; he's an animal, and he will turn on you, just like –"

"ENOUGH!" Alaric's voice crackled through the air with raw anger. "Cease your prattle, Gatekeeper, or I shall force you to do so."

The Gatekeeper's amused smile did not fade as he stopped speaking. With a wide, exaggerated bow, he spoke once more. "Oh, Lord Garaunt, perhaps I should start on you..."

"Perhaps you would do well to remember who I am, and obey my command."

"I am the Hand of the Gods now, Alaric," the Gatekeeper said, a look of indignity appearing on his face. "You would not dare."

Alaric's helmet masked his expression, but as he stepped forward in the shallow water to look up at the Gatekeeper, the Gatekeeper took a step back. "And when has invoking them ever stopped me in the past?"

The Gatekeeper's sallow face hardened, and his look turned to anger. "I have opened the gate before you to the island of fire, but I will return when you are not watching, Alaric. You cannot shepherd them all, and I will claim some for my own amusement - because I can."

"You will interfere no more." Alaric's helm came off in his hand, and his sword was drawn. "And you damned well know it. Go, fool." He waved his hand. "Your amusement is to be found elsewhere, lest we find out how strong the Hand of the Gods really is."

"In the interest of civility and of fulfilling my role as Gatekeeper, I will depart," he said with a dark look. "But do not think I do this because I am afraid of any reprisal you may summon."

"I know what you fear, Gatekeeper," Alaric said darkly. "You claim to know all, but I know *your* soul. I know *your* sins. Never forget that."

The Gatekeeper folded in on himself once more and vanished. Silence filled the air around them as Alaric donned his helm and strode through the shallows back to the corpse of the eel. With a nod at the others, he lifted once more.

"So, is anyone going to say anything about what just happened, or are we going to pretend it didn't?" Menlos said, voice betraying his curiosity.

"I should be fine with never mentioning it again," Thad said.

"I applaud your courage, Thad," Alaric said. "To stand up to him and take his abuse to remove one of your comrades from his fire is an act of great courage."

"I agree," Vara said in a hushed tone. "I found myself unable to speak, paralyzed by the memory of previous conversations I have had with him."

"Me too," echoed Terian.

"If I had thought for a moment we could have attacked him physically, I would have been less reticent to insert myself in the conversation," Cass said with a shake of his head. "I dislike verbal jousting. It's a coward's means to avoid combat."

Alaric shook his head. "He would have welcomed the opportunity. As mentioned, he is the Hand of the Gods, and he has powers far beyond anything else we would face in this Realm."

"Then why aren't you afraid to confront him?" Cyrus asked. "And why is he afraid of you? Are you more powerful than he?"

Alaric smiled. "I knew him before he was the Hand of the Gods, and I know his darkest secrets, lies and fears better than anyone - and many times those are worth more in a battle than a sword."

"How did you know him?" Cyrus asked.

"A matter for another time," Alaric said. "We have business to attend to."

"You know what that means, right, Cy?" Terian said with a chuckle.

"Yes," Cyrus said with a sour expression. "It means 'don't bother asking later, either'."

Alaric chuckled. "In time, gentlemen, all will be revealed... to those who are patient."

"Guess that rules me out," Terian snarked.

As they approached the shore, others from their army waded out to join them in carrying the eel. Larana stood quietly at the fore, with a smile on her face, and a cutting knife in her hand. Her eyes followed Cy as he led the party carrying the eel and dropped it at her feet. "All yours," Cyrus said. Her eyes flicked down at his approach, then flitted back up for just a moment, giving him a hint of vivid green before she averted them from his gaze once more.

He walked back on dry land and threw himself down next to his armor. He watched as Thad embraced Martaina, and she began to help him put his armor back on, piece by piece. The warrior's expression was still haunted, listless, in spite of trying to smile for his wife.

Cyrus looked for Aisling, but she was not to be seen. Erith was aiding Cass in putting his armor back on, as J'anda helped Terian. Nyad assisted Menlos, causing Cyrus to shake his head at the odd sight - the usually filthy, wandering northman and the composed elven princess.

He looked up with a start as someone approached him. Vara stood before him, dripping. "Do you require assistance with your armor?"

He smiled. "You wouldn't mind being my squire?"

She sighed and rolled her eyes. "I am offering my assistance. Do you wish it or not?"

"I would love it. It's easier when I'm pulling the pieces off the bust I have in my quarters, instead of trying to strap it on and bend over to pick up the next piece."

She rolled her eyes again. "I have been known to wear armor myself, from time to time."

"Yes." He nodded, staring absentmindedly at her chestplate, still gleaming in spite of having been so recently submerged in dirty water. "And you wear it well," he said without thinking.

She stopped fastening his pauldrons. "What is that supposed to mean?"

He cringed. *Oh, screw it.* "I didn't mean to say that, but it means that in addition to being damned handy with a sword and a nightmare to argue with, you're also very pretty."

She resumed fastening the straps on his armor, but her eyes looked down. "You forgot to mention how intelligent and charming I am."

He grinned. "And they say I have a big ego." She pushed him roughly, but had a sly smile to match his.

"We've done well so far," she admitted, changing the subject. "The final two islands will be more difficult, but I have confidence we will prevail."

"Next is fire," he said. "I'm not much looking forward to it."

"It is not an enjoyable battle," she admitted, fastening the straps on his breast and backplate. "I recall my armor getting hot enough that it burned me even through my undergarments."

A moment's thought gave him pause as he considered her undergarments. Shaking that thought away, he fastened his belt and adjusted his scabbard. "How do I look?" he asked her with his best dashing smile.

Her eyes only half-rolled and she placed his helm on his head with undue force, jarring him. "Better if we could get a helmet that covered your face, like Alaric's."

He sighed. "I just called you pretty. I don't suppose there will ever be a moment when you'll let your guard down and say something nice about me that's not related to my performance as an officer or a General?"

She did not speak, but her gaze softened and she hesitated before turning and walking away, one slow step at a time.

"No insult?" he said to her retreating back, then lowered his voice. "It's a start."

Chapter 25

"All right," Cyrus called out to the army. "Next is the island of fire." He outlined in a few sentences what he expected of them, and they set out on a path over the lake with the aid of Falcon's Essence, floating a foot above the water. They reached the far gate, already open for them, and Cyrus marched through first. On the other side was a much smaller island, and instead of dry dust or rock, scorched earth greeted them, alight with scattered flames burning on the ground. The air smelled of acrid smoke, of burnt things, flesh and wood and metal.

"It looks like a battlefield," Vaste said with a tone of awe. The troll stood to Cyrus's side, looking over the burnt ground as Niamh moved behind them among the Sanctuary army, dispelling the Falcon's Essence - it was not an easy matter to fight while floating.

In the middle of the island was a pit in the ground, filled with fire. "That's it?" Cyrus looked for Vara. She was not in the front ranks of the army.

Alaric caught his eye, nodding. "That is the Siren of Fire."

"Where's Vara?" Cyrus asked, surprised. *She never leaves the front line of battle.*

"Here," she announced, pushing to the front. "I was checking with some of our spell casters to ensure they were ready. Alaric is quite right. Approach the flame and she will come for you."

"All right." He nodded and shifted his attention to the army. "Move into position, encircle the flame, and wait for my signal to move in."

"What's your signal?" Terian asked. "A girlish scream of, 'It burns, it burns'?"

"No," Cyrus said with a shake of his head. "I wouldn't want to be mistaken for you using the lavatory."

Terian flinched. "You can hear that? Through the walls?"

"I can." Cy clapped the dark elf on the back with a broad grin that was not shared by Terian and stalked off toward the flame in the middle of the island.

Cy watched out of the corner of his eye as the Sanctuary army encircled him. He slowed his walk to give them time to complete the circle. He looked to the flames, burning in the pit. The fire stretched above his head and seemed to be emanating from the ground itself. As he closed on it, something began to take shape in the bottom of the fire.

With a screech so loud it made him look away for a second, the flames rose into the air and coalesced into a female form, a little taller than him. The fire slid up to reveal flesh beneath, red skin and a scathing look as the face was revealed. The flame settled at several points around the body, enshrouding both hands, both feet, and becoming the creature's hair.

"I am the Siren of Fire," came a voice that was melodic but tinged with a note of chaos. Without any warning, it flew at him, eyes burning and her hands grasped him by the armor, heating it to an unbearable temperature. He brought his sword down against her flesh but she knocked his hand away with almost no effort and battered him with a flaming slap across the face that sent him reeling.

"Good enough signal for me!" Terian shouted as he attacked. She parried his overhand axe blow and grabbed the dark knight by the neck and hurled him bodily into three other Sanctuary attackers. One of them, a ranger, was killed by Terian's spiked pauldron upon impact.

Cyrus felt his chainmail burning through his undershirt as he pushed to his feet and checked his armor. It was hot but not melting. He blinked and watched as the Siren threw her hand out as though she were tossing a ball and a wall of fire ten feet high sprang up in a line leading through a densely packed group of spell casters. Screams filled the air as robes caught fire. Several of them ran, in flames. Alaric and Curatio charged toward the chaos. The smell of seared flesh filled the air.

Fortin stomped through the flames, bearing down on the Siren along with a half dozen other fighters. Smoke began to flow from her eyes and a burst of angry red shot forth, sending another half dozen combatants to the ground with blistered and blackened skin where the beam hit.

She moved her stare to Fortin, hitting him in the chest. The rock giant stopped moving forward. The intensity of the light from her eyes increased and he took a step back, then another. She moved, a subtle bob of her head, and the beam from her eyes knocked the rock giant onto his back.

Vara jumped at the Siren while her back was turned. As she was about to land, the Siren spun and caught the paladin with a blow that sent her rolling across the ground. Cyrus watched as she came to rest, blood trickling from her nose and a cut on her forehead, eyes closed, and his sword shook in his hands.

He charged, blood pounding in his ears, narrowly dodging the Siren's perfectly timed answering blow. *I will carve your flaming head off!* he thought. He didn't even raise the short sword, catching her instead with an offhand slash that was so quick she didn't have time to riposte.

A flurry of blows came at him, two of them glancing off his armor, heating it up and rattling him from the force. He countered with another slice, another small gash, this time across her muscled abdomen, and blood sizzled as it dripped onto the ground.

She raised her arm, outrage blazing on her face. Her aim was true but just as she was about to connect, a blast of ice encapsulated her. Cyrus blinked in surprise and looked to see Mendicant, hands raised, a blast of freezing spell energy still flying from his long, clawed fingers.

Cracks began to appear in the ice and an explosion rocked the island. The Siren of Fire burst forth, cloaked in flames once more. A hail of arrows greeted her from the rangers holding position at the edge of the island, standing apart from the chaos in the middle.

Her feet returned to the ground and the flames retracted from her body, but the fire remained in her eyes. The red beam she had shot from them now honed in on him, hitting him in the center of the chest and left him clutching his sides and gasping as though he were hit by a battering ram operated by a host of trolls. He spit out a mouthful of blood and watched as Sanctuary army attacked again.

Thad and Cass moved toward her, each plunging their sword at her from opposite sides. Her arms moved quickly enough that on her left, Thad scored only a minor slash before she slammed him to the dirt, but on her right Cass managed to dig his blade several inches into her thigh before being backhanded head over feet.

Terian and Vara flanked her next, distracting her with a frontal assault while several newer warriors that Cyrus knew only by face attacked from behind, stabbing her in the back. The eyes flared once more and the Siren of Fire screamed, her flaming hair extending and taking on a life of its own, whipping back the attackers behind her while she moved forward to deal with Terian and Vara.

One of the Siren's hands reached between the spiked pauldrons and grasped Terian by the neck while she fended off Vara with her other. Terian raised his axe and she knocked it away. Her eyes flared once more and Terian took a full blast to the face as her hand jerked him forward. Something flew through the air, landing near the burned and wounded spell casters. It rolled to a stop as she dropped the dark knight's body, the head now missing.

Vara let out a howl of outrage and brought her sword down before the Siren of Fire could pull back the hand with which she dropped Terian's body. The slash was powerful, cleaving the elemental's hand from her body and forcing her to stagger away after backhanding Vara once more.

Vara stumbled and recovered. The paladin's face was covered in blood and dirt. Cyrus pushed himself to his knees then fell down, unable to breathe. He looked to Terian's body, decapitated, and felt rage, pushing himself to his knees once more, fighting for another breath. *All my ribs are broken*, he concluded, feeling agony in his chest.

The Siren screamed and flung her remaining hand at Vara, sending another wave of fire, which the paladin dodged. Cyrus watched as the dozen or so combatants behind her, who did not have the dexterity given her by her armor, were consumed in the wall of flame, screaming and tossing themselves to the ground.

"Curatio," he muttered, but the Healer was far from him, across the battle, and tending to the spell casters that had been burned by the last wave of fire thrown by the Siren.

A swell of relief filled his chest and his lungs inhaled; most of the pain vanished, leaving only an echo behind. He drew himself to his feet and looked behind him to see Erith shaking her head. "Go," she said, worried look written on her face.

Cyrus threw himself into battle again, rage burning through his veins like the fires scattered across the island. Vara was drawing to her feet again as well, he saw, and her face was crisscrossed with open cuts, blood dripping along her cheek and chin, but her jaw was set and her sword was raised.

The Siren of Fire drew her hand back as if to throw another burst of flame but Cyrus lunged, crossing the last of the distance between them and plunged his sword into her side. He brought it across her stomach, slitting her belly as she brought her remaining hand across and knocked him six feet into the air.

He landed with a thump a few feet away and Vara moved in to attack as the Siren was hit with another flight of arrows, peppering her body. The shafts and fletchings burned upon impact and the wounds dripped with melted metal from the arrowheads.

Vara struck from behind, bringing her sword down overhand and cutting several inches into the Siren's shoulder. The elemental's eyes blazed once more and Vara went flying from the blast, almost to the edge of the island. Upon landing, she did not move.

Cyrus rolled from his back and jumped to his feet, ignoring the dozen pains he felt. A figure shoved him back roughly and filled his view.

Alaric Garaunt stepped forward from where he had pushed Cyrus back, sword in hand. The Ghost took two quick strides forward and brought his blade down more quickly than Cyrus could have imagined possible for the old knight as he parried her attack. She struck again and once more he avoided it, scoring a stabbing blow to her midsection in return. His hand reached out and she staggered back from the spell he had cast, and he moved toward her again, almost a blur of motion, sweeping in to close range.

His sword swung again, but the Siren of Fire blocked it and countered with a blow that did not even seem to impact the Ghost. He swung with another strike, leaving another gash, this time across the Siren's chest, drawing more blood and exposing bone. She staggered but threw another punch that he parried as he brought her arm down, breaking it and flipping her sideways to the ground, where he placed a boot upon her chest. He brought his sword to her throat and it hovered there.

"I have met you," Alaric said with a cold indifference, "I have bested you, and in the name of Sanctuary, I send you back to your god." A cool understanding lit the Siren's eyes, the Ghost's sword plunged down and the fires on the Siren's body flickered and went out like blown candles, with only wisps of smoke drifting over the corpse.

Cyrus looked around at the detritus of the force around him. Three quarters of them were wounded in some way and at least half were on the ground, moaning or worse. Cyrus's eyes looked across the island to find Vara, still unmoving. He rushed to her, feet thudding across the dusty ground.

He dropped to her side and rolled her over. She coughed and blood trickled down her chin from her mouth. She tried to speak but gasped and more blood poured out. "Healer!" he shouted. Her eyes rolled back in her head.

A sparkle of light ran up her body, and Cyrus turned to see Alaric standing behind him. "Do not be concerned; I can tend to her wounds. Our Healers are otherwise occupied."

Vara sat up in Cyrus's arms, breathing heavily. "I am in your debt once more, Alaric." She looked around and a glimmer of sadness crossed her face. "Just like old times."

Alaric's expression was nearly unreadable through his helm, but Cyrus could have sworn he saw a flicker of some deep emotion run across the Ghost's face, but when he looked again, it was gone. "Indeed," he responded.

"What about Terian?" Cyrus asked.

Alaric held up his hand to stay the warrior. "Curatio is working on him as we speak."

Cyrus stood and ran to the spot where Curatio, Vaste, Andren and Erith stood, looking down with a small crowd gathered around them. Cyrus broke through the observers and saw the dark elf, eyes open wide and staring at him.

"We brought him back," Curatio said. "Tricky thing, the timing of the spells - a resurrection spell, a heal to rejoin the body parts - which, with a decapitation, usually causes death again, then another resurrection spell and another heal, some incantations to restore vitality."

Cyrus looked to the dark knight laying prostrate on the ground. "How do you feel?"

"I feel like I just got the hell beat out of me by a living fireball until my head popped off." Terian scowled at him. "How do you think I feel?"

"Crabby."

The dark knight's scowl lessened. "And thirsty."

Curatio winced. "I wouldn't drink anything for a bit. Reattaching a head is tricky business. We're going to need to do some targeted healing to your neck later to make sure there aren't any holes."

Terian sighed. "So you're saying that if I take a drink right now, I might spring a leak? Marvelous."

"At least it won't burn," Cy added with an innocuous

expression.

"I hate you," Terian said, scowl deepening.

"Because my expedition got you killed?"

"Please. I hated you long before this." Cyrus laughed. Terian tried and ended up with a coughing fit.

Erith spoke up from behind them. "Andren, I didn't think you knew the resurrection spell?" she said with a frown.

"No, I do," the healer said defensively.

Her frown deepened. "You didn't before. And I know you haven't been gone for two years to learn it."

"Hey!" Terian said. "Can we please focus on what's important over here - namely, me?"

"Sorry," Erith muttered, but did not sound remorseful. Her eyes followed Andren, narrowed to suspicious slits.

"All right," Cyrus said, looking over the carnage around them. "When can we be ready to move?"

Curatio looked with him. "Probably in a half hour if you want everyone at full strength. I'd prefer an hour."

Fighting back internal pressure, he nodded. "An hour it is. I want everyone at their best."

Vara hobbled up behind him at that moment and rested her hand on his shoulder. He looked at her in surprise and she blushed. "I am still unsteady and require some support to stand."

He blinked and looked down at her hand, small and delicate but covered in dirt. Cyrus caught sight of Alaric walking across the flaming ground as he tended to wounded. "I've never seen a paladin cast spells other than for healing before. Can you do what Alaric did back there underwater?"

She stared back at him with a look of practiced incredulity. "The force blast spell? Of course. All paladins can."

"Then why didn't you?"

She deflated slightly. "I know many of the same spells as he does, but I haven't learned sublingual casting - how to cast spells without speaking. It's a rather advanced skill, one that I did not learn during my time with the Holy Brethren."

Cyrus's eyes followed Alaric as he picked his way across the island. "Do many spell casters know 'sublingual casting'?"

"No." She shook her head. "It takes quite a bit of additional study and by the time I reached the point that I could have learned it I was eager to get out into the world." He chuckled, bringing a look of annoyance across her face. "What?"

"Nothing," he chuckled again and waved away her inquiry. "I was just imagining you as a young paladin, sick of learning in a League and desperate to get out of there."

She shrugged. "It happened very much that way." A look of discomfort crossed her face. "I don't know if you've noticed this or not, but I am not comfortable in any situation where I feel I'm not in control."

He remained expressionless, but only with greatest effort. "I hadn't noticed." She glared at him but broke the effect of it with a half-smile of acknowledgment. "I guess Alaric must have been more patient if he took the time to learn sublingual casting before leaving the Holy Brethren."

Cyrus saw a wall spring up in her expression, guarding her emotions. "Alaric is capable of more than any other paladin I've ever met," she said with a note of awe. "For most paladins the force blast only stuns your opponent; Alaric's can kill." She paused, her words hanging in the air between them for a beat. "We have details to plan for the Last Guardian. He has a death glare and it will kill one combatant for each of his two eyes."

Cyrus nodded. "Yeah, I figured I'd take the hit again."

"That is unnecessary. There are a dozen people you could order to do it - it's not as though they're in any great danger. A resurrection spell shall sort them out in moments."

Cyrus exhaled, and eased her hand off his shoulder as he walked to the pit where the Siren had sprung from. With a sudden weariness he sat, feet dangling into the hole. "I know you haven't died, so I don't think you realize how much it hurts - and how much you lose when it happens."

She reddened. "I've heard it can be disconcerting -"

"Disconcerting doesn't begin to cover it." Cyrus looked out at the horizon beyond the islands, at the sky in perpetual twilight, with a dark orange glow filling the air around them. "Death hurts. Resurrection is almost worse. But you also lose memories. Things just disappear from your mind." She flushed and looked away. "Things you don't want to forget, things you'll never get back."

Cyrus looked over the Sanctuary army. "Thad would willingly throw himself into the guardian's death glare if I ordered him to. He's so gung-ho he'd die a dozen times over if ordered. Should I tell Martaina that the reason he can't remember the moment they met is because I needed him to die 'for the team'?" He looked at her soberly and shook his head. "No. I'll do it."

"How sweet and poignant," came the voice like ice from behind him. The Gatekeeper appeared at Cyrus's shoulder. "I am beginning to be somewhat impressed by your rabble and their consistent refusal to die. However, you cannot endure what you face next."

Cyrus waved him away. "You told me a while ago that I could become the greatest warlord that Arkaria had ever seen. I'm about to show you why."

A deep guffaw filled the air and the Gatekeeper's eyes lit up. "Or perhaps you're about to show me why I used the conditional phrase 'could'."

"Well," Cyrus said with a sickeningly sweet smile that betrayed the turmoil and anger he felt inside, "why don't you just open up the next gate for us and we'll see?" Something gripped him, an instinct to draw his sword and gut the old man that had taunted them from the moment of arrival, someone who had hurt Vara badly in the past...

The Gatekeeper stared at Cyrus and the expression on his face showed a flicker of uncertainty. The Gatekeeper blinked at him, concentrating. "Who... are you?"

Cyrus met his glare and a laugh escaped him. "I thought you knew our destinies, our sins, our past and all that rubbish?"

The Gatekeeper took a step back, a look of undisguised shock filling his features. "I can't - how are you -?" The Gatekeeper composed himself, severe expression returning. "I will open your gate, and you will face the death you so richly deserve."

"You don't sound as sure of that as you did a few minutes ago," Cyrus said with a growing confidence. "What are you afraid of, Gatekeeper?"

"I am the Hand of the Gods!" the Gatekeeper barked. "I do not fear you - nor any mortal!"

"Hand of the Gods, eh?" Cyrus said with a sudden streak of recklessness. "Why don't you open the gate and then go do whatever a god's hand does?"

The Gatekeeper muttered something and folded in on himself once more, leaving them in silence. Cyrus turned to Vara, who wore a shocked expression. "I have... never, in all my excursions here, seen what you and Alaric have managed to do to the Gatekeeper today. He is never less than arrogant, full of threats and taunts." She shook her head in amazement. "And he never retreats before striking a final verbal blow."

"It would appear," Cyrus said with a frown, "something about me disturbed him."

"One sympathizes with him," Vara said, "but I agree, it would seem something you said or did - I know not what - put him ill at ease." A smile broke across her features, lighting up the twilight. "That bodes well for us."

Erith appeared at Cyrus's elbow. "The dead are healed. Curatio says we may be ready to move sooner." She lingered, looking at the two of them. "Did I interrupt something?"

Vara stared at her in disbelief. "No. No, I suppose not. I have other matters to attend to." She walked off and Cyrus watched her go, disappointed.

When she had left, he wheeled back to Erith, who was still standing there. "Yes?" he asked.

"Nothin'," she said with a shrug. Her eyes shifted left and right, seeing if anyone was near them. "Okay, question - officer to officer, do you ever get tired of the whining and the stupidity and all the garbage that comes from running a guild?"

He blinked, caught off guard. "Uh... no? Although I admit being banished from the cities of western Arkaria is causing some stress."

"The officers of the Daring do what we can," Erith said, ignoring his reaction, "to grow our numbers, to find new members, to put together a program of expeditions - small scale ones, trying to keep our heads above water and grow. There's no appreciation for what we do; just bitching and moaning; complaints about the other guilds in the Alliance, and how you and Goliath are expanding and we're not."

Cyrus nodded, a creeping feeling of familiarity washing over him. "I understand. I led a small guild once, and when you're stuck in a bad situation, people would rather gripe than try and fix it."

"Exactly!" she said. "Elisabeth is great with people; she's smooth and sweet, and agrees with everybody, and everybody loves her, and Cass is all big and tough but pulls back on saying what needs to be said. So," she went on, brow furrowing in annoyance, "I'm the bad guy. I get to speak the truths that they don't want to, and have everyone hate me. I'm sick of it."

"It's tough," he agreed. "I respect that; you're willing to fight the good fight, even when sometimes it may not seem like it's worth it."

"What if it's not worth it?" she asked. "What happened to the other guild you ran?"

"There were three of us and when Sanctuary offered, we did some thinking and jumped ship. Of course," he chuckled, "Sanctuary was in a better spot then than we are now."

"I don't know about that," Erith said. "You've got a lot of forces arrayed against you, but that could help you - you know, buckle down together, have each others' backs, focus on the bond you have with people you fight alongside. I think you'll come out of this crisis stronger than ever."

He laughed. "I hope you're right."

"I'm always right," she sighed as she wandered off. "I only wish they saw that in *my* guild."

Chapter 26

A sense of foreboding filled Cyrus as he watched the Sanctuary army recover and prepare to face the Last Guardian. Vara found him only five minutes before he was set to order reassembly of their formation. "You are still intending to be the first to take the death glare?" she asked.

"Yes," he nodded. "I have to find a second."

"No, you do not," came a voice from behind him. Alaric strode up and placed a hand upon his shoulder. "I will join you."

Cyrus flushed. "Alaric, I don't think you should... what about Fortin? Won't he turn on us when you die?"

The Ghost waved his hand dismissively. "So long as I am resurrected, he will not. Do you think I would ask one of my other brethren to die in my stead?" The Ghost's glare penetrated Cyrus even through the helmet.

"Very well," Cyrus agreed. "Once we enter the gate, you and I will charge. The guardian stands in the middle of the island." He looked to Vara, whose expression was masked. "Right?"

She nodded. "The first two to catch his gaze will be killed instantly. His death glare will strike again every fifteen minutes until the guardian is dead."

"Got it," Cyrus nodded at her. "You lead the battle while I'm gone."

"You would be better suited to this than I," she said.

"But I'll be dead, so you're in charge."

A look of argument came over her face, then disappeared. "Very well."

Cyrus bellowed to get the attention of the Sanctuary army, reformed them and they marched toward the next gate, already opened. The officers, as usual, gravitated to the front of the formation. As they passed underneath the gate, Cyrus ordered the army to halt.

"The island of evil," Niamh said with a gasp, then she straightened and looked around with a cocked head, face more curious than afraid. "It doesn't look that evil."

"Rest assured," Vara breathed, "evil is here."

The island looked like the ones before it; a long stretch of dust hanging in the air, unremarkable in every way but one: spaced around the far end of the island were a number of portals, similar to the ones scattered throughout Arkaria, save for one detail: they each pulsed with energy of different colors, like the entryways he had seen to the Realms of Darkness and Death.

In the middle of the island before them stood a pool of black, viscous liquid. It writhed, coalescing and taking shape, a thick tar that rose out of the puddle to form a dark figure that rose to the height of a titan, twenty feet into the air, and solidified. The Last Guardian's body was not quite shaped like a human - it had four arms and four legs, with an unrecognizable head. Its skin glowed a shade of black that Cyrus had never seen, not even in the Realm of Darkness.

"Are you ready?" Vara asked from just behind him.

"Alaric?" Cyrus asked, looking at the Ghost, who shot him a sly smile and nodded. "We're ready."

"Good," Vara said. Without warning she kicked Cyrus's legs from under him as she hipchecked him to the side. He landed on his back, hard, the weight of his frame and his armor knocking the wind out of him. He watched her leap over him and blaze across the ground toward the guardian as he gasped for breath and struggled to retake his feet. Alaric followed behind her, and by the time Cyrus was upright again, he knew he would never reach her in time.

The Last Guardian's head spun on the top of its neck, in ways that no living being could move. Two eyes gathered on the front of its head as Vara and Alaric approached.

"Charge!" Cyrus spurred the army of Sanctuary into motion, running toward the guardian.

A flash from one of the eyes lit the air around them and a cry of victory came from the guardian as Vara crumpled to the ground. Another flash and Alaric seemed to become hazy for a moment, but kept running, sword in hand.

As Cyrus closed the distance, Alaric engaged the guardian. Four arms swung down at him and two of the guardian's legs moved to kick. Alaric dodged every blow that came his way. The guardian's arms seemed to slide across the torso, positioning themselves all on one side to better strike at the Ghost.

Cyrus made his way past the Ghost, buffeting the leg with glancing strikes as he passed, not doing much damage. Fortin thundered up to the guardian and launched into it with a powerful fist, striking a blow that glanced off. Cyrus looked at the rock giant for a split second – there was a black scoring on his chest. Finally, all four of the guardian's arms lined up and struck a flurry of punches at Fortin.

Cyrus could hear a cracking noise as the attacks landed one after another. The last hit the rock giant in the face with the force of an explosion. Chips of stone from the impact hit Cyrus in the face and drew blood. He watched Fortin drop to a knee. The arms struck again and when they withdrew, cracks like gashes could be seen along the rock giant's chest and dark fluid oozed out.

Fortin's red eyes faded and he slumped at the guardian's feet, dead. He landed with a thump that forced Cyrus to step back, during which time the guardian waded into a cluster of Sanctuary attackers gathered behind it. It stomped its spider-like legs that had suddenly grown pointed at the ends and flailed its arms as it attacked much softer targets than Fortin.

Bodies flew through the air, whole and in pieces. Cyrus watched Terian duck one attack only to be flattened by another while Thad was not even fortunate enough to dodge the first: he was impaled by one of the guardian's legs and flung off into the crowd, knocking over several spell casters upon impact. Aisling's assault was cut off midway as one of the guardian's arms struck her a killing blow.

Spells impacted upon the guardian's skin and attacks continued by the survivors of the guardian's assault. Cyrus dodged another round of strikes from the fiend and joined Alaric in attempting to attack the legs, the only reachable part of the creature.

Cyrus sensed another arm coming his way and swung his sword into it with all his force. The appendage cleaved in two but withdrew, leaving a slight residue of dark gray liquid behind on the blade. "I think I hurt it," he muttered, more to himself than anyone.

"Excellent," came Alaric's reply over the chaos of the battle. "Keep doing so." The paladin brought his sword back for another strike and Cyrus could see the Ghost's weapon was coated in the same fluid that his was.

Does this thing have a weak point? Cyrus wondered. *Vara seemed to think if we hacked away at it, it would eventually die – but she was used to fighting it with mystical weapons. But surely there must be a weak point...*

He looked up, to the top of the creature, where two eyes stared down, rotating around the ovoid, formless head. "I need a ranger to strike those eyes!"

"With pleasure," came a voice, breaking with anger. Cyrus looked back to see Martaina taking aim, a look of malice on her face. Arrows flew, one after another and peppered the head of the guardian. She placed four arrows in each eye, but still the head spun. The arms swept around, but with less purpose than before.

"At least he's blinded now," Cyrus said as he blocked another strike with a sword blow, cleaving an arm and then watching it reform before his eyes.

The guardian shuddered and pulled away from them, legs sliding back into something approaching a line. The guardian's torso widened in one direction and flattened in another, becoming human-like but with four arms. The legs coalesced into two legs from four. The head disappeared for a moment and then sprang back up, eyes missing.

Cyrus brought his sword forward and was knocked off balance when it hit with a *clang!* and his short sword bounced off the guardian's skin. He brought it back for another swing and was rebuffed once more with a shock of pain that rattled his teeth.

Cyrus looked over to see Alaric chipping away at the metallic skin with his sword, doing a little damage. Sheathing the short sword he dodged a swing of the guardian's arms and ran to Vara's body. He rolled her over gingerly and froze for a moment. Her eyes were closed and a peaceful expression lay upon her face. With a grimace, he pulled her sword from its scabbard and touched her hand, which was already cold.

Her sword was almost twice the length of his, with a blade almost as thick as his bicep. Serrated edges curved on either side, giving it an elegant appearance lacking in his simple short sword. The curves of the blade continued into the guard, which came to pointed edges. The hilt was all metal, cold in his hand, and the pommel was the head of a wolf, cast from a dark metal.

He swung the blade around, admiring the balance as he charged back into the battle and the Last Guardian's arms came after him again. The closest was taking aim; a hand sprouted at its end, individual fingers balling into a fist. He smiled as it flew toward him and he sidestepped, bringing the sword sideways into a strike that split the arm once more, all the way to elbow. He used his weight and dragged the sword down, stripping half the lower arm off the guardian.

Another hand swung at him, palm open for a vicious slap and he brought the sword across the wrist, cutting the hand off. The other two arms avoided him as he crossed back to the leg to join Alaric. He plunged Vara's sword into the upper thigh of the guardian, eliciting a sound of grinding metal on metal before pulling the blade out at the kneecap, creating a three foot gash. Grey fluid oozed from the wound, dripping onto the dusty ground and forming pools in the contour of the landscape as the guardian moved about.

Alaric mirrored Cyrus's attack, pitching the guardian off-balance, then cast a spell. The same blast he'd used underwater was even more devastating now – the force blast flew from Alaric's open palm, tilting the guardian at the waist and knocking it onto its back. Cyrus did not hesitate; he jumped, imitating a move he'd seen Vara execute many times. He flew through the air and landed on the torso of the felled guardian, plunging the blade into the side of its neck and dragging across it four times before a reprisal came from one of the arms. He blocked the attack with the sword, mangling another of the guardian's hands.

He attacked the neck once more. He could sense Alaric behind him, warding off the arms as Cyrus brought the sword down again and again, until the head rolled free and stopped a few feet away, dissolving into the gray slag that had been oozing from the body.

Alaric brought his sword down on the torso, and channeled a spell through the blade, rocking the Last Guardian. It shuddered again and Cyrus felt his feet begin to slide into the body. He jumped free as it melted, losing its solid form and spreading across the ground in all directions, a thick sludge.

He sighed a breath of relief and returned to where he had left Vara. Curatio stood above her, hands glowing, magic already surging to revive her. She came back with a lurch and her head jerked forward as she gagged. He knelt next to her and she opened her eyes, squinting against the twilight around them.

"Alaric?" she gasped, looking around, disoriented. "Where am I?" Cyrus looked up to see the Ghost standing there, leaning on his sword.

"It's all right, lass," he said in a soothing voice. "We're in the Realm of Purgatory."

A beat passed before she seemed to comprehend. "Again?"

"You took the death glare of the Last Guardian," Cyrus

interjected. "Knocked me on my ass so you could do it."

"I don't..." She squinted at him, a look of confusion on her face. "What are you doing here? Am I wounded?"

"You died," Curatio said.

"Curatio," she breathed, and turned her eyes toward Cy. "Cyrus Davidon."

He grinned. "Glad to see you didn't forget me."

She managed to roll her eyes. "I could scarcely forget you, but not for lack of trying."

"Why did you knock me over?" he asked, a flash of annoyance welling in him.

She drew a breath before answering. "Because if I hadn't, your thoughtless gallantry wouldn't have allowed me to take the death glare," she answered as she sat up. Wobbling on her arms, she stabilized herself by leaning against him. "You did not exaggerate the effects of resurrection." Her eyes fell on her sword in his hand and irritation darkened her already wan features. "What are you doing with that?"

"I needed it," he said, "to win the battle." He slid it back into her scabbard, prompting an offended look from her.

"How dare you slide that into my scabbard without permission?" She blanched. "Oh, never mind."

Cyrus laughed, prompting a weak smile from Vara. "So did you get all that curiosity out of your system? Don't feel the urge to go dying again anytime soon, do you?"

She shuddered. "That was quite a bit worse than I'd anticipated. No, I don't intend to try that again. Who took the other death glare?"

Cyrus looked up at Alaric, who was strangely calm. "Excellent question. Alaric was supposed to, but it doesn't seem to have taken hold on him."

Alaric shrugged. "It would appear that the guardian failed to attack with death glare a second time, for I am still here and feel quite well, I assure you."

"I have no doubt," Cyrus said with no small amount of irony. "I believe the guardian did reach out with a death glare a second time. How did you avoid it?"

"What you describe would seem impossible. I assume it somehow missed," Alaric said. "If there were any other explanation, doubtless it would reveal itself –"

"In time, yes," Cyrus said with an air of resignation. Alaric smiled, bowed and strode away to Larana, who was stooped over a puddle of the Guardian's remains with a bottle, collecting it.

Vara watched him go. "Did the Guardian speak to you? Try to tell you anything? Try any of the things that the Gatekeeper has been doing?"

"No," he said, unable to take his eyes off hers. "I haven't had anything speak into my mind since the Realm of Darkness."

"Peculiar. Every time we faced it the mental attacks were intense." She frowned. "It doesn't make sense. Why wouldn't it attack that way?"

"I don't know," he said, gritting his teeth. Her grip, enhanced by her armor's power, was crushing his fingers.

"Perhaps you're special," the Gatekeeper's voice came from behind them. They turned to find him sneering, with something sitting across his hands. He tossed it at Cyrus's feet, stirring up a cloud and causing both he and Vara to blanch from the dust.

"What is that?" she asked.

Cyrus pulled away from her, eyes fixated on the object in the dirt. He reached down and picked it up with delicate hands, holding it as one would hold a newborn baby, covetously, taking in every line of the intricate styling. The paladin's words rang in his ears, but the warrior was far beyond hearing them.

It had been a blazing hot day in the slums of Reikonos, years before he'd met the forces of Sanctuary. The heat swelled, sweat dripped down his skin, soaking his undergarments. In the places where his armor touched skin it burned, even in the shadowed light of the canyon-like slums. The smell of mortal refuse from the latrines overwhelmed the air, so strong it turned from smell nearly to taste, gagging even those with the strongest stomachs.

Cyrus walked the streets at midday. All but the most courageous vendors had abandoned their carts due to heat. The normally vibrant, noisy slums, teeming with life and merchant activity – legitimate and not – had given way to a mere whisper of its normal volume.

Turning a corner into a quiet alleyway, a racking pain filled his head, as though a sword had been driven into his temple. He reached out to a nearby wall for support, blinked, and another shock of pain seized him, bringing him to his knees.

A hazy figure had appeared before him as the light from above swelled. ***"Cyrus Davidon,"*** *boomed an all-consuming voice. The pain in his head was paralyzing, but the words were a soothing balm, and the angry tautness in his skull faded at the sound.* ***"My loyal servant."***

"Who – who are you?" Cyrus's mouth was dry and each word had to be forced out.

"You have served me for years, making war, giving combat and offering your prayers with loyal heart. I am here to help you achieve your destiny - becoming the most powerful warrior in Arkaria." *The figure's eyes lit with an unknown power, blotting out anything but a faint, human-like outline.*

Cyrus looked up, trying to discern details through the fog surrounding him. "Bellarum?" Even through the pain, a sense of palpable awe filled him. "You... you are the God of War?"

"I have watched your growth into a warrior since the days you took up my cause in the Society of Arms. You have been a good and faithful servant and I see great potential in you. I come to you now to assist you in obtaining a weapon of power unlike anything wielded since the ancient times."

A scrap of parchment drifted from the cloaked figure's grasp, landing at Cyrus's feet. His hands darted forward after a moment's pause, scooping it up from the dirt and bringing it close enough for his eyes to read.

> ***Serpent's Bane*** *– The guard and grip are in possession of Ashan'agar, the Dragonlord.*
> ***Death's Head*** *– The pommel is held by Mortus, God of Death.*
> ***Edge of Repose*** *– The Gatekeeper of Purgatory holds the blade as a prize for one who knows to ask for it.*
> ***Avenger's Rest*** *– G'koal, Empress of Enterra has the Scabbard.*
> ***Quartal*** *– The ore needed to smith the sword together is found only in the Realm of Yartraak, God of Darkness.*
> *Brought together by one who is worthy, they shall form* ***Praelior, the Champion's Sword****.*

"What... what is this?" Cyrus asked, confused.

The figure held out a hand, eyes blazing in that magnificent shade, overpowering everything. He gestured to the parchment Cyrus held. ***"I give you a test. It is no idle test fit for lone warriors - this task will require you to assemble or co-opt an army."*** *The figure paused, solemnity filling Cyrus with a palpable sense of awe.* ***"Gather the pieces and the prize will shape your very destiny. Pass through the trial which I have set before you and I will guide your blade. Let us see the strength that you possess - if you are worthy of being called Warlord."***

Cyrus blinked and the pain that filled his head was gone, along with the figure. He was back in the alley in Reikonos, one hand against a wall for support, and in the other was clutched a small scrap of parchment - and a curiosity, a drive to know if what he had seen was real.

"The Edge of Repose," Cyrus whispered. He turned to Vara. "It's the blade - for my sword. I only need the scabbard now."

"So glad I could grant your fondest wish," said the Gatekeeper with a healthy dose of sarcasm. "Now if you'll excuse me, I have others to attend to." Before he turned, he favored Vara with a malicious look, mouth upturned in a smile. "And what about you? What do you want? Same as last time?"

"As I recall, you did not grant my request last time," she said, dry lips smacking together.

"Ah, but it was granted, though perhaps not in the way you intended." The smile grew larger on the Gatekeeper's face.

Vara did not return it. "Not through any action of yours."

"Well," the Gatekeeper said lightly, with a shrug, "think about it and get back to me." He smiled and strolled off to the next nearest member of the Sanctuary army.

"So he starts by trying to pinpoint your darkest fears and ends by giving you what you ask for?" Cyrus said with a shake of his head. "Bit strange."

"Not really." Vara stared at the Gatekeeper, now speaking with Thad and Martaina. "It's all about what drives you - for good or ill. It's not as though he will grant a wish," she said, a tinge of sadness in her voice. "He'll give you things. Tangible objects. Easy requests for things you covet that can be created with godly power. It's not as though he can bring back the dead." She paled.

"It takes a while for the effects of the resurrection spell to wear off," he cautioned her.

"It's not that," she said. "Never mind. It is quite overwhelming."

Neither of them spoke for several minutes as they watched the Gatekeeper. A line of their guildmates had formed in front of him. Whenever one of them made a request, the Gatekeeper would turn away for a moment and something would appear in his hands, much like the disappearance when his cloak seemed to fold in on him. After an hour, the line had been depleted.

"I think we are almost done," the Gatekeeper said with the thinnest air of relief. "One left, I believe." He turned to Alaric, who was standing at a distance. "So, Lord Garaunt, what would you have of me?"

"I would have nothing of you," the Ghost said. "Unless you would be willing to offer your head, stuffed and mounted on a wall."

"That would be asking a bit much."

"I thought so."

"Very well then," the Gatekeeper said with a clap of his hands. He hesitated and stepped closer to Alaric. "Perhaps I could offer... just one thing." His hands disappeared behind his back and his face went blank. When his hands re-emerged there was something clutched in his fingers, something small. The Gatekeeper held it out for Alaric to see.

It was a lock of hair. Brown, wispy and delicate, bound together at the middle by a white ribbon.

The Ghost did not react visibly. Stonefaced, he stared down at the Gatekeeper's hands before reaching out and taking what was proffered. "Thank you," he said in a voice without inflection. "I assume you mean for this to taunt me, but be assured I take it with gratitude."

"Take it however you'd like." The Gatekeeper's voice was hushed. "It matters not to me." The Gatekeeper paused, some twist of emotion almost unrecognizable passing over his weathered face. "You'll want to leave through this portal." He gestured to the one directly behind him.

"Why don't we go through one of the others?" Terian said with an air of suspicion.

The Gatekeeper grinned. "You are most welcome to exit through any of them, but I wouldn't recommend it, even for you."

"He is right," Alaric said with certainty. "The others will not take us anywhere that we wish to go. We will leave through the portal he indicated."

A mutter ran through the crowd but upon Cyrus's call to formation, the Sanctuary army assembled in front of the portal. "Remember," Cyrus called out. "We'll be appearing in the middle of Reikonos. If we encounter hostility, the front ranks will hold them off while the rest of the army exits the portal. Nyad," he said to the wizard, "you'll be the last one into Reikonos and as soon as you appear, cast the teleportation spell. We'll have dealt with any... interference by then."

"What's the likelihood we'll be seeing battle?" Thad asked.

"We just broke the big three's monopoly on the Trials of Purgatory and we're already wanted by the Reikonos guards,"

Vara said. "I would say... high."

Cyrus looked at the faces of the army standing before him. "We just became the fourth guild in Arkaria to claim victory over the Trials of Purgatory. Whatever we face on the other side of that gate is nothing compared to what we went through on this side of it." Excitement infused his words. A roar of triumph from Fortin broke the uneasy tension and a small celebration rippled through the crowd as the realization of what they had accomplished spread over the expedition.

"I'm proud of you," Cyrus said. "One last thing and we can go home as heroes." He turned toward the portal and raised his hand. "Forward!"

Chapter 27

The light of the portal flickered on the walls of two massive guildhalls on either side of them as they emerged into the Reikonos guildhall quarter. The sun was behind the buildings, the chill of early evening was in the air and the sky was the same twilight color that had been present in Purgatory. The smells of cooking meat wafted as Cyrus looked from the raised platform the portal was mounted on down the street in front of him. A few souls were scattered on either side of the avenue.

Cyrus had passed through these streets many times; large guildhalls towered above the dainty structures of the markets and spread out for entire blocks of the city. He looked down the street to an intersection only a few hundred feet away, a place where the entrances to the four largest guildhalls in the city looked across a square at each other.

They varied in styles, one taking its appearance from ancient elven architecture like that of Pharesia while one across the street favored the more modern elven architecture seen in the city of Termina. Reikonos had almost no style of its own, an eclectic mix of different types of buildings that did not blend well. One of the halls even appeared to be human architecture with dwarven decorations ringing it.

As they emerged from the portal, Cyrus kept the army marching forward. The spectators watching had looks of awe. Whispers filled the air along with the crackling of energy from the portal behind them. Cyrus saw a few people run, some down side streets, some into their guildhalls.

"That is Amarath's Raiders' hall," Vara said tightly, pointing to their left. She moved her hand toward the intersection, pointing at a building across the square. "That one belongs to Burnt Offerings; that one belongs to Endeavor." She moved to point to the building to their right.

Cyrus eyed a structure almost as big as the other three, situated on the forth corner of the intersection. "Whose is that?"

"Take a guess," Vara said with utter contempt as a dark elf in a cloak emerged from its doors followed by a dwarf and a host of others.

Cyrus stared at the dark elf as he moved forward, almost

gliding. "Malpravus," he whispered. "Goliath?"

"None other."

The streets were filled as the four biggest guildhalls in the quarter emptied and others came from side streets, most keeping their distance, perhaps remembering the last time this had happened. Cyrus cast a look back to see only a little more than half his army had emerged from the portal.

The flow of people from the Burnt Offerings guildhall had slowed to a trickle; a mammoth clot of their members stood before Cyrus on the street. Endeavor's and Amarath's Raiders' doors were open and their hall was still emptying. Cyrus continued to shuffle toward them, pushed by the growing numbers of his guildmates appearing from the portal behind him.

"Keep a tight formation," he whispered, and heard the command passed row by row through the army. There was some movement on the street as a few figures pushed to the front of the crowd. A female elf that looked oddly familiar led the group. Her blond hair hung loose around her shoulders. Robes of the purest white were draped over her and held snug at her midsection by a belt that was black leather with a buckle of one of the finest and most intricate designs he had seen. A blue scarf was draped over her shoulders that matched her sparkling eyes and a smile stretched across her face.

She was flanked by a human dark knight, a man whose build was similar to Cyrus's - he stood taller than most humans, had dark hair and light eyes, and a scar crossed his face diagonally from his forehead to chin. His armor was a dark shade, not quite black but polished to a sheen and made from a metal with a texture different than any Cyrus had seen before.

A dwarf stood next to them, a mighty warhammer slung across his back and a braided beard that stretched past his knees. Next to him was the most vicious-looking troll Cyrus had ever seen. Slitted yellow eyes peered at them, scuffed and battered armor spoke of a thousand battles won, and a sword big enough to be carried by a titan was slung across the troll's back.

"It's good to see you," said the lady elf, voice sincere. "Congratulations on conquering the Trials of Purgatory." She kept a distance between them, but even from ten feet away Cyrus caught a hint of an intoxicating lilac scent wafting from her.

Cyrus nodded warily. "Thank you."

"You are Cyrus Davidon, an officer of Sanctuary?" she asked.

Cy raised an eyebrow. "Yes. And I believe you are Isabelle, officer of Endeavor."

Her smile broadened. "So nice to be known."

"I'm surprised you know me."

Isabelle shrugged, again stirring a feeling of familiarity in Cyrus. "I know the names of all of Sanctuary's officers. Allow me the pleasure of making your introductions." She pointed to the troll behind her. "Grunt is also an officer of Endeavor." The troll scowled at Cyrus. Cy did not return the troll's glare but kept an eye on him.

She pointed to the dark knight standing at her shoulder. "This is Archenous Derregnault, the Guildmaster of Amarath's Raiders." She tilted her head to Vara and a strange tone filled her melodic voice, as though she were trying to keep it neutral. "I believe you have met." Turning to indicate the dwarf with the warhammer, she said, "This is Larning, the Guildmaster of Burnt Offerings."

Cy nodded at each of them in turn, but his eyes were drawn back to Archenous, the human. He met Cyrus's gaze, and there was something indefinable between them. Cyrus could feel a deep loathing spring up within him, something more powerful than he could have imagined from nothing but a shared glance.

"You need not worry," Isabelle said, drawing his attention back to her. "We have no ill intentions toward you or your army." Something in the way she said it made Cyrus believe her.

"You can trust her," Vara said from behind him. "Probably."

"Such kind words," Isabelle said with a laugh. "How are you, little sister?"

"Not so little anymore, I'm afraid," Vara said.

"You should come home more often." Isabelle's expression did not change. "Father misses you. Mother too, though she doesn't say it."

"I'm sure she hides it well under snide, judgmental remarks about how I'm wasting my life," Vara replied.

"She does indeed," Isabelle agreed. "That doesn't mean you shouldn't come home more often."

"I'm afraid I won't be doing that for the near future; you see –"

"You've been banished?" Isabelle said. "I heard. A flimsy excuse for so great a holy warrior. It's not as though the Termina Militia would stand against you, since you are –"

"That's enough," Vara said, her voice a warning. "I will consider it."

"Very well." Isabelle turned to see Malpravus standing at a distance behind her, eying the Sanctuary army almost hungrily as they filed out of the portal. "It would appear you have no shortage of admirers."

"Oh, yes, we're very popular," Cyrus said with a final backwards glance. The light of the portal had stopped flaring. He looked to the square to see a small assemblage of Reikonos guards, standing at the end of the crowd, glaring toward them.

"Perhaps you should go," Isabelle said with a look of sadness. "I suspect they are assembling more guards as we speak and you wouldn't want to have to kill them all."

"Excellent work conquering the trials," came the hoarse, guttural voice of Archenous Derregnault. "You are, as always, a master tactician, Vara."

If she heard, she did not acknowledge him. Turning to Cyrus, she nodded. "My sister is quite correct: we have outstayed our welcome."

"Agreed. Nyad?" he called out.

Before the words had left his mouth an orb of teleportation appeared in front of him. A loud clapping filled his ears as Isabelle applauded, then Archenous joined in and everyone on the street followed. The noise was thunderous, drowning out any other sound. He looked back to see his army begin to disappear in flashes of light as they grasped the orbs.

Malpravus caught his eye. The necromancer was not clapping, a motionless figure in a sea of movement, his hands hidden in his sleeves and the same gleeful, malicious smile filled his lips.

Isabelle looked on with an air of sadness as Vara disappeared. She turned and pushed past the entourage of guildmasters and officers behind her to disappear into the crowd.

Cyrus's eyes fell once more on the dark knight, Archenous Derregnault, whose gaze was locked on him. A small smile cracked the knight's stony facade, and he bowed his head to Cyrus. That same sense of loathing filled Cyrus as he stared down the human. *It feels like I know him. I definitely dislike him. But why?*

A last look confirmed that the rest of the Sanctuary army had disappeared save for one. Alaric stood at his shoulder. "I appreciate you staying behind to ensure safety for our comrades, my brother. But now," the paladin said with an eye toward the Reikonos guards, who were moving through the crowd toward them, "it is time to go."

Cyrus reached up to grab hold of the orb as Alaric did the same. The last Cyrus saw before disappearing was of a small guard force halted in their tracks, surrounded by a crowd of thousands, still applauding and shouting their congratulations to the army of Sanctuary.

Chapter 28

Cyrus felt his boots land with a gentle clank on the stone floor of the foyer. The noise of approbation he had left behind was replaced by the applause and cheering that filled Sanctuary's entrance and was spilling over into the lounge; the beginnings, no doubt, of a party that would last into the night. Across the crowd Cyrus caught a glimpse of Andren, opening a cask of wine and a keg of ale simultaneously, seesawing back and forth between the two.

A smile crept across Cyrus's face as the infectious nature of the atmosphere took hold of him. He felt hands clapping him on the back, voices crying out in excitement and exultation, and saw a flash of blond hair wrapped in a ponytail as Vara disappeared up the stairs.

"We did it!" Thad yelled across the room from a position atop a table in the lounge, Martaina at his side, looking no less jubilant. The warrior already had an ale in his hand. Menlos Irontooth stood in his shadow, nursing a flagon of his own, talking to Nyad.

A door banged open on the far end of the hall and Belkan stood silhouetted in the entryway, hands in the air in triumph. "Well done!" the armorer shouted, narrowly missing tripping over Mendicant as he made his way across the hall toward the lounge. Mendicant dodged expertly and backed up into a wall, startling himself. The goblin watched the celebration with as pleasant a smile as Cyrus imagined a goblin could produce, but eventually reached under his robes and pulled out a book, which he proceeded to read in the corner, sitting by himself.

Cyrus watched with amusement until he felt a gentle hand glide around his waist. He turned to see Aisling with her hand on his short sword, examining it. "This is unbefitting a warrior of your station," she said, shaking her head. She looked up, dark eyes meeting his, a playful look on her face. "Would you like me to steal a better sword for you? I know lots of brigands and troublemakers that have very nice things and well deserve to be parted from their weapons. All I want in return is just..." The face got more playful and she leaned in close, whispering in his ear – something foul and yet pleasant.

He closed his eyes for a moment at the feel of her breath on his neck – it smelled of sweet cinnamon – then opened them again to roll his eyes. "No."

"Well," she said with a shrug as playful as her look, "at least you didn't yell at me for suggesting it. Does that mean I'm making progress?" With a laugh, she darted through the crowd toward the lounge and the center of the party. Music had begun to fill the air from a few enterprising members who played instruments.

Cyrus shook his head at the dark elf's persistence. *No, it doesn't mean you're making progress,* he thought. *It means I'm grateful to you for saving my life in Purgatory. And I haven't felt the touch of a woman in that way... outside of a mesmerization... in years.* He sighed.

He turned, leaving the noise of the celebration behind and ascended the staircase, exiting in front of the Council Chambers. He opened the door to hear a loud whooping akin to what he had left behind and a blur of red as something small hit him squarely in the armor.

"WE DID IT!" Niamh shouted after kissing him on both cheeks. She let go of him and stepped back, her face flushed. She seemed to vibrate with excitement.

"I saw you give that treatment to Alaric and Cy, but not for me?" Terian asked with a frown. "I lost my head in Purgatory!"

"Nor for I, either," Vaste agreed. "Although I am pleased to report I did not lose my head. At least not literally. I did freak out a little bit when the Siren started burning through the Healers like wildfire through a rotting forest, but I made it out okay. I only screamed once – maybe twice."

"Oh, fine," Niamh said and circled to the dark elf and the troll, giving them both strong kisses on each cheek. A deeply offended look by J'anda prompted her to go to him, followed by the surprised Curatio and even more surprised Vara, who had the look of a cat thrown into water.

"Do not expect me to kiss any of you on the cheeks," Vara said archly as Niamh took her seat. "Nor anywhere else."

"Come now, old friend," Alaric said with a grin from the head of the table, "We would worry if you ever showed a sign of affection for anyone."

"If you did, I would assume you were feverish and attempt to drown you in the nearest pond in the middle of the night," Cyrus said with only the trace of a smile.

"Oh, yes, very droll," she said with an expression that mirrored his own. "While we are all very pleased with ourselves – as well we should be – this does not solve our problems."

"On the contrary," Cyrus said. "It could solve one of our problems right now." He turned to Curatio. "Did you get the tally?"

The Healer nodded. "Larana thinks that between a few of the rocks from the golems – they have some enchantments, I suppose – the skins and some other parts of the pegasi, pieces of the eel, embers from the Siren of Fire and all the liquid she managed to bottle from the Last Guardian, we will net somewhere in the neighborhood of 30 million gold pieces when we sell them through her contacts in the Dwarven Alliance."

Vara frowned. "It should have been more."

"I agree," Curatio replied. "It would have been considerably more if we could sell in Reikonos, Pharesia or Saekaj – probably somewhere in the neighborhood of 60 million gold. But..."

"This could solve that problem," Cyrus said, looking around the table. "We could pay off the fines without any difficulty – at least in Reikonos and Pharesia and have some money left over."

Alaric's hand hit the table as loud as if lightning had struck. "We will not buy our way out of this, like a thief bartering for his life! This is our honor and we will fight for it with our very lives, if necessary."

"So... more battle, then," Vaste quipped.

"I am quite serious," Alaric said, eyes cool.

"So was I. Unless you see some way out of this that doesn't involve us staring down armies from three hostile countries?"

Alaric stood, forcing his chair back from the table. He turned, helmet crooked under his arm and walked to the window behind him. "No, I do not see a way to avoid that conflict until we have proof that we are not behind the attacks."

"Let us not forget," Curatio said. "We still haven't placed Goliath's proposal before the members. We have a few months yet."

"How could we forget that our allies have placed us in such a fun position?" Vara retorted. "I am only thankful we have no more 'friends' like Goliath, if this is what 'friends' do to you."

"Let us discuss these matters tomorrow. We should be down there with our guildmates, celebrating." Alaric stared out the window across the plains, helmet cradled beneath his arm. "Tomorrow, we begin the search for these bandits anew. We will catch them, even if we have to use every resource available to us."

"Agreed," J'anda said. "Tonight we eat, drink and be merry, for tomorrow we sit upon the plains for long periods of time, staring at the grasses and waiting for someone to attack a convoy." The enchanter stood, followed by each officer in turn, until Cyrus and Alaric remained the last two in the Council Chambers.

Alaric turned. "For once it is not I who halts you at the end of a Council meeting." A slight upturn of the lips gave the Ghost an amused look. "You have questions, I presume. I will answer what I can."

"When we were in the water, the Gatekeeper said something about my destiny, about me becoming a Warlord greater than any in Arkaria," Cyrus began. "Was he taunting me with idle words, or can he see the future?"

Alaric gaze met Cyrus's, but the gray of the Ghost's eye hid his thoughts. "The Gatekeeper – the Hand of the Gods – whatever you would like to call him – does possess some clairvoyance. But if you ever asked – and if he ever answered you – it would likely be something equivocal about how your choices shape your destiny, and that you are in control of whether you become a great Warlord or simply a great Warrior."

"So he would have answered it like you," Cyrus said with an air of amusement.

A smile split Alaric's lips. "Likely. He, too, is enigmatic."

"There was something else." Cyrus rested his hands at his sides, nervous energy causing him to flex them unconsciously. "There was a moment where the Gatekeeper stared at me, and he seemed to get disconcerted, and asked me who I was."

"Yes," Alaric nodded. "Vara described the incident to me in some detail. I would not let it concern you."

Cyrus's eyebrows recoiled. "The Hand of the Gods became lost for words in my presence, Alaric. According to Vara, he's never lost for words. And the only other person who can do that to him – and we're talking about someone touched by the gods, who stares down the toughest, meanest fighters in Arkaria – is you. What am I supposed to think about that?"

The Ghost turned from him to face the window, and placed his helm on his head before answering. "In the interest of bringing the full facts to the table, you were also able to block the mind control efforts of the Dragonlord – an impossible feat for most. You can assume whatever you'd like about these curiosities. I cannot give you an answer."

Cyrus felt his internal temperature change with a possibility he'd mulled over. "Am I the son of a god?"

Alaric turned back to him. "No. You are the son of a warrior that died in the Dismal Swamp campaign of the troll war."

"How did you know that?" Cyrus stared at him with an air of suspicion.

"Belkan served with your father," Alaric said, watching him through the slits in the helmet. "He knew your mother as well; well enough that we can rule out any godhood in your blood."

The Ghost smiled. "There is no denying you have powers that others do not. You are special - and not just because of whatever gift you have in your mind, but because of your abilities as a warrior, a thinker and a tactician. Temper them with wisdom, courage and mercy and you have the elements of the greatest warrior in Arkaria."

Cyrus let Alaric's words hang in the air. "I need to know about these abilities. I need to know how to control them."

Alaric stared at him from across the chamber. "I have no answers to give you." The paladin turned back to the window. "You should rejoin the party."

The words tasted bitter in Cyrus's mouth as he spat them back at Alaric. "You 'have no answers to give' me? Or none you're willing to give me?"

Alaric did not turn to face him, nor did he make any motion at all. "The result is the same."

Head spinning, Cyrus left the Council Chamber. *Is he lying to me? Holding something back?* Cyrus wondered as he descended the stairs. He found himself at the back of a crowd, standing in the foyer while the party raged on in the lounge, but his thoughts stayed dark, brooding.

"You don't look like you're having any fun at this celebration," came Vara's voice at his side. He turned to face her. She still wore her armor, although she had cleaned some of the dirt and blood from her face after the Council meeting.

"I'm not," he agreed. "I have a lot on my mind." A sudden shock ran through him. "You never told me you had a sister!"

She did not smile. "You never asked."

"You're right, I didn't. Any other questions I've forgotten to ask?"

"Many."

"So your sister is an officer of Endeavor?" he probed. "And you were an officer of Amarath's Raiders?"

"We might have been slightly competitive in my family."

"She seemed pleased to see you."

"Why would she not be, when I am such a pleasure to be around?" Vara's expression was straitlaced, with only a hint of irony. She pointed a finger at him. "Let me not hear a word of disagreement from you, General Davidon, lest you discover tonight a reason to be displeased at seeing me." The party hummed in the lounge, but even at a whisper, he could hear her perfectly in the foyer.

"General?" he laughed. "Feeling formal?"

She took another sip from the cup in her hand. "Actually, after that resurrection earlier and all its lovely side effects, I'm feeling rather tipsy. I can only conclude I should have eaten something before I had this. Or that perhaps I should go to bed."

Glazing over her statement, he thought to ask a question that he had pushed to the back of his mind. "If you were an officer of Amarath's Raiders, then you know that dark knight - Archenous Derregnault - that runs the guild?"

She stiffened and all trace of mirth was gone in an instant. "I do. Why do you ask?"

He thought about it for a moment and shrugged. "I don't know. I got this sudden, deep, inexplicable loathing for him. I have no idea where it came from; it's not as though he gave me cause."

Vara stared at him, mouth slightly agape. Without warning her hand reached up to his cheek and held it still while she kissed the other. A quick peck, and she turned and walked away, leaving him standing in the foyer with a stunned expression.

"What was that all about?" came Fortin's rumbling voice from the grating below.

At any other time, Cyrus might have snapped back at the rock giant. So stunned was he that he absentmindedly answered, "I don't know." He stared at Vara's receding back as she climbed the stairs.

Chapter 29

He did not see Vara the next day to ask her about what she had done, nor the day after that. When he asked about her, Curatio mentioned that she had gone home for a few days to Termina. They had stood in the Halls of Healing, Curatio cleaning while waiting for any patients that might appear. The strong smell of lye filled the air as the elf scrubbed every surface with it. Light shined in from broad windows on the beds, lined up in rows.

"Isn't she concerned that we're banished from the Elven Kingdom?" Cyrus asked.

The Healer dismissed him with a smile. "I doubt they'll arrest Vara."

"Because she's shelas'akur?" Cyrus asked.

Curatio looked at him shrewdly before answering. "Yes. But technically you would say 'the shelas'akur'."

"Care to explain what 'shelas'akur' means?"

"If you really thought about what you know of the elvish language," the Healer said, tugging a bedsheet into place, "you could probably figure out what at least part of it means."

Cyrus thought about it for a minute. "I don't know anything about the elvish language."

Curatio guffawed at that, a low laugh as he put a feathered pillow into a pillowcase. "You spent several weeks in the Kingdom last year; you learned nothing during that time?"

"Ha! I spent most of my time in the Kingdom on my back, recovering in Nalikh'akur –" He stopped. "Nalikh'akur. Shelas'akur." His eyes wheeled to the healer, who went about his work with a faint smile. "What does Nalikh'akur mean, Curatio?"

The healer looked up, and his faint smile turned knowing as his eyes filled with a calmness. "Last bastion."

"So what does 'shelas' mean?"

"Ah," the elf said with a wag of his finger. "That would be telling - and you know elves don't talk about that; it's not seemly to discuss it with offlanders. However, I have heard that in Reikonos, someone has gone to the trouble of putting together a dictionary that would translate from the human tongue to elvish, if someone were interested."

"As I cannot go to Reikonos right now under pain of death,

that doesn't help me," Cyrus said with a frown. "But thank you - you've come closer to explaining it than any other elf."

Curatio nodded, still smiling. "I've given you nothing but hints. From here, it's up to you."

"Thank you," he said with a genuineness that he felt to the heart. "I was beginning to think that the Sanctuary Council was filled exclusively with enigmas."

Curatio laughed. "I still have my secrets."

Vara had not appeared again for a week, during which Cyrus patrolled the Plains of Perdamun on horseback with groups of his guildmates. The only exception was one day that he took to travel to Fertiss, the dwarven capital, with the ore and components of his sword to have them forged by a blacksmith that Belkan knew.

"Not much to look at," the Sanctuary armorer said when Cyrus showed it to him. "But she'll likely do a sight better for you than that short sword." He held out his hand expectantly.

"I can't give you the short sword back yet," Cy argued. "Without the enchantments, the balance is wrong on this blade; it's too heavy for the amount of damage it renders."

"Mortus take you, Davidon!" Belkan said with a dismissive wave of the hand. "Fine, keep it a while longer, but I'll not hear any more bleating about how much you hate it!"

"I'll return it when I get the enchantments on the other one - unfortunately, I suspect it will be a while before I make it to the depths of Enterra to pay my respects -" his jaw tightened at the thought of killing the goblins responsible for Narstron's death - "and get the scabbard to enchant this blade." He turned to leave the armory but paused. "You never mentioned that you knew my parents."

Belkan grunted. "Your father and I served in the war together. Knew your mother because when we'd go back to Reikonos from the front she'd put up with the both of us carrying on 'til all hours of the night, so long as we didn't wake your sorry baby arse."

"You stayed in our house?" Cyrus looked at the armorer, face guarded.

"Many times," Belkan answered. "My home was near Prehorta, and I rarely had a long enough furlough to make my way down there and back. So your mother would tolerate me staying with you lot. I still owe her quite a debt for that - and other things." He looked down. "I was the one who told her when your father died. I brought back his armor to her." Belkan nodded at the black mail

Cyrus wore. "She went... mad with rage at the sight of it." His eyes looked haunted. "Never seen anything like it before... or since," he said with a shudder.

"I barely remember her," Cyrus said with a far-off look. "I don't have any memory of my father at all."

"Good folk," the armorer said. "Your father was the finest warrior in the Confederation army. Shouldn't have died at Dismal, but the trolls had a shaman leading their troops and he was fearsome. Your father took him on in single combat while he weaved his wicked spells." The armorer shuddered again.

"What's a shaman?" Cyrus asked with a frown.

"Troll magics," Belkan scoffed. "Spirit talkers, they are. Kind of like a healer, but with some foul twists. They use the powers of the dead."

"Like a necromancer," Cyrus whispered. "Like Malpravus."

"The shaman your father fought, he was powerful. Made your dad delirious, sick, but your dad near killed him anyway before he fell. Rest of us finished the job, but the shaman and his troops had killed ten thousand men at that point." He shook his head. "We never stood a chance in that battle."

"If this shaman was so dangerous," Cy said, "why didn't the Confederation general order a retreat?"

"Pretnam Urides order a retreat?" Belkan snorted. Cy bristled at the mention of the Reikonos Councilor's name. "That glory hound would never! But it wouldn't matter if he had: your father was on the other side of the battle. When word got to us of a troll shaman killing men by the hundred, Rusyl charged headlong toward it. Couldn't have stopped him if we'd all had a hold on him." Belkan stared at Cyrus. "He was stronger than any ten men. One of the few that could stand toe-to-toe with a troll and come out ahead. Rest o' us attacked in groups."

"You said you brought my father's armor back to Reikonos," Cyrus said. "What about his body?"

Belkan looked down. "What that shaman did to him, with his plagues and horror, wasn't a fit end for anyone. I couldn't have Eri – your mother – see him like that. We buried him on a hummock near the battlefield. I marked it with a stone." He shuffled behind his counter. "If you'd like, someday, once this damned banishment ends, I'll get my daughter to teleport us out there. It's a few days' ride from an elven town on the edge of the swamps."

"Your daughter?" Cyrus looked at him in confusion.

"Larana."

"Ah." *How did I not know that?* "I'd like that," Cyrus agreed. "Thank you... for telling me." He left the armorer, who did not seem upset at an end to the inquiries.

Late one night, after returning Windrider, his favored horse, to the stables after a long patrol of the plains, Cyrus entered the foyer to find Andren waiting with an ale in hand. "She's back," he muttered nonchalantly.

"What?" Cyrus said with a start. "Where?"

"Where she always is when she's among us unwashed masses," he said with a subtle nod toward the lounge.

Cy's eyes followed Andren's nod to where Vara sat in the far corner of the lounge, without her armor, staring out one of the windows with a book in her lap, unopened. He crossed the ground between them and stood behind her.

"Cyrus," she said, staring at his reflection in the window.

"Hello," he said. "How are you?"

"I'm well." When she turned to him, the look on her face did not match her words. "Yourself?"

"Just got back from a long patrol."

She studied him. "I trust I haven't missed anything terribly important, such as us catching the raiders?"

"No." He stared out the window. "We found the remains of more convoys in the last week, but still no sign of our mysterious bandits."

"I spoke with Alaric. He's asked me to lead patrols as well, beginning tomorrow morning, early."

"I'm leading one then as well," Cyrus replied with a glimmer of hope. "I'm heading north. You?"

"Southwest. Toward Aloakna." Her voice remained neutral and her eyes met his but revealed nothing. "I should turn in. Thank you for breaking my reverie; there's no telling how long I might have been staring pointlessly out that window if you hadn't interrupted."

"You're welcome, I think," he said, unsure of what else to say.

"Goodnight," she said, picking up her book and crossing various rugs that dotted the stone floor as she moved toward the foyer.

"Goodnight," he echoed, voice a whisper.

For the next weeks, frustration grew heavy in the halls of Sanctuary. Cyrus spent upwards of sixteen hours per day on horseback, riding around the southern plains, searching for any sign of the raiders. On the rare occasions he did see Vara, it was in passing in the stables as she was either leading a patrol out or coming in. She greeted him cordially on all occasions but they never had a chance to speak.

The weeks of banishment turned into months, as the winter winds swept down the Plains of Perdamun. Far too temperate for snows, the plains received a liberal dousing of cold rains that settled over the open lands for days at a time. Almost four months since the day of banishment Cyrus found himself on a patrol in the early spring evening with Terian at his side. The grounds were still wet from heavy rain and the horses hooves could scarcely be heard as they journeyed through the quiet night.

"The rain may work to our advantage," Cyrus said to the dark knight. "Our foes are more likely to leave obvious tracks, they're less likely to hear us approach - perhaps we'll finally get lucky."

"That's the difference between you and me, Davidon: I get lucky all the time. Speaking of which," Terian said with a grin, "what is going on between you and Vara? Every time you pass in the stables..."

"Nothing," Cyrus replied. "She gave me a kiss on the cheek then disappeared for a week and since then we haven't had a conversation that's lasted over two minutes."

"How long do you really need? Anything worth doing can be done in less than two minutes."

Cyrus pulled back on the reins. "I've heard that's your philosophy in many areas."

"Ha ha," Terian replied without mirth. "In all seriousness, why don't you be as direct in speaking with her as you are with your sword in battle?"

"I don't know," Cyrus said. "By the way, I've been meaning to ask you since we got back from Purgatory - what did you do after you left Sanctuary last year?"

"I told you," Terian said, tension in his voice rising. "I wandered the lands."

"If you don't want to talk about it -" Cy began.

"I don't."

"All right," Cy agreed without argument. "But if you ever need to talk about it -"

"Please don't say anything else," Terian said with a bowed head. "You're making me feel like we're about to bond, and I'm a dark knight, which means I'm supposed to project an aura of danger. Bonding really interferes with that."

"I see." Cyrus thought about the knight's words. "You probably shouldn't wisecrack so much; it undermines that 'danger' aura you're supposed to be projecting."

"Davidon," Terian said with an air of annoyance, "there are some sacrifices I'm not willing to make in my career as a dark knight, and giving up being a loudmouth smartass is one of them."

"What about –" Cyrus was interrupted by Terian holding up a hand. The dark elf pointed to his ear, concentrating, and without warning spurred his horse into a ninety degree turn. Holding up his hand in a signal to the hunting party following them, Cy took off after the dark knight with the rest of his group close behind.

In the clouded night he could barely see Terian as the dark elf cut across the long grasses of the plains at high speed, galloping into the night. Ahead, Cyrus could hear the smallest noise above the beating of hooves, a noise that grew louder the longer they rode.

Screams. Of pain and terror.

Terian pulled the reins of his horse, too quickly for Cyrus to stop. He charged past the dark knight and burst onto a dirt road. Scattered wagons littered the ground around them and one last scream cut off as Cyrus jumped from his horse. Figures moved through the wreckage of the caravan. Too dark for his human eyes to discern features, Cyrus chased the nearest with a sword as it darted around the edge of a wrecked wagon.

Cyrus turned the corner and swung his sword, making unmistakable contact with the figure's upper arm as it slid away behind the wagon and into a group of the raiders, all too dark for Cyrus to see. A grunt from the figure he had been chasing told him his attack was more than a grazing blow. He raised the sword again, prepared to leap forward when something hit him in the side, knocking him into the wagon he had just rounded.

Cyrus reached out in the direction of his attacker and grabbed hold of them in his gauntlet at he fell. He dragged his assailant down with him as a flash of light exploded in the air around them – a blue glow that lit the wagons and cast the face of his attacker in stark colors. His jaw dropped as the angular lines and pointed ears gave way to the sharp teeth. Yellow eyes stared back at him.

An orb of teleportation shot in front of him and a clawed hand reached up and grabbed it before he could react. His assailant disappeared in the flash of the wizard's spell, leaving Cyrus flat on his back in the middle of the wrecked convoy, shocked into silence.

How? How is this possible?

Terian rounded the wagon, followed by Martaina and Thad, weapons drawn. "Did they get away?" When Cyrus did not move or respond, the dark knight dropped to a knee and pulled him to a sitting position. "Where did they go? Did you see them?"

"Yes," Cyrus whispered. "Yes, they got away - and yes, I did see them."

"My gods, man, don't keep us waiting - who the hell was it?"

"It was... a goblin. There was a raiding party... of goblins... in the Plains of Perdamun."

Chapter 30

"I am telling you," Cyrus said in a defiant tone that filled the Council Chambers, "it was a goblin. A gods-damned goblin!"

"It's not that we don't believe you," Terian said with an air of quiet skepticism. "It's that you've been having nightmares about goblins for months, your best friend got killed by them and you've been riding a horse sixteen hours a day, every day, for months with no break and lots of time to think. If I were you," the dark elf said with an unmistakable - and uncharacteristic - air of sympathy, "I'd likely have seen a goblin too. But it was awfully dark out there. No moon, no starlight because of the clouds..."

"I saw it when the wizard cast the teleportation spell! An orb of teleportation parked itself in my face, between mine and his, and he was this close to me!" Cyrus moved his open palm to a position just inches from his nose. "I don't care if it was a goblin, a dark elf, a troll or Pretnam Urides, at that distance and with the light of a teleportation orb, I know what I saw, and it was a goblin!"

Alaric sat at the end of the table, fingers steepled. "We were unable to resurrect any of the victims of the attack?"

"No," Terian said with a shake of the head. "We're so light on healers, we didn't have one with us. Curatio was south with Vara's group, Andren was with Niamh's group and Vaste was..." He turned to the troll.

"Vaste was tired," came the reply from the green-skinned healer. "I had just gotten back from riding for 36 hours straight, and when you've got my frame –" the troll's hands rested on his ample belly – "you eventually have to eat something."

"They've started doing something new," Cyrus said, voice hushed. "In the last few convoys we've found, they've dismembered the bodies to prevent resurrection."

"Yuck," Niamh opined.

"How?" J'anda leaned forward with grim interest.

"Decapitation," Terian replied. "The raiders are keeping the heads."

"Yuck more," Niamh said, face skewed with a look of disgust.

"What now?" Vara sat back in her chair, eyes on the Ghost.

Alaric stared at his gauntlets. "I, for one, believe that Cyrus may well have seen a goblin. Unfortunately, without a body, we have no evidence. Reikonos and the other powers will have difficulty believing that goblins are responsible for these assaults, especially since Enterra is far from here and goblins traditionally keep to their cloister."

The Ghost shook his head sadly. "If we were near the Confederation's Riverlands or the Gnomish Dominions, it would be no difficulty believing that these attacks are goblin-related. Since we are many months of travel on foot from Enterra and goblins have no magic users for teleport..."

"They're as likely to believe us as if we said the Goddess of Knowledge came back from the dead and did it," Cy finished bitterly. "But they are using teleportation spells. And we have a goblin wizard in our own ranks."

"Indeed," Alaric said, hand moving to his mouth in pensiveness. "We should send for Mendicant to ask some questions about goblin involvement in this."

"I'll fetch him," Niamh said, pushing back from the table. Alaric nodded and she slid through the door.

"So you believe me?" Cyrus asked Alaric.

"I am open to the possibility," the Ghost said. "However, there are many questions to be answered, and we must have evidence if we are to clear our name. This is, of course," he continued, mouth curling downward in displeasure, "in addition to the other unpleasant duties in front of us."

Cyrus looked at the Ghost in mild confusion and turned to find Terian and Vara sharing his look. Curatio's eyebrow was raised.

"While you were gone," J'anda answered for Alaric, "one of our members asked to address the entire guild tonight at dinner in regards to our current crisis."

"Who was it and what about?" Curatio stared straight ahead.

"One of the applicants that joined us after Ashan'agar," J'anda said. "Ryin Ayend – a druid if I'm not mistaken. Human."

"I know of him," Curatio said. "He's a good druid."

"Perhaps one of us should have a conversation with him?" Vaste suggested. "To get a feel for his topic?"

Alaric shook his head at the end of the table. "We have never inhibited our members from speaking their minds, even when the consequences are not pleasant."

"What do you think he's going to say, Alaric?" Terian stared at the Ghost.

"I suspect that he will discuss the proposal to merge with the other Alliance guilds – the one we have shelved for the last four months." Alaric's gauntlet clanked as he made a fist. "I think he will bring up the topic of paying our way back into several of the cities now that we have the means to do so, and he will make mention of the fact that three hostile armies still circle our location, able to strike at any moment. I suspect, in short, the worst, and will be pleased by any result less than that."

"It's nice to see you've set your expectations at a manageable level," Vaste said with a nod. "We don't have to stifle him – but wouldn't it be nice if we had an officer talk to him first to see if these are his intentions?"

"I will not stop any of you from doing so," Alaric replied, head bowed as he studied his gauntlet. "But I reiterate that I do not want his right to speak to be squelched in any way."

The door opened as Niamh returned with Mendicant. She escorted the goblin to an empty seat next to J'anda at the round table and took her seat. Alaric wasted no time. "Mendicant, during last night's patrol Cyrus became entangled with one of the raiders and before it vanished using a wizard's orb of teleportation, he claims to have seen a goblin."

Mendicant receded in his seat. "It wasn't me. I was with Vara's patrol at the time!"

Alaric exchanged a look with Vara, who nodded. "That wasn't the reason we called you here, but thank you for vouching for your whereabouts. Our question pertained to the idea that goblins would be involved in attacks here in the plains."

"Oh." Mendicant's eyes glassed over for a moment and his lips began to twitch. "Spellcasters among goblins are not tolerated nor trained in the Imperium because of the royalty's love of strength above all." He receded further into his chair, a gesture Cyrus thought odd until he realized it indicated embarrassment. "I am the only goblin wizard that I know of. And the idea that the royalty would send an expedition this far from Enterra, well..." He hesitated. "...it doesn't make a great deal of sense."

"I saw a goblin. I would swear it right now even if you demanded my life were I wrong," Cyrus said with total conviction.

"It could be an outcast, like me," Mendicant suggested.

"I saw the outline of several of the others; they were the size of goblins as well," Cyrus said, shaking his head.

"It would be rare to see more than one or two goblin outcasts at a time," Mendicant said with deference to Cyrus. "Coupled with the idea of a goblin wizard it becomes... impossible." He looked around the table at the officers. "Goblins pull off secret attacks of this type, even down to the complete lack of evidence regarding the attackers afterward - but they are limited to human and gnome convoys and villages that sprinkle the areas around Enterra. This is far from the empire, several months journey for an armed force of goblin warriors," Mendicant finished. He bowed his head to Cyrus in a gesture of supplication.

"You need not fear my wrath for disagreeing," Cyrus said to the goblin. "You know your people and the points you make are well taken. But I say nonetheless, there was at least one goblin with the raiding party last night and likely more."

"Could they have been dwarves?" Mendicant asked. "Dwarves have captured some of our number and could be using a goblin to advise them on attacking with stealth."

"You think one of your warriors would betray their people and work with the dwarves?" Alaric looked down the table.

"Unlikely," the goblin said, bowing his head. "But the Dwarven Alliance is far to the north of us, and not nearly the enemy that the Gnomish Dominion is. If the Imperials of Enterra were of a mind to raid convoys, they could find them much closer to home and I see no means for them to acquire a wizard without outside involvement," Mendicant said with a note of regret, unable to look at Cyrus.

The goblins continued to stare at his lap. "As we have no alliances or ties to the outside world, that seems unlikely. If there was a goblin involved in this attack, I would guess it to be a rogue rather than an effort sponsored by the Empire." He bowed his head. "I am sorry, Lord Davidon."

"You don't have to apologize, Mendicant," Cyrus said softly. "You speak the truth. But I know the truth of my eyes and though it defies explanation, I know that I saw a goblin."

"We come back to a search for evidence," Alaric sighed. "We are no closer to proving our innocence, even if we had seen a hundred goblins slaying every convoy from here to Prehorta. No," he said with great finality, "we will continue on our present course until we find evidence - not only testimony -" he held up a hand to Cyrus - "but something firm that we can take before the Council of Twelve and the King of the Elves."

"And the Sovereign of Saekaj?" Niamh suggested.

"That will not turn out favorably, regardless of evidence," Alaric replied. "Let us go - and if you intend to have a *peaceful* discussion with this Ryin Ayend, now would be the time," he said with a gesture toward Vaste.

They broke, Mendicant scurrying to the door and holding it open for all of them. "Mendicant," Alaric said gently, "there is no need, brother. We are here to serve you, not vice versa. Thank you for your time today."

"Oh," said the goblin with an embarrassed nod. He did not relinquish the door, but bowed. "Thank you, Lord Garaunt. Lords, Ladies," he said, bowing to each of them in turn.

Alaric sighed as the goblin left. Cyrus had made it out of the chamber without a word from Alaric when he felt a heavy hand land on his shoulder. He turned to see Vaste staring down at him. "Let's go," the troll said with a jerk of his head toward the stairs.

"Go where?"

"To Reikonos. I've had my eye on this exquisite pair of leather boots, and I saw a cuirass last week that would look just *fabulous* on you!" The troll rolled his eyes. "To talk to Ryin Ayend - where else?"

"Oh," Cyrus said in surprise. "I thought maybe you were serious about the Reikonos thing for a second."

"I don't fancy the thought of fighting my way through a wave of guards right now, thank you, and certainly not so that you can solve your fashion woes."

Cyrus frowned. "I do not have 'fashion woes'."

"Please," Vaste said with an aura of impatience. "You wear black all day, every day. I'm not the most in-tune with style, but even I know the monochromatic look is not in vogue."

Cyrus looked down at his black armor with a tinge of self-consciousness. "Why do you need me to come along to talk to this Ryin?"

"Because I need someone less intimidating than I am."

"Shouldn't you ask one of the women? Like Vara?" His frown deepened as Vaste laughed. "Maybe Niamh. I meant Niamh."

"Let's go."

They descended the stairs and found Ryin Ayend in the lounge, surrounded by five of the newer members Cyrus recalled from the recruiting trip that had carried him across a good portion of Arkaria. There were three humans, a dwarf and a dark elf sitting around the druid. Vaste caught the attention of Ryin. "We'd like a word," the troll told him.

"All right," the human said with a nod.

"You want us to come with you, Ryin?" the dwarf sitting across from him watched Cy and Vaste. "In case they try something?" The dwarf's chest puffed out, an indignant look on his face. Some of Ryin's other associates sat forward, hands lingering near their weapons, or in the case of spell casters, hanging free.

"We're guildmates, toerag," Cyrus said to the dwarf with a welling sense of rage. He looked at the others. "What exactly do you think we're planning to do? Rough him up? Kill him? Say unkind things about his mother?"

The dwarf deflated. "You can never be too careful," he murmured, his hand moving away from his weapon and creeping nonchalantly to his shoulder, where it sat as he pretended to scratch himself.

"Can we have a word in private?" Vaste emphasized, staring down at Ryin.

"Anything you have to say to me can be said in front of my friends," Ryin replied, looking up at Vaste with the frostiest eyes Cyrus had ever seen.

"Fine," Vaste said. "We want to know why you want to address the guild tonight."

"I need to speak," Ryin began. "There are issues that need to be addressed in Sanctuary. Things are broken."

"We're a guild that's been operating for twenty years without difficulty. You're here for six months and you think we need fixing?" Vaste's face turned a dark green shade, darker than the leaves of the trees. "Thank the gods you came along to fix us, then."

"You cannot look at the situation Sanctuary is in and claim that all is well," the druid replied, voice raised.

"Fine, fine," Vaste said, taking his voice down a notch. "What... things... are not working in Sanctuary in your... opinion?" The last word came out as a sort of muttered curse.

"Let us not even address the fact that spell casters get treated worse in this guild than in any other guild I've been in –" Ryin began.

"It must be tough, being treated equally with the meatheads that use swords and maces," Vaste interrupted, words dripping with sarcasm.

"Every other guild accords certain privileges upon those who are blessed with the gift of spell casting, in acknowledgment of their value - preferred looting rights, gold bonuses -" Ryin ticked them off on his fingers, one by one.

"I recognize that spell casters are rarer than those of us who fight with weapons -" Cyrus began.

"In a normal guild, 1 in 10 of their members would be a spell caster," the druid said, voice heated. "Here, it's easily 1 in 20."

"And out there in the non-guild world, it's 1 in 1000," Vaste said, sounding bored. "You want more money and preferential treatment because you can wave your fingers and make the trees dance?"

"The spell caster Leagues - the Circle of Thorns, the Commonwealth of Arcanists, the Healer's Union and all the rest - are a 5,000 year old tradition," Ryin said with a glimmer of pride. "The Society of Arms and Wanderers' Brotherhood didn't even emerge until 2,000 years ago, and only then because warriors and rangers wanted to elevate themselves to the same level of importance that spell casters enjoy! They don't even have to learn from those Leagues; they can be taught outside them, such is the lack of sophistication for their teachings!"

"So you want to be treated better than your guildmates because people who lived before you established fancy clubs that taught you everything you know?" Vaste nodded, expressionless. "Makes sense. You've certainly *earned* favorable treatment, based on that argument."

The druid reddened. "That wasn't even my original point. You interrupted me before I could make it, sidelining us into this discussion."

"Oh, I'm sorry," Vaste replied, voice dripping with a mock-apologetic tone. "Please, let us discuss something outside your raging elitism. What did you intend to talk about tonight - other than how you're brutally mistreated and forced to stay in a dungeon room while the warriors have wine and dance and song every night, and women delivered to their palatial quarters by the dozen?" He turned to Cyrus. "How was the wine and dance and song last night?"

"Not as good as the dozen women."

"This is going nowhere," Ryin stood, face red.

"Why don't you just make your point?" Vaste bent down to look the druid in the eyes.

"Fine," Ryin spat. "We're banished from our homelands, and we have a way to solve that problem. The leaders in our Council have refused. We have hostile armies circling us like vultures around a dying soul, waiting for gods know what to attack and destroy us. We have patrols that have operated for months without ceasing, trying to prove our innocence in a futile search –"

"It occurs to me," Vaste said with a low rumble, "that these patrols are voluntary, and I haven't seen you on one."

"It would be easy for you to think me a whining coward," Ryin Ayend said, glaring at the troll with a fire in his own eyes. "But I have been on patrols every day for the last four months and will continue to do so until they are called off. If you don't believe I am, ask Niamh; I ride with her every day."

All eyes in the lounge now turned to the argument going on in their midst. "We have a way out. We could either pay the fine ourselves and work to redeem our own name, or we could merge with the Alliance and let Goliath pay the fine and use the merger as an opportunity to bury the disgraced Sanctuary name and start anew." Ryin must have sensed Cyrus and Vaste bristle at the pairing of 'Sanctuary' and 'disgraced' because he held up his hands in a gesture of surrender and waited before speaking again.

"I am not admitting guilt," Ryin said, determination filling his eyes. "I know we have had nothing to do with these attacks. But that doesn't change the perception of the rest of the civilized world that we are responsible. And our own guildmates –" he pointed at the three humans sitting with him – "can't even go home right now because of events that are within our ability to control!"

His voice became impassioned. "Every day we delay costs our guildmates beyond measure. Jesha." He pointed to one of the humans, a glum looking young woman. "Her father is on his deathbed in Reikonos, and she cannot go to him because of this banishment." He pointed to another human, a scared-looking boy who was barely old enough to be in Sanctuary. "Corin has not seen his parents in six months, the longest he has ever gone without renewing these family ties. And Yeral –" his finger swiveled to the dark elf in his group – "his wife is in Saekaj and he cannot go to her and see his newborn son."

Cyrus spoke up. "I feel for their plight – every one of them. But you are wrong. To pay our way out of this would be to admit guilt for something we had no part in. There is no disgrace on the

Sanctuary name right now but that which we would bring by cowering before the bullying powers of the west, and paying them a toll like you would pay a bandit on a bridge to avoid a fight."

"That is pride!" Ryin said, pointing at Cyrus. "That is akin to the highborn who watches a lowborn get pummeled by thieves but won't involve himself because he's afraid his robes might get dirty!"

"Strange metaphor for an elitist to use," Vaste commented.

"I feel the pain of those you call brothers and sisters," Ryin said with a sneer, ignoring Vaste's jibe. "I sit down here every night while you sit in your high-and-mighty 'honorable' Council and hear none of the heartache and separation and loss that your guildmates feel."

The druid composed himself, wiping the emotion from his face. "Change is coming. The moment will soon arrive when you in the Council will be forced to accede to our wishes - to take the actions necessary to remove this banishment - or we will find new leaders. Either from within Sanctuary, or from without."

Ryin Ayend returned to his seat. A smattering of applause filled the lounge, and grew louder as Cyrus and Vaste left and entered the foyer. Cyrus looked back to see a swarm of guildmates huddled around Ryin, who was talking to them while casting a look over his shoulder at the retreating officers.

"That went well," Vaste said as they entered the stairwell.

Cyrus grunted. "I don't think he liked your attitude."

"I have no time for anyone who claims to represent the people and then tries to rally for additional rights and privileges to be bestowed on a group that includes them." Vaste stopped, bringing Cyrus to a halt a few steps above him. "That sort of elitist thinking may start soft, but it ends with one group thinking they're better than the other."

Cyrus shrugged. "I don't know. It sounds innocent enough to me. If other guilds treat spell casters better because they're rare, it makes them a valuable commodity."

"There are two problems with that thinking," Vaste argued. "First, if they're better than us, what does that allow? Because for someone who buys into that 'superiority' thinking and takes it to an extreme, it becomes perfectly acceptable to kill an inferior - because they looked at me funny, because they got in the way of what I needed, or because they opposed me and my 'superior' thinking. You marginalize them, write off their opinions as stupid and worthless, and say the same about them as people. Or the other problem," the troll said with an odd expression, "is that you begin to treat people like a commodity."

Cyrus stood back, looking at the troll with mild surprise. "You feel strongly about this."

Vaste nodded. "I saw the same stupid thinking in my people the last time I was there. It nearly got me killed."

"How?"

"You know how the last war played out, right?"

Cyrus nodded. "We studied the basics at the Society of Arms. The trolls started a war of conquest, invaded the Elven Kingdom, then they crossed the river Perda and began raiding human territories, which united the humans into the Confederation, who joined the elves against them and the trolls got well and truly shellacked."

"I'm not surprised the Society of Arms teaches a different version than I learned growing up," Vaste said with a healthy dose of irony. "However it started, yes, the trolls began invading other territories, enslaving people and all that. They were doing well as I understand it. Until just after the Dismal Swamp Campaign."

"I'm somewhat familiar with that one."

"Quite right," Vaste acknowledged. "Just remember, my father died there too. Anyway, your people were losing. Dismal Swamp was a rout; the elves and the humans were running scared, retreating on all fronts until your dear father killed our most powerful shaman. Even still, the troll armies could have marched all the way to Saekaj and not met any resistance until they came up against the dark elf army. The human and elven forces were broken by that battle."

"Fine." Cyrus nodded. "I've heard it differently, but what you say may be true. So what happened after Dismal Swamp?"

"The Sorceress Quinneria, more powerful than any other, raised an army of magic users from the guilds, paired them with the tattered remains of your human and elven armies, and proceeded to kill almost a million troll warriors in a series of twelve pitched battles that annihilated most of our fighting force." Vaste smiled. "Not that I'm sorry you won, because living under troll rule is not pleasant."

"This relates to superiority how?"

"After their defeat, attributed to Quinneria's unfair use of magics versus their infinitely more powerful warriors –" Vaste beat on his chest with exaggerated emphasis – "the trolls turned against all magic users, wiping out or exiling our few surviving shamans, claiming spell casters as cowardly and inferior – that they have to resort to nasty trickery because they are weak. Any magic user in our homeland is marked for death."

"The scarring on your face, from your last visit to your homeland, when you were recruiting for us..."

"Yes," Vaste said with a nod. "Not only did I represent a foreign influence, something that's not popular, but while on the streets I watched two children playing our version of a kid's game – fighting – and one accidentally killed the other. I resurrected and healed him and was soundly pummeled for it by a mob that included the child I'd just saved."

His expression hardened. "They feel they're superior in some way to spell casters. I don't care if it comes from some true, deep-seated feeling of inferiority; it doesn't matter. I've seen what that sort of thinking can do, and I despise it."

"So you mocked and berated a druid who was expressing the mildest form of that elitism?"

Vaste shrugged. "Mighty trees start as seeds. Same thing with elitism."

"We need to warn Alaric," Cyrus said. "So we can prepare a response to what Ryin's going to say."

"I've already got a response to Ryin." Vaste climbed the stairs, passing Cyrus as he watched, waiting to hear what the troll was going to say. A string of profanities reached the warrior's ears, ending with a a suggestion that was anatomically impossible for a human.

"Well, that will certainly salve the situation," Cyrus muttered to himself.

Chapter 31

Dinner that night was a grim affair at the officers' table. The rest of the Great Hall was filled with hushed anticipation, eager voices cutting through the heavy atmosphere that had surrounded every meal for weeks. Cyrus looked around, realizing that as the banishment had dragged on, the Great Hall had become less and less festive with each passing day. Meals were eaten in near-silence; but the impending speech by Ryin had spurred the first sign of life in weeks.

"Are you ready to respond to his bullshit?" Vaste said, leaning toward Alaric, who sat in silence, not eating.

"I am prepared to address the concerns of our brother and guildmate," Alaric said with a note of rebuke. "Can any of you say that you have not had the same doubts about this course of action?"

Vara bristled. "I don't think any of us at this table have ever considered a merger with Goliath as anything other than lunacy."

"Other than that, can any of you say his concerns are not valid?" Alaric surveyed the gathered officers. "That you would not be willing to pay any price to go home again?" He steepled his fingers as he leaned back in his seat. "Were it not such a black stain upon our honor, I would have paid the damned gold already." He shook his head. "I think it is time."

Alaric stood and conversation in the hall abated. "My brothers and sisters, this evening one of our guildmates would like a chance to address us about matters of great concern..."

Cyrus did not wait to hear the rest of the introduction. He stood as Alaric complimented Ryin as a thoughtful, concerned member of Sanctuary. Cyrus passed between tables and heard the scattered applause fill the hall as Ryin stood. He did not look back.

He exited the Great Hall, intent on heading up the stairs to his quarters but stopped at the doors from surprise. Standing in the middle of the room, enormous pile of boxes and bags around her, was Erith. Perplexed, he crossed the distance between them. "What in the hells is all this?" he asked without preamble.

She looked at him crossly. "It's my luggage. Where do I put it?"

Cyrus was nonplussed. "Outside, where it came from, I would

suggest. Perhaps the stables if you must."

"Ha ha," she said, not laughing. "Seriously, where do I go?"

"I'd pick a spot on the map," Cyrus quipped, "that is uniquely *you,* that encapsulates your personality and the feeling you bring people. I'd say the Great Dismal Swamp. What do you think?" She glared at him. "Realm of Death? Darkness? Realm of Evil?"

"No one even knows if there even is a Realm of Evil," she scoffed. "And you should be nicer to me; it's not every day you have a first-rate Healer apply to join your guild, especially in these times."

"Excellent," he said with glee. "And where is the first-rate healer of whom you speak? I would be most eager to meet him or her."

"Would you like me to leave and apply to Goliath, smart ass?" Her glare increased in potency.

"No, no. I'm sorry for teasing you."

"No you're not. Don't apologize if you don't mean it."

He thought about it for a moment. "You're right: I'm not sorry; I so enjoy mocking and derision."

"I do too, which is the only reason you're forgiven." She smiled.

"Give me a minute," Cyrus said, turning to look back into the Great Hall, hearing cheers for Ryin as the druid finished speaking. From the brief snatches that Cyrus had heard, it had all the markings of an impassioned plea similar to what he'd heard from the druid in the lounge. "I'll show you to the applicant quarters."

"You know," she said, puffing up, "most guilds, even those not currently under embargo and banishment everywhere in the known world," she emphasized the last part, "would be ecstatic to have a new healer - especially a princess that is truly a joy to be around. They might go out of their way to kiss her ass a little. You know - even more than they normally do for spell casters."

Cyrus shook his head, not even deigning to look back at her as he stared into the Great Hall. "Everyone's treated equally here, princess."

She deflated. "So I don't get my own suite?"

The applause filling the Great Hall was loud; maybe louder than anything Cyrus had heard since the Purgatory victory. He watched Alaric take his feet to respond. The sun sank below one of the windows to the side of the foyer and the light in the room dimmed as the sun's rays faded. Torches began to light of their own accord around them.

"That's amazing!" Erith said, staring at the walls. "How do they do that?" Her voice carried an awe that Cyrus couldn't help but chuckle at.

"Magic." He strained to listen as the Ghost began to speak.

"You're an ass."

"Come with me," he said, walking back toward the Great Hall. He entered the room, sliding along the back wall with Erith behind him as Alaric spoke. He watched the Ghost, helmet on the table behind him, eye focused ahead as he seemingly prepared himself for what needed to be said.

"I hear the words that Ryin Ayend speaks, and I cannot deny their truth. These are troubling times, and anyone with family in the lands from which we are banished would be heartless if they did not long to see their own kin." His hands met in front of him, clutching onto each other, fingers intertwining. "I feel the pain inflicted on every one of you, and it troubles me.

"These last twenty years we have seen peace in these lands. A lack of war and strong economies among the powers meant prosperity for the peoples of Arkaria, and that has flowed to the southern plains. In recent years I have seen this area grow in population and watched as its people have built lives from what was empty ground.

"But the world changes on us," Alaric continued. "We have seen turmoil brought to the southern plains. We have seen traders and soldiers lose their lives without cause or provocation and we have seen the powers of western Arkaria align against a most unfortunate enemy – us.

"They would force us into a corner because they have no strength here and because they – three armies between them! – have failed to stop the raiders." Alaric looked around the room, moving from person to person, reaching their eyes, looking into their souls. "Three governments, three armies, one supposed purpose – to find the guilty souls responsible for these attacks – and they have found not one shred of evidence to link anyone to them – let alone us, the ones they have blamed."

His hands broke apart. "They have exiled us from our homelands, separated many of us from loved ones and demanded – without reason or provocation – that we make restitution. As though draining our treasury and insulting us were not enough, they would consider our payment to be admission to a crime we have yet to be proven guilty of! They stain our honor with these accusations, smearing our name to the world."

He pointed to Ryin. "His words ring true. All we need do to end this pain and anguish, at least for now, is to bow to the governments that have scorned us, kiss their hands, swear allegiance once more, and promise that should they ring a bell in the future, we will come running to fight in whatever pointless conflict they intend to start on that day."

Alaric's brow creased, his countenance turned stormy. "I would not have it so. I did not start Sanctuary with the intention of turning us into a mercenary band, doing the bidding of whatever master offered us the greatest reward. We are our own masters! The name Sanctuary is meant to stand for something greater than the nations around us! Something greater than the other guilds, greater than our Alliance!

"We stood against the Dragonlord, racing to defeat him when no others understood the threat. We stand now at a crossroads, where the armies of the three greatest powers in Arkaria play games around us, charging ever closer to each other - and war."

"Pay them then!" Ryin's voice cut through Alaric's, interrupting him as the druid took his feet. "Pay them and they would go away, and this war you speak of could be averted before it begins!"

Alaric smiled. "It is not that simple. Convoys brought their armies here. Conquest will keep them here. Foolish men have their eyes set on expanding their empires and this is the first step. Pay them all they demand and more, there will still be war, whether it begins here or elsewhere. And you will have the stain of blood on your hands as well as the stain of treachery forever upon your honor. Our integrity stands upon what we do, what we say and who we are. If we pay their blood price, we admit we are thieves, and we consign our names to the shame of being the bandits who start this conflict."

"Even with all this in the balance," Ryin said, looking at the Ghost with a sort of numb shock, "you will still not consider paying them? You could end this!" the druid shouted, a betrayed look on his face. "Your stubbornness and refusal to yield will leave us with nothing!"

Alaric stared him down. "Except our honor. Every one of you must decide if looking your families in the eye now is worth never being able to look another soul in the eye ever again without being associated with a guild of admitted thieves and bandits." He straightened. "There is no course for me but to clear our names - and then you can see your families with your heads held high, knowing that when things were at their worse you did not yield to the lies that others might tell and believe about you."

"And how long should we continue to be pariahs, Alaric?" Ryin's face was laced with bitterness. "What if we never find the raiders? How long are you willing to stand out here in the cold, with everyone arrayed against us? How long do you expect they'll let us sit here, with their armies growing every day? They'll come for us, come to slaughter us - and then it won't matter if we know the truth of our honor and goodness, because no one will be alive to tell it!"

"Very well." Alaric bowed his head. "There is a motion before the Council now, as you are all aware. It is for a merger with the Alliance guilds. It will be before you - the members - to decide whether to accept it or not." He held up a hand with two fingers aloft. "In two months, you will have the right afforded every member of Sanctuary, to guide the direction of our guild. It will be your choice, not the Council's, that will determine how we proceed."

"Why not now?" came a voice from the crowd, not far from Ryin. "We want to go home now!" A chorus of agreement rang across the hall.

Ryin looked across the crowd at Alaric. "No. Two more months is acceptable," he said to the crowd surrounding him. "We may not be able to wait forever to see our families, but two months would be worth it and more - if we could prove ourselves innocent."

Ryin looked down at the human next to him, whose name Cyrus remembered to be Jesha. "I am sorry, but he is right. And for two months..." Ryin's eyes fell to the floor. "I am sorry, Jesha." Cyrus could hear her sobbing from the back of the room.

"Very well," Alaric said from his place by the officer's table. "The next two months will decide the fate of our guild. Patrols will double. Officers... we are in Council in five minutes."

"I just leave an Alliance guild that's kowtowing to Goliath and I walk into another one," grumbled Erith from beside him. "You damned sure better find these bandits."

"Maybe with your help, princess." He dodged past her and out the door, beating the crowd. He caught Andren's eye as the Healer left the Great Hall.

"I would not want to be an officer right now," Andren said.

"I'm not worried about it."

"Why's that?"

"Because in a couple of months, Malpravus could be leading us, and then my only trouble would be trying to find a new guild to join," Cyrus fired back, ignoring the flinch from Andren. "I need you to show Erith to the applicants' quarters. I have to get to a meeting." The healer nodded and Cyrus left them, following Alaric into the stairway as the Ghost passed.

"All or nothing, Alaric?" Cyrus grimaced. "I don't like it. I'd rather they elected a new Council from within Sanctuary and used our funds to pay the fines. At least then Goliath wouldn't own us."

"Goliath would own us, regardless," the Ghost replied, taking the stairs more quickly than Cyrus. "Malpravus has many spies in our ranks; he would ensure it in whatever manner possible. The new Council's first act would be to approve the merger."

Cyrus's jaw dropped. "How do you know?"

"I know."

"Because they are treacherous rats and it is likely they would waste their time in such weaselly matters," came Vara's strident voice, echoing up the stairwell from below Cyrus. He looked back to see her and the other officers following close behind.

Alaric halted mid-stride, bringing Cyrus to an abrupt stop behind him. "Are all the officers here?" He looked down the spiral of the stairs. "We need not venture to the Council Chambers. You have all heard what I have promised. It is now incumbent on us to deliver. Double patrols. Our healers will not sleep much in the next weeks, and for that I apologize."

"I'll sleep plenty," Vaste said from below. "But it'll be on my horse."

"We have two months to prove our innocence or we face something too unpleasant to contemplate," Alaric said, words echoing. "We will make every effort, exhaust every possibility." His face hardened. "If this is to be the end of Sanctuary, then let it not end with anything other than a fight to the last."

Chapter 32

A month passed in the blink of an eye. Ryin Ayend had held to his word and been on patrol every day without fail. Some of his followers had not been so pleased at the bargain the druid had struck; Jesha disappeared within the week, along with the glum youth Corin. Shortly thereafter the dark elf Yeral had gone missing. A handful of others trickled out the door openly, renouncing ties to Sanctuary, while others disappeared under the cover of darkness.

The departures continued for the first two weeks after the confrontation in the Great Hall and came to a halt with the arrival of ill tidings. Dinner, returned to the deathly quiet affair it had been before the night of Ayend's speech to the guild, was interrupted by the squeak of both doors to the hall opening with violence. Thad Proelius made his way through the scattered tables with unusual urgency.

Alaric rose to meet him; Thad was posted to the detail that stood watch along the walls that ringed Sanctuary. For the first time since Cyrus had been part of the guild, the great gates that had always stood open were now closed against the possibility of attack. Thad cut through the Great Hall, stopping at the officer's table and whispering into Alaric's ear.

The Ghost remained stoic. Those who knew him well could read his anger in the clenching of the fist he held at his side, but his face gave no sign.

"The Council of Twelve in Reikonos holds Jesha, Corin and a half dozen others that have fled in the last fortnight," he announced. "They will be executed unless we pay our fines and admit guilt." He looked through the crowd, gauging reaction.

A voice in the back shouted, "Pay them!" and the call was taken up by another. Cyrus felt a pain in his gut.

"No," a calm voice cut across the hall. Ryin Ayend stood. "It was agreed that we would wait two months before taking action. Their intemperance pains me, but they acted of their own accord." The rumblings of the crowd settled. "We wait. We hunt. The day will come when we will make our peace with Reikonos and Pharesia, but it is not today." The druid seated himself.

"I appreciate your patience," Alaric said with a cool demeanor.

"This is an intolerable state of affairs; Reikonos even holds captive several of the individuals who renounced all ties to us, refusing to acknowledge their renunciation." The Ghost shook his head and returned to his seat as well; the rest of the meal passed in silence.

The next two weeks were hard. Word came that Yeral and other dark elves had been executed in Saekaj. The captives in Reikonos remained imprisoned but survived. No word had reached them from Pharesia about any captives after the first month had passed, and Cyrus found himself on a long patrol with Andren and Terian one day, curious about it.

"The King of the Elves is loath to upset his youngest daughter by detaining her guildmates," Andren suggested.

"Doesn't he have countless daughters?" Terian asked.

Andren shifted the reins of his horse to one hand so he could reach his flask with the other. "He does. But Nyad is the youngest, and that means much in the Kingdom."

"That would count for nothing in Saekaj," Terian said. "The Sovereign has more bastard children than he knows what to do with."

Andren raised an eyebrow. "He cares nothing for his heirs?"

Terian snorted. "He hasn't got any heirs. The Sovereign will never step down."

"So he'll die on the throne?" Andren asked.

Terian did not answer and looked away.

There had been no sign of raiders in the weeks since Cyrus had spied the goblin in the wrecked convoy, but his dreams had been haunted by the red eyes, green skin and shrill voices of the Emperor and Empress in his nightmares, as well as whispers and shouts of "Gezhvet!" The face of Narstron came to him, bloody and wrecked, whispering to him.

He always awoke in a sweat, crying out. Cyrus knew it was loud enough to wake all the officers, but they remained silent about his nighttime difficulties. He rarely managed more than a few hours of sleep a night and his dreams began to bleed into his waking thoughts.

Avenge me.

The three of them led the patrol up a hill and looked down upon the plains. The green grasses waved in the early summer winds and far in the distance, there was movement on the horizon. Cyrus drew Windrider's reins, pulling him up as the other two halted.

"An army," Andren said, squinting. "Looks like the elves to me."

"We'll be heading the opposite direction then," Terian replied, sour look pasted on his face. "Having all these armies running around is interfering with our ability to hunt bandits."

"You could go ask them nicely to clear out, but odds are they'd take that as proof that we're the bandits they're looking for." Andren grinned as he took another swig.

"I doubt they think they need any more proof, so best we avoid them and the gallows they'd take us to," Terian answered back. "West?" he asked Cyrus.

"Agreed," the warrior replied. He'd kept quieter on this ride than any other. As if the hellish dreams of Narstron and the goblins weren't enough, his days were spent obsessively focusing on finding the raiders. He rode hard every day, thinking of goblins, and went to bed every night dreaming of them.

They moved west and rode in silence for an hour or so before catching sight of another group on the horizon, smaller this time. "Vara's patrol," Andren said after a studying the horizon. "Looks like she's got Niamh, J'anda and Vaste with her."

Cyrus frowned and exchanged a look with Terian. "Niamh and Vaste were supposed to be on their own patrol."

They rode closer, and as they approached, Cyrus could see that Andren had been right. "Hail," Niamh said with a smile.

"Hi hi," said Vaste across the short divide between them. "There's a really big army of humans coming from the other direction, and we all know how they feel about trolls."

"That they're worthless and smell bad?" Terian asked with a smile.

"Just another area where you have it all wrong. Elves, they're the ones who smell bad."

Cyrus chanced a look at Vara, who was looking back at him with a blank expression. "I do not smell bad," she said with a raised eyebrow.

"Uh... I never said you did. It was Vaste."

"You looked at me accusingly."

Cy reeled. "I... looked at you... I wouldn't say it was accusingly. And in my experience, you have a lovely scent. Of course, I rarely get close enough to tell."

Her eyes narrowed. "As it should be."

"So the human army pushed you in this direction?" Cy asked.

Her wary look gave way to one of frustration. "Indeed. The noose tightens, it would appear. They may be reluctant to ride us down and confront us, but their patrols bring them closer to Sanctuary – and each other – day by day."

"Which brings an interesting question," Andren said. "Why haven't they attacked Sanctuary yet, if they think we're responsible for this mess?"

"Isn't it obvious?" Terian said with a snort of derision. "Either their governments don't really believe we're guilty or they're still hoping we'll pay. Or both."

It was Andren's turn to frown. "Then why haven't they attacked each other yet, if it's like Alaric says and the humans want war?"

"They want justification," Vaste answered. "To be able to parade their grievance in front of the world, cloak it in righteousness, to be able to say that they didn't start it but they'll damned sure finish it."

Andren shrugged. "I don't know. It's been a few months and we've yet to see a war. I'm starting to think they're all just blustering."

"They are, make no mistake," Vaste replied. "But you cannot have this many soldiers this close to each other and so far from a brothel and not expect a war to start." Laughter echoed from the ranks around them as well as from the officers.

"I suspect our patrols in this direction will be fruitless for the rest of the day," Cyrus said. "Perhaps we should reassemble at Sanctuary and head out again on the morrow."

"I agree," Vara said, pulling the reins of her horse, a beautiful black stallion that belonged to her, not Sanctuary. "Heading in this general direction is sure to mean a visit from one army or another."

They readjusted their course and set their horses at a trot toward home. Cyrus found himself riding next to Vara, a little apart from the rest of the patrol. "So," he tried to break the ice, "how have you been?"

She had been looking straight ahead, but upon his question she froze and her head turned toward him, a look of incredulity on her face. "Is that the best you have? 'How have you been'?"

He flushed. "You're not the easiest person to talk to, you know that?" He began to lead his horse away but her voice stopped him.

"Wait," she called out. "I am sorry," she said with a flush of her own, scarlet creeping up to her normally white cheeks. "I should perhaps be more kind to you." She looked down. "It is difficult for me to avoid the verbal jousting, as well you know."

"Yes, you're like one of those creatures that has spikes jutting out in all directions from its body." He struggled for the words. "What do they call them?"

"Dragons?"

"That too," he agreed, "but I meant something else. Anyway, my point is –"

"That I wall myself off from attempts at conversation, friendly inquiries and the like," she interrupted, staring ahead once more. "I know this. It is intentional, after all." She turned her head to look at him, and her armor glinted, distracting him from the earnest expression on her face. "Let us perhaps try and have a pleasant conversation on our way home, shall we?"

"I'm game if you are."

"Very well." She seemed to straighten in her saddle. "How have you been?"

He chuckled. "You just remonstrated me for asking that question."

An abrupt exhalation of impatience from her was followed by a swift rolling of her eyes. "Yes, very well, I did. Fine, have it your way." She paused. "So, how are your nightmares treating you? Still terrible, I would presume, judging by the screams that keep awakening me at odd hours," she snapped, annoyance consuming her words.

He paled for a moment but did not respond. Her fiery look softened and her eyes widened and sunk downward, looking forward again. "I apologize," she said after a moment. "That was unworthy."

"Yeah." His voice was strangled; her brusque mention of his nightmares brought on the guilt he felt for his failure to avenge Narstron and his discomfort at awakening the officers quartered around him. "I don't think today's our day for having a conversation." He urged his horse forward, away from her.

"Wait." A note of pleading entered her voice. "You still long for revenge on the goblins, do you not?"

He did not look back. "I do."

"It is as I feared. You cannot bow to this craven desire. It could consume you at a time when we have more need of you than ever before."

"These attacks and the goblin involvement have given me more reason than ever to want to finish them as a power."

"Don't you see?" The note of pleading had increased. "This is a reckless path. If we go to Enterra, it should be to prove our innocence - if what you say is true."

"I always hear that kind of talk from people who have the least reasons for wanting revenge on anybody."

Vara's eyes hardened. "I assure you that I have more reason for revenge on someone than you could possibly imagine, but I have deigned not to claim that vengeance, as much as I would have liked to at times."

His jaw set, eyebrows arched and eyes narrowed. "Then I guess you're a better person than I am. Because I'm going to kill them. As many of them as I can. I will kill the Empress and Emperor, and anyone foolish enough to guard them." He urged Windrider forward, widening the distance between them.

Looking back, he saw her bow her head. She did not speak to anyone for the rest of the ride home.

Chapter 33

When they returned to Sanctuary, Cyrus ran up the steps without speaking to anyone. He gathered his most commonly used belongings as well as the bust that he hung his armor on and packed a bag. Carrying the bust under his arm and the bag across his back, he returned to the foyer to see Erith enter with another patrol.

"Ran into the dark elven army," she said with a scowl. "What the hell is that?" She pointed to the bust, a figure of wood, carved from head to upper thigh, with no facial features and an androgynous body.

"It's for hanging my armor."

"Oh." Her face split wide in a grin. "I thought maybe it was a practice dummy."

"For what?" Cyrus said. "Swordplay?"

"Nah," she said with a nasty grin. "I heard you've been lonely. Figured you'd need some companionship."

He raised an eyebrow as the bile of annoyance returned from his earlier conflict with Vara. "If so, I think I could find something prettier and more womanly than this." He held up the faceless figure.

"I don't know," she said with a shrug. "You've been rejecting Aisling over and over; maybe womanly isn't a concern for you."

His eyes flicked up. "It is. Which is why I'm not interested in you." He turned, pushing the bust back under his arm.

"Don't be jealous!" she called from behind him. "You couldn't handle all this!" He turned to see her waving at herself while gyrating slightly.

"Nobody could handle all that –" he mimed her waves, pointing at her – "for very long." He turned the corner and headed down the stairwell to the dungeons.

They were twice as dark as he remembered from the day he had ventured through with Alaric. The twists and turns led him through a host of paths, running against locked doors, until finally he found himself standing before the cell block where he had first met Fortin. A long hallway lined with cells stretched before his eyes, all the doors open. A rumble greeted him from inside Fortin's chamber. "What brings you down here?"

"I'm looking to switch quarters," Cyrus admitted, peeking his head inside the rock giant's room. "Are there any that don't have grates looking up into other rooms?"

"The cells," the rock giant said. "But those are not nearly so entertaining."

"I need some peace and quiet, where I can't hear anyone and no one can hear me."

Fortin waved toward the end of the hall. "Down there, past the big locked door. Those are all under the meeting rooms toward the back of the building; no grates, no noise."

Cyrus left him, walking to the far end of the hall, passing an ornate set of double doors with a heavy bar across them and a series of locks. Cyrus picked out a cool, dark cell as far from Fortin as he could find. He pulled the key from the door and pocketed it, distributing his belongings around the room.

The walls were of the same dark stone as every other room in the guildhall, but most of the cells he had seen were considerably darker. This one had several lamps scattered around and looked bigger than the other cells. It had a sink and privy, to his relief. He lay down on the cot after unpacking, and could not hear any noise - not of the bells that rang in half-hour intervals during the day to mark time, and not a whisper of dinner, in spite of being certain it was being served above.

The next two weeks dragged, as Cyrus felt himself become isolated from everyone around him. He spoke less and when he did, it was with few words. When not on patrol, he had Larana send his meals to the dungeon cell. She delivered them herself, always with a beseeching look and not a word spoken.

In spite of the best efforts of the lamps, the cell was a gloomy place, perfectly reflective of his mood. The tinge of the stones was burned into his mind by the end of the second week.

There had been no Council meetings since the day that they first learned that former members of Sanctuary had been arrested and imprisoned. Alaric was scarcely seen, but when he was his mood was somber. An Alliance officer meeting had been scheduled, much to the dismay of the Sanctuary officers, and with no other option, Alaric had agreed with greatest reluctance to host it.

"Let us be clear," the Ghost snarled to the messenger in the Great Hall. "This is our guildhall, and it will be on my terms - none other."

The messenger had nodded and disappeared in a blaze of energy. The day of the meeting came quickly, only two weeks before the guild vote on the merger. Patrols had been hemmed in tighter and tighter by the movements of the armies around them, cutting their effectiveness. Even an attacked convoy was a rare sight in the small area left to them to monitor.

Cyrus entered the foyer on the day of the Alliance meeting in the hour before dinner to find Malpravus and the other Alliance officers standing before him. Elisabeth and Cass from the Daring, as well as Carrack, Tolada and another figure stood behind Malpravus – a ranger, dressed in a cloak and tabard of green and a helmet of solid metal that covered his face from top to bottom with the only holes being two narrow slits for the eyes.

Orion. In Sanctuary.

The sight called forth a rage in Cyrus. His hand found his short sword and it was unsheathed in a second. He lunged even as Elisabeth screamed "NO!" and Cass moved aside to let him pass with a slight smile. Carrack and Tolada moved to block him from Orion, while Malpravus stood to the side, hands wrapped in his sleeves.

Avenge me.

Tolada moved forward, warhammer unslung from his back, but Cyrus kicked him, hard, before he could strike, smashing his nose and face, blood spurting everywhere as the dwarf crumpled to the stone floor, limp as a boneless fish.

Cyrus's sword came up of its own accord as Carrack raised his hand, fire already pulsing in his palm. The slash caught the wizard mid-wrist and sent his hand flying across the room in a low arc as he grasped the stump with his other and fell to his knees with a cry. With no conscious thought, Cy whipped his sword across the wizard's neck, slitting his throat. A gurgle came from beside him as the elf fell to the floor.

You and me, now. His eyes burned into the masked ranger, who had yet to move. Cyrus brought his sword up and forward with a slash that Orion dodged, but only barely. "Looks like you need a longer sword," came the familiar voice. "It would appear that your time with Sanctuary has not been kind to your wallet, if that is all you can afford."

With a visceral cry, Cyrus plunged the sword forward in an impaling blow, but it glanced off the ranger's doublet. *SHIT! I forgot his gods-damned chainmail!* He tried to bring the sword around for another slash, aiming for the gorget that was wrapped around the ranger's neck but a dagger at his throat brought him up short.

"This is unacceptable, Cyrus!" Elisabeth's voice hissed in his ear. Her blade at his neck held him back. He felt her other knife poke him in the small gap between his backplate and greaves. "You've attacked three Alliance officers and killed two of them!"

"Let me go and we'll see about a trifecta." His words came out in a low growl.

She threw him forward with a hard shoulder check that brought him to his knees, then stepped between him and Orion. He looked around to see a small crowd of Sanctuary guild members watching in shock. Terian and Vaste were holding back Andren, who was straining against them to no avail. The remnants of a broken glass of ale lingered on the ground at his feet.

A chuckle from behind caused him to whip his head around. Malpravus stood, unmoving, in the same place he had been when Cyrus began the attack. "I see that today we receive the full hospitality of Sanctuary." His sleeves parted to reveal his skeletal fingers, steepled. His grin was from ear to ear. "I should have expected nothing less from anyone who would stoop to attacking convoys for plunder."

"Cyrus!" The voice, like a thunderclap, filled the air around him. Alaric entered the foyer, Vara at his side. Her expression was tight and his unreadable, but they were both focused on Malpravus. The Ghost did not look at him as he passed the prostrate warrior. "You are excused from this meeting. Go elsewhere."

Curatio and Niamh followed in the wake of Alaric and Vara, and the Healer was already casting the resurrection spell. His eyes found Cyrus's, and he bowed his head in deep disappointment, flicking his gaze from the warrior. Cyrus tasted bitterness in his mouth and saw Vara cast him a contemptuous glance for only a second before looking away.

Cy pulled himself to his feet and left the way he had come. He passed the stairs to the dungeons at a fast pace, then felt as though he nearly flew down the hallway to his cell and slammed the door with a fury that echoed through the dungeon. He locked the door from the inside and did not answer any of the insistent knocks that came in the next few minutes and hours – not Terian's, nor

Andren's, nor even Vaste's. He had almost fallen asleep when a small but insistent tapping came from the other side of the door.

He ignored it for several minutes, until an exasperated sigh caught his attention for its unfamiliarity. "Who is it?" he asked.

"Dear boy," came the voice of Malpravus, strong and clear through the heavy steel door, "there is only so much discourtesy I can take from you in one day without becoming deeply offended."

Chapter 34

Cyrus walked to the cell door and swung it open. Standing before him was the Goliath Guildmaster, face impassive, dark robes covering him from neck to floor. "What do you want?" Cyrus asked, voice slow and curious.

"What does anyone want, really?" the necromancer asked, brushing past Cyrus to enter the cell. "For some, the answer is riches; for others, power. For me, it's to answer needs. And you," he said with a tight smile, "have a clear need."

Cyrus stared at the dark elf who had invaded his room almost without permission. "And what is that need?" He folded his arms in front of him.

The necromancer's eyes glistened. "Rumors have reached even my ears about your difficulties lately, dear boy. Trouble sleeping? Guilt eating at you for the loss of a dear, dear friend?"

Cyrus grew still, holding himself back with every bit of restraint he possessed. "What of it?"

Malpravus walked the length of the cell, looking it over. His eyes fell upon the sword in the corner, scabbardless and waiting for enchantment. His eyes looked it over hungrily, then flicked back to Cyrus. "When it comes to matters of death, you should consult an authority. And there is no greater authority about death," he said in a lilting tone, bringing his fingertips to rest, palms down on his chest, "than I."

Still Cyrus did not move. "My friend has been dead for over a year. So it would be a bit late for a resurrection spell, even assuming you were capable of casting one."

The necromancer's eyes danced and he made a tsk-tsk sound. "I see you still have grave misunderstandings about what I am capable of. Allow me to explain." Malpravus reached into his robe and pulled out a small object, no larger than a peanut. It was red and glistened even in the light of the lamps. "This is a soul ruby. Very rare items, these," he said with a smile, "and thus more valuable than you could imagine."

When Cyrus did not respond he continued. "With the proper spell, performed by a necromancer, of course," he said with something just short of delight, "this can bring back the dead, regardless of how long they've been departed."

Cyrus stared back at him, unimpressed. "I've seen you bring back the dead. I'd sooner die a thousand deaths myself than have that fate befall my friend."

"No, no, no." Malpravus's voice was as smooth as poured honey. "I agree: that would be a terrible way to live. A soul ruby," he said, smile returning, "brings them back *as they were,*" he said with a flourish. "All their memories, their skills, their knowledge. A bit cold to the touch, it's true, but a soul ruby truly does bring them back."

Malpravus's hand remained outstretched, the soul ruby dangling. Cyrus's eyes were locked on it, suddenly hungry. *What if it worked?* Cy thought. *What if I could bring him back, just as he was?*

"I see you're considering my offer." Malpravus's smile danced.

Cyrus's face grew guarded again as he remembered who he was speaking to. "There's nothing that comes without a price from you, Malpravus. What do you want in return?"

If the necromancer was offended, he did not show it. "That's a wise perspective, dear boy. You recognize that there's always a price, always a trade – power for power, this for that." His smile faded. "I have made no secret of what I desire. This Alliance could be the most powerful guild in all of Arkaria, and dare mighty things that the 'big three' could not fathom." He licked his lips. "But just as here, power has its price. I cannot create the most powerful guild in Arkaria without the support of Sanctuary's officers – at least one of them.

"It is also no secret, I hope," the necromancer said, "that I consider you to have great potential. Great ability. You could be the finest warrior in all Arkaria, and a great leader. I would cultivate that. I would help you grow, in the right directions, assist you in growing more powerful." His hand still stretched out, the ruby shining red against his blue palm. "All I require is that you help me bring Sanctuary into the fold, and I will make you an officer of the new guild in return – and you can be my General – my Warlord."

"And if I don't?" Cyrus looked evenly at the necromancer. Caution prickled at the back of his mind, even as he continued to move his gaze back and forth from the Goliath Guildmaster's face to the ruby in his outstretched hand.

The necromancer's expression never changed at Cyrus's words. "Now, dear boy," he whispered, "do we really need to reflect on the possibilities of that answer?" His hand closed around the ruby, slowly pulling his arm away, cradling it as though it were an item of incalculable value.

Something in the way he moved, in the way he pulled his hand back into the sleeve, the darkness of the cell casting shadows on the fabric of the dark elf's cloak spurred a memory in Cyrus. It was the nightmare again.

The black cloaked figure emerged from behind the thrones of the Emperor and Empress, gliding across the floor... the Emperor pulled *Terrenus,* the Hammer of Earth from his belt and handed it to the figure in black...

... with blue hands...

... and the figure pulled the Hammer away, cradling it... just like Malpravus did with the soul ruby.

"Someone in the Alliance," Cyrus whispered. His eyes were glazed over.

"Give it some thought, dear boy, and let me know your answer." Malpravus turned and slid from the cell, down the hall. Cyrus did not even bother to watch him go. The warrior's mouth was dry. Thoughts of what he had done earlier in the foyer held him back from attacking the necromancer. *I can't prove it,* he realized. *But now I know who betrayed the Alliance to Enterra. And if he betrayed us to the goblins once...*

Chapter 35

Cyrus sat on his cot after Malpravus left. His head was spinning and a raw feeling of annoyed disappointment filled him. *I knew there was a traitor in the Alliance. Of course it was the most evil bastard I've ever met. He has no qualms about using the corpses of his guildmates to save his ass; why would he have a problem with betraying every member of Sanctuary to death?*

He felt his hand shaking. A moment later he sat up, realizing that he was not shaking from anger, but because the cell was moving. A crashing of footfalls could be heard coming down the hall and his door burst open, revealing the face of Fortin, peering in at him.

Cyrus jumped to his feet. "You know, it's rude not to knock."

The rock giant looked at him, expressionless as always. "Knock knock," he said.

"What do you want, Fortin?"

"It's dinnertime," the rock giant said, squeezing himself through the door. "Since there's nothing to entertain me in the foyer, I came to find out what the necromancer wanted."

Cyrus's head was still spinning from his conversation with Malpravus. "He... he offered to bring back my friend."

Fortin's rocky eyelid slid up a few inches. "Narstron? Yeah, I heard that."

Cyrus paused and looked at the rock giant in surprise. "You heard all that? From down the hall?"

"Rock giants have exceptional hearing."

Cyrus sat back down. "How did you know Narstron's name?"

"You don't sleep quietly."

"Oh," Cyrus said with chagrin. "I'm sorry if I disturb your sleep -"

A giant, craggy hand dismissed him. "When I'm sleeping, your nightmares, loud as they are, would not wake me. I hear them if I'm not sleeping. I've had those kinds of dreams before."

Cyrus looked away, focusing on the stones in the wall. "It's not something I really want to discuss."

"Fine," Fortin said. "Any more kisses from the ice princess?"

Cy's head snapped around. "Why would you call her that?" He thought about it for a beat. "Never mind."

He felt his mind drift back to that simple motion from Malpravus of drawing the ruby back to him, and saw again the similarity to the hand in Enterra, drawing the hammer to the cloaked figure. He saw the red eyes of the Emperor and Empress, felt the raw bile of hatred fill his throat and mouth, and in that moment he wanted nothing more than to kill them all, Malpravus as well.

Glee filled him as he remembered driving Tolada's nose into his face, of slitting Carrack's throat. He wished he had been able to knock Orion to the ground, to throw off that ridiculous helm and plunge his sword into him over and over. And then turn, and strike down Malpravus with a single blow, sword slicing through the cloak - why did everyone keep telling him he should avoid vengeance when it would be so sweet and satisfying?

"I sense that our conversation is not first priority in your mind right now," Fortin said.

He looked up in surprise at the rock giant, one of the greatest warriors he'd ever seen. A moment of insecurity crossed Cyrus's mind. "Let me ask you something, Fortin," he began. "I think you'll understand better than anyone."

"Proceed," came the rumbling answer.

"I've been wanting... revenge against those who killed... my friend," he managed to choke out, unable to say Narstron's name. "Everyone keeps urging me against revenge." He shook his head and stood. "I've listened, so far, but the cry for vengeance does not leave my mind; I can't even sleep without dreaming about it." He turned and placed his hands against the walls, felt their coolness and roughness against his palms. "If it were you who were wronged, you'd pursue vengeance at all costs, wouldn't you?"

A rumble of amusement filled the cell. "No."

Cyrus froze and turned back to the rock giant. "No? Why not?"

A moment of silence filled the air. "I am the youngest brother of five in my family. My oldest brother was like a father to me after my real father died. He taught me to fight and when he entered the service of the Dragonlord, I followed him with my other three brothers. All of them with the exception of my oldest brother were killed in the last battle with Sanctuary in the Mountains of Nartanis."

The rock giant paused. "My oldest brother was killed a year before when you pushed him into the lava while he was guarding the bridge to Ashan'agar's den."

Cyrus turned and felt a cold, gut-clenching sensation of warning slip through him as he faced the rock giant. His sword was not in easy reach; by the time anyone could get to them, he would be a smear on the walls; permanently dead. "And you don't want revenge?" Cyrus asked, frozen in place, eyes fixated on the blade leaning against the wall between him and Fortin.

"Stop eying your sword like I'm going to splatter you across the dungeons; it's insulting." The rock giant guffawed, a deep, guttural sound akin to stones clacking together. "We were the sworn guardians of a dragon that everyone in the world wanted to kill. It'd be a fool who didn't know the risks when they swore their loyalty and chose their path. I do not regret my service, and nor would my brothers - any of them. You are an adventurer, someone who dares death every day. You should understand."

"I don't think I do." Cyrus sat back on his cot, head bowed.

Fortin took one massive stride to the door, where he turned to face Cyrus. The rock giant's eyes glowed in the darkness as he spoke. "If you charge willingly into death and send others to it, you shouldn't be upset when it comes for you the last time. Revenge for my brother would be pointless. He's dead. The master we swore to serve is dead. They cannot help me; they cannot teach me. Sanctuary can give me a path. If I were to strike all of you down - and be assured I could - my desire for short term satisfaction would have cost me the infinite possibilities I could have pursued instead."

Fortin cocked his head at Cyrus. "Let's say you could kill the goblins, kill the traitor in the Alliance that you tried to earlier in the foyer - yes, I heard and saw it - you should have lunged harder on your first attempt - and even bring back your friend with that necromancer's help. Only one of the three actions really matters. Everything else is just getting in the way of what you're trying to do." The rock giant ducked and stepped through the door. He turned back and looked at Cyrus before leaving. "Unless, of course, you want to spend every day for the rest of your life plotting and scheming at killing goblins, traitors and other people who have offended you in some way."

"What if it didn't take that long?" Cyrus said. "What if it could be over soon? Then it could be done. And I could... find peace." He exhaled, heavy air rushing out of his nostrils and mouth as he sagged.

"Hell of a way to live your life, even for a short period of time," the rock giant said. "I'd hate to think of what you might cost yourself in the meantime - expeditions, a guild, even ice princess kisses." The loud crash of the rock giant's steps faded as he retreated down the hallway, leaving Cyrus to his thoughts.

Alaric called them to Council the next morning. It was a short meeting. "We have nothing left to discuss. Malpravus's intentions are plain; he will use this situation to take our guild. We have two weeks before this happens. Every hand should be ready."

"I have... an idea," Cyrus said quietly.

Heads swiveled to him in surprise. Curatio gave him a smile of encouragement, as did Alaric, in a patronly sort of way. "What is it, brother?" the Ghost said with an air of friendship.

Cyrus explained his plan, keeping out any mention of his suspicions regarding Malpravus. *I'll tell them when they're ready to hear.*

"If you are correct," Alaric said with a nod, "this may indeed be our best chance to catch them."

Vara had remained silent. "I have something that may help." She laid a piece of parchment on the Council table. "My father sent this from Termina - it is a shipping manifest and schedule for a convoy that will pass through the southern plains in a week, coming from Termina to Aloakna." Her eyes slid around the table. "It is ripe for the plucking. With this, we will have a general idea of where it will be and when. We could send a patrol to ride close by, waiting for the raiders."

Alaric nodded. "I have received similar manifests from acquaintances in Reikonos; unfortunately I have had to dismiss them all as I suspect they are a trap." His eyes narrowed. "Are you certain that this is not?"

Vara shook her head. "Not certain. But I don't think my father would betray me; not ever. I explained our plight when last I was in Termina and he sent me word today of half a dozen shipments planned for the next months from his employer. The rest will not happen for several weeks, so this is our best chance."

"Even if it is a trap," Terian conceded, "we have nothing to lose."

"Agreed." Vaste nodded. "We have two weeks until we'll involuntarily be forced to admit complicity; we might as well stalk a convoy now." He grinned. "We could always hit it and make off with the proceeds; at least have some gold to start our new lives with."

Scattered laughter around the table was brought to a halt by a harrumph from Alaric. "Not funny," the Ghost said.

"Too soon?" the troll asked with a shrug.

"Very well," Alaric nodded. "We will continue our patrols at an increased level over the next week, keeping Cyrus's strategy in mind. Should we not achieve the desired results, we will follow this caravan that Vara's father suggests." A grim look crept over the Ghost's face. "Trap or no, it may be our last chance to save Sanctuary."

Chapter 36

The next week went the same as the previous: no attacks sighted, but the armies of the Elven Kingdom, Human Confederation and Dark Elven Sovereignty edged ever closer. By the day that Vara's convoy rolled through the plains, there were no other options.

"So how do we get past the armies?" Terian said from the wall, looking out with Cyrus at his side.

"We teleport to the portal with our horses," Cyrus said, looking down at the armies moving in the distance as dusk approached the plains. The armies clashed with the flat horizon, little bumps of darkness against the flat edge of the sky. "And we ride out from there."

The two of them descended the steps in one of the wall's towers, then stalked toward the stables. "So," Terian said nonchalantly, "how's life in the dungeons?"

"The beds are terrible and when Fortin snores it sounds like Ashan'agar's den collapsing around me."

As they crossed the grounds, Cyrus watched as the front doors opened and disgorged a host of members. Every horse was being taken from the stables and every rider would be part of the same patrol. His eyes saw Erith, Andren, Niamh, J'anda, Curatio, Vaste, Nyad and a hundred others. Alaric came last, helm on and sword at his side.

Cyrus waited at the doors to the stable for the Ghost. "Would you care to do the honors of leading us out?"

Alaric's mouth twisted in a smile. "This is not Sanctuary's last ride. I trust you to deliver the results we are seeking."

"I hope you're right." He followed Alaric into the stables and watched as the Guildmaster mounted his horse, a gorgeous pure-white mount that looked as though she had never seen a spot of dirt.

Cyrus found Windrider already saddled. Longwell rode up to him, lance in hand. "I took the liberty of making ready your horse, Lord Davidon."

Cy looked at the dragoon with nod of thanks. "I'll need you and that lance of yours up front with me if we go charging into battle."

Longwell nodded and fell into formation behind him. Cyrus

rode Windrider out of the stables and through the mass of assembled riders. Ryin Ayend was there, sick look on his face as he sat atop his horse. "You should look more gleeful, Ayend. This may be our last chance to avoid the fate you seem determined to bring down on us - the dissolution of Sanctuary."

The druid glared back at him, disgust written across his fair features. "If you think I want this guild wrecked, you can go to the hells. I pray to all the gods that we find these raiders tonight, goblins or otherwise."

Cyrus gave the druid a grudging nod of respect. The patrol formed, officers in front per usual. He nodded at Niamh, who began to cast a spell. A burst of wind grasped hold and shook him, dropping his horse onto the plains, portal at his back. The rest of the patrol was behind him, still in perfect formation. He nudged Windrider into a gallop, heading north.

Vara had made clear the path the convoy was to take. He looked back and his eyes found her, atop her black horse, eyes vacant, staring into the distance. They set a pace that would allow them to meet the convoy, even if it were early. Cyrus sent riders ahead as scouts to report. As night fell, they found themselves on a ridge, looking down at the winding road below, barely visible in the last rays of sunlight.

Vara and the other elves stood forward and Vaste cast a spell on Cyrus, giving him night vision. J'anda shrugged as the troll cast. "It's easier than handing you one of my orbs of lucense, I suppose."

Cyrus peered into the distance. The patrol was quiet, as though a grim vigil for Sanctuary were taking place. After an hour of waiting, the scouts returned to report the convoy moving toward them. Minutes later they caught sight of it, a collection of thirty wagons with a few outriders - elven guards and humans mercenaries, well armed. The convoy moved at a slow gallop, wagon wheels bouncing in the ruts of the well-traveled road.

"It's carrying mostly silks sewn in the Kingdom to be shipped from Aloakna across the Bay of Lost Souls to Taymor and up to the human settlements along the desert and mountains," Vara said from behind him. "They'll be easily spooked and I can almost guarantee that they're more ready for raiders than previous convoys."

"Good," Cyrus said. "If they get attacked, it would help us if they could hold them off until we get there."

The patrol rode down the small ridges, keeping a distance of a few miles from the convoy. "The road goes into a small canyon ahead," Niamh warned them. "We won't be able to see them for a minute or two."

"That's no good," Cyrus said. "That'd be the place they're attacked."

"I don't see what you can do about it," Niamh said.

"I can go through the canyon before them," Cyrus said as he spurred Windrider to a full gallop. "Longwell, Terian, Vaste, you're with me; the rest of you split – half the formation ride ahead past the canyon, the other half stay here and keep watch on the entrance."

Windrider galloped at full speed, the others following behind Cyrus. With a friendly wave, he cut in front of the convoy almost a hundred yards before they reached the canyon and heard the cursing of the outriders. "Sorry," he shouted over the rattle of the wagons, "I'm in a hurry."

He raced through the canyon – a short, shallow lowering of the terrain to coincide with an old riverbed before the road turned south. His eyes scanned the walls and rocks for any sign of movement. Seeing none, he relaxed for a moment as he emerged from the canyon on the other side. With a frown, he pulled up the reins, bringing his horse to a halt. "I thought they'd hit them there," he said to the others as they pulled up behind him.

"Maybe we spooked them?" Terian suggested.

"These raiders are cowards," Longwell agreed, clutching his lance. "They would likely hide at the sight of an unexpected force."

Cyrus did not have a chance to reply to the dragoon as a bolt of lightning struck the warrior, coursing through his armor and blasting him clear of the horse. His teeth rattled with the power of the shock and his head ached beyond description. A slow pain spread across his back and he blinked the spots out of his eyes and heard the spooked horses around him.

Another blast of lightning seared the air and Terian flew from his mount, then Longwell. Cyrus watched Vaste jump from his horse, using it for cover against the next blast of lightning, aimed at him. His horse screamed and bucked, but the troll dodged out of the way. Cyrus watched Vaste cast a spell and the scorched skin around Cy's hands faded to pink.

The convoy was almost to the end of the canyon and the low,

guttural noise of voices could be heard. Goblins poured down the sides of the canyon, swarming among the convoy defenders, and another blaze of lightning lit Cyrus's view, skipping over his head. A fire started, walling them off from the canyon. A figure in a cloak stepped behind the wall, flames flying from his fingers. *A wizard,* Cyrus realized. *Their transportation.*

The warrior was on his feet and running across the ground. A whinny caused him to turn his head, revealing Windrider running beside him at a trot. He jumped, landing a foot in the stirrup and swinging the other over as he urged the horse toward the fire. "You're not a normal horse," he whispered. Another whinny came back to him and the horse bore down on the wall of flames and leaped over it.

The image Cyrus saw as Windrider jumped was of goblins looking up in awe as he flew through the air toward them. His sword was in his hand, and upon landing he swung, sending foes flying left and right. He rode forward, eyes on the convoy, watching as goblins hauled elves and men off horses. The wizard was at the end of the caravan, cutting off the convoy's retreat with another fire spell.

The outriders' horses were spooked, throwing their masters to the ground where goblins were swarming over them. Cyrus rode to the end of the convoy, attacking and killing a half dozen goblins from horseback. He swept around the last wagon and passed the wizard too quickly to bring his sword around. He landed a heavy kick on the wizard's chest. Though he could not see the face he was virtually certain of the identity of the spell caster. A grunt of pain came from the cloaked body as it tumbled to the ground.

He rode along the side of the canyon, screams of the convoy's defenders ringing in his ears. Cyrus jumped from Windrider as he reached a concentration of goblins and began to cut his way through. Three goblins blocked his path forward. The first came at him while the other two held back. He dodged a two-handed attack and brought down the pommel of his sword on the goblin's uneven skull, cracking it and sending him to the ground.

The next two goblins stepped forward, slashing and stabbing. One landed a claw under the armor at his elbow joint; the second glanced off his breastplate. He butted his chest forward, knocking the goblin back a few paces and giving him enough room to swing his short sword to decapitate the goblin's comrade. He leaned forward and kicked the survivor and the force of his blow lifted the small body off the ground, causing it to carom off a wagon and come to a rest on the ground, motionless.

A warcry came from in front of him as the fire was extinguished by a blast of wind and rain. He could see the forward element of his patrol riding past the first wagons, attacking. A strangled cry came from behind him, and a light filled the air as half a hundred orbs of light shot past him to each of the goblins standing around the convoy. They began to wink out in a flash of light, leaving behind only their dead and wounded.

Cyrus saw a dozen goblin bodies interspersed with the wounded and surviving members of the convoy detachment. "My gods," came a voice to Cyrus's right. An elf lay wounded against a wagon wheel, eyes wide in fear, blood trickling down a corner of his mouth. "Those were goblins, I'd swear to Virixia! And... and..." His eyes found Cyrus, who looked down at him. "You stopped them! My thanks, sir! Who are you and where do you hail from?"

"My name is Cyrus Davidon and I hail from Sanctuary," he said in a calm voice. "My healers will resurrect your dead and assist you and your convoy in getting back on the road. Make for the elven army - my riders will guard you until you reach them. Tell everyone what you have seen today," he said, fire in his eyes. "Take some of the goblin bodies with you for proof." He whistled, and Windrider was at his side.

"I will," the elf promised, eyes still wide. "I will tell everyone. We all will."

Cyrus climbed back into the saddle and dashed to the rest of the patrol, issuing orders as he came. "Vaste, Terian, stay here and escort the convoy; the rearguard should be here momentarily. Everyone else, you're with me!" Vara made her way to him, looking him over with unease.

His eyes brushed past her as he looked for Niamh, finding her still on her horse. "You know where to take us." She nodded, and began to cast a spell. "Longwell," he said to the dragoon, who had returned to his side, a few of his hairs sticking up, singed from the lightning, "get your lance ready..."

A tornado of wind swallowed him and the patrol, leaving the last remnants of the convoy behind them.

Chapter 37

Cyrus urged Windrider out of the maelstrom that accompanied the teleportation spell. The horse stumbled for but a moment in gaining its footing on the unfamiliar grounds and whinnied as screaming filled the air around them.

Behind them, the Sanctuary forces moved forward from the portal, weapons drawn, spells already streaking through the air.

Before them, a horde of goblins squealed at their sudden appearance. The night was lit as the wizard accompanying the goblins raised his hands, magic arcing from his fingertips as he cast a spell.

Cyrus did not even get a cry out before a lance streaked through the air and caught the wizard square in the chest, knocking him backwards, spell energy already dispersing. A smile broke across Cyrus's face as he watched Longwell pump his arm in victory.

"There is no retreat for them!" Cyrus called to his forces. "Ride them down!" His sword flashed in the light of the spells cast around them and hacked into goblin after goblin. The area around the portal was flat, filled with volcanic rocks and dirt, and in the distance, volcanoes spewed magma in the air and pooled in the ground.

"So nice to be back in the Mountains of Nartanis," Terian breathed as his axe felled two more fleeing goblins. "It seems like we always find a victory here."

"Except once," Cyrus muttered. "They'll flee towards Enterra!" he shouted. "Kill them here!"

Screams and whinnying filled the night as they gave chase to the goblins. The goblins' meager efforts to defend themselves resulted in several wounded horses, but the only injuries to Sanctuary riders came when a pair of newer members were thrown from their mounts. Cyrus swept down on the goblins responsible before they could do any more harm.

Within minutes, the battle was over. Goblin bodies lay strewn across the ground and Cyrus sat atop Windrider, viewing the carnage with a feeling of odd dissatisfaction.

Niamh picked her way over to him. "You guessed right. They did head for home after the attacks."

Cyrus nodded. "Now we've got some proof. A surviving convoy that can tell what they've seen, a host of goblin corpses and even a surviving conspirator." He turned to look at the body of the fallen wizard. "If we choose to resurrect him."

The other officers cantered over on horseback, Longwell and Andren in tow. "Where's Alaric?" Cyrus said with a frown.

"He was with the rear guard," Vara replied. "He's back at the canyon. Any idea who our mystery wizard is?"

"Yeah," Cyrus admitted. "I'm pretty sure."

"Did you see him in the battle?" Niamh asked.

He shook his head. "No. Just a guess."

The druid looked at him in amusement. "You're guessing? Would you like to bet on it? Because I'm betting you can't figure out which wizard, in all Arkaria, is under that cloak."

Cyrus smiled even though he didn't feel it. "I'll bet you a hundred gold."

"And you didn't see him?" Niamh said, skeptical.

"On my honor, I have not seen his face nor anything but his cloak."

"I'm in," Longwell said.

"Me too," Niamh agreed. "Unless that's too rich for you?"

"That's fine. Any other takers?" Cyrus asked, looking over the crowd of raiders milling around him. He looked to Andren. "You?"

"Nuh-uh." The healer shook his head. "You've burned me with these tricks before."

"It's called perception."

"It's called me losing money, and I need every piece of gold I can get."

Cyrus looked to Vara. "What about you?"

She looked at him evenly. "I wouldn't care to bet against you – in this or any other matter."

A small smile crossed his face at the memory of provoking her to an outburst to win a bet. "Because I change the odds?"

"Because you're likely right."

"All right," Niamh interrupted. "All bets are in, so who is it?"

Cyrus smiled. "Carrack from Goliath."

"That horse's ass?" The druid looked at him in astonishment. With a flash of her red hair she dismounted and crossed the ground, Longwell a step behind her. Cyrus led Windrider at a slow canter toward the body, Vara and Andren behind him.

Niamh and Longwell stood over the corpse, having pulled back the hood. "Impossible," Niamh gasped. Her red hair suddenly matched the color that her cheeks brought forth, anger filling her eyes.

"Damn," Longwell breathed. He dropped his lance in surprise.

Cyrus looked down from Windrider into the still face of the Goliath wizard, eyes bulging from his head. "You just couldn't resist taking a shot at me, could you? That was a mistake; if you'd kept it impersonal you'd have knocked out our healer first; he wouldn't have been able to heal me and you would have made a clean getaway. If you were really smart, the minute you saw us you would have teleported out, but now you see what vengeance... gets you..." His words drifted off and he felt a sudden dryness in his mouth.

"Indeed," came a whisper from Vara.

"We should get out of here," Cyrus ordered, voice suddenly hoarse. "Gather up half a dozen of those goblin corpses and Carrack's body, and let's get back to Sanctuary."

His orders were carried out and within minutes they were dissolving into a teleportation spell. The light faded and Cyrus found himself on Windrider, in the foyer.

"I'm afraid I'm going to have to ask you to park your horses outside," came the amused voice of Alaric from behind them on the balcony. Cyrus looked around to see the members of Sanctuary assembled in a ring around them, having moved aside when the light of teleport appeared. "We were just having a guild meeting in regards to what our evening's efforts revealed."

"Wait 'til you see this, then," Niamh said with a nod at Longwell, who threw the corpse of Carrack into the middle of the floor. The wizard's dead eyes stared up at the ceiling.

"I don't understand," came the voice of Ryin Ayend. Cyrus looked back to see the human staring, eyes dull.

Cyrus dismounted. "We suspected Malpravus was pushing the governments toward the action they took; now we know why."

"I don't get it," Ayend said numbly. "Why would... our ALLIES... do such a thing?"

"It was the only way that Malpravus could ever get Sanctuary to merge," Niamh said. "He brought all this down on us just so he could take over our guild."

"None of you were there but Alaric and Curatio," Cyrus began, "but in my first Alliance officer meeting, Malpravus proposed to merge the Alliance guilds. Alaric voted it down, as did the Daring, but with us disgraced I'm sure he found it easier to get the Daring to move."

"Vultures," Vara said under her breath.

"This is beyond circling the carcasses of your enemies, waiting for them to die," J'anda said from his place on the balcony. "We've known Malpravus was capable of some evil things, but he's been bringing goblins into the Plains of Perdamun, killing countless traders and guards on these convoys... all so he can absorb us?"

"And now, the last piece of the puzzle falls into place," Alaric said from above.

"Not quite," Cyrus replied. "I didn't want to tell any of you without proof, but I remembered something from our night in Enterra - you know, the one I've been reliving every night for the last year." His voice turned ironic. "I believe Malpravus was the one who conspired with the goblins." A muttered gasp of shock filled the hall.

"He's already conspired with the goblins to kill hundreds of people in an effort to get us banished and shunned from every civilized town in the west, and you all act shocked that he'd have sold us out before?" Vaste shook his head in amazement.

"He's the one who betrayed us the night that Narstron died - he must have known we'd have at least one dwarf with us, so he played the Emperor and Empress, saying that their 'gezhvet', this prophesied harbinger of doom, was coming with us. He collected the Hammer of Earth as a reward -" Cy clenched his gauntlet - "and they killed Narstron thinking he was going to be the death of their Empire."

Alaric answered with a nod. "It would make sense that he would have ties to them before proposing this scheme. So now the question becomes, what do we do about it?"

Cyrus looked up at the Ghost. "Is this sufficient evidence? If we resurrect Carrack - maybe cut out his tongue so he can't teleport and heal him when we want him to talk?"

"There are less violent ways to restrain a wizard from teleporting, my friend," Alaric said with a smile.

"Not as much fun," Terian added.

"With the word of the survivors, the bodies of the goblins, and Carrack," Curatio said from beside Alaric, "that will convince the King of the Elves."

"Even Pretnam Urides would have difficulty ignoring all this evidence, but I would not be surprised if he tried very hard in spite of it," Alaric agreed. "It might be best to have something more."

With a sigh, Cyrus looked up at the Ghost. "If there's any more evidence, it's either in Goliath's guildhall or in the depths of Enterra with the Imperials."

A glisten lit the Ghost's eye. "Precisely. It would seem unlikely we could storm Goliath's guildhall, being as it is in the heart of Reikonos, so if you would please... General... make ready the guild for an expedition to Enterra." Alaric surveyed the room. "We will clear our name - and make warning to all about what happens to those who attempt to stain our honor."

A low, grinding feeling in Cyrus's stomach filled him with unease but he looked up at Alaric and nodded, as a cheer filled the hall. *At last, I'll have revenge,* he thought with a feeling of intense trepidation - and no excitement.

Chapter 38

Alaric dismissed them after announcing that they would reassemble for the invasion of Enterra in one hour. Cyrus left, wandering downstairs, ignoring the roars of approval at impeding battle that resonated from Fortin's chamber, shaking the corridor as he made his way to the end of the long, dark stone passage in the dungeons to his cell.

I've wanted vengeance on these beasts for almost two years, he thought. *Now we're going... and I don't know what to think. It's not as if they don't deserve it... killing Narstron... killing all those traders... but why? What's in it for them? I know why Goliath is doing this, but why would the goblins send warriors across Arkaria?* He thought again of the soul ruby in Malpravus's hand, and shook his head. *What if it worked? What if I could bring back Narstron?*

He stared ahead and his eyes alighted on the sword, the Champion's Blade, assembled and waiting for the scabbard that would make it whole. He shuffled toward it, almost afraid to approach it for fear that his hopes would be dashed. *Last time I died in Enterra. So did everyone else. And Narstron never came back.*

He reached down and grasped the hilt; it felt cool to the touch. He tossed his gauntlets aside and felt the pommel, stared at the carving, ran his fingers up to the swordguard, and finally the blade. It was sharp, but heavy, even for him. It was made of material that was stronger than any other he'd seen, but it was not light of weight.

"Reflecting on your impending triumphs?" Cyrus turned to see Vara leaning against the frame of the cell door. Her posture was almost relaxed, something he hadn't seen from her in a long time.

"Worrying about my impending battle," he admitted, tying a strap of leather across his back and tucking the sword into it. "In case you forgot, last time we were in Enterra, it did not end in triumph."

"I have a very clear memory of that night," she replied, straightening up and tucking her hands behind her back. "We also had a much smaller army at our disposal."

"They still have us outnumbered ten to one."

"Which are very bad odds, on an open field of battle," she

conceded. "But in the confined spaces of Enterra, the victory goes to the strongest fighters – which we have."

"I don't know," he said, slumping onto his cot. "We won't be able to sneak through the gates like we did last time; we have far too many fighters for that." He looked up at her in surprise. "You didn't come down to my cell to discuss strategy for the battle."

She looked at him for a long moment before her eyes flicked down. "I did not. I have all the confidence in the world that whatever your strategy, it will be more than adequate to give us a great victory. I came..." she began with an air of reluctance, "...not to see what you planned to do when we get there, but what you planned for yourself when we come to the end of this. I need to know... if you're going to let your personal feelings cloud your judgment."

"I don't know," he said. "I still want to kill them, the Emperor and Empress. I'd like to wipe out their whole army and disassemble that damned city stone by stone."

She crossed the distance between them and lowered herself to sit next to him. "I... understand your feelings. I doubt anyone would begrudge you the right to feel that way. But in pursuing your revenge, what are you willing to sacrifice?"

"I don't understand."

She leaned her head against the wall behind them, armor making a slight scraping noise against the stones of the cell. "Carrack attacked you against his better judgment, I would think, embarrassed because a lowly warrior had killed him. If anyone else from Goliath had been running that attack party, they would have seen you coming and assumed you had others waiting with you." She laughed lightly. "Actually, they should have seen you coming and assumed somehow you would crush them regardless of how many people you had with you."

"Kind words," he said, still expressionless. "But Carrack had to do what he had to do –"

"But what he did was wrong, don't you see? It cost him his life – again – and fouled the whole raiding party and their plan in the process! They would have gotten away with it if not for his desire to pay you back for some nonsensical incident that he walked away from with no lasting damage but to his pride."

She stood. "And that's what's happened to you. Your friend died, and it hurt. You felt it, in your guts, in your heart, and it stung. But you know what stung worse? Your pride – that you, the warrior, the strongest man I've ever met, couldn't save him. And that sticks in your craw worse than anything else and leaves you with nothing left to do but strike out at the ones you think are responsible.

"It won't bring him back – and it won't make you feel even a whit better. And if you do something stupid while gaining your revenge, something that gets others killed in Sanctuary, I promise you'll feel worse than you ever did with Narstron, because this time it will be something you could prevent."

Her words came spitting out at him like howling winds of a tornado. He looked at her in wonderment. "I'm really the strongest man you've ever met?"

She froze. "I did say that, didn't I? Oh, bollocks. Yes, you are." She paused, and annoyance took root on her face. "I deliver an impassioned speech that's incisive and cuts to the heart of your character and pain and *that* is all you got out of it?"

"No," he said. "I heard the rest, too. And you're right. Carrack acted foolishly and doomed his whole force because he wanted revenge on me. I promise you, that no matter what else, I won't put our army in danger for my revenge."

She bowed her head. "I believe you. I just wanted to make sure you thought about it before going down there." She paused and looked down at him. "So what *is* your plan for Enterra?"

A rueful smile crossed his face. "I thought you had faith in my strategy, whatever it might be?"

She made an exasperated sound. "Just because I have faith in your ability to lead the attack does not mean I wish to charge blindly into a mountain filled with goblins."

"I'll spell it out for the officers as we're riding there. I have something important for you to do."

She raised an eyebrow. "Truly? Then I suppose I should prepare." She turned to leave.

"One more thing," he said and she turned back. "When you leave, Fortin might ask you if you kissed me."

She looked aghast. "*What?!*"

He shrugged. "I don't know. Just tell him yes."

"I already know she didn't," came the rumbling from down the hall.

Vara bristled at the sound of the rock giant's voice. "He heard everything?"

Cyrus shrugged. "Rock giants have unusually good hearing."

"Our sense of smell is pretty decent too," came Fortin's voice. "Did you know she put on a lilac scent before she came down here? I've never known her to do *that* before a battle."

Vara's pale cheeks reddened; she was more embarrassed than Cyrus had ever seen her. "Say nothing," she snapped.

He stared at her and she stared back, and for a moment the silence hung between them unbroken. "You smell nice," he conceded.

With a snort of fury, she turned and stormed out the door. Down the hall came the short, sharp laughs of a rock giant who had been soundly entertained.

Chapter 39

After a journey of a few hours the Army of Sanctuary was concealed behind the edge of a crater on the slope of a mountain. Inside the crater, jutting up to the mountainside was a keep. Grey stone walls stretched fifty feet into the air above the crater, backing up to the mountain's sheer edges. It was a perfectly defensible keep, wooden gates standing ten feet tall, all defending a secondary gate built into the side of the mountain.

Cyrus looked down at the walls from his vantage point, hiding at the crater's rim. "All right," he announced to the force behind him. "Everyone knows what to do?" Nods greeted his statement. "I'd like this better if we had a battering ram, some siege engines and catapults, but we'll make do." A half-smile curled his lip. "Archers, to your places. Vara..." He looked over at her and she nodded, a little uncertainly. "You'll do fine."

Her expression turned severe. "I am not worried about my part in this endeavor. I am concerned about you, cannon fodder." She sniffed and turned away, leaving him with the same half-smile.

He turned back to Alaric, who stood at his side. "We'll be ready in a moment." Drawing his sword, he took a moment to look at the Ghost's weapon, not for the first time. A long, heavy sword, it had runes inscribed along the blade and a detailed pattern carved into the hilt. The pommel was a skull, with black onyx inlaid into the eyes. "I never have asked you about your sword - it's very impressive."

The paladin hefted his blade and flipped it, pommel first, to Cyrus. "It is called *Aterum*. Would you like to try it?"

Cy took the sword by the hilt and swung it in front of him. The blade was perfectly balanced and felt light in his hands. "It's mystical, isn't it?"

"Quite." The Ghost took the blade back and held it at his side. "Your archers are in place, I believe."

"Vara will be ready in a moment." Cyrus turned to the army. "Once we get inside, I'll need rangers to scout down the tunnels ahead of us."

"I volunteer," Aisling said, stepping forward.

"You're not with the archers?" Cyrus asked her.

She gave him a wide grin. "Couldn't find my bow and arrows.

Care to search me for them?"

He looked down at her with a weathered look of resignation. "If you can disappear as well as your bow, you can be our first scout."

Her eyes lit up. "I accept. And not only can I disappear, I can make other things disappear if you like."

His eyes narrowed. "I sense a veiled reference. Still not learned our lesson yet?"

She covered her mouth, hiding the wide smile beneath. "I'm a slow learner. I'll stop now. Thank you for entrusting this duty to me." She seemed to hover for a moment, vibrating with excitement, then she surged forward and kissed him on the cheek, so soft he scarcely felt her touch. He could not ignore her warm breath on his neck as she passed him, though.

The flare of a fire spell lit at the base of the gates of the goblin keep. "That's the signal," Cyrus said. "They're in position." He waved his hand at the archers on the far rim of the crater, and saw an acknowledgment from Martaina as a volley of arrows filled the skies above the crater.

Shouts came from the keep as the gate began to close. "All right, we charge," Cyrus called out. "Be loud; move around a lot; do everything you can to get them to watch us." He thrust his short sword into the air. Bellowing a warcry, he jumped over the lip of the crater and began to half-run, half-slide down the sloped wall.

As he descended, in all the shouts before and behind him, he could have sworn he heard another, familiar voice once more in the clamor of the charge.

Avenge me.

He pushed it out of his mind as he reached the bottom of the crater. The portcullis was down, its latticework design dark against the fading strips of light disappearing as the gates behind it were shut. He smiled as he looked to the tops of the walls and saw goblins peering down through the gaps in the parapet.

Cy began to stride across the ground toward them. The army behind him slowed to match his pace, although some were still descending the slope. Arrows fell upon the keep in waves, keeping the goblins under cover.

"Hail, goblin folk," Cyrus called out. "We are willing to accept your surrender. None of you need die." There was no response but for a peal of laughter from behind a parapet. He sighed. "I'm going to need our battering ram up here."

"We don't have a battering ram," Erith snapped from behind him. "So what do you plan to do now, genius?" She looked up as something brushed past her. "Oh."

Fortin walked to the front of the army as the Sanctuary combatants made way for him. Cyrus smiled at the rock giant. "Would you prefer to open the gates or open the walls?"

"I think the walls would surprise them more," the giant said in a quiet timbre. "They are short, somewhat like gnomes; may I eat my kills?"

Cyrus's eyes widened at the suggestion. "I... uh..." He looked to Alaric, who nodded. "I guess so."

"Excellent." The rock giant interlaced his fingers, stretching his knuckles. His arms dropped back to his sides and for a moment Fortin looked completely at peace. Then a bellow filled the air that was louder than any war horn but just as resonant, and the rock giant was in motion, a blur streaking across the ground, aimed at the tower nearest the gate.

Cries of alarm filled the air on the walls, and the sounds of battle echoed from inside. All this noise was drowned out by the impact of a rock giant hitting a stone wall, a blasting noise as horrendous as any explosion and the sound of stone buckling and breaking. Cy looked away, covering his eyes as a shower of pieces no larger than slivers fell around them. When he looked back up, there was a hole in the wall of the keep tower roughly the size of a rock giant, and the stones above it began to crumble and fall.

Cyrus could hear fire and lightning being cast about inside the walls, and the screams of the goblins increased in intensity and pitch.

"Oh my," Alaric said. "It sounds as though we are winning."

Another explosion of stone marked the exit of Fortin very near to his entry point, and the tower next to the keep's gate collapsed as though it were made of flimsy wood. The rock giant charged back to Cyrus, stopping short of the warrior, resting his hands on his knees as though he were out of breath. "They tried to retreat, of course, but the ice princess and her force have them cut off. The inner gate is sealed and its defenders are dead at the hands of her fighters. There will be no warning to the goblin city that we are coming."

"Good," Cyrus reassured him with a smile. "You mind opening that keep-gate for the rest of us now?"

"Certainly," Fortin said and turned, charging this time at the portcullis.

"I'll give two to one odds that says he bounces off," Andren said from behind Cyrus. "That's got to be worked dwarven steel."

"You think they brought dwarves down here to craft it?" J'anda replied. "I'll take your odds."

"I'll bet that it is dwarven steel, and I'll bet that he breaks it down," Cyrus added.

Before Andren could reply, the rock giant hit the portcullis. Dwarven steel or not, it broke free with the force of his impact and ripped into the gate behind it. Fortin's momentum carried him sailing through the keep's gate, ripping it off its hinges, and the rock giant landed in a lump just inside the gates.

A cracking noise filled the air. Pieces of heavy stone began to rain down as the wall above the gate began to collapse from the damage Fortin had done to the arch when he broke the portcullis. It fell with the sound of a rain of multi-ton stone blocks. When it finished, there was a pile of rock ten feet high where an open gate had stood moments earlier.

"Sorry," came a rumbling voice from behind the wreckage. "I'll make another door."

Goblin screams came from above on the wall as a section of the keep burst open near the top of the parapets. Fortin had climbed the wall and was demolishing it piece by piece to clear a path. Stone blocks the size of Cyrus flew into the crater a few at a time as the rock giant broke the wall down. It took five minutes, by which time the goblin voices had faded and Cyrus saw Vara look down on them from the top of the keep, Niamh and Curatio at her side.

"It would appear you are unable to carry out your part of the plan, which was the simplest. I fear for our efforts from here on," she needled at him, smiling down.

"What?" he called back to her.

"You were supposed to walk through the gate and meet us once our work of securing the inside gate was done. Even this modest task appears to be too much for you." Her words were teasing rather than vicious, and her mood was light.

"You want to try climbing over the wreckage here?" he asked.

"I do not. That's why I consented to lead the task force inside. I had a suspicion Fortin might not make your entry the cleanest."

"Oh yes," Fortin replied, clearing the last stones out of the wall, making a perfect V-shaped hole in the keep, wide enough for even him to walk through. "Blame the rock giant for shoddy goblin construction. I can't help it if this place is as delicate as... a lilac," he finished with gleeful laugh.

Vara cut short any reply she might have made, disappearing out of sight behind the wall. Cyrus rallied the army and they moved through the opening into the yard of the keep and found the gates to the mountain already opened. Vara stood at the door with her arms crossed, tapping her foot. As he approached, she extended her arms toward the open gates. "After you," she said with a bow.

"I would normally say, 'ladies first', but if there're goblins on the way down, I'd rather face them," he said as he walked past her. She fell into line at his shoulder, and Aisling squeezed past him, Martaina at her side.

"I brought another ranger," Aisling said as she passed. "What do you want us to do?"

"Aisling, you go scout ahead of us, let me know what's coming," he began. "Martaina, I want you to keep an eye down the side tunnels as we pass; let us know if there are soldiers. If you see any, spur our army to kill them. Pursue if necessary. Draft some other rangers to go with you if you feel like you need help, but keep it quiet. I don't want the goblins to know we're coming."

"Maybe you should have avoided using a rock giant as a battering ram then," Erith mumbled, barely audible.

He glared at her for a beat before turning back to Aisling. "Let me know if there's any hint they know we're coming. Vara," he said and the elf appeared, "did anyone get away from you at the gate to the mountain?"

"No," she said with shake of her head so vehement that it tossed her ponytail around. "The mountain gate was open when we snuck in so I placed our force in the tunnel before breaking invisibility and attacking. We hit them from behind before they knew what was happening. Between us and your friend the walking boulder, there was no escape."

"Good," he said, not breaking his pace down the tunnel. "Where's Fortin now?"

"At the back," Terian said, a few paces behind Cy. "He barely fits in these tunnels."

"Have him be our rear guard. I want warriors spread out along the line. It's a long way to the depths of the mountain. Lots of side tunnels where trouble could crop up, and I don't want us vulnerable."

With a nod, Terian dropped back to issue orders to the formation. The tunnels were narrow - only big enough for a few people to walk side by side. The walls had a shine of phosphorescence from the algaes living on the rock. The light of a spell that gave him vision in the darkness was the only thing that allowed him to avoid a sudden drop as the floor stepped down. He smiled in memory of the last time he had missed that step, and remembered what had happened after.

Aisling appeared from the shadows to his right and he halted. "There's a half dozen goblins walking patrol routes between here and some sort of keep built into the cave walls. If you want to keep this party quiet, I recommend you do something about them."

"J'anda," Cyrus called quietly, and the enchanter emerged from behind Vaste. "I need you up front in case we get anyone who decides to run. Niamh," he said to the druid, "can you send some vines to slow them down if need be?"

"Absolutely," she said with a nod. "I can even make it a small patch instead of a big old mess of 'em."

"Eyes open, then. We're going to charge down the tunnel and kill them as we go."

Cyrus descended the tunnel. He rounded a corner to find a goblin looking at him in shock from just behind the wall. He reached out, grabbed the goblin and impaled it on his sword before it had a chance to respond. Squeals down the tunnel told him that it had not been alone.

Vines burst from the dirt on either side of the tunnel walls and grabbed firm hold of two goblins. Cyrus struck both down with casual slashes as he passed.

"This seems easier than last time," Erith said.

"We have more people and we're not sneaking," he replied. A shock ran through him. "I met you here for the first time, didn't I?"

"Aww," came her mocking reply, "you remembered."

"Yeah, I remember," he said. "I remember you told me I'd only get three healing spells for the entire expedition."

She shrugged. "What can I say? I lied. I'm a sucker for a hopeless case like you."

"Hopeless now, am I? What does it say about you, who

followed me here –"

"Children, perhaps keep you voices down so we don't bring down a whole army of goblins upon us?" Vara looked daggers at both of them.

"My apologies." He waved her off.

"You threw a goblin head at me last time," Erith said with a pouty look.

"I actually decapitated the goblin with such skill that it hit you," Cyrus whispered back.

"Bullshit," came Vara's succinct reply. "I remember those days; you were not so elegant with your sword strokes as to be able to accomplish such a feat."

Cyrus exchanged a look with Andren. "Did Vara just say 'bullshit'?" The elf nodded. "You've been hanging around me and my ilk for too long, shelas'akur."

She rolled her eyes. "You shouldn't use words you don't know the meaning of. Which, if you followed that simple rule, would actually cut down on the amount of pointless conversation spewing from your drivel hole."

"I know more than you think," he replied. "You remember that nice little elven town where you tried to drown me in the local watering hole in the middle of the night? Nalikh'akur?"

She regarded him with suspicion. "What of it?"

"Nalikh'akur?" he asked. "'Last Bastion'?"

"So which is it?" she asked. "Is 'akur' 'last' or 'bastion'?" She did not smile. "And what does 'shelas' mean, out of curiosity?"

"I don't know," he admitted, "but do you think it's impossible to figure out?"

"Well, it's been roughly a year and you're still in the dark, so yes, I believe it may be impossible for you to figure out." She surveyed the crowd around them. "Unless anyone would care to throw him a hint? Anyone? You?" Her gaze turned to Andren, who shook his head when she stared at him. "I didn't think so." She turned back to Cyrus. "Good luck in your search for the answer. Your best friend won't even tell you, and he knows."

"While I think I speak for all non-elves here when I say I'd love to understand the tantalizing mystery that Vara is torturing Cyrus with," Vaste spoke up, "I suggest we instead focus our efforts on the pack of goblins that's lingering ahead of us." He pointed down the tunnel as it widened into a small chamber. "Right there. Looking at us. They're pointing. Their faces are covered with awe... and... they're running."

Cyrus bolted after them, Vara and Alaric on his heels. Twin flashes of light from spells cast by J'anda and Niamh streaked by on either side of him, but Cyrus honed in on the first goblin. A lance sailed over his head and perfectly speared the rear goblin, but a half dozen more were still running. "Nice job, Longwell," Cyrus yelled, running to catch the shorter creatures.

"I thought you sent scouts ahead to apprise us of their positions?" Vara yelled, slashing into a goblin trapped by Niamh's vines as they pursued down the tunnel.

"I did!" He beheaded one mesmerized by J'anda as he passed it. *Four to go.*

"There is no time for recrimination! Clear the way!" Alaric shouted and thrust his palm forward. A blast of concussive force shot by Cyrus, sending a stir of air as it blew by. It hit a goblin squarely in the back, knocking him to his knees with such force that he flipped. Another burst from Alaric missed, blasting an inch of solid rock off the tunnel wall.

Vara answered with a stun blast of her own. It grazed one of the remaining goblins, spinning him off balance into the wall, where she knelt and killed it.

A shadow moved in the distance, just in front of the last two goblins, reaching out for them as they ran down the tunnel. A figure emerged, dark blue skin almost invisible even with his spell-enhanced eyesight, and two daggers stabbed into the sides of the goblins as they passed, causing both to stumble. The feral shadow stepped delicately out of the way to let them drop, then pounced on one after another, stabbing them until dead.

Cyrus slowed to a walk. "Aisling," he said, "I thought you were going to tell me when there were goblins ahead."

She picked over the bodies and he saw her slip two coins into a small purse at her belt. "These weren't in the main passage as I went down. They must have come out of a side tunnel after I passed." She shrugged. "I wouldn't worry, though; they won't be telling anybody about us."

Alaric nodded. "Well done, lass. I was beginning to worry they'd get away."

"Yes, well done indeed," Vara said with an icy tone. "I could have leaped forward and killed them both if not for this lumbering beast in my way." She pointed at Cyrus.

"Lumbering beast?" he said with a look of great offense. "I

thought I was the strongest man you know?"

Her eyes became narrow slits. "Perhaps you are, but it would be in addition to being the most petty, vain and self-reverential man I know."

"If you don't want him," Aisling said with a sly smile, "I'd be glad to take him - over and over -"

"Oh, stop it," Cyrus said. Vara shook her head in irritation. "We have work to do, more ground to cover, innocence to prove and all that."

"Agreed," Alaric said. "We also have several miles to go before Aisling's last uncomfortable statement purges itself from my memory," he said without looking at the dark elf. "The sooner we begin, the better."

Elements of the army began to catch up to them as the tunnel narrowed once more. "How are we doing?" Cyrus asked Terian, who had rejoined them at the front of the army.

"We're starting to spread out," the dark knight reported. "These tunnels were not meant to be invaded by an army of over a thousand. I don't know for certain, but I have to guess that Fortin and the rear guard are at least a mile behind us."

"What's slowing us down?" Cy asked, brow furrowed.

"Lots of attacks out of side tunnels," Terian replied. "We've managed to run them all down so far, but elements of our force keep splitting off to deal with these ancillary threats and it costs us time."

"I want every element accounted for, and every single person accounted for within each element." His grip tightened around his sword. "We will not leave anyone behind."

"Are you sure?" Terian asked lightly. "Enterra seems like a great place to spend... uh..." The dark knight's voice faded as he thought the better of his jest. "...about five minutes before deciding to go somewhere that doesn't suck."

Cy ignored him, marching down the corridor. The cave walls twisted and turned at bizarre angles, like a snake bending back on itself. No rock jutted out from the sides of the cave, but neither were they smooth or polished. Whoever had tunneled it had made it functional but not aesthetically pleasing. A smell of sweat and stale air lingered.

Upon reaching a corner Cyrus halted and peeked around. "Damn," he breathed. "Glad I remembered."

"What?" Vara asked, leaning past him to look. She crossed his midsection, her neck not far below his face. The faint smell of lilac wafted up to him and he shut his eyes for a moment. She glanced for a few seconds, withdrew and sighed. "Damn. That's the complex where the Emperor and Empress are?"

"Yeah." He nodded. "I counted about ten guards around the top wall - if we screw this up, they'll seal the gate and we'll be stuck here until we can bring up Fortin." He frowned. "If we can bring up Fortin. They can hold that position against attack for months against conventional enemies." Around the corner lay a long stretch of open tunnel leading up to a ten foot high wall built across a wider chamber. A small gate with a portcullis lay in the middle of the wall and goblins stood arm to arm across the parapets. "This will require coordination and precision."

"I would have assumed given our efforts thus far, haste and violence would be in order." Her eyebrow crooked and a smile tugged at the corners of her mouth.

"Perhaps some combination of all," he replied. "Where's Aisling?"

She slipped from the shadows in front of him with a bow in hand, arrow already notched. "I can take two, perhaps three of them before they realize what's happening and take cover."

His eyes fixated on the bow in her hands - it was almost as tall as she; a long length of hickory, with a taut string running down it. The only concession to beauty was a carving of a leaping fox running along the top end of the handle. "Where did you get that?"

She shrugged but did not bother to hide the impish smile that dotted her features. "I told you I had one."

He shook his head. "All right, you take two of them." He turned to Vara. "Can you hit any of them with that stun spell of yours?"

She shook her head. "The tunnel is too long; they are out of my range."

"But not mine," Alaric said, making his way forward to take a look. "Three of them are clustered together at the right side of the wall; I may be able to hit all of them with a force blast."

"J'anda," Cyrus called.

The enchanter made his way forward and snuck a peek around the edge. "Two, perhaps three if luck favors us. I think you would want me to go first?"

"Before the others start flinging arrows and spells at them?" Cy smiled at the enchanter. "We have a means of dealing with somewhere between six and nine of them, depending on how fortunate we are. I don't know about the rest of you, but I don't feel that fortunate." A quick look around revealed shakes of the head. "Niamh? Vines?"

She looked around the corner. "I can get one, maybe two of the ones close to the wall on the side Alaric's not attacking, otherwise, no. They're pretty far off the ground."

Cy nodded. "Now we've got between seven and ten sewed up. Still not feeling lucky. Any other rangers close to the front of our line?"

Aisling shook her head. "They're helping keep the side tunnels secure. Arrows tend to hobble runners. I can deal with the last ones." She turned to J'anda. "I'm going to start shooting in thirty seconds, so get your targets mesmerized by then." Without waiting for a response, she melted into the shadows.

The enchanter turned to Cyrus in alarm. "She's not serious? We haven't settled this plan yet!"

"Aisling?" He looked at the shadows with undisguised annoyance. "Yes, she's serious," he said to J'anda, "move!"

The dark elf slid into the shadows at the bend, hands already in motion, casting an incantation through unmoving lips. A faint light surrounded one of the goblins, then another, and then a third.

Cyrus watched as one of the goblins fell to his knees without warning, then dropped off the wall face first. "Alaric, Niamh," Cy muttered warningly.

The Ghost stepped around the corner and unleashed a blast of force from his hand that caused Cyrus to sway. Another goblin near the back of the wall fell, and Cyrus could see a thin arrow shaft protruding from his eye. Alaric's blast hit the goblins on the far right side, flinging two of them off the wall like stick men in a hurricane wind, limp bodies broken against the rocks behind them.

"Got two," the old knight said through gritted teeth. "The other one moved to check on his fallen comrade before my spell hit."

Niamh's hands waved with fervor, and roots burst forth from the tunnel above the left side of the wall, enveloping one of the goblins, pulling him against the roof of the tunnel.

"Two left!" Cy yelled, watching as the last goblins dodged

behind parapets. The portcullis began to descend as he, Vara and Alaric ran to cross the ground between them. It closed, leaving the three of them standing in the shadow of the wall. Cyrus drove his fingers under the bottommost iron segment and tried to lift. Alaric and Vara joined him, adding their strength to his own, but the portcullis did not budge. "They'll have warned the defenders in the keep. We have to get this thing open now, before they swarm out or we're screwed!"

"One more try?" Alaric suggested. "On three... one... two... three..." At the count of three, the portcullis jolted, moving upward with their insistent pushing.

A clanking noise could be heard behind the wall, and Cyrus stopped pushing. The portcullis continued to move upward. "Where are the goblins?" he asked. Vara and Alaric ceased their lifting efforts, and still the portcullis continued to rise.

A small mass hit the ground in front of Cyrus, followed by another, each with a muffled thump. After staring at them for a moment, he realized they were bodies - goblin corpses.

With catlike grace, Aisling dropped down after them, landing with a nimbleness that Cyrus could have predicted. "I killed the ones that were mesmerized too," she said as she sheathed her daggers. "Niamh's vines choked the other one to death. I snuck in while you were distracting them."

"Once again, lass, well done," Alaric nodded. "Your tactics of distraction and deception are... quite impressive. But I have to ask, must you stab them in the back unknowing?"

She shrugged, an air of unconcern. "It's the fastest way."

"And the most treacherous," spat Vara.

"War's not a pretty thing," Aisling said to the paladin, tensing as if bracing for an attack. "And we can't all be tall and graceful and strong as you."

"Enough," Cyrus said. "Beyond this door is an antechamber to the throne room. It's big enough we can reassemble and prepare for the assault on the Emperor and Empress." He walked to the handle and turned it.

"Are you quite certain you should do that?" Alaric asked. "Perhaps we should have Aisling scout the room first?"

"You're right," he agreed. His fingers left the knob but it continued to turn of its own accord. A moment of curiosity - *How is the door handle turning itself?* - flashed through his mind, replaced by the horror of realization as the door opened and he found a goblin looking up at him, mouth agape, sharp teeth gleaming.

Cyrus brought his sword down in a flash, but the goblin let out a startled cry that turned into a scream as he twisted away from Cyrus's blow. The short sword caught the goblin between the ribs and caused him to squeal in agony, throwing himself backward off of the warrior's sword. Cyrus looked past his foe to see a room half the size of the Great Hall at Sanctuary, balconies around the edges, and goblins staring down - dozens, maybe hundreds of them scattered throughout the room, all staring at the open door - and him.

Chapter 40

A howl of fury came from a hundred goblin throats as Cyrus thrust the door open. *So much for a plan.* "Get the army down here now!" he shouted back, sword in his hand.

He moved to the first rank of goblins, huddled in a cluster only a few feet from him. They stood on a rich, red rug that Cyrus barely took note of before bringing his sword down and making it redder still with the blood of two goblins caught unprepared. He heard a loud WHUMP! and to his right a half dozen goblins went flying with the power of Alaric's spell. A few to his left were knocked asunder by Vara's less powerful burst.

Stones cracked on the far side of the hall and entangling vines reached out, dragging goblins away from the impending fight as the room turned into a frenzy.

Cyrus raked his sword across another three foes, not killing any of them but wounding them enough that they stepped back. He saw a goblin streak at him to attack his flank when a light came over it. A glance back showed J'anda working his magic, sending a courteous nod toward the warrior as he mesmerized another goblin.

"They'll be warning the Imperials!" Alaric shouted over the melee. The Ghost had waded into the growing number of enemies scampering forward to fight them. Cy watched Terian and Thad enter the fray, and felt a healing spell run across him as Erith sealed the small wounds that his foes had inflicted.

Vara hacked a great bloody swath across the packed crowd and pieces of four distinct green bodies flew across the room. Her next swing produced similar results, and the next. She moved too fast for them; the goblins' mob attacks were causing them to trip over one another and limiting their effectiveness. Alaric and Vara kept them at arms' reach without great difficulty; Cyrus was not so fortunate.

He swung his short sword again and again, and the goblins came crushing in at him with greater force. They were four deep now, all in a line, bunching up toward him and snapping and clawing. He felt a thousand tiny pinpricks as their claws found purchase in the gaps in his armor. Blood dripped from between links and plates, a hundred small wounds. His short sword found targets, over and over, yet still they came.

Another blast from Alaric knocked over the horde swarming Cyrus and gave him a moment to breathe as a heal, this time from Vaste, patched his wounds. The blood stopped flowing, but the aches remained. He nodded to the Ghost, who raised a hand to him before bringing around *Aterum* again and devastating another rank of goblins.

A rush of flame blasted forth to his left. He could feel the warmth, as though he had come too close to an open fire. It streamed into the tightly packed goblins, searing them, causing several to fall dead. Cyrus chanced a look - Mendicant stood behind him, hand raised, fire jumping forth, and a cool smile baring his teeth as he killed goblin warriors with the magics his people had scorned.

Into the gap rushed three blurs of white and gray, and Cyrus heard the goblins squeal in pain and terror. *Wolves.* A leather bound northman let out a howl and charged into the battle, a sword no longer than Cyrus's clutched in one hand and a leather apparatus with claws mounted on it strapped to his other. Menlos Irontooth waded into the fray, a smile upon his lips that matched the snarl of his wolves.

Aisling had slipped through the line and was attacking the goblins at the rear. Her daggers found target after target, foes cut down by the lethal placement of her blades. Her bow was not in evidence anywhere on her person. The hall grew fuller as the forces of Sanctuary entered a few at a time, and the line of goblins fell further and further back. As they broke and ran, Aisling dispatched them; only a few made it from the room alive.

Alaric brought down the last goblin with a force blast that would not have been a killing blow but for the goblin's proximity to a wall. It bounced against the stone, leaving a red streak on the stone as it slid to a final rest.

"No reinforcements," Vara noted, looking at the far hallway leading toward the throne room.

"They're waiting for us in there, I would guess," Cyrus said. "We need to move now, before their Emperor and Empress can escape, or the garrison from their barracks can fill the room. There's a passage that leads directly into the throne room; it's how we were overwhelmed last time."

He took a look around - less than a tenth of the Sanctuary army was present in the hall. "I'd prefer to regroup first, but we have no time. We have to storm the throne room now."

"Agreed," Alaric said. "Lead on, and let the word go back to the tail of the army that we have engaged the enemy and will need everyone as quickly as possible."

"I'll go," Niamh volunteered. In a beat, she was gone, running through the door to the gate in a flash of red, shouting at the top of her lungs. "We're in it now, hurry, hurry, hurry, we're engaging the Emperor –!"

Vara moved to Cyrus's side. "You've killed a great many of them now. Do you feel any better?"

Cyrus hefted the short sword. "Ask me after."

He took off down the hallway at a jog. He passed countless doors, ignoring them, until he reached the end of the hallway, and a double door that stretched from floor to ceiling and had a carving of the history of the goblin empire on it. He cracked a door and looked in.

"The Emperor and Empress are still in there," he breathed to Vara, who stood behind him.

"They are the foremost warriors of the empire," she acknowledged. "It does make sense that they might want to be involved in the battle."

Cyrus watched the Sanctuary forces pooling behind him, the hallway filling. "Alaric," Cyrus said and the Ghost focused on him. "I think it might be best if you head for the door to the barracks, see if you can keep it closed." He looked to Vara. "You feel like going head to head with the Empress of Enterra?"

She smiled. "I think I could teach the old biddy a thing or two about fighting."

"Be careful," he cautioned. "She killed me herself last time, and she hits like a titan." He looked to the army filling the hall behind them. "Everyone be cautious. Remember, we're looking for evidence..." He cringed internally at the admonition. "So try not to completely trash the place."

"Who are you and what have you done with Cyrus Davidon?" Andren asked with a broad smile.

Without bothering to respond, Cyrus turned and kicked the door open, following through with his sword already in motion. The goblins were bigger than in the last chamber, the personal guards of the Emperor and Empress, and he had already felt a dozen grazing wounds by the time his sword claimed its first victory.

Vara and Alaric waded in behind him, both their swords in motion, merciless in their assault; yet still they were halted inside the door by the ferocity of the goblin attack. More soldiers poured through the door that Cyrus had told Alaric to guard; the Ghost was nowhere near it, weighed down by goblin opponents from all sides.

A sound of thunder filled Cyrus's ears and a jagged bolt of lightning streaked through the open doors behind him, arcing through the goblins, knocking them back. Mendicant came forward, lightning flying from both hands, sending shrieks of pain from the mouths of a hundred of his own people as the current ran through them, pushing them back from the door.

Thad, Menlos, Terian, Scuddar and Longwell entered into the space the wizard had cleared for them. Thad moved into the battle, rough swings of his sword dislodging goblins from the half-circle line they had formed around the door. Menlos lit into them with a ferocity that was only matched by his wolves, which were moving through the room, finding prey of their own.

Cyrus saw Samwen Longwell, three goblins skewered on the end of his lance, and watched as the dragoon tossed the unwieldy weapon aside and drew his sword, swinging it in a style Cyrus couldn't quite place. The dragoon wielded it in circular motions, almost as a shield and a sword.

Terian's axe was slow to swing, but caused great havoc every time he brought it down, splitting the heads of goblins around him. Scuddar In'shara followed close behind the dark knight; his scimitar flashed with great speed, sending goblin parts raining in all directions.

The gap was widening now; more of Sanctuary's forces were filling the throne room. The Emperor and Empress stood silent and still before their seats, waiting to prove themselves, and Cyrus caught a glimpse of the scabbard on the wall behind them. When last he had seen it, it had been on a belt on the Empress, close to her body as one cradles a child to them.

My scabbard, he thought.

Another heal mended a bone he hadn't realized he'd broken and absolved him of a hundred cuts. He threw an elbow, catching a goblin unawares as it moved to attack him from the side, sending it to the floor in pain. His next sword strike killed another, but two more moved forward and drove him back a step, claws rattling against the metal of his armor.

The room was filling fast; dead goblins were on the floor all around, and Sanctuary attackers were wading in amidst the pile of the dead and the motion of those still fighting. Cyrus watched as goblin after goblin was swallowed by a blue glow and stopped, mid-battle, expressions serene as J'anda trapped them inside their own minds.

Alaric had taken the barracks door now, and was holding it against a steady stream of goblin attackers. *Aterum* flashed through the air and another goblin lost its head. The door swung open again and the Ghost fired a concussive blast through it before he slammed it shut once more.

Mendicant advanced through the crowd, throwing lightning and fire in turn, cowing the goblins in the front rank with the display of magic.

Vara favored the five goblins closest to her with a swipe of her sword that decapitated all but one of them and then leaped over the heads of the rest in her way to land a few paces from the Empress. Cyrus watched her and saw the Emperor move to attack before the paladin had steadied herself from her leap; the goblin moved with more speed than even Vara could boast. He clipped her and sent the paladin to her knees, sword skittering out of her grasp.

"Vara!" Cyrus cried out, scrambling to make his way through the line of goblins arrayed against him. He watched the Emperor pick up the elf by her throat, watched Vara look back with the dull, dead eyes of someone who had been stunned by a heavy blow. She threw her hand up but the Emperor batted it away and a stun spell knocked the Empress's throne over backward. The Emperor's hand twisted and Vara went limp, dangling from the grasp of the goblin, dead.

A howl of fury filled Cyrus's lips and a storm took over his blade. His sword moved of its own accord, left and right with stunning precision, hacking a path to the elevated platform the thrones sat upon. The Emperor threw Vara's corpse to the side where it crumpled against a wall, staring back at him with unfocused eyes.

Vara...

Avenge me...

Cyrus used his left fist in concert with his blade, knocking aside the last of the Imperial guard and stalking up the steps to where the Emperor and Empress stood watching him, coiled for attack. A warcry flew from his lips at such volume that it echoed through the chamber, the halls of Enterra, and the rest of Arkaria for all he knew. He threw himself at the Emperor, felt the goblin's claws grasp hold of him on both arms, halting his thrust of the short sword.

The claws dug into the armor gaps on his forearms, and blood began to run. The floor below them was swarming, the throne room filling from the open door of the barracks. Alaric was in the middle of the room, a small space cleared around him, and a few bodies of Sanctuary members were scattered among the countless goblin corpses. J'anda, Andren and Thad were among the dead he could see. Menlos's wolves moved like whispers among the goblins while the northman himself had his back against the wall close to the door of the chamber, Longwell at his side.

Cyrus saw the Empress enter his peripheral vision, moving toward him to help her husband. A flash of light distracted he and the Emperor both as Mendicant fired a lightning bolt from across the room that pulled a shriek from the lips of Enterra's Empress. Cyrus butted his head forward, hitting the Emperor with his helm and knocking the goblin back a step.

He wrenched his hands free but dropped the short sword, bringing his shoulder down for a tackle that knocked the Emperor to his back. Cyrus pounded him with a flurry of blows, blood hammering in his ears as he pummeled the leader of the goblins. Cyrus felt strong hands drag him off the Emperor and fling him against the wall. With a crack, he felt teeth break in his mouth when he landed. He looked to his right and saw Vara's body next to him. With a cry of sorrow lost in the sounds of the battle, he reached out a mailed hand and stroked her cheek.

Hatred filled him. *Again. They've done it again.* He pulled himself up, leaning against the wall for support, reeling from the horror inside him. With a howl of inarticulate rage he plunged forward again and hipchecked the Empress to the side, knocking her over her already fallen throne. The Emperor took a step forward, hands moving, and Cyrus felt the claws dig into his flank as he slammed into the goblin, tackling him. He brought his elbow across the goblin's face, breaking three pointed teeth out.

Cyrus reached back and slammed his fist into the mouth again and again. The goblin snapped at him and Cyrus grabbed the Emperor's arm and pulled it as hard as he could. A popping noise echoed as he dislocated the shoulder and slammed a knee into the goblin's groin. Claws still dug into his sides but his chainmail slowed their progression and he felt them begin to relax. He grabbed the Emperor's dislocated arm by the hand and pinned it under his knee.

Holding the Emperor's other hand down with his left, Cyrus brought his right fist down on the goblin's face. He felt the Empress's hot breath behind him and backhanded her before she could strike. His next blow broke the front structure of the Emperor's nose and jaw; the next after that changed the shape of the face entirely. He struck again, then once more, and again... he hated that face, those damned teeth, what few of them were left, those yellow eyes, rolling back in the Emperor's head - those were the eyes that presided over the death of Narstron... and now Vara...

Avenge me. The words played in his head with every punch, every blow to the Emperor's face.

"CY!" A voice cut across the clamor in the room, shaking him out of his trance. The room was filled with goblins, swarming from the door to the barracks. Sanctuary's forces in the room were down to Alaric, holding his own in the midst of a crowd of goblins. Erith screamed at him from the doorway, protected behind the dual swords of Scuddar and Terian Lepos, retreating from the sheer force of goblin numbers weighing them down.

His eyes took stock of the situation in the throne room. Thad was dead. Andren - dead. J'anda, Mendicant, Vaste - Cyrus saw the outline of a large, green-skinned body in the corner of the room. Menlos - he could see the unmoving tail of one of the wolves, and a smear of blood on the wall where the northman had been defending, along with the top of Sir Samwen Longwell's helm crowning the slumped figure of the dragoon. Before his eyes, Scuddar fell at the doorway, bleeding from a torrent of wounds and was swept down by the raging army of goblins, followed by Terian, then Erith.

Again. It's happened again. And it's all my fault. His eyes fell once more to Vara. Her blond hair ran along the floor where her body lay, looking like a river of gold running from the stone floor to her head to the prettiest face he had ever seen. With a final punch he caved in the skull of the Emperor of the Goblins and stood up. The Empress surveyed him warily, claws at the ready, and he looked at her with fury and murder in his heart.

Without waiting for her to move, he kicked the corpse of her husband to her feet and took two quick strides to the Emperor's throne, stepped up and ripped the scabbard off the wall. He pulled the sword from the strap on his back and thrust it into the casing. The Empress watched in stunned silence as a light grew from within the scabbard, shining out onto his hand and lighting the semi-darkness of the room, drawing the attention and a moment of silence from the goblins rampaging toward the door.

The silence ended as Cyrus thrust the scabbard into his belt and drew *Praelior*, the Champion's Blade.

The Serpent's Bane was the hilt, inscribed with symbols across the sword guard and wrapped in a soft and pliable leather that gripped better than any Cyrus had felt. The Death's Head was the pommel, forged to the bottom of the grip; it jutted out in a circular pattern, hollowed with a cross in the middle and came to a sharp point at the bottom – sharp enough to be used for a weapon of last resort. The Edge of Repose was the blade, and had been dull as old iron until he pulled it from the scabbard –

Now it shone. Where once had been a dull and tarnished edge, bereft of sharpness, there was now glistening metal, shining as though it were new, and glowing with an aura of energy that lit the walls around him. Quartal, the hardest metal in Arkaria, held it all together with a strength no normal blade could claim. The scabbard in Cyrus's hand glowed with the magical power of a force beyond anything man – or goblins – could cast.

The soft blue glow of *Praelior* cast Cyrus's face in relief from shadow; his jaw was set and the anger was visible on every line of his face. He did not wait for anyone to make the first move; he struck at the Empress with a warcry that caused G'Koal, one of the most powerful warriors in the Goblin Empire, to take a step back in fear for her life.

Cyrus's first overhand strike with his sword was true – the blade was long, at least a foot longer than his short sword, and it met meat and bone at the shoulder of the Empress. In a contest between the strength of an enraged warrior and his mystical sword on one side and the sinews, scales and ligaments of the goblin Empress on the other, the winner was clear.

Empress G'Koal's severed arm spun from her body as she screeched in pain, falling backward off the steps of the raised platform upon which she and her husband ruled an empire. Cyrus did not wait to see her hit the floor; he was already in motion.

Praelior swept through the flesh and bone of his enemies as if they were made of air. Arms and heads flew before him; the screams of his victims echoed as he worked his way toward the doors where his allies were falling. Still, the goblins came, more and more of them. The doors had swung shut and were opening and closing as more goblin soldiers moved forward to push back the Sanctuary army through force of their numbers.

Cyrus looked down and saw more of his fallen brethren than he cared to count - more than a hundred bodies lying on the stones of Enterra, no healer close by, and more enemies filling the room by the moment. Hope grew distant.

The doors flew open once more and a shout crackled through the air in a low, rumbling tone. "GET OUT OF THE WAY!"

Cyrus flung himself, blade first, to the side, killing goblins in his path as the throne room doors blew off their hinges. Fragments of wood and metal ripped through the air, tearing a path of destruction ten feet wide in front of the entryway.

A blur of brown moved through at high speed, hitting several goblins and turning them to smears on the floor before coming to a stop next to the shattered remnants of the doors. Fortin looked around at the destruction he had wrought and a smile of satisfaction crossed the face of the rock giant, standing far above the goblins that surrounded him.

His hand reached down and plucked three of them up, dashing them against the nearest wall. With another wave of his hand, four more of them became messy splatters of blood that dotted the floor around the rock giant.

"Fortin!" Cyrus called with a smile. "Would you mind closing that gods-damned barracks door? It's feeling a bit drafty in here."

With a salute of his mammoth, rocky hand, Fortin charged once more, this time into the door at the far end of the room that led into the barracks. Once more, he blew the door off the hinges and sent it spiraling down the hall in front of him as a harbinger of the destruction that was to follow.

Cyrus cut once more into the goblins in the room, watching them reel from his attacks, now more lethal and painful than ever, watched them flash with pain and agony, watched them die... like Narstron...

Alaric was still alive, fending off a rapidly diminishing host of goblins. With their reinforcements cut off by Fortin and Cyrus's and Alaric's vicious, destructive attacks, their numbers dwindled. The Army of Sanctuary pushed back into the room, Martaina and

Aisling at the head. The dark elf struck three goblins from behind in rapid succession, assisting Cyrus while Martaina dropped four in a row from across the room with her bow. Ryin Ayend blasted fire at a cluster of soldiers dogging Alaric's steps while Niamh sent a lightning burst from her hands that turned another to a cinder.

Cyrus watched the last few goblins form a protective ring around the Empress, who was lying, armless and wounded, next to the body of Vara. Her defenders kept their distance from him. He closed on them without patience or mercy, and *Praelior* cut the first one in half at the waist while it tried to feint away from Cyrus.

The second guard went on the offensive, as did the third, and the blade caught one with a gash across the chest and the next with the spiked pommel to the head as he clawed into Cyrus's ribs between the gap in his armor.

The body fell away and Cyrus struck the last defender with a long stabbing blow that impaled the goblin, then sliced him halfway apart as Cy removed his sword. He advanced on the Empress, who was crawling back, hissing. Her arm was gushing blood, missing at the shoulder, but her teeth were bared. She reached the wall and propped her back against it. She looked up at him and lashed out clumsily with her remaining hand.

He drew back and cut it off at the elbow with a flick of his wrist. She screamed again, a terrible, gnashing sound. He looked down at her, rage filling his heart. *She's the last... do it...*

His eyes alighted once more on Vara's dead eyes and he flicked his gaze back to the Empress. "Remember me?" he taunted. "Last time we met, this is how you left me. Back against the wall, dying, and you cut my throat with your sword. I remember looking up and seeing this –" he gestured down at the scabbard tucked in his belt – "right before I died." His face tautened with the hatred he felt coursing through him. "Isn't this ironic?"

With a gasping, heaving sound, the Empress of Enterra spoke. "You invaded my home... you were already dying... I killed you... it was a mercy... grant me the same." It was not the dark, demonic voice of his nightmares. It was a cracking, strained voice, pleading for release.

"I invaded your home because you were a threat to everyone around you!" he yelled back at her. "How many gnomes and humans have you and your kind killed just because they were there! You were plotting a war with your neighbors... and I meant to stop you." He relaxed for a moment, sword still pointed at her neck. "And now I have."

She rasped back at him. "You came... brought the gezhvet... our doom."

He leaned down and threw his helmet aside to look her in the face. "You don't get it! You killed HIM! He's dead! He was noble, and good, and forgiving – he would have settled for kicking your ass and being on his way to the next challenge!" His face convulsed as anger of every sort ran across his features. "But you killed him! And because of that, I'm your doom, G'Koal! *I'm* the death of your empire!"

He gestured at the door behind him. "Right now, my rock giant is in your barracks. And he will kill every one of your warriors, if he hasn't already. Your husband is dead. There's the ruin of the goblins. Narstron was the gezhvet because you made him the harbinger of your doom when you killed my best friend... and sealed your own fate." He drew the blade back.

"Be done, then." The pleading in her voice was worse than any angry words he could imagine. "You have destroyed my world, warrior. Do this final thing..." she coughed, "...and take your vengeance."

He hesitated. *Why are you waiting?* he railed at himself. *DO IT! She killed him! She and her people! SHE WANTS TO DIE! DO IT!* The thoughts broke through his mind like a torrential flood sweeping through an old, dry stream bed.

A strange sense of calm filled him, his fury abated. He lowered his sword and got to his feet. "You know what?" he said with an air of grim realization. "You want to die more than I want you to." He sheathed the Champion's Blade. "You will come with us... and you'll tell everyone why you sent raiders halfway across Arkaria to attack convoys. And you'll tell them who colluded with you to do it."

She looked up at him, yellow eyes slack, staring into his. "And why would I do this...?"

"Because I conquered you." He looked down at her without any trace of anger. He felt only pity for her now, this broken, hollowed out shell of a warrior. "I bested you. Me. You fought for years to become the chosen Empress of Enterra. Out of all the goblin women, you were the strongest. And I beat you *and* your husband. Respect my strength, for I have conquered you, and you will do as I say."

Her head bowed and the yellow eyes slipped away from his. "I will do as you say," she repeated, voice breaking.

He turned from her to see Alaric next to Vara. The Ghost graced him with a nod of respect and turned away. From all across the throne room, the dead of Sanctuary were rising, Curatio returning them to life.

Sitting in the shadow of Alaric, Vara was staring at Cyrus, holding her hand to her neck. Light had returned to the shining blue eyes and they were fixed on him, a look of relief washing over her. Warring emotions fought on her face until it finally returned to her practiced stoicism. "I'm glad to see you didn't let the desire for revenge overwhelm your good sense."

A wan smile crossed his lips as he went and knelt down to her. "You just implied I had some form of good sense. Are you sure you're feeling all right?"

Blood oozed from between her fingers at the place where they met her neck. "I was just resurrected from an abrupt and brutal death; it's only natural I might be prone to confusion. When I said good sense, I meant –"

"Don't go taking back a compliment once given," he chided her.

She paused and looked into his eyes, earnestly. "Then the next time I proffer one, take it humbly."

"I will... try." He reached down to her hand and gently peeled it back from her neck. A thin trickle of red slid down to her still-shining armor. Looking at her wound, he frowned. "Can you heal yourself?"

"I have no magical energy left," she said with a shake of her head. "But this is nothing. Let me see your sword." He stared her down, and for the first time since he'd known her, her expression turned impish. "Let me see it. I did die so you could acquire it. At least do me the courtesy of letting me see what my blood bought."

He drew the blade from the scabbard and handed it to her. A wearying feeling hit him, as if he were feeling the weight of his armor on his shoulders for the first time and he slid to the ground next to her, tired and overwhelmed.

"It's a very fine blade," she admitted, swinging it in front of her. She passed it back to him with a look of regret. "I don't know that I've held one better."

He took it back in his hand and felt strength fill him as he held it. His armor felt lighter, the sword felt like it weighed nothing in his grasp, and he stood almost without effort. "It has a powerful enchantment on it," he said with awe.

"Do you know its origin?" she asked, eyes transfixed on the slight glow of the blade.

"No," he half-lied.

"A pity," she said. "But hardly the first time an object of power came to a bearer through mysterious means." With great effort, she pulled her gaze from the blade and back to him. "I am... pleased... that you did not cave to your darkest desires and turn the Empress into a poorly cut meal for buzzards."

He did not seem to register her comment for a moment, so intense was his stare at *Praelior*. "It was a very near thing," he said at last. "When I saw the Emperor kill you..." His voice trailed off. "It looked very dark for a few minutes while you were dead."

"You killed the Emperor?" she asked.

"With my bare hands, I think," he said with a note of surprise at the memory. It felt like someone else had done it. Staring into those yellow eyes as they faded had given him no real joy. "It doesn't matter; it's done now." He took a deep breath and the wan smile returned. "It's done."

Chapter 41

Hours later, he stood on the platform in the throne room, surrounded on all sides by the dead of the battle. Dull, yellow eyes stared up at him from the floor. The brave fighters of Sanctuary had left, and he was alone in the middle of the carnage. He turned back to see the Emperor's body, still lying where he had kicked it. Blood pooled in between bodies and pieces, and his boots made a soft sucking sound as he walked through them, as though his feet were drinking it in as some bizarre spoil of war.

"You really did it for me, didn't you?" The voice shook him, causing him to turn his head. There, picking through the debris of battle, was a familiar face. A dwarf, only waist-high to him, beard flowing from beneath a metal helm, with rough skin, but an unmistakeable grin. His eyes were dark, as Cyrus remembered him in life, instead of the red of his nightmares.

"Narstron," he breathed. "I did. I killed them... but I have to tell you... when it came to the moment, I didn't do it for you. I did it to stop them. I did it because I was angry."

"Aye," the dwarf said with a shake of his head at the bodies surrounding him. "That was a bit weak of you to falter before killing the last... but we can work on that as time goes on."

The dark eyes found him again, but this time they were different, glowing deep crimson, as though the darkest fire Cyrus could imagine was burning behind them. The outline of Narstron became blurry, changing into something else, something familiar – a memory from a day years ago in Reikonos.

"You carry my sword now. You have completed my quest. You are my faithful servant. Now go forth and unleash havoc – in the name of Bellarum. And perhaps, in time, I will forgive you your weakness today."

With a jolt Cyrus awakened. His eyes adjusted to the darkness, and he realized he was in his officers' quarters, back in the tower of Sanctuary. A thick silence hung in the air around him, punctuated by a loud snore from Vaste, far down the hall. He listened for any other sound, but none was evident.

This time when he awoke, he hadn't been screaming. He turned over and lulled back to sleep, a deep, dreamless slumber from which he did not stir until after noon the next day.

When Cyrus arose, he donned his armor and slipped the scabbard onto his belt with a smile. A sense of pride filled him; Vara had not been false when she said it was perhaps the finest sword ever.

He descended the steps to find a celebration ongoing in the Great Hall, foyer and lounge. Niamh was the first officer he saw and he caught her by the arm as she flitted past. "What happened?" He paused, rethinking his question. "Other than our victory?"

A heady smile cracked her face. "While we were in Enterra, Alaric sent the evidence we had with messengers to Pharesia and Reikonos and they cleared our names!"

"What about Saekaj?"

She shrugged. "I don't know that we'll ever be welcome there until the Sovereign dies. Whoever he is, he must be one damned spiteful son of a bitch."

"I suspect the Sovereign wasn't born to a woman so much as spawned from a darkness you can scarcely imagine. But as for being spiteful, he's all that and more," Aisling said, appearing behind Cyrus. Cy's hand instinctively reached down and caught hers on the hilt of his sword. He held it up in front of her and she made no move to pull it away. "If you wanted to hold hands, you need only ask," she said with a taunting smile. "Can I see it?"

He humored her, and his display of *Praelior* drew admiring looks and comments from all around the foyer as his guildmates came to see the new weapon.

"You know," came the voice of Alaric as he descended from the balcony above with a twinkle in his eye, "I don't begrudge you that excellent weapon you've assembled, but do try to remember that an officer of Sanctuary must be humble, and not a braggart of any sort."

Cyrus hesitated and began to sheath the sword until Alaric laughed. "I was teasing you, brother. Be proud of your weapon. Your quest was long and arduous to acquire it and we all celebrate your success with you. But," he said, "I must speak to you about a different matter. It would seem that in light of recent events, we have a host of meetings to prepare for."

Cyrus broke free from the crowd that had gathered around him and walked with the Ghost, who led him out the doors and onto the grounds. "What sort of meetings?" he asked as they descended the stairs.

"Mere formalities," the Guildmaster assured him. "I presume you have heard that Reikonos and Pharesia have absolved us?" When Cyrus nodded, he continued. "Now we must go to Reikonos and cast the blame where it belongs," the Ghost said with an air of deep satisfaction. "We leave in an hour. And then, after that, I have scheduled an Alliance officer meeting in the Coliseum at Reikonos. There was a guild meeting this morning while you were sleeping and we have... results to report to them."

"We'll be taking the Empress with us, I presume?" Cyrus asked.

"Indeed," Alaric said with gusto. "She is with Nyad and Curatio right now in Pharesia, and Niamh informed me that before she teleported back to us, the Empress was filling the air of the King's Court with a compelling tale of deceit and treachery."

He smiled. "I confess, it has a twist in the tale that I did not quite expect, but should not surprise - after all, so busy were we proving that the goblins were the raiders that we never did ask ourselves what possible motive the goblins could have in participating in the attacks."

Cy frowned at the Ghost in confusion. "I thought it was for the treasure that the convoys were filled with?"

"I would have thought so too," Alaric replied, "but the Empress insists that Goliath received the majority of the proceeds and that the caravans grew poorer and poorer as the attacks dragged on, until their worth was but a fraction of the rich bounties they brought at first. No," he said with a shake of his head, "something else was promised to the goblins."

"What?" Cyrus asked in genuine curiosity.

The enigmatic smile that embodied the persona of the Ghost filled Alaric Garaunt's face. "You will hear for yourself in only a few hours," he promised, turning back toward the front steps. "Oh, and by the way... I am proud of you for reining yourself in at the last."

Cyrus felt a rush of embarrassment. "Alaric, I still killed... hundreds of goblins. I beat the Emperor to death with my own hands in a rage that would put a bloodthirsty troll to shame. I ordered Fortin to kill the reinforcements that the goblins sent from the barracks, and I didn't stop him from killing them even after we won."

"All true," the knight conceded. "But let us examine motives for a moment - were the goblins you killed attacking you at the time you killed them?"

Cyrus blinked. "Without exception."

"And if you had called off Fortin from his attack on the barracks, do you think the goblins within would have given up and retreated?"

Cyrus looked at the Ghost. "No."

"And had you relented in your battle with the Emperor, unarmed as you were, do you think he would have yielded to you?"

"No." Cyrus shook his head. "I looked in his eyes as I killed him. There was no surrender in him, only defiance."

"And which were you more upset about when you attacked him – the death of Narstron or the death of Vara?"

Without a moment's hesitation Cyrus whispered his reply. "Vara."

"Here is what I see," the Ghost said, adopting a pensive tone. "You were attacking a clear enemy of Sanctuary, one which you had a long and bitter personal history with, but when it came down to it, they were an implacable foe in battle, and when you struck down their leader you were more upset at the plight of your comrade that died that day than the one that died over a year ago." His eyes found Cyrus's, and the Ghost's look cut through him. "And when you found a foe that you had beaten, totally, you offered her mercy rather than slaughter her without it."

"Yes, but the only reason that I did it is because I felt pity for her!" Cyrus felt the flush of embarrassment, as though he were confessing to a particularly filthy crime.

"Pity and mercy go hand in hand, for it was your pity that awakened the realization that you should be merciful – and you did not let your hatred wreck any hope for us to prove our innocence."

Alaric stepped closer and placed a hand on the warrior's shoulder. "Revenge is a dangerous obsession; and it is most dangerous because it *is* an obsession. Someone truly out for revenge at all costs – someone that irredeemable – would not have had their hand stayed by pity. They would have struck down the Empress, swift and true, and we would still be proclaimed innocent but the guilty would go free. All for the sake of fleeting revenge."

Having said his peace, the Ghost turned again from Cyrus and marched up the stone steps into Sanctuary.

They left for Reikonos an hour later, teleported once more by Niamh into the city square. A frenzy of activity greeted Cyrus as he stepped away from the portal. Wagons were moving through the square and up and down streets at a much quicker pace than usual, but voices were hushed as people went about their business. Cyrus saw a cluster of dark elves around a wagon loaded to bursting, heading through the square toward city's west gate. A few more dark elven parties were behind them, all heading in the same direction.

They walked to the Citadel, finding themselves once more at the base of the gargantuan gray tower. The guards waved them through, and the elevator moved just as slowly as the last time they had been here. Upon stepping out of it at their floor, Cyrus steered G'Koal from the lift and into the corridor. She walked without much prompting, feet bound by ropes just enough to slow her should she decide to run. Her arms were severed and she had refused reattachment, saying she would prefer to carry the scars of her shame for the rest of her days.

As they stepped through the door, Cyrus involuntarily reached for his sword, squeezing the hilt for reassurance that it was still there. He glanced behind the elevator and saw the balconies that opened up with a view of the entire city spread before them. *Long way down,* he thought. *But it might be preferable to surrendering my sword.*

Entering one of the sets of double doors, they marched the Empress down the aisle before them as the Council of Twelve looked on. Pretnam Urides's jowled face stood out, a satisfied smile resting upon his lips. "Gentlemen," he called out as they opened the waist-high wood gate that separated the floor before the Councilors from the benches where the audience sat, "I hear you have brought us evidence of treachery by one of the guilds in our city. I am eager –" the Councilor's voice betrayed no sign of insincerity – "to see justice done."

"Indeed," Alaric began. "We appreciate your review of the evidence we provided you earlier; the testimony of the elven caravan leader and men, the bodies of the goblin raiders and the surviving wizard who brought them to the Plains. Were you able to coerce anything from him?"

"No, our guards have as yet been unable to loosen his tongue," Urides admitted, jowls shaking along with his head. "But he is known to us; Carrack, officer of Goliath." Pretnam Urides smiled.

"Which is why I am so very interested to hear your evidence."

"Behold the Empress of Enterra," the Ghost said. "She had intimate knowledge of the planning and execution of the attacks on convoys and will tell you herself who was involved."

Without prompting, the Empress spoke, in a low voice that did not sound female at all. "For over two years we have been allied with Goliath. Malpravus, their Guildmaster, came to us with a warning of an attack that was about to fall upon our city. With his assistance, we were able to stave off this danger to our realm in exchange for *Terrenus*, the Hammer of Earth."

"I see," Urides interrupted. "And did Malpravus express interest in other of the godly weapons?"

The Empress's dull eyes looked up at the Councilor, uncaring. "He wanted to acquire them all, yes."

"I see, I see," Urides said. He shifted his focus to Alaric. "This seems to back up your assertion that Goliath assisted in stealing our spear. Please continue."

"A few months ago, he came to us again, with another proposition." The goblin's voice was dull; she sounded like a broken thing; her voice dragged. "Over a year ago we were preparing to invade the Gnomish Dominions, but were concerned that with the Human Confederation as their chief trading partner, any attack on the gnomes would prompt a human response."

Her eyes stared straight ahead, not acknowledging anything she saw. "We were not prepared to handle that threat; the might and numbers of the Human Confederation are known to us, and they are great.

"Malpravus came to us, promised us that with our help he could redirect human attentions for the next few years, giving us free reign to destroy the gnomes and claim their territory for our own. He claimed that his plan would distract the rest of the world for so long, we would be able to consolidate our power for a few years and conquer the dwarves when we were ready, adding their mountain halls to our territory."

"And the human riverlands between you and the dwarves?" Urides had a look of indignation.

"He promised us," the Empress continued, "that you would be so ground down by the war that he would begin that we could take them at our convenience." She shook her head. "But we had no interest in riverlands when the mountains around Fertiss still stood, ripe for the conquest."

"Do not think that coy words and denials will bring you any mercy!" Urides warned. "Threats to our territory are taken very seriously indeed and carry the death penalty in the Confederation."

"I don't think she much cares at this point," Cyrus observed.

The Councilor looked at him with an air of surprise. "No one wants to die."

Cyrus held his tongue. *She does.*

"Malpravus proposed that we should provide the forces; our goblin soldiers are known for their stealth. Our attacks are the stuff of legends." Her voice betrayed the first hint of emotion – pride. "We can disappear without a trace, leaving the afflicted party to wonder if a ghost struck from thin air and attacked them."

"It is much easier to disappear with a wizard to aid you," Urides snorted.

"He provided the wizard." The Empress's voice returned to her flat, dull tone. "We provided everything else. We split the rewards with 70 percent going to Goliath and 30 percent to us, after Goliath sold the goods in the markets of Reikonos."

"Did you hear that?" Urides remarked to the Councilor next to him, who was nodding. He leaned forward at his bench, looking down the row of Councilors to the place where their recordkeeper sat. "Trading in stolen goods. Theft. Murder. Conspiracy." The recordkeeper nodded as she scrawled on the parchment before her.

"To make no mention of the fact that Goliath likely kept more than 70 percent," Alaric added. "The goblins' proceeds came from Goliath's accounting, after all."

"Yes, yes," Urides jowls wobbled. "Find a charge for that as well," he said to the recordkeeper. "Unfair dealing, or perhaps larceny."

"Do you truly care that the goblins were treated unfairly in this transaction?" the Ghost asked without emotion.

"Of course not!" Pretnam Urides snapped. "They were engaged in attacking and destroying our convoys and selling the proceeds! I want more charges for Goliath, however, so I am willing to hear her complaints, real or perceived. Is there anything else?" He peered down at the goblin Empress.

She shook her head, her eyes focused on the floor. The pity that Cyrus felt when he spared her life grew in that moment, and he realized that whatever she had been responsible for, he no longer felt anything but sorry for her.

"Very well," came the hurried voice of Pretnam Urides. "You will be taken into custody by the guards of Reikonos and placed in jail until trial. As for Goliath..." he said, voice trailing off as three of the Lyrus guards came to lead the Empress away.

With a start Cyrus realized one of the guards was Rhane Ermoc, haughty sneer ever present as he grasped the bandaged stump of the Empress's arm and began to drag her away. She did not protest, trying to keep up with the bigger human's strides. Cy watched as Ermoc gripped her around the bandage and squeezed. Blood oozed from between the fingers of his metal gauntlet but the Empress did not acknowledge any pain or cry out.

"I think for Goliath we should issue the following sanctions: their treasury shall be drained to pay damages. I want all their assets and all their members' assets seized," Urides began. He turned to another Councilor. "I believe you already spoke to the banks; their accounts totaled north of 400 million gold pieces?" A nod met his question.

"Very good. Goliath will be forced from their guildhall and exiled from the Confederation - all members, never to be allowed within our borders again. And this time, the executions will be upheld rather than stayed," he said with a nod at Alaric. "We have already released your people that were detained."

"Much appreciated," said Alaric.

"No business shall be transacted with any member of Goliath by any merchant or citizen of the Confederation, under penalty of 50 years in jail. All in favor?" He surveyed the Council of Twelve with a quick glance. "None opposed? Good. Seize their assets, eject them from the Confederation and let us be done with this. Send a messenger to inform them of the findings of this Council."

Cyrus let out a laugh, a short, sharp bark that was unintended but caught the attention of the Council. He covered his mouth. "Sorry," he said with chagrin.

"Davidon, I believe it is... have you something to add?" Urides glared down at him, clearly unused to being challenged or interrupted.

"I was just... curious," Cyrus said, "about how you planned to remove Goliath from the city."

"With the greatest ease," Urides said with cool assurance. He turned to the clerk at the opposite end of the bench from the

Recordkeeper. "Send for the Guildmasters of Endeavor, Amarath's Raiders and Burnt Offerings. Tell them I am invoking their Homestead clause in order to remove an undesirable element from within the city." A smile lit Pretnam Urides's fat face that Cyrus suspected came from the Councilor savoring the exercise of his power.

"My apologies, Councilor," Alaric said with a bow of his head. "You will not find the Guildmaster of Goliath at his hall presently to deliver the message. He is waiting for us at a meeting in the Coliseum."

"I see." Urides's eyes lit up. "Could I impose on you to deliver our message?" The Councilor seemed to relish the thought of Alaric twisting the knife on Goliath; his eyes glowed with excitement.

"It would be no imposition," the Ghost admitted, keeping his expression neutral. "If there is nothing else?" After a moment's pause, he began to leave.

"There is one last, small matter," Urides admitted. "Some further service you might be honored to perform for the Confederation."

Alaric turned back, wary. "And that is?"

"Our armies are withdrawing from the southern plains," Urides said with a certain stiffness.

"An excellent decision, Councilor, if you mean to avert war," Alaric said with a slight bow.

Pretnam Urides smiled. "There is no averting war now. The dark elves attacked our Sophisan Infantry regiment last night not far from your guildhall. War is declared, sirs, and armies are already on the march. No, the service we require of you is quite different," he said, ignoring the stunned reactions on both their faces. "Our forces are moving to positions of great strategic importance elsewhere so that we may win this war quickly, and make the dark elves regret their aggressiveness.

"I require... a steward," Urides said. "A force that can keep a close eye on the trade routes of the southern plains and keep them open against raiders and others that may decide to halt the flow of necessary commerce at an hour when it would be costly to us to strip forces from our other efforts. Be assured –" the Councilman's smile returned – "when the war is concluded, we shall return our garrisons to the plains, likely by the end of the year – but until then, someone will need to guard the peace."

Alaric stared, unblinking, at the Council of Twelve, drawing his eye across them all in a slow, long look that took each of them in. Whatever might have passed through his head, only a few words came out of his mouth. "As ever, Sanctuary will steward the southern Plains of Perdamun to the best of our ability."

"Excellent." Urides rubbed his hands together. "I am pleased we can count on your assistance." He looked toward the back of the chamber. "You are dismissed, then. By all means, send us updates on your progress and stewardship. We look forward to reading them," he said without enthusiasm. "Next matter..."

Cyrus led the way out of the chambers. Alaric was muted, and as they passed through the double doors into the room containing the elevator, Cyrus was surprised to see Rhane Ermoc standing beside one of the balconies, same malevolent smile on his lips. Upon seeing the two of them exit the Council chambers, Ermoc called out, "Your Empress tried to escape, but we stopped her."

Cyrus looked around, sensing something unpleasant. "Where is she?"

Rhane Ermoc's smile grew wider and more mocking as he stuck his thumb over his shoulder toward the balcony. "She fell. Accidentally," the guard said with a laugh. "At least she didn't escape."

Cyrus's jaw clenched and he felt Alaric grip the back of his armor, restraining him. Cyrus's hand clutched the hilt of *Praelior*, ready to draw. Ermoc looked at him in mild amusement. "That's right, Garaunt. Restrain your dog of war or I'll teach him a lesson in respect."

"And while that would end in your not-at-all-tragic and well-deserved death, I think perhaps you should realize that I am only assisting my comrade in remembering that some fleas are simply too insignificant to scratch." The Ghost smiled. "I used your dog metaphor because I felt that if anyone could understand a comparison to worthless, bloodsucking insects, it would be you."

"What's that supposed to mean?" The guard captain's face had turned into a scowl not shared by his compatriots, who were trying (in vain) not to snicker.

Alaric guided Cyrus back to the elevator. "Take it to mean what you will. Good day, Rhane Ermoc. I hope you see the front line of the war soon. I suspect they will need your guidance and martial prowess, honed to a fine edge by killing armless goblins half your size." The Ghost cast a final look at the guard as the elevator began to lower, and released his hold on Cyrus's backplate. "You must get a better hold on yourself, my friend."

"What he did," Cyrus spat in rage. "That was unnecessary."

"I do not disagree," Alaric replied.

A moment of silence passed between them as the elevator crept downward. "She should have died in battle," Cyrus said.

"That would have been what she wanted," Alaric cautioned. "She schemed the murder and dishonor of our guild."

"I'm aware," the warrior said, tense. "But you know that Malpravus fed the imperial ambitions of the goblins until they couldn't see anything but the possibilities. And he took advantage of them. He stole their most powerful weapon while feeding them a falsehood about some ridiculous prophecy –"

"That, as you pointed out, came true."

"But –"

"There is no but," Alaric said. "She made her own choices, as did her husband, as did her people. If you don't believe that, look no further than Mendicant, who chose to go in the opposite direction of the Goblin Imperium. She and her husband ruled the non-soldiers of that empire with an iron fist, by the way of the warrior. Do not mourn for their destruction, and be glad of the mercy you found for her."

"Why?" Cyrus said, a bitter tinge in his voice. "She's just as dead as if I had killed her myself."

"Not the point," the knight replied. "It's not the effect on her that mattered when it came to the mercy you showed. She would have been happier dead. The importance of what you did for her was the effect the mercy had on *you*." Cyrus's quizzical look was met by a knowing smile. "You and I have talked about purpose many times. Becoming a harder man, a killer who would destroy lives without mercy or provocation, is a hard path on the soul and sensibilities. You are a warrior. Your mercy kept you from becoming a murderer. Death is an awesome power. Make certain you have reason to wield it when you do, or be slow to employ its means."

They passed the rest of the ride in silence as Cyrus contemplated the words Alaric had spoken. They returned to the square, where Niamh waited with Windrider as well as Alaric's mount and one for herself. The journey to the Coliseum took longer than usual. The streets of Reikonos were filled with travelers, mostly dark elves leaving the city laden with horses, wagons or even packs on their backs.

They exited the city's eastern gate and Cyrus's gaze fell on an enormous circular building that was almost as tall as Sanctuary, and could nearly fit the Citadel lying on its side, within the walls. They entered through the square archway, finding their allies waiting in the dirt floor, where the spectacle of combats took place. Cyrus wondered when last the Coliseum had seen use for gladiatorial sport; for as long as he could recall it had been used largely for public events.

Malpravus stood waiting to one side, with Tolada and the helmeted Orion flanking him at each arm. Orion's helm protected and covered his face totally, with only small slits for his eyes. Tolada had a bored look on his face and was fingering the handle of his warhammer.

To the other side stood Cass and Elisabeth. Cass's arms were crossed and a look of disgust was evident on his face. He shifted to a slight smile and nod at Cyrus when the party from Sanctuary entered. Elisabeth also graced him with a faint smile, but the look in her eyes was cooler somehow than in their previous meetings; he assumed the memory of his attack on Orion was fresh in her mind.

Malpravus spoke first. "As you have summoned us here, Alaric, I can only assume you either have a death wish or you have managed to free yourself from the troubles encumbering you these last months. Tell me, have you decided to embrace wisdom and pay what they have asked?"

"I have not," Alaric replied, dismounting. "But nor am I any longer banished from Reikonos."

"Oh?" Malpravus's eyebrow perked up in interest. "Do tell."

"Malpravus," Cyrus called out, catching the necromancer's attention, "where's Carrack?"

Malpravus let out an exasperated sigh, somewhat uncharacteristic of the usually cool dark elf. "Dear boy, how should I know where all my officers are at every hour of the day? I brought the three normally requested for Alliance meetings..." He grinned. "Although, if you should feel the need to assault them as you did last time, Alaric should perhaps pick differently when next we meet..."

"'When next we meet'?" Alaric said, seizing upon the necromancer's words. "I'm not much concerned about that. I have a message for you from the Council of Twelve." He smiled as the

Goliath Guildmaster froze. "Your assets are being seized as we speak; you are banished from the Human Confederation, and you will be removed from your guildhall by tomorrow at noon under pain of death. Whatever you cannot carry with you will become property of the Confederation." He tossed the scroll from the Council's clerk in the dirt at Malpravus's feet.

The necromancer stared down at it, all mirth gone from his gaunt face. "If this is some form of a joke, I can only assume that my sense of humor is not quite up to the modern standard."

"It is no joke," Alaric replied as Tolada reached down and seized the parchment, unrolling it. His eyes widened as he read it, and Malpravus snatched it out of his hands before he was finished.

"Carrack blew your whole plan," Cyrus said to the necromancer with a smile. "He was still mad at me for cutting his throat at our last meeting – mad enough that he made a really bad decision to go after a convoy that we had a clear watch on."

"I see," Malpravus said with cool indifference. "The word of one wizard is nothing. He lies."

"That would be more persuasive if we hadn't killed all the goblins you sent," Cyrus answered back. "And then we stormed Enterra and brought the Empress back, and she told quite an interesting tale."

"Goblin deceits," the necromancer said with a small laugh. "You cannot possibly believe what any of them would say? They did kill your friend, after all..."

"They did," Cyrus admitted. "But only after you warned them that the 'gezhvet' was coming to attack them." The warrior's voice grew icy. "Tell me, did you know that Narstron was with Sanctuary? Or did you just assume that there would be some dwarf on the Enterra invasion that you could pass off as the 'gezhvet' to get your hands on the hammer?"

Malpravus's smile was gone. No evidence of laughter was present on his face, which had grown stiff, his eyes cold as the death he claimed mastery over. His expression was calculating and aimed right at Cyrus. "That is a powerful accusation to make."

Cyrus met the necromancer's cold stare with one of his own. "I'm a powerful warrior." He gestured at Orion. "He told me last year that there was another traitor in the Alliance. It figures that the two of you would end up thick as thieves. After all, you both served the Dragonlord."

Malpravus did not flinch at the accusation, but Tolada did. Cyrus could see Elisabeth out of the corner of his eye. "That's enough, Cyrus," she called out to him. "You go too far!"

"The Council of Twelve has spoken, as has the King of the Elves," Alaric said matter-of-factly. "They have found the testimony of the Empress of the goblins and the presence of Carrack at the raid to be compelling enough to find Goliath guilty of these crimes, and levied sanctions accordingly. By the way," Alaric continued, "Pharesia is also demanding payment, should you ever want to set foot in the Elven Kingdom again."

"So we see how the wheel turns," Malpravus said. He looked back to Cyrus for but a moment. "You have lost your chance, boy, and now your friend will rot forever."

"I think he'll rest in peace, actually," Cyrus replied, "knowing that the treacherous dogs that got him killed have finally faced some justice - and knowing that I didn't have to sell out everything I believed in just so you'd use your precious bauble to bring him back to life."

"Bauble?" Cass said with a frown. "What are you talking about, Cyrus?"

"His soul ruby," Cyrus said with a dismissive wave at Malpravus, who stiffened once more. "He claimed he could bring back Narstron."

"Soul ruby?" Cass's eyes hardened, a line of suspicion etched across the warrior's brow. "You traffic in soul rubies, Malpravus?"

"Utter rubbish," the necromancer replied. "The boy is mistaken."

"He showed me one," Cyrus said. "He had it in his sleeve."

"That's dark magic, even for a necromancer," Cass said with contempt. "You have to sacrifice a life to make a soul ruby, Malpravus."

The necromancer scowled. "I do not have –"

"Have you ever seen someone brought back to life by a soul ruby?" Alaric asked. "It is a not a life - it is a twisted, dark reflection of life, not even fitting for the worst of criminals as punishment."

"This is ridiculous," Orion protested, voice heated through his helmet. "The Council of Twelve and the King of the Elves have exiled us based on what? Your word, the ramblings of a goblin and some arrogant wizard?"

"Plus my word that you're traitorous, malevolent, sell-your-mother-for a piece of chainmail –" Cyrus began to rattle off an insult but did not get a chance to finish it. Orion charged at him, blades already drawn, two of them, each the length of Cyrus's borrowed short sword.

The warrior could feel the strength and speed of *Praelior* coursing through him; Orion moved as slow as if he were underwater. Cyrus drew the blade as Orion closed on him and brought it across in a purely defensive blow that knocked both the ranger's swords out of his hands. He staggered from Cyrus's strike, and with a knee to the abdomen, Cyrus spun him about and brought the ranger's charge to a halt.

Orion lay on his back, gasping for air as Cyrus stood over him. "I took your advice and got a longer sword," he said coolly. "I could scarcely afford better, as I have yet to be paid a large bounty of gold for being faithful to my friends and guildmates, rather than selling their lives to the highest bidder." He swung the sword delicately across Orion's doublet, peeling back the cloth with the blade. "You know, like you did to buy this fine, fine chainmail of yours."

Cyrus stared down at the ranger. No one moved around him. Alaric stood back and watched, arms folded. Niamh bit her lip. Cass had an arm out, holding Elisabeth back from intervening. Tolada stood open-mouthed, but neither he nor Malpravus showed any sign of moving to help their fallen comrade. The necromancer stood with his hands crossed in front of him, eyes still cold.

Cy edged *Praelior* down with a push, splitting the first of the links of Orion's armor with a sword harder than any other metal. "It's a funny thing, honor," he said as he brought his blade down from the neck of the chainmail to its terminus below Orion's waist. "You pledged yours to your guildmates and allies, then made a pact with the Dragonlord who would have killed us all."

Orion's shirt of links fell from him and Cyrus brought his blade down, snagging the ranger's chainmail pants at the hip. He dragged the blade along the ranger's leg on each side. Orion's priceless, finely crafted armor fell away from him, but still he made no move to stop Cyrus.

"We fought and in some cases died to check your insane ambitions, and you got away without a mark, without justice, without consequences." Cy knelt down and looked the ranger in the eyes through the helmet. With a sneer he tipped the sword under Orion's chin. "I'm sick of this ridiculous mask. I want to look at you when I call you a traitor." With a flick of his wrist, he pushed the helm up and over the top of the ranger's head, and it fell to the ground. Cyrus gasped.

"That's not exactly true, is it, Cyrus?" Orion looked at him, eyes burning.

The ranger's face was a ruined mess; his lips were split open in an exaggerated ovoid, showing far more of his teeth and gums than should have been visible. Heavy, ugly scars showed on his forehead, gashes grown over with new flesh, but ridges stood out on his brow and ran diagonally, and another from his left eye down to his mouth that ended in a peculiar V-shaped split that looked like a river running into the lake that was his mouth. His chin lacked almost any definition, as though there were no bones in it at all, and his right eyebrow seemed to have suffered the same fate.

Elisabeth looked away from the grotesque sight with a gasp and Cyrus could hear Niamh retching behind him. "I didn't get away without a mark. You left me scarred for life. Selene got me out of the mountains alive, but she passed out and wasn't able to heal me in time to fix the damage you caused." He looked down, bowing his head. "Now my wife cannot even bear to look at me." The ranger's eyes turned defiant. "So do your worst. Tell me how I've wronged you. Take your revenge at last."

Cyrus stood up, leaving his sword pointed at Orion and shook his head. "I don't need revenge against you, Orion. Look at you. Revenge would be beneath me. If the day comes when we cross blades again, it will be because you provoked it, and it will be the last in a long line of your foolish mistakes."

"Forgive and forget, Cyrus?" Orion brought his eyes up, looking at the warrior. "Is that it?"

"No," Cyrus said. "Never forget." Cyrus pivoted on his heel and brought *Praelior* down on Orion's helmet, neatly cutting it in half. He cast a look at Orion, but the ranger showed no emotion on his ruined face.

He pointed the blade at Malpravus, who did not move or react in any way. "The same goes for you, necromancer. My business with you is done. What you tried, you failed, and it has cost you everything. If I ever catch you in wrongdoing again... I won't let you survive."

"I think that it goes without saying, but I will mention it anyway," Alaric interjected, stepping forward. "Sanctuary voted unanimously this morning to reject a merger with the Alliance. In a second vote, we decided that we no longer desire to be affiliated with this Alliance, and so we are leaving it."

A smile crossed the face of the Ghost, slow and sweet, full of a deep satisfaction. "We wish you all the very best." He angled his head to Cass and Elisabeth. "Should you require our assistance in the future, we would be pleased to render it in honor of the bonds of fellowship we once shared."

He turned his head to the Goliath officers. "I would hope that these events will bring to light the fact that some ambitions are not worth pursuing and that some bargains come at far too high a cost. Should that lesson not have sunk in to your thick skulls - *we will be watching you.*" A hard edge crept into Alaric's voice, and even though the threat was not aimed at him, Cyrus was intimidated.

With a bow, Alaric led the way out of the Coliseum. Cyrus took a last look at Malpravus, still unmoving, and Orion, who sat in the dirt, head still bowed, his face forever marked with the wounds suffered in his treachery. Alaric waited until they had passed the gates until he spoke. "You're passing up opportunities at revenge left and right."

"You sound impressed," Cyrus replied with a deep amusement. "Perhaps I've grown as a person. Best not to mention it to Vara; she might die of shock."

Alaric shook his head. "If you wish to hide your best, most noble deeds..."

"Okay," he said. "You can tell her. But don't make it sound like I wanted her to know."

The Ghost regarded him, impassive for a moment as they continued their walk. "I never cease to be amazed at the lengths two supposedly mature adults will go to in order to avoid the possibility that their feelings might be bruised by the possibility of rejection. I mean - gods, man, just tell her how you feel already and get it over with."

"I second that," Niamh said from behind them.

Cyrus shot her a glare that caused her to look away. "Perhaps I will." He frowned. "I didn't think about it at the time because of all the other things that happened in our meeting with the Council of Twelve, but Pretnam Urides said that the Confederation is already at war with the Dark Elf Sovereignty. Won't that change things for us?"

"Worse than that," Niamh said. "I heard in the square before you both showed up; the Dark Elves must have been ready before they made a move - they hit a dozen towns and outposts in the last fifteen hours all along their border. I guess the humans weren't as prepared as they thought. There are armies marching through the Confederation as we speak, sacking everything in their path."

"Pretnam Urides was so arrogant that he assumed that the war would start and stay confined to the southern plains," Alaric said. "I suspect that the Sovereign of Saekaj has other plans, especially if his opening gambit was this ambitious. The elves will remain neutral, and the Sovereignty will take the lead in this war for the foreseeable future."

"You don't think the humans will be able to mount a counteroffensive?" Cyrus asked.

"Perhaps in time," the Ghost said. "I believe Pretnam Urides was more ready for the war than the Confederation was," he said with a sad shake of the head.

"Will this change things for us?" Cyrus asked.

"Of course," Alaric replied. "We do not go about our business untouched by the outside world. As Reikonos and Saekaj Sovar make war against each other, all the powers and the peoples of Arkaria will be affected in some way. I doubt we'll see the carnage show up on our front doorstep - yet - but be assured, the fires of war burn hot, and they consume all in their path. It will be a matter of time, and we will become involved in some way - willing or not. But for now, we will remain as we have been for all these years: a Sanctuary for those who need it most."

Chapter 42

War news consumed the conversations in the lounge and Great Hall that evening, and carried over through breakfast the next day. The names of the human towns that had been destroyed in the first attacks were on the lips of everyone. Some members left to join the armies of their respective homelands; more applicants began to show up at the door as the truth spread faster than war news through the lands of Arkaria.

Cyrus found Niamh at the appointed hour the next day, waiting in the foyer for him. "You're early," she said with a hint of surprise.

"Wouldn't want to be late, would I?"

"Not for this." Her smile spread almost from ear to ear. "I doubt I'll stay for the whole thing; I'm going home to Pharesia to see my family."

"I didn't know you even had family," he said with a shake of his head. "We've known each other for two years, traveled the world together and you're still just the girl who keeps saving my ass whenever I get into trouble." She gave him a look that evidenced her six hundred plus years. "Woman," he corrected.

"Family's not a hot topic for those of us that have been here a long time," she observed. "Sanctuary becomes your family after a while. I haven't been home in years. Hadn't felt a sudden urgency to, until I couldn't anymore because of the banishment." Her face grew solemn. "Then, suddenly, I wanted to see my mother and father, nephews and nieces and brothers and sisters more than anything.

"What about you?" she asked after a beat. "Do you have any family left in the world?"

A vision of hearth and home flashed before his eyes - of his childhood, of a fireplace, of the warm smell of meat pies cooking and a mother with green eyes and a laughing smile, whom he hadn't seen since before he was dropped off at the Society of Arms at the age of six. "No."

"Would you like to go home with me?" She had a half-smile, pity that she couldn't quite conceal edging into her expression at the corners of her eyes. "They're preparing quite the feast, I'm told."

"You're too kind, but I have some errands to run while I'm in Reikonos."

She nodded, a wistful look on her face as a half dozen others joined them in the next minutes. Terian, Vaste, Andren, Nyad and more. When the last arrived, Niamh cast the teleportation spell and Cy felt the warm air of Reikonos hit his skin as the fountain in the square appeared when the wind of her teleport spell faded. They walked through the streets of the city unnoticed; even now, a steady line of dark elven refugees filtered out from the slums toward the city gates.

The guildhall quarter was buzzing with activity even though it was not yet noon. At the four corners where stood the biggest guildhalls in the city, the streets were already packed with people. He and the others picked their way through the crowd, ending up on the raised platform of the portal that exited from Purgatory. The portal was lifeless now; no energy crackled within the ovoid rock.

"You know, I still say it'd be a fine day for a mass public execution," Andren said with not a little acrimony. Terian nodded along with the healer.

"I wonder how many members of Goliath actually knew what was going on?" Niamh said.

"I would guess few," Vaste commented. "Enough to make it work and no more. Malpravus is no fool and this is the sort of plot that is best kept secret; the more people that knew, the worse chance of keeping it quiet."

Cyrus watched the crowd. A bored assemblage stood guard at the doors to Goliath's guildhall. Even from this distance he could see Archenous Derregnault, sour expression on his face. Larning, the Guildmaster of Burnt Offerings, stood next to the human, warhammer slung behind him. Isabelle was not far from them, standing at a distance, arms crossed and golden hair flowing around her shoulders. She chanced to look up as he was studying her and a slight smile filled her lips. Her arms uncrossed and she offered him a salutory wave. He returned it.

"Look who's here," Vaste said with a smile, nudging Cyrus in the ribs. Vara picked her way through the crowd, caught sight of them and hesitated for only a moment before moving to join her guildmates on the platform.

"You never come to Alliance events," Cyrus said as she climbed the steps to join them.

"I decided to make an exception," she said. Her expression softened. "You know I wouldn't miss this."

The doors to the Goliath guildhall opened, and the first of a procession began to file out, all of them laden with bags and boxes. Hoots and jeers filled the air, as did a few rotten vegetables. Orion was near the front, face uncovered.

"You'd think they'd take wagons or horses," Niamh wondered aloud.

"All seized. Part of the restitution; they killed an awful lot of horses in their raids," Andren said. "Serves them right."

"The goblins are finished as a power. Goliath is cast out, bankrupted and homeless." Vara looked at Cyrus with a smile of undisguised pleasure. "I would say you got your revenge."

Cyrus shrugged. "I would say justice was done."

Andren remained sour. "Still galls me that Malpravus and Orion are allowed to walk free when they should be rotting in a Reikonos jail or hanging from a gallows. Your human justice system makes me sick."

Vara rolled her eyes. "As I recall, Pharesia let them walk free as well."

"Oh, yeah," the healer said, taking a drink from his flask. "What's wrong with people nowadays?"

"The Confederation couldn't sort out exactly who in Goliath was guilty, and I doubt they could contain that many spell casting prisoners for very long," Cyrus replied. "I think we've hurt them all more than you can imagine. It's true, their schemes have killed quite a few people, but we've taken everything from them."

Vara stared him down. "You know they'll be back."

"I know. But like Alaric told them - we'll be watching, and waiting. And when they do come back, it'll be the end for them. No more mercy, no more forgiveness." He touched his sword, and the power of it flowed through him. "I'm not worried. If they come, we'll stop them."

"Only if you see them coming," Vaste retorted. "They aren't known for declaring hostilities before knocking us flat. It's always treachery - the way of the sidewinder."

They all chewed on that for a moment as the procession grew, the line from Goliath's door stretching down the street. Cy turned to Vara. "Can I talk to you for a moment?"

She nodded and followed him away from the group, behind the portal. "It is well that you asked me to speak, I have something

I've been wanting to tell you as well."

He blinked at her. "You go first."

She pursed her lips. "Very well. Do you recall how you had mentioned your intense dislike of Archenous Derregnault?"

He frowned. "I do. I just saw him a few minutes ago, actually."

She looked at him with curiosity. "And?"

"I still feel the same."

She breathed, letting out a small laugh, then turned serious again. "I dislike him as well, obviously, though unlike yourself, for clearly defined reasons."

His mouth felt dry. *She's letting me in,* he mused. "Which are?"

"You know that I was an officer in Amarath's Raiders." She waited for his nod and continued. "When I was there, Archenous was also an officer, and we were proteges of the Guildmaster, a paladin named Trayance Parloure.

"He was a legend, and his personal honor was unquestioned. Archenous and I were both rising stars, new out of the Holy Brethren, deeply ambitious and clamoring to take over for Parloure when he stepped down as Guildmaster."

"Archenous is not a paladin," Cyrus said with measured uncertainty.

"Not any longer," Vara agreed. She seemed to hold on to every word until the last possible moment, as though keeping them on her tongue longer might prevent her from having to finish her story. "We began our expeditions in Purgatory and spent months learning how to overcome the first battles, enduring the taunting of the Gatekeeper the entire time."

She took a deep breath and paused, as if trying to decide whether to go on. She looked in his eyes and he could see the pain and vulnerability coming to the surface. "On the day we defeated the Trials, Archenous slew Trayance Parloure after we killed the Last Guardian. He did it at the behest of the Gatekeeper, who had been slowly turning Archenous to the path of the dark knight through the months we had spent there."

"He betrayed his Guildmaster?" Cyrus said, stunned. "Didn't anyone step up to defend him?"

"A few," she said with a shake of her head. "He killed them all. I was mortally wounded, left for dead. The Gatekeeper taunted me as I lay dying, alone. I pleaded for life as my reward for completing the Trials."

"You're still here," he said, hands open, gesturing toward her.

"I survived," she said with a trace of a smile, "but only just." She looked away from him, back toward the procession leading out of Goliath's guildhall. "I hope... that story does not make me appear weak in your eyes. I have never pursued revenge against Archenous, though I wanted to more than once."

Cyrus's eyes flitted to the Guildmaster of Amarath's Raiders, standing watch in the shadows of the Goliath guildhall. "To attempt it would be suicide," he said. "How many guildmates does he have... and they're the best equipped and most powerful fighters in all Arkaria." He shook his head. "I don't think less of you for it, nor do I think you're weak. I would say –" he looked into her eyes and saw the faintest drops of water forming in the corners – "that you are wise... and strong... because sometimes it takes more courage to avoid foolish action than to charge into it."

He reached for her hand and found it, and she stared at his fingers, intertwined with hers and did not pull away. "Thank you for telling me," he said.

She looked up at him, blue eyes staring into his. "By your word and deed you continue to prove yourself to be the kind of man... that I *can* trust." She looked at him for a long moment, then her hand pulled from his and brushed across his face, a slight touch that sent a strange quiver down his spine. She let it linger for only a moment, then slid past him to rejoin the group watching the last members of Goliath retreat from Reikonos.

Cyrus left them all behind, pushing his way through the crowd, out of the guildhall quarter. He slipped through side streets that he had walked for most of his life, passing landmarks that he could recall from childhood. He crossed the square on the opposite side of the long line of Goliath's refugees, taking the same path out of the city as the dark elves that were fleeing.

He turned at the square, heading toward the Citadel, but veered down an avenue before he got there. He found the building he was looking for, sitting in the shadow of the Citadel, a multistory structure that bore a pillared facade that stretched across its entrance doors, cut from quarried marble, with an arched roof that was filled with stone statues of gods in varying poses.

The library.

He entered and made inquiries at the desk in the foyer, where the curator pointed him in the right direction. After a short search, he found it, holding in his hands a leather bound tome, thicker than a loaf of bread with pages so thin they were almost insubstantial. He placed it upon a stand and opened it. The pages were new, the ink still bold, and the words stood out at him - both the words he understood, written in short paragraphs, alongside the words he did not know.

He opened to the first word he searched for, sounding it out. "'Akur'," he said. His fingers ran through the pages until it jumped out at him - a definition as short as any he had seen. "'Last'," he repeated, reading off the page. A smile half-crooked his face. "'Akur' means 'last'."

He flipped toward the back of the book, still seeking. Page after page he turned, until finally he found the one he sought. His finger skipped down the page and a nervous tension filled his stomach. His finger stopped and he blinked, then read, then blinked again.

"'Shelas'," he breathed. He read the translation once more, just to be sure he had it right. "'Hope'," he said, then pieced the words together. "'Shelas'akur,'" he repeated, turning the words over in his mouth. A strange feeling filled him, a sense that he now knew more - and yet somehow less - than he had before he had found the words.

"Last hope."

NOW

Epilogue

Clouds filled the skies out the window of the Council archive. Pain gnawed at Cyrus, the memory of all that had come from those days. The ache was one of deep regret; most of all for things not said. He turned his eyes back to the journal and forced himself to read, trying to drown out the thoughts of what had come later. He flipped to a different page, then rifled back a few pages, until he reached a passage that answered a question he had long asked.

I left the Holy Brethren in a fury, sick of schooling, sick of memorizing spells, and sick of arrogant paladins droning on about their damned self-righteous holy crusades. I was eighteen years of age; a baby in the eyes of the elves, yet a legend because of my status as shelas'akur.

Whilst in the Kingdom I was seldom refused anything – which made me sick in and of itself. So I fled, leaving Termina behind for Reikonos, striking out on my own to find my path with the Holy Brethren, something that had been arranged for me since it was discovered I had magical talent as a young child. I left behind the home that I had known for the anonymity of the human world, and found something I had not expected: damned human arrogance.

It manifested in their belief that their efforts had resulted in the defeat of the ancient and powerful trolls, it stemmed from their annoying pride in that gaudy Citadel that jutted above all else in their deformed city (they didn't even build the damned thing!) and worst, it sprang full grown from every human male that ever wielded a sword – a sort of cockiness that spawns from some unfathomable pit in their depths, possibly born from an insecurity so far buried that you would need to extract their gallbladder to find it.

It was annoying, to say the least.

But the talk of the crusades was worst of all. One would proudly proclaim his undying devotion to the ideal of freeing every slave in Arkaria while another would bleat about the plight of the suffering poor and how they deserved to be fed and clothed while another whined about advancing their god above all else – worthy causes, I am sure, with the possible exception of the evangelism (who wants to preach the gospel of the Goddess of Love? Truly.) – but in me they found no suitable audience. I am certain the Lord Knight who taught the Crusader Philosophy course could hear my teeth grind from the back of the room.

When the day came that I was forced to proclaim my crusade, I mumbled something about smiting the self-righteous and left. The Lord Knight let me get away with it; he was an elf, after all. But I never found that damned, insufferable arrogance an attractive quality until the day I met Archenous Derregnault. Tall, handsome and with a deep-seated conviction in the rightness of his cause, I found myself putting aside the word 'arrogance' in favor of 'confidence'.

I do not know whether he pretended not to notice me since I was a year behind him in my studies or whether he genuinely did not, but when, by chance, we were introduced, I can honestly say I fawned over him.

Me.

Fawned.

Over him.

I'm embarrassed by the thought now. But he did some fawning of his own, and it worked out well. We became lovers within a fortnight; he was my first, and tender, and sweet, and his confidence was charming.

He, being a year older, of course left the Brethren before I did. He secured a spot as an applicant to Amarath's Raiders, one of the foremost guilds in all of Arkaria. I was impressed, but not surprised – it's not as though I would have wasted my time falling in love with an untalented warrior destined to spend his life on the bottom, devoid of ambition. He climbed quickly from applicant to member, and by the time I left the Brethren, six months later, bored out of my mind by the excruciating minutia of their curriculum, he welcomed me lovingly back to his arms as an applicant of Amarath's Raiders.

The months passed quickly. The guild was large, but not so large that you didn't know everybody. In fact, in my first two months I had become acquainted with nearly everyone in the guild. I was polite, I was friendly – upon reflection, probably something like a giddy schoolgirl. In love, excited to be there, eyes wide with possibility and danger and living a life of thrills. We would adventure throughout the day in small groups and come together as a guild at night to tackle challenges unfathomable to most.

Then came the Trials of Purgatory.

We found a spell on one of our excursions that opened the gates of that Realm to us, and spent months trying to conquer it. I had known the Guildmaster, Trayance Parloure, in passing, but more by reputation than personally. In our first attempt on the trials, we lost eighty-five percent of our force to the golems on the first island and were forced to retreat. I say with all the humility I can muster that it was only through my quick action that we fared as well we did. Trayance was impressed; he involved me in planning, sought my council.

Archenous became an officer at the same time I did, both of us favored by Trayance to help run the guild as we faced this new challenge. The officers would meet to discuss the intricacies of strategy until late in the night and Archenous would continue our discussions in bed after we made love, long after the other officers were sleeping.

It was through our late night debates that we finally hit upon the ideas for defeating the golems, then the pegasi and Wind Totem. All the while, I felt him drawing away from me. We talked of the battles ahead but made love less and less; Archenous became obsessed with defeating the Trials, of gaining the reward promised by the Gatekeeper.

I watched him, sometimes, when we would take a break after one of the battles. He was always with the Gatekeeper. That bastard. Always taunting us, humiliating people by revealing their secrets and sins to their guildmates.

I know of more than one person that killed themselves in shame after that treatment, after feeling the burn of his words, of feeling their innermost secrets - things they would die rather than admit – given voice and paraded in front of their comrades. He sickened me.

But Archenous... Archenous talked to him. Constantly. When I asked, he said not to worry, he was trying to get the Gatekeeper to part with secrets, things to help us along.

Liar.

When I came up with the strategy to defeat the Siren of Fire, on my own, it came on the heels of a bitter defeat Archenous had led us into. His strategy for battle with the Siren was so poorly executed that it cost us thirty members, permanently dead. Based on his success with the eel, Trayance had put his faith in Archenous without reviewing the plans and it ended in disaster.

I can still hear Trayance's voice in my head, tearing a hole in Archenous in the officers' meeting. I had known him better than anyone – I should, perhaps, have recognized the look in his eyes when Trayance berated him over and over, but by that point he was so distant to me that I can honestly say I had no idea. Archenous was removed from his position as General and placed in charge of applicants.

When I led us to victory against the Siren, Trayance praised me with effusive, pretty words, just the opposite of what he had done to Archenous only days before. I noticed a seed of darkness growing in Archenous, a bitterness, but I hoped it would pass. He took me savagely that night, and I let him, hoping that we could go back to the way it used to be. But when we were done, he felt... empty.

I focused my attention on the Last Guardian and ignored my flagging relationship. I could fix it later, I assumed, and defeating the trials was what Archenous wanted more than anything, right? Right.

Right.

Right?

It took dozens of defeats. Dozens, to get my strategy right. But they were conservative, always, and we never lost a single person to permanent death, even in my wildest experiments.

The day we defeated the Last Guardian was a day of triumph. There was celebrating, wild, frenzied excitement at the fact that after months of blood and tears and defeats, we could finally claim our reward. Archenous had eyes for my sword since the day we met in the Brethren, and when he stood before the Gatekeeper, he received one very similar. He turned and embraced me, sword still in hand.

All the strain, all the worries, all the concerns were gone in that instant. He kissed me, and it was a blissful washing away of all my fears for our relationship. In that moment, I felt that a return to the days when we had begun was possible. He muttered something under his breath and I felt his hand slip up my backplate, tempting me, I thought, with a possibility for later.

Imagine my surprise when his new sword slid into the space between my armor that he had made for it and slid out my belly.

He dropped me unceremoniously, and the applicants that he had been training for months turned on the staunchest defenders of Trayance Parloure. My mentor was killed by a pack of hungry dogs, led by a demon in crusader's clothing. He took my sword, the one given to me by a noble elf with no children of his own, and threw down the one he'd just received from the Gatekeeper. Then he looked down at me. He knew I was still alive while all the others were dead, and he walked out the portal without a backward glance, taking all that was left of my guild with him.

I couldn't move, could barely breathe. The minutes passed like hours. There was a fire in my belly, an agony I couldn't control. I could barely remember the words to a healing spell, and whenever I used them it did nothing to help.

Of course the Gatekeeper was there. "Such a brave effort," he said in that damned, taunting voice of his. "Such a glorious victory, and you showed them the way! You should be proud."

At that moment, I would have been proud if I had possessed the strength to impale him on the damned sword that Archenous left me with, but unfortunately, I was in far too much pain. Hours passed. Maybe days. It felt like years. The Gatekeeper faded in and out along with my consciousness, and I found myself hating him and Archenous more and more. He taunted me while I lay there, fed me tender lines about how he had bent Archenous against me, fed his arrogance leading up to the defeat by the Siren and his desire for revenge at being embarrassed by Trayance.

He knew Archenous well; after a few months he had a grasp on the heart and soul of the only man I had ever loved better than I did. And he used it. Archenous knew I would turn on him if he attacked Trayance. And he wanted my sword. Do you know what you can become if you're prepared to betray and sacrifice someone who loves you?

A dark knight.

And the Gatekeeper talked him into it. Fed him on thoughts of power, of ability to fight off death in ways a paladin never could. Of abandoning your holy crusade and focusing on what's important – you.

Well, half of it isn't bad, I suppose.

So he pushed him. And Archenous bought into it – waited until we were weary at the moment of ultimate triumph, waited until he had enough applicants with him to turn against us, and took me out first with a blade to the back. And he cast aside his holy crusade (yes, it was evangelizing for the Goddess of Love) in favor of power and a love for himself before others.

And the bastard stole my sword.

I lay there forever, I swear. We were the only guild to beat the Trials, after all, and the Gatekeeper did not seem eager to help me, regardless of how much I begged. I knew no one would come, and I wondered how long it would be before I succumbed to my wounds. I prayed to Vidara for salvation, over and over. When the pain became too great, I prayed for death.

The Gatekeeper left for a long time. When I saw him again, he was touching my cheek, and he looked different. He was missing an eye, for one thing, and he wore battered armor for another. He stared down at me, eye searching. "Please... help me..." I muttered, or something of the like. I hardly remember. I was dying, after all.

Then the real Gatekeeper appeared at the man's side. "Life is about choices, isn't it?" he said in the mocking, cruel tone of someone who thinks they've just told the funniest jest of all time. I still wanted to kill him. Other sounds came from around me, but I could not identify any of them.

A glow of light filled my vision, but no warmth entered my body. It was still a miserable cold, chilling me through the skin. I felt strong arms wrap around me.

"There was never a choice," the man in armor said. He cradled me in his arms, picked up the sword that was next to me, and carried me through the portal. I woke days later in a far different place. And nothing was the same again after that. Ever.

Cyrus looked up from his reading. A sharp intake of breath filled the air as it all settled in. "Archenous," he said with grim finality. He read a little further, then flipped ahead, reading a section at a time. Another passage drew his attention.

I looked at Alaric with rage. He was possessed of no arrogance, but Cyrus had enough for both of them. "He's going to make the wrong decision," I told the man they called the Ghost. He had looked at me just as enigmatically as he had all those years ago, when I lay on my back in Purgatory, then told me I was wrong.

"And if you are not wrong," he went on, "and he does, at least be sound in the knowledge that you are an astute judge of human character."

"Don't be an ass," I told him. "Cyrus fills the quotient of that for the Council at present."

He shrugged in that infuriating way that he has when he's trying to be flippant. "I counseled you about revenge. I will counsel him as well. Perhaps the reason you're so upset by this is because... you're hoping you haven't fallen in love with the same man twice."

I flung the stupid sword into the wall. It embedded a few inches into the stonework, and I felt warmth in the corners of my eyes. I hate crying. I don't do it often. I never sob if I can avoid it. Damn the man, he knows. He just knows. "I..." Didn't know what to say.

"Cyrus and Archenous are not the same person," Alaric said. "To confuse them or paint them as the same man would be folly on your part."

"I was betrayed, Alaric," I snapped at him. "Being gutted, literally, by your first love does not make it easy to trust again. And in this case, perhaps I see the similarities because I know what to look for – and none of the rest of you do."

"You are hardly the first among us to be betrayed," he replied. "But keep watching. You'll know soon enough."

Cyrus sat back for a moment. He had been aware at the time of the debate raging inside Vara, but not of the substance and depth of it. He found another passage – from Termina. *Right after she kissed me on the cheek and left,* he realized.

I sat with Isabelle in my room long after my parents had gone to bed. She still labors under the illusion that because we are sisters, we should share our every prattling thought, every heartfelt desire and every girlish whim. I cannot believe she is older than me by two centuries. She acts like a child.

"Well done helping Sanctuary through Purgatory," she said, lying next to me on the covers. "Everyone in Reikonos is talking about what you did."

"Excellent," I replied. "You know that my sole ambition in life was to not only be the talk of the Elven Kingdom but of all Arkaria. It's why I left Termina in the first place," I deadpanned.

"You still don't take compliments well," she said with a hint of resignation. She paused for a moment and brightened. "Tell me about Cyrus Davidon."

I bristled at the name. "What is there to tell?"

"His name comes up often in my circles," she said. "A rising star in the Sanctuary firmament, helping to lead your guild to prominence."

"The thing about rising stars is that they tend to burn brightest just before they disappear."

"So are you interested in him?" Her impish smile annoyed me.

"Hardly," I snorted.

"Hm," she said. "Then I might be."

"Marvelous. I'll introduce you, you can get married and raise fat halfbreed babies with pointed ears and lantern jaws." My acid tongue has no effect on my sister. I know it. Nonetheless, she stopped trying to make conversation. When she reached the door, she turned back to me and started to say something, but must have thought better of it, because she left instead. I might have been mistaken, but I believe I caught just a hint of sadness in her eyes before she walked out the door.

Cyrus marveled at her admission; even among her family it seemed Vara did not bother with diplomacy. He frowned. Or was it because of her close intimacy with them that she didn't bother?

"You were right," I said, edging into the room. I felt as humbled as I could be, but relieved. The events in Enterra had born out Alaric's belief in Cyrus – and my hope that I was wrong about him.

"You think so?" the Ghost said mysteriously.

"I know so," I replied, giving him a confused look. "You saw what happened – he resisted it, the urge to kill the Empress. He held back."

"Indeed, that is what I saw," Alaric agreed. "But just because he won that battle today does not mean that it is won forever."

My smile must have disappeared at that point, perhaps replaced by that fearsome expression I get when challenged, or annoyed, or sometimes when I have stomach pains, because he raised an eyebrow at me. "Alaric, this foe had hurt him more than anyone – as bad as Archenous hurt me, at least. You think that he'll face a worse test in the future and fail it?"

"The only thing I said," he reiterated, "is that a battle won today is not won forever. There is a war raging for the heart and soul of Cyrus Davidon. We stand on one side – those who would see him do great things, hold mercy and purpose in his heart and act in that spirit – while on the other side, there are those who would have him act from petty, cruel, self-serving motives. He is young – and impressionable. And that battle is not decided today. It goes ever on."

"You are damnably cruel," I told him. "And I care not what you say, I believe he has faced his worst trial and shown his true character."

"If that is the case and you feel that way, then perhaps you should tell him how you truly feel – about him – and stop dancing around the subject."

"Oh?" I asked. "And how would that factor into your belief that there is a war for his soul?"

"Favorably," he replied. "I believe he would fight harder to please you than for anything else in his life right now – including his new sword."

I blinked. Damned swords. But all I said was, "I'm not ready... yet. Perhaps soon. Perhaps I'll start by telling him... something. And then," I said with a hope that ran the length of my soul, "perhaps someday I'll tell him... everything."

I looked at the man who had been called the Ghost for as long as I have known him, and hesitated. He stared back at me, with that one, cold gray eye of his, looking into the depths of my soul. For as long as I have known Alaric, our relationship has been based on a mutual respect. He doesn't write me off every time I swear and throw things and I don't press him continuously with questions I know he doesn't want to answer.

"What?" His look was wary, guarded. I think he sensed one of those unpleasant questions in the offing.

"Alaric... I have been through the Trials of Purgatory, many times. When we went through them with Sanctuary, they were only a fraction of the difficulty that I had experienced previously." I looked at him, uneasy. "The Golems were slower and hit less hard, the Wind Totem and its pegasi were almost pathetically weak, susceptible even to arrows – and the Last Guardian was a joke; it never even made an attempt at using its mental abilities to influence the outcome of the battle."

I looked at him and he sat unmoving, expressionless. "I have yet to hear a question."

"Alaric..." I looked at him and he refused to meet my gaze. "How did you reach the last island of the Trials of Purgatory when you rescued me? And why were you there?"

A deep sigh filled the air and Alaric's head turned to look out the window. The silence filled the room like the mist he creates when he appears and disappears. When he finally answered, it was in a voice just above a whisper.

"I will start by telling you some of it... and someday, when the time comes... I will tell you the rest."

Cyrus looked up from the journal. The dark skies outside the window finally broke loose and cold autumn rain poured down outside.

A Note to the Reader

If you enjoyed this book and want to know about future releases by Robert J. Crane, you can go to my website (robertJcrane.com) to sign up for my mailing list! I promise I won't spam you (I only send an email when I have a new book released) and I'll never sell your info. You can also unsubscribe at any time.

I also wanted to take a moment to thank you for reading this story. As an independent author, getting my name out to build an audience is one of the biggest priorities on any given day. If you enjoyed this story and are looking forward to reading more, let someone know - post it on Amazon, on your blog, if you have one, on Goodreads.com, place it in a quick Facebook status or Tweet with a link to the page of whatever outlet you purchased it from (Amazon, Barnes & Noble, Apple, Kobo, etc). Good reviews inspire people to take a chance on a new author – like me. And we new authors can use all the help we can get.

Thanks for reading.

Robert J. Crane

About the Author

Robert J. Crane was born and raised on Florida's Space Coast before moving to the upper midwest in search of cooler climates and more palatable beer. He graduated from the University of Central Florida with a degree in English Creative Writing. He worked for a year as a substitute teacher and worked in the financial services field for seven years while writing in his spare time. He makes his home in the Twin Cities area of Minnesota.

He can be contacted in several ways:

Via email at cyrusdavidon@gmail.com
Follow him on Twitter - **@robertJcrane**
Connect on Facebook **- robertJcrane (Author)**
Website **- robertJcrane.com**
Blog - robertJcrane.blogspot.com
Become a fan on Goodreads -
http://www.goodreads.com/RobertJCrane

The Sanctuary Series
Epic Fantasy by Robert J. Crane

The world of Arkaria is a dangerous place, filled with dragons, titans, goblins and other dangers. Those who live in this world are faced with two choices: live an ordinary life or become an adventurer and seek the extraordinary.

Avenger
The Sanctuary Series, Volume Two

When a series of attacks on convoys draws suspicion that Sanctuary is involved, Cyrus Davidon must put aside his personal struggles and try to find the raiders. As the attacks worsen, Cyrus and his comrades find themselves abandoned by their allies, surrounded by enemies, facing the end of Sanctuary and a war that will consume their world.

Available Now!

Champion
The Sanctuary Series, Volume Three

As the war heats up in Arkaria, Vara is forced to flee after an ancient order of skilled assassins infiltrates Sanctuary and targets her. Cyrus Davidon accompanies her home to the elven city of Termina and the two of them become embroiled in a mystery that will shake the very foundations of the Elven Kingdom - and Arkaria.

Available Now!

Crusader
The Sanctuary Series, Volume Four

Cyrus Davidon finds himself far from his home in Sanctuary, in the land of Luukessia, a place divided and deep in turmoil. With his allies at his side, Cyrus finds himself facing off against an implacable foe in a war that will challenge all his convictions - and one he may not be able to win.

Coming Fourth Quarter 2012!

Savages
A Sanctuary Short Story

Twenty years before Cyrus Davidon joined Sanctuary, his father was killed in a war with the trolls and he has never forgiven them. Enter Vaste, a troll unlike most; courageous, loyal and an outcast. When Cyrus and Vaste become trapped in a far distant land, they are forced to overcome their suspicions and work together to get home.

Available Now!

A Familiar Face
A Sanctuary Short Story

Cyrus Davidon gets more than he bargained for when he takes a day away from Sanctuary to visit the busy markets of his hometown, Reikonos. While there, he meets a woman who seems very familiar, and appears to know him, but that he can't place.

Available Now!

Alone
The Girl in the Box, Book 1

Sienna Nealon was a 17-year-old girl who had been held prisoner in her own house by her mother for twelve years. Then one day her mother vanished, and Sienna woke up to find two strange men in her home. On the run, unsure of who to turn to and discovering she possesses mysterious powers, Sienna finds herself pursued by a shadowy agency known as the Directorate and hunted by a vicious, bloodthirsty psychopath named Wolfe, each of which is determined to capture her for their own purposes...

Available Now!

Untouched
The Girl in the Box, Book 2

Still haunted by her last encounter with Wolfe and searching for her mother, Sienna Nealon must put aside her personal struggles when a new threat emerges - Aleksandr Gavrikov, a metahuman so powerful, he could destroy entire cities - and he's focused on bringing the Directorate to its knees.

Available now!

Soulless
The Girl in the Box, Book 3

Available now!

Family
The Girl in the Box, Book 4

Coming Fourth Quarter 2012!

Trust
The Girl in the Box, Book 5

Coming Fourth Quarter 2012!

23207363R00189

Made in the USA
Middletown, DE
20 August 2015